brutal EMPIRE

brutal empire

A.J. FALLOW

Also by AJ Fallow

Boston Kings Series

The McTiernan Clan Trilogy

Dark Empire

Saint

Cruel Empire

Brutal Empire

The Moretti Syndicate Trilogy

Deadly Secrets

Book Cover by Pretty Little Design Co.

Map by Maxim Gertsen.

First edition 2024.

Author's Note

Brutal Empire is the final book in the McTiernan Clan Trilogy and ends with a HEA. *Brutal Empire* is a dark romantic suspense novel, and it contains content and situations that could be triggering for some readers. This book is explicit and has explicit sexual content. It also contains graphic violence, and the on screen death of a parent from cancer. Please check the trigger warnings carefully. This book is not intended for readers under the age of 18.

The following is a list of potential triggers and explicit/graphic content. This list contains spoilers but is intended to better inform and pre-warn readers.

Graphic violence, blood/injuries, cancer, onscreen death, onscreen death of a loved one/death of parents, fear of losing loved ones, smoking, slurs, illegal activities (related to mob/mafia lifestyle), gun trafficking, assult, self-harm, alcohol abuse, grief, depression, anxiety, panic attacks, alcohol abuse, foul language, sexually explicit scenes

Character List

The McTiernan Clan

Territory - South Boston - Waterfront to Shawmut

Tommy Quinn: Clan Chief

Sloane McTiernan: Arbiter, owner/bartender of Lady Devine's, Callum McTiernan's daughter.

Grady: Master-at-Arms

Callum McTiernan: Retired Clan Chief, father to Sloane and Aiden, uncle to Connor

Connor McTiernan: Former warlord, Callum's nephew, married to Cassidy

Aiden McTiernan: Warlord (Deceased)

Michael Quinn: Former Clan Chief, father to Tommy and Cassidy

Cassidy McTiernan (Quinn): Trauma resident at Boston Medical Center, Connor's wife and Tommy's sister

Alfred "Alfie" Doyle: Former Master-at-Arms, Connor's best friend, married to Emilia Russo.

Teagan Kelley: Reaper

Dr. Jerome Carter: Chief Trauma Surgeon at Boston Medical Center, Cassidy's boss

The Moretti Family

Territory: North End – Downtown from the Charles Town to Beacon Hill. Ties to the Giordano Family in Providence by blood

Lorenzo Moretti: Former Don, father to Dominic and Angelo

Viviana Moretti (Giordano): Lorenzo's wife

Salvatore "Sal" Giordano: Consigliere, acting Don

Isabella Giordano: Sal's wife

Dominic "Dom" Moretti: Underboss

Angelo "Angel" Moretti: Capo

Luca Mariano: Capo, Emilia's best friend

Julian (Jules) Russo: Capo, Sofia's brother and Emilia's cousin

Sofia Russo: Emilia's cousin and Julian's sister

Emilia Russo (Moretti): Lorenzo's adopted daughter, Alfie's wife.

The Volkov Bratva

Territory: Jamaica Plain to Brookline. Ties to the Sointsevskaya Bratva in Moscow through Uncle Dmitri Volkov

Aleksandr Volkov: Pakhan (leader) of the Volkov Bratva

Misha: Soldat (soldier)

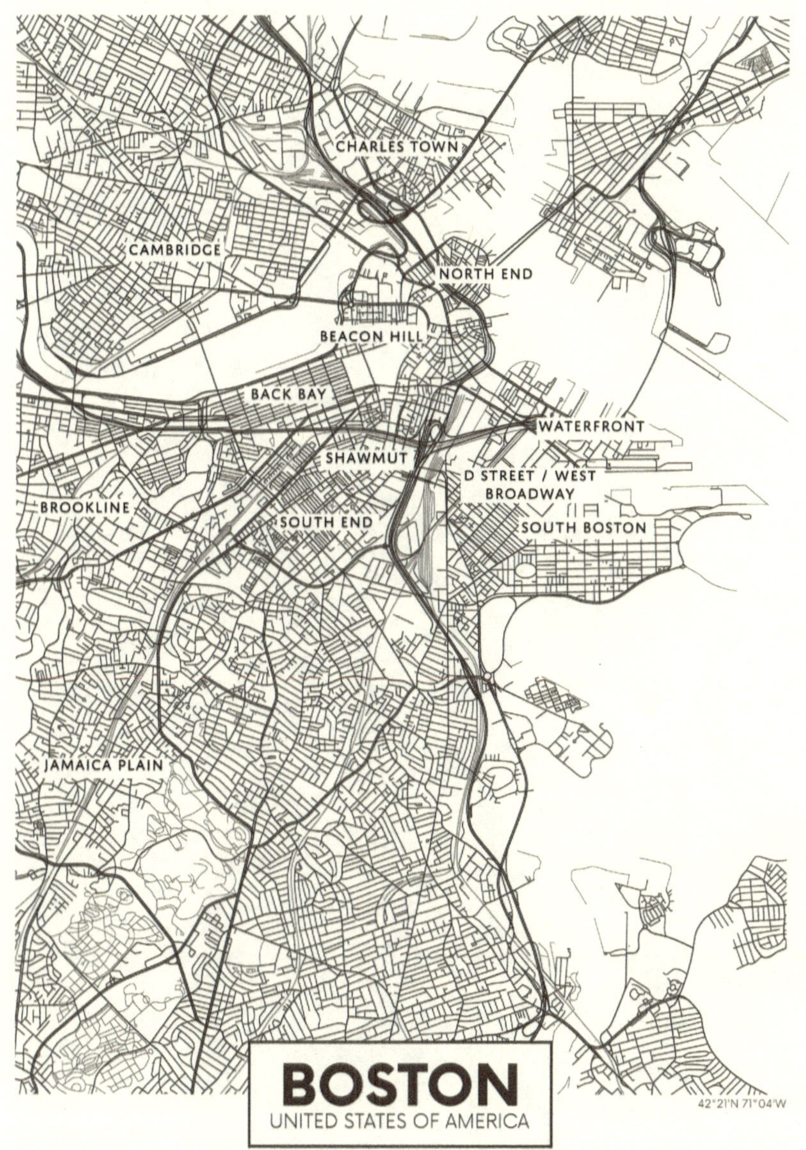
CHARLES TOWN
CAMBRIDGE
NORTH END
BEACON HILL
BACK BAY
WATERFRONT
SHAWMUT
D STREET / WEST
BROADWAY
BROOKLINE
SOUTH END
SOUTH BOSTON
JAMAICA PLAIN
BOSTON
UNITED STATES OF AMERICA
42°21'N 71°04'W

Playlist

Listen to the playlist on Spotify HERE

Blood – *Dropkick Murphys*

Heartbreaker – *The Rolling Stones*

Kiss With A Fist – *Florence + The Machine*

Psycho – Muse

Short Change Hero – *The Heavy*

Part Goddess Part Gangster – *Madalen Duke*

The Sky is a Neighborhood – *Foo Fighters*

Glitter & Gold – *Barns Courtney*

Howlin' for You – *The Black Keys*

Beat the Devil's Tattoo – *Black Rebel Motorcycle Club*

Warriors – *Imagine Dragons*

Royals – *Otep*

Prologue

Kennebunkport, ME – 1998

That girl was here again.

Her daddy was friends with mine, although Mom said that friends was "stretching it." I wasn't sure what that meant, but I wasn't going to ask her to explain, because that was the fastest way to end up scrubbing the kitchen floor with a toothbrush. Cassidy and I weren't supposed to talk about what Daddy did at the office. All we knew was that he was a Very Important Man, and that sometimes, we got to visit the McTiernans at their summer home in Maine.

Mr. McTiernan's house was the nicest house I'd ever seen. And this was just the one for *summer*. It had a pool and a beach and a big green area for tennis, but that was boring. The gardens were my mom's favorite. She would always point and sigh at them when we drove up the driveway and they came into view. I thought they were boring, too. There were about a million rooms in the whole house. I'd tried counting them once, but I'd gotten lost and confused, and I ended up falling asleep on a couch in the basement. They even had a room just for watching movies.

Those weeks were the best. The grownups would sit by the pool and drink grownup drinks, which meant us kids did pretty much anything we wanted. Once, Mr. McTiernan flew in his brother and his family all the way from Ireland. They had a son named Connor. He was pretty cool, but he talked funny.

The McTiernans had a son named Aiden, who was the same age as me. He was a lot of fun. He liked to play football like me and swim in the ocean. Sometimes, we would get bored and go exploring around the estate and try to find things. We found a cave once. Well, not a real cave, but it was dark and deep, and it had a stream running through it. It was down by the beach, and it was the perfect spot to look for pirate treasure.

At least until his sister showed up and ruined it.

Mom told me Aiden and his sister were twins. I said they didn't look the same to me, and she laughed. Whatever. I couldn't remember her name, but she was always hanging out with my sister, Cassidy. She had the darkest hair and these weird green eyes that looked kind of creepy. Today, she was wearing a purple t-shirt with a unicorn on it. She was sitting cross-legged on the sand, braiding daisies into a chain.

Today, Aiden and I were supposed to go digging for clams. Mr. McTiernan said he'd pay us a whole quarter for each one we'd find. Mom said that wasn't a good job for a seven-year-old, but Dad just ruffled my hair and said, "Let him go, Rosie. The sooner the boy learns the value of a hard day's work, the better."

That had been hours ago. Aiden had gone up to the garage to look for gear, and I was supposed to be scouting for spots along the beach, but I was getting bored.

Instead, I found myself drifting closer to the girls. They had sticks and were battling imaginary enemies, laughing and shrieking. It looked like fun. Cassidy was wearing her favorite yellow dress and had a crown of daisies on her head. The sun glinted off her light red hair as she jumped and twirled. Aiden's sister had a daisy crown on too, but she was taking the game a lot more seriously, shouting and slashing so fiercely I had to stop and stare for a minute.

I took another step closer, not meaning to spook them. But the second my foot hit the sand, both girls whirled around and brandished their weapons at me.

"Who goes there?"

"Halt! In the name of the king!"

I threw up my hands. "What? I don't care about the king. I'm going to dig for clams."

Aiden's sister stepped forward, her face serious as she held her stick sword to my throat. "You shall not pass, foul beast."

I snorted. "What are you going to do about it? You've got a daisy crown on your head."

"Girls can be knights, too." She whacked me across the arm to prove a point, and I clenched my teeth. I didn't want her to know that it had hurt a little bit.

"Mom says we're not supposed to hit anyone with the sticks." Cassidy pouted. "You're going to get us in trouble."

"But he's an evil dragon," Aiden's sister replied, her eyes wide. "He's going to eat us if we don't stop him!"

Cassidy looked at me with narrowed eyes. "Can you please be the dragon?" she begged. "Aiden won't play with us anymore. He said it's a stupid game."

I rolled my eyes. "Fine. What do I have to do?"

"You're the dragon," Aiden's sister explained, "and we're the knights. We're here to slay you and save the princess from the tower." She pointed her stick at the sand. "See? That's the tower."

The girls' sandcastle the girls was pretty good. There were even shells on top for the archers to hide behind then they shot their arrows. I looked back towards the house, but Aiden was nowhere to be seen. "Okay, I'll play. But you'd better run quick, because I'm hungry and I just might eat you all up!"

Cassidy squealed and ran for the safety of the castle. Aiden's sister chased after her, laughter filling the air. I grinned and took off after them, roaring and flapping my arms. The girls fought off each attack bravely, and right when I had them cornered, Aiden's sister stepped forward and rammed her sword into my chest, skewering me through the heart.

"Argh!" I cried out, clawing at the sky as I tumbled to the ground, taking her with me.

We hit hard and rolled to a stop near the water's edge. The sand was cool against my overheated cheek, and I licked the salt from my lips. We lay there on the sand for a minute, catching our breath.

Finally, I peeked an eye open and looked at her. "You're good at this."

"So are you." She stood up and brushed the sand from her hair. That's when I noticed her flower crown had fallen onto the sand.

I tried to pick it up, but I made it worse. "I broke it."

"It's okay, I can fix it. Look." She took it from me and carefully started to untangle the chain. "See? You just have to be gentle."

"Oh."

I watched her work, oddly fascinated. When she finished, she placed the crown on my head. "There. That means you can't be the dragon anymore."

"Why not?" I frowned. The flower crown was stupid, but I kept it on because it seemed to make her happy.

"Because we're friends now, silly." She took my hand and pulled me up. "I'm Sloane."

"I'm Tommy. But if I'm not the dragon, then what am I?"

"A knight."

"But you're a knight, too." I looked down at her.

She nodded, her dark eyes wide and serious. "That's right. We're both are."

I smiled. "Cool."

SOUTH BOSTON, MA – 2003

"Fight! Fight! Fight!"

The chant echoed down the halls, growing louder as the crowd surged forward, pushing and jostling for a better view. The school's hallway was a mess of bodies, all of them shoving and jockeying for position.

I grinned and joined the fray, elbowing my way towards the front. I had no idea what the fight was about, but that didn't matter. A fight was a fight. Besides, it wasn't like the teachers were going to do anything about it.

I pushed my way through the crowd, ignoring the dirty looks I got. I knew I was bigger than the other kids, but so what? It's not like I asked for it. And it's not like I was the only one who had grown a few inches over the summer.

As I got closer to the center of the circle, I saw two guys trading punches. It was Alfie Doyle and Mickey Sullivan, one of the biggest bullies in our class. I wasn't too surprised to see Doyle there. His scrawny stature and hand-me-down clothes made him a popular target for teasing, but at least he was quick with his fists. The kid spent more time in detention than he did in class, I swear.

Sullivan, on the other hand, was a different story. He was big and dumb and mean. He used his size to get what he wanted and he wasn't above pushing around anyone smaller than him. In fact, I had seen him do it a dozen times.

Not that any of the teachers cared.

"Get him, Doyle!" someone shouted.

"Kick his ass!" another voice yelled.

Beside me, Sloane pushed through the crowd with her brother in tow. "We've got to do something! They're going to kill each other!"

"No they're not," Aiden laughed. "Besides, it's about time someone taught Mickey Sullivan a lesson."

Sloane glared at her brother. "This isn't a joke, Aiden. Look at them! We can't just stand here and watch."

Aiden rolled his eyes, but I had to admit that Sloane was right. Doyle was getting his ass kicked. But Dad always told me that you didn't have to be the strongest guy in the room to win a fight. You just had to be smarter.

"Let them alone," I said to her, grabbing her arm to hold her back. "A guy's got to fight his own battles. We wouldn't be doing Doyle any favors."

"Yeah," Aiden agreed. "We'll step in if things start to get out of hand."

Doyle had Mickey in a headlock, but Mickey was twice his size, and he had Doyle on the ground in seconds. The bigger boy pounded Doyle's face into the linoleum floor. The crowd smelled blood in the air and pressed closer as two of Mickey's friends joined the fight.

Sloane pointed at what was quickly about to become a murder scene. "How about now? Is this out of hand enough for you?"

"Yep," Aiden and I said together as we waded into the fight.

Aiden took on Mickey's two friends. I went after Mickey, who had Doyle down on the ground again, kicking him in the ribs. Doyle was bleeding from a cut on his forehead, but he was still fighting back, flailing at Mickey with his fists.

"Hey! Asshole!" I shouted. Mickey turned and swung at me, but I ducked under his wild punch and came up swinging. I hit him square in the jaw, and he staggered backward.

Just as I was about to hit him again, one of Mickey's cronies got away from Aiden and jumped on my back. His arms locked around my throat as I heard shouts from teachers echo down the halls.

Suddenly, I could breathe again. I whirled around. Sloane had tackled the kid on my back, knocking him loose. She circled her arms through his from behind and hauled him back in a surprising show of force from someone so small.

"Well? What are you waiting for?" She shouted.

I punched him in the face. Blood spurted from the kid's nose as the teachers rounded the corner, and I grabbed Sloane's hand, scraping what was left of Alfie Doyle off the floor.

"Come on!" I shouted to Aiden. He caught my eye and nodded, following me as we barreled through the crowd of kids, dragging the other two behind us.

We ran down the hall, taking a hard left at the lockers and then another at the bathrooms before cutting through the empty cafeteria and out the side door. We stopped running once we reached the janitor's closet. No one was following us. I heard the bell ring, signaling that lunch was over, and I grinned at Sloane and Aiden, breathing hard.

"You okay, Doyle?" Aiden asked, helping the smaller kid to his feet.

Doyle smiled through bloodstained teeth. "Yeah. I'm okay. Thanks, guys."

"No problem," I shrugged. "Anytime."

Sloane shook her head, trying to catch her breath. Her face was flushed and her dark hair was coming undone from its braid. "That was crazy."

"Yeah, it was," I agreed. I looked down at her, suddenly feeling self-conscious. I wasn't sure why, but the sight of Sloane, her cheeks red and eyes bright from the fight, made something stir inside me. "But you were really good. Thanks for the assist, spitfire."

She smiled shyly at the nickname, ducking her head. Then the second bell rang, and her eyes went wide. "We're going to be late to class. I've got to go."

She took off, leaving Aiden and me behind. I watched her go, a strange tightness blooming as she disappeared down the hallway. Beside me, Aiden elbowed me in the ribs.

"What?" I asked.

He scowled at me. "Whatever you're thinking about, don't even go there."

"What? Ew. No way. Gross."

Aiden snorted. "Whatever, man. Just keep your hands to yourself, okay?"

I rolled my eyes. "Relax. I'm not gonna make a move on your sister."

Still, I turned and watched until she'd disappeared around the corner. Yeah, Sloane was pretty cool.

For a girl.

SOUTH BOSTON, MA – 2008

The Rolling Stones' *Heartbreaker* blared from the bar's jukebox as I stood outside Lady Devine's, smoking a cigarette. May had finished out unseasonably hot, but tonight was finally starting to cool off. It was the first time all week I'd been able to step outside and not feel like I was being baked alive. Only a few more days and I would finally be free for the summer.

I took a long drag on the cigarette, enjoying the burn in the back of my throat. The smoke curled lazily into the air, hanging heavy around my head. I breathed it in, letting it soothe my nerves.

This wasn't exactly how I'd planned on spending my Friday night, but what the hell. When Aiden's old man asked if he and I wanted to earn some extra cash, I was down. A little bit of extra scratch on the side would be pretty cool this summer.

Besides, it wasn't like we were doing anything illegal. Just a few deliveries. How bad could it be?

I blew a smoke ring into the air, watching as it dissipated into nothingness. The streetlights cast pools of amber light on the sidewalk, illuminating the cracks and potholes in the pavement. I leaned against the brick wall, watching as cars drove by, their headlights cutting across the brick like searchlights.

Across the street, a group of college girls walked by, laughing and talking loudly. They were all dressed up, on their way to the bars no doubt. I watched them go, taking a moment to enjoy the view. One of them looked over her shoulder and smiled at me.

I grinned and took another drag of my cigarette. Winked.

A few minutes later, I walked back inside with her phone number in my back pocket.

"Hey, Tommy." Mr. McTiernan was behind the bar, and he pointed to one of stools. "Have a seat. Where's Aiden?"

"Parking the car, sir. I needed a smoke."

He waved his hand. "None of that 'sir' shit around here. Call me Callum."

From the keg room behind the bar, Sloane appeared, carrying a rack of clean glasses. Her dad was starting to let her barback for him on the weekends to 'learn a trade', he said, but really I think he just wanted to keep tabs on her. I didn't blame him. If I had a daughter who looked like that, I'd keep her under lock and key.

I watched as she stacked the glasses on the countertop, her pretty green eyes focused on the task at hand. Her dark hair fell across her face, and she pushed it away, tucking it behind one ear. She was wearing a pair of tight black pants and a low-cut top, and I couldn't help but notice the way the fabric clung to her curves.

Sloane glanced up and caught me staring. "Hey, Tommy."

The smile that she gave me made my heart beat a little faster. "Hey yourself."

I flashed a smile back at her, and she blushed. It looked pretty on her. Her jet-black hair, so distinctively McTiernan, was cut into a short bob, and the summer sun had brought out the scattering of freckles at the corner of eyes darkened with eyeliner. Pouty lips, quick with a snarky comeback and perfect for kissing. Not that I knew anything about it.

I'd thought about it, though. Kissing her. I mean, she'd always been pretty, but now it was like...I don't know. Like I was really noticing it for the first time.

Sloane was just so different from other girls. She wasn't afraid of a little dirt or hard work. She was funny and smart and I knew for a fact that she had a wicked right hook. I'd gotten into plenty of scuffles alongside her and Aiden, and I'd have her back me in a fight any day.

And she was beautiful. Not the kind of beauty that needed lipstick or mascara to complete, but the real kind. The kind of beauty that made your breath catch when she walked into the room. The kind that made you want to stay up all night, just talking, because you couldn't bear to miss a single moment with her.

Yeah, I really liked Sloane.

But she was Aiden's sister, and I had to play it cool. If he knew I was thinking about her like that, he'd kick my ass, or at least try to. So I just smiled at her and said, "Good crowd tonight."

She nodded. "Yeah, it's busy."

"You doing anything tomorrow?" I leaned a little closer to her until I could catch the faint scent of her shampoo. I wondered how good she'd smell with my buried my face in her neck.

Sloane perked up. "I'm going to the Sox game. Alfie's got tickets."

My heart fell, but my smile didn't. "Alfie? That guy from school? I didn't know you guys were friends."

"We're just hanging out. Nothing serious. You should come."

"Nah," I said, trying not to sound disappointed. "Baseball's not really my thing. Besides, Aiden was talking about going to get in a little sparring time down at Big Saul's."

"Oh. Right. Maybe we can all meet up later?"

"Sure thing, spitfire. Maybe."

Sloane flashed me a smile, and I felt my heart skip a beat. "Okay then. See you around."

I watched her disappear into the kitchen and cursed myself. What was wrong with me? I was acting like a fucking pussy. It was just Sloane. She was Aiden's sister, for Christ's sake. We'd been friends our whole lives. Why was I getting all tongue tied around her now? This wasn't like me.

Callum reached behind the bar and pulled out a bottle of whiskey, pouring two glasses. He pushed one towards me and took the other for himself. "Cheers."

I hesitated for only a moment. Of course, I'd drank before—I'd been big enough to pass for twenty-one since I had been sixteen—but never in front of our parents. Mom would have skinned me alive.

I clinked my glass against Callum's and took a sip. The whiskey burned going down, but it warmed my belly and settled some of the nerves.

"Atta boy. You work like a man around here, you get to drink like a man." Callum jerked his chin at me. "You got the goods?"

I nodded, pulling the envelope out of my pocket. It felt heavy and full in my hands as I handed it over to him. He thumbed through it, counting the money. Then he tucked the envelope into his pocket.

Aiden slid onto the barstool next to me. Callum nodded at his son, then leaned back to study us. "You boys did good tonight. Listen, next Friday I want you to take Connor with you. Kid's maudlin as fuck. He needs something to get his mind off things, understand?"

Connor's parents had been killed in Ireland two months ago. Word was, the IRA had blown them both to kingdom come. Wrong time, wrong place sort of thing. Callum had shipped the boy across the pond and had taken him under his wing. The guy had barely said two words to me since getting here, most notably 'fuck' and 'you.'

I liked him immediately.

"Sure thing, pops," Aiden said as he tossed back his own drink, trying to pretend it didn't burn all the way down.

"Cal! Why're you givin' them that rotgut?" My dad was coming down the stairs with a stack of papers in his hand. He dipped behind the bar, nudged Callum out of the way, and reached under the bar, pulling out a bottle of top-shelf scotch and three glasses.

Dad poured a glass for himself and Callum, then he poured two for us. He winked. "Don't tell your mother."

"She'd skin us both," I agreed, taking a sip.

A year later, my mother will be murdered by a car bomb and my family will be destroyed because of the foundations that had been laid in this very bar. But we didn't know that then.

The scotch went down like butter and warmed my belly, coating my tongue with smoky goodness. I smiled, thinking maybe getting in on this side gig wasn't the worst thing in the world.

KENNEBUNKPORT, ME – 2013

No matter how hard I tried, I couldn't get Aiden's blood off my hands.

The four of us were still gathered at the graveside: Connor, Sloane, Alfie, and me. Cassidy left right after the funeral. Callum had taken his wife back to the car, both nearly prostrate with grief. Rain dripped from the edges of the umbrella I was holding over Sloane's head, and leather creaked as I gripped the cheap plastic handle tighter. Ever since that night, I'd taken to wearing gloves. I couldn't stand the sight of my hands anymore.

I don't think anybody even noticed.

I didn't dare look at Sloane. Not now. The pain in her eyes was too much to bear. Instead, I stared at the black lacquer casket in front of us, at the spray of roses adorning the lid that covered the man that I hadn't been able to save. Callum had trusted me with his son's life. Sloane had trusted me to have her brother's back. Instead, I'd been an arrogant fool, and Aiden had bled out on a filthy side street in South Boston. Twenty-two years of life, gone in the blink of an eye.

It should have been me.

"I...I can't believe he's gone," Sloane sniffed, covering her mouth with her hand. "I keep thinking I'm going to wake up and this will all be a bad dream."

Connor and I didn't say anything. We'd seen enough death to know that there was no waking up from this nightmare.

Alfie put his arm around Sloane, and she wept into his shoulder. I turned my face away.

"Tommy." I turned at the sound of my father's voice. He was waiting a few yards away, and he jerked his chin towards the car.

I handed the umbrella to Connor. He shifted it over Sloane's head, taking my place without a word as I jogged after my father.

Six years had turned Michael Quinn into a hard man. We'd lost Mom, and we nearly lost Cassidy. Somedays it felt like my sister was gone, too. She hated what our father did. Gone was that old rule about not mentioning Dad's work. Now, that was all we ever talked about. Fought about.

The McTiernan Clan was a powerhouse in South Boston. Business was good. Aiden and I had been rising stars in the organization, with

Alfie on our heels. Only Connor had been reluctant to get in while the action was good, although since Aiden's death, he'd changed too, throwing himself into the job like Satan himself was on his ass.

The only person who hadn't changed was Sloane. She was still as pretty, smart, and snarky as ever. But that would probably change, now, too.

I closed my eyes and let the rain drench my face. Sometimes there were moments I wished I could bottle. To hoard for later, enjoy and savor like fine whiskey. Every moment with Sloane was like that.

My father called my name again, impatient. I turned towards the car. Time waits for no man, and the devil must have his due.

"Leave them to their grief, son," my father said. "We have work to do."

SOUTH BOSTON, MA – 2023

"I'm not going to abandon Emilia. I love her!"

Silence descended, cloyingly thick in the wake of Alfie's declaration. For a moment, the only sound in the back room of Lady Devine's was the ticking of the wall clock, and I looked over at Sloane to see how she was taking this.

Not well.

Her face was parchment white, gauze still clenched in her hand from where she'd been patching up Alfie after the fight at the club tonight. The fight had been about Emilia, who apparently was Alfie's new girlfriend.

Oh, and by the way, she also happened to be the daughter of our archrival.

I wouldn't trade places with Alfie for all the money in the world. Connor looked seconds away from murdering him.

Sloane stood and left the room.

"Sloane, wait!" I jumped up and jogged after her.

She was already down the hall and halfway through the kitchen doors by the time I caught up to her. She pushed open the emergency exit and stepped out onto the alley behind Lady Devine's.

"Sloane. Stop. Talk to me."

"How could he be so stupid?" She whirled at me, tears glistening in her eyes. "He's in love with *her*? Are you kidding me? Of all the women..."

"Hey, come on. He didn't do it to hurt you. I don't think he thought it through at all. Obviously. Besides, it's not like you guys were ever really together."

That was the wrong thing to say. Sloane's eyes narrowed, her face turning red. "Fuck you. You know how I felt."

"Yeah, and I know how Alfie felt, too," I said, bristling, jealousy making me mean. "He was never into you, Sloane."

I knew I'd gone too far as soon as the words left my mouth. But I couldn't stop myself. Sloane was so perfect, so beautiful, so...untouch able. And I knew Alfie would never look at her the same way I did. It had eaten at me for years, and I was just drunk enough to finally let the jealousy out.

"You're the last person who should be giving me relationship advice. Mr. 'Different Girl on his Arm Every Night?'" Sloane scoffed. "Like you're some great expert in matters of the heart."

"I am when it comes to my own! And I know that Alfie could never feel a fraction of the way I do. But you're just too stubborn to see it."

"What...what are you talking about?" Sloane paled and stepped back.

I walked towards her, leaning down into her space. I needed to be close to her. I needed her to know how I felt. To know that she was the one who made my heart race and my palms sweat. She was the only one who made me feel alive.

"I'm in love with you, Sloane. *I am.* Not Alfie. I have loved you since we were seven years old playing knights by the sea." My face was inches from hers, her breath trembling against my lips. Gently, I cradled her cheek, and her pupils widened. "And I will love you until the day I die."

I kissed her.

The instant my lips touched hers, I realized that this was the kiss I'd been waiting my entire life for. Sloane's breath caught and trembled. Angling my face, I cupped her head and drew her deeper, my tongue touching hers, tasting the sweetness of her mouth. Her hands went to my chest, her palms against my wildly beating heart. She softened, opening to me, inviting me in as every sexual impulse I had went wild. This was it. This right here, finally holding Sloane in my arms, kissing her, this was where my life truly began.

Until she froze, broke the kiss, and shoved me away.

I tried to reach for her, but she held up a hand. It was trembling. "Don't. Don't touch me."

"Sloane—"

"Stop."

I stepped back. "I'm sorry. I thought—"

"What—you thought you loved me?" Sloane laughed bitterly. "Tommy, you don't know the first thing about love. You think you're in love? Newsflash, you're not. You're just like every other guy. You can't stand that someone else might be interested in me, so now you've got to make a move. You know, I see how you are with women, but I never thought you would stoop this low. I thought we were friends."

This was all going so wrong. "We are, but—"

"Friends don't shove their tongue down their friend's throat! God, you're such an asshole!" Sloane turned away, tears glistening in her eyes. She wiped them angrily with her sleeve.

"Come on, spitfire. Don't do this."

"Don't call me that!" Tears were falling down her face freely, now. Fuck. I had made her cry. "God, Tommy, just...just go. I can't even look at you right now."

Sloane whirled and fled the alleyway, her boots splashing through the puddles as she stomped away. I watched her go, my heart cracking in two.

What just happened?

I went back into the bar and headed straight for the bathroom. I locked the door behind me, then I stood there, staring at my reflection in the mirror. My hands were still shaking, and I had to clench them to steady them. I hadn't felt this much in years, and it was fucking terrifying. I wanted to throw up.

I stared at the stranger in the mirror, the man who'd just blown it with the only woman who'd ever mattered. How could I have been so stupid? She was right. I was an asshole.

I punched the wall, and blood stained the paint. My knuckles throbbed in agony, but the pain felt good. It was something to focus on other than my aching heart. I leaned my head against the cool tile, breathing deeply.

Well, that was it. Cassidy had been wrong. I'd gambled, put my heart out there, but all I had done was make matters worse. I'd be lucky if I didn't lose Sloane forever over this. The thought made me anxious and unsettled.

What the hell was I going to do now?

I took a few more minutes to collect myself, then I splashed some cold water on my face and went back out into the bar. Connor and Alfie still needed me, and there was only one thing I could do.

Forget about Sloane, roll up my sleeves, and get back to fucking work.

1

Sloane

South Boston, MA – NOW

I slid a glass across the polished wooden bar, the amber liquid sloshing the dim light as it settled in front of one of the regulars. The clink of glasses and conversational hum filled the bar as I wiped the worn wood top down with a white rag. The bar was packed tonight.

Most people didn't know this, but Lady Devine's belonged to me. Sixty years of history sat in front of me in the form of faded photographs and worn wooden booths, and the weight of it settled around me, grounding and real in a way some things in this life never seemed to be.

It was all mine, now.

Faded signs and photographs lined the walls in memorial to the generations of Southie Irish who had frequented this place. Behind me, shelves stocked with liquor bottles gleamed in the low light, while I expertly poured pints of Guinness and Boston Lager for the regulars. Lady D's was a dive, but it was more of a home than my own apartment was, than all the properties my father owned. I wasn't sure if that was ironic or just sad.

I cashed out a customer and drew another draft. Ironic. Yeah. Let's go with that.

You see, the percentage of Lady Devine's that actually operated as a bar was relatively minute compared to its true reason for existence—as a front for the McTiernan Clan, the notorious Irish mob factor that controlled South Boston from Shawmut to the Seaport, formerly headed by my father, Callum McTiernan.

My hands moved on autopilot, sliding drinks across the counter to familiar faces. My grandfather had started the bar and passed it down to his son. Back in the late sixties, Lady Devine's really had just been a neighborhood bar, precisely located to cater to the wave of dockworkers who came in for a quick drink or two before heading home to the wife and kids. Then came the seventies and the big cranes. Mechanization. Automation. Jobs became scarce, the neighborhood went to shit, and everybody turned to an Irishman fresh off the boat, looking at him to solve all their problems.

This man's name was Michael Quinn. He and my father went into business for themselves back in 1973 in the upstairs office of Lady Devine's, and they hadn't looked back since.

At least, not until two years ago.

For decades, The McTiernan Clan ruled South Boston. On paper, we had the bar. We provided protection to local businesses and residents and received a cut under the table. A look the other way. A good word to the cops. On the flip side of things, we ran guns. Sure, we dabbled in the rest of your standard organized crime fare, but guns were our thing. Shipped from overseas through our port of control, then distributed to all points west and south. And for a long time, it worked. Until one young doctor with a chip on her shoulder witnessed a mafia hit from our rivals and everything went south.

"Another round, Sloane?" called out a patron from the end of the bar, his Boston accent thick as he raised his empty pint glass.

"Coming right up, Jimmy," I replied with a practiced smile, pushing back a stray lock of my black bobbed hair. My hands moved with efficiency, pouring pints of Harpoon IPA and shots of Tullamore Dew, the familiar scents mingling with the salty tang of the harbor that crept in through the open doorway.

I frowned at the tap. I was going to have to grab another keg of Boston Lager soon. A year ago, we didn't go through nearly this much alcohol, but, then again, most of our time was spent in the back room trying to fight our way through a situation that went from bad to worse. The doctor, who was none other than Tommy's estranged younger sister, got a price placed on her head and was married off to my cousin Connor for safekeeping. That turned into another debacle when Connor actually fell in love with her, and one of our own men, Teagan Kelley, turned coat, abducted Cassidy, and brought her to our rival in the north, Lorenzo Moretti.

Connor had nearly burned down Boston to find her, and the fallout had been immense. Southie was crawling with cops. The Italian doubled down. Murders started popping up with signatures loosely tying them to us, and just when we thought it couldn't get worse, our Master-at-Arms, Alfie Doyle, fell in love with Lorenzo's adopted daughter and started seeing her in secret.

"Hey, Sloane," Grady greeted me as he approached the bar, his good-natured smile a welcome sight among the sea of faces. "Busy night, huh?"

"Tell me about it," I replied with a wry grin as I handed him his usual. "Summer's here and everybody suddenly wants to party. It's a Friday, which is great, but it's been like this all week, and it's driving me nuts."

"You should consider getting some more help," he suggested, taking a sip of his beer. "You can't do all this yourself."

I huffed a breath and shook my head, tucking my black bob behind my ears as I finished up the drinks for the three guys down the bar. "I can't afford anyone else right now."

"I know somebody! He just got his license and is practically foaming at the mouth for a job," Grady offered with an eager smile.

"I don't know, Grady," I hesitated, leaning my elbows against the counter. "I've been burned enough times in the past. I have to be careful who I bring in here, now."

"I wouldn't steer you wrong, Sloane," Grady promised. "Trust me. He's a good guy, and he could use the work. What do you have to lose?"

Honestly, if I was going to let anyone behind my bar it was going to be my friend Kat, who worked as a bartender uptown. But if it made Grady feel better, I guess I could try his guy out.

"Fine," I relented with a sigh. "If you think he'd work out, bring him in on Monday night, and I'll give him a try."

I watched Grady take a sip of his beer, smacking his lips in satisfaction. He was a short, paunchy, balding man in his late thirties, who inexplicably always seemed to wear an expression of bemused contentment at his situation in life. No one would ever expect him to be a key player for the Irish mob.

Two overdressed women sat at the bar next to Grady, and he straightened up a little higher. I smirked and turned, pretending I didn't see.

"Hey, can you believe this place?" the twenty-something woman said to her friend, her voice threaded with excitement. "It's so authentic."

"Real Southie vibe, yeah." Her friend nodded, sipping a craft cocktail.

I couldn't help but let out a quiet snort. Authentic? Sure, but if these walls could talk, they'd tell tales that would have half these folks running for the hills. They didn't know the blood that had seeped into the floorboards or the echoes of whispered secrets that lingered like spirits in the air.

"Is it always this lively?" another newcomer asked, leaning against the bar with interest glinting in his eyes.

"Only when the company's good," I shot back with a wink at Grady, encouraging him. His wife had divorced him two years ago, and he guy could use a break. I motioned to the empty glasses in front of him. "Another round?"

"Sure thing," he replied. "Keep 'em coming."

As I pulled his beer, I surveyed the crowd. Ever since Callum stepped down as head of the clan last year, we'd become just another hole in the wall. The neighborhood was changing around us, shiny new condos and craft breweries popping up like weeds and pushing out the grit that had defined this part of South Boston for decades.

But the neighborhood wasn't the only thing that had changed.

The events of last year had led up to an all-out war with the Italians that left Lorenzo and his two sons dead. Connor and Tommy had been taken hostage by the Italians, Alfie had been seriously injured, and Connor nearly died in the back of a van while his wife gave birth prematurely to their son.

The fallout had been immense. Lorenzo's death left a vacuum in North Boston where the Italians once reigned. Callum retired. Connor and Cassidy moved to the suburbs with their baby son, Aiden. Alfie and Emilia ended up faking their own deaths and moved down to North Carolina, a rather dramatic move if you asked me, but at least it kept them safe.

And Tommy?

He was here, picking up the pieces along with me.

At least, that's what he was supposed to be doing.

I eyed Grady across the bar. Too bad, the two blonds had moved on.

"How's the new gig treating you?" I asked.

"Keeping me on my toes," he admitted, taking a sip and nodding in approval. "But you know how it is—gotta keep the peace somehow."

I chuckled dryly, polishing another glass until it shone under the dim lights. "Peace is a rare commodity around here."

"True enough." Grady leaned against the bar, his gaze surveying the room like a hawk. Master-at-Arms suited him, though no one would replace Alfie Doyle.

Alfie. The thought of him sent a sharp pang through my chest. He had a way about him, all dark red hair and tattoos, with that sarcastic wit that could disarm you at fifty paces. My heart had been foolish enough to fall for him, but his was already spoken for.

Grady's eyes narrowed, noticing my distraction. "Everything okay? You seem...I don't know. Off."

I shrugged, wiping down the bar. "Just thinking about the old days, that's all."

My gaze drifted to the photos again, lingering on a familiar face. Sharp blue eyes, a crooked smile, and tattoos peeking out from under a leather jacket. A twist in my gut, as fresh as the day he'd ridden out of my life for good. I'd loved him with a fierceness that stole my breath, but in the end, I couldn't compete with Emilia. Not for Alfie Doyle.

I had moved on from Alfie, or so I told myself. But moving on felt like trying to wade through molasses—slow, sticky, and leaving traces of bitterness behind.

Grady nodded, knowing. "It's not the same without them. Aiden, Connor, and now Alfie..."

I sighed. "No, it's not. I miss the old days, you know? When it was just us against the world, and we didn't have to worry about shit like this. It was simpler, then. We were younger, I guess."

"Well, I'm older and fatter," he pointed out, patting his belly.

I laughed. "You're not that old, Grady. And you're not fat, you're just big boned."

He snorted. "Right."

I smiled, but it faded quickly. It was true, though. Things had changed. The clan wasn't what it used to be. And while I knew it wasn't fair to heap the blame solely on Tommy's massive shoulders, he certainly wasn't helping.

"You hear from Callum lately?" Grady asked.

My eyes drifted toward the wall clock, and I thought about Callum up in Kennebunkport, Maine. He was living a life I could hardly picture—retired, spending his days fishing with Michael Quinn. Michael was dying of pancreatic cancer, and Dad... Dad was just gone in a way that wasn't about distance. They were playing grandparents to little Aiden, teaching him how to fish on his little practice pole and making sandcastles on the beach. Simple pleasures of a life I didn't seem to fit into anymore.

"Your old man's doing what he needs to. Its good he's there for Michael," Grady said quietly, as if reading my mind. It was eerie sometimes, how he did that. "He's earned a rest. They both have."

"Yeah, good for him," I muttered, not sure if I meant it. It was hard to reconcile the image of the man who had once led the McTiernan Clan with a vengeance, now content to live out his days in peaceful obscurity. It was like he had shed his skin, and the father I knew was just another layer discarded and forgotten.

"Change ain't always bad," Grady continued, as though it was his mission to pull me out of the quicksand of my thoughts.

"Isn't it?" I challenged, meeting his steady gaze. "Feels like losing a piece at a time."

"Or finding new ones," he countered, taking a thoughtful sip of his beer. "I heard Cassidy's pregnant again."

"Oh, really?"

"Tommy told me. Looks like little Aiden's going to be a big brother."

I tried to infuse some warmth into my smile, but it fell flat. "That's great news. I'm happy for them. How's Connor doing?"

"Seems all right," he replied, taking another sip. "Can't say I blame him for staying out of the way. Adjusting to live without all the...drama."

My eyes strayed to the faded photograph on the wall, one of the last pictures taken of my twin brother Aiden. My throat tightened as a familiar pang of grief bloomed. Even now, so many years later, I still missed him. Missed his smile and his laughter, the way he always knew how to cheer me up on my darkest days. He'd been my partner in crime, my confidant, the one person who'd known me even better than I knew myself.

Aiden had been dead for years, now. The memory of that fateful night still haunted me—how he'd taken Connor's place at a drop with Tommy. They'd been ambushed by the Russians, and Aiden had ended up dying in Tommy's arms. Losing him had been like losing a part of my soul. And the worst part was, it had been so senseless—the result of a stupid mistake that never should have happened. If Connor hadn't backed out at the last second...if Tommy had been paying closer attention...

It had been years, but I was still angry. Angry at Tommy, at the Russians, at the whole damned world. But most of all, I was angry at myself. Because if I'd tried harder to talk Aiden out of that run, if I'd refused to let him take Connor's place...he might still be here.

With an effort, I pushed the thought away. No amount of wishing would change the past. Aiden was gone, and nothing I did would ever bring him back.

Still, it rankled that Tommy never talked about him. Never seemed to show an ounce of regret for his role in Aiden's death. They'd been friends once—as close as brothers—but in the aftermath of that awful night, Tommy had retreated into a shell of cynicism and indifference, and it had only gotten worse since Callum retired and left him in charge.

The clink of glasses and low hum of conversations swirled around me like a comforting blanket, but the ache remained. I had just finished wiping down the counter when Grady's nasal voice pulled me out of my thoughts.

"Tommy! Good to see you, man!" He called out, raising his hand in greeting as Tommy pulled up a barstool next to him.

Speak of the devil.

Tommy looked worse for wear, as usual. That once strong jawline was looking rather scruffy these days, giving him the look of a man who'd lost track of time, or maybe just stopped caring. His clothes were rumpled, probably slept in, and a fresh bruise was blooming along his jawline, complemented by a busted lip that had definitely seen better days. But it was the blankness in his gaze that unsettled me most.

Once, Tommy had lived as loudly as anyone I'd ever known, full of cocky charm and wry humor. The man had been a walking, talking, exclamation point. Now he was a ghost of his former self, and it really pissed me off. Did he think he was the only one struggling? The only one the past few years had worn down? Our eyes met from across the bar, and for a second something flickered in Tommy's gaze. Regret? Longing? It was gone before I could guess, replaced by his usual indifferent mask.

"What do you want?" I asked flatly.

Tommy shrugged, sliding onto one of the barstools. "Same as everyone else. A drink."

I arched an eyebrow at him.

He narrowed his eyes. "Whiskey."

"How'd you get that?"

"What?"

"The busted lip."

"Fightin'."

"Jesus, Tommy, you're a menace. You ma must've had her hands full with you."

My head shot up when Tommy wasn't ready with another rapid-fire comeback, and I immediately realized what I'd said. Tommy's mother was killed when he was barely out of high school by a car bomb intended for her husband, Michael. Her death had torn the family apart, causing a rift that perpetuated for the better part of a decade. A rift that had only barely begun to heal.

I sheepishly looked down at the glass in my hand. "Sorry."

"Don't be. Cass never wants to talk about her, half the time I think she'd rather pretend we never had a mother at all. But I...I like talking about her."

"I know," I murmured, swallowing hard.

He cleared his throat, clearly uncomfortable. "Besides, you're right. I was a shithead as a kid."

I nodded. "You're still a shithead, Tommy."

He smirked. "Then how about another round for this shithead? You can leave the bottle this time."

I rolled my eyes but poured him another shot anyway, watching as he tossed it back with ease. I hated to admit it, but he was good at his job, at least when he wasn't off fighting or fucking his way through half of South Boston. Tommy was ruthless and efficient, able to cut through the bullshit and get to the heart of the matter, whether it was a negotiation or a firefight.

But there was a darkness in him that seemed to grow with every passing day. It scared me, to be honest. He'd always had a temper, like a powder keg set to explode, but this was something darker. Deadlier.

Tommy reached for the bottle.

"Moving right along tonight, aren't you?"

"Wouldn't be the worst way to go," Tommy said, the corner of his mouth twitching up as he lifted the glass to his lips and took a deep swallow.

"Sure, if you're the live fast and die young type." I leaned against the bar, arms crossed. "But some of us are still hoping you'll pull your head out of your ass."

"Keep hoping, Sloane," he snorted derisively. "It's what you're best at."

"Asshole," I muttered.

Tommy just shrugged. He poured himself another shot of whiskey and downed it in one gulp, hissing as the alcohol burned its way down his throat.

I glared at him, trying to ignore the tug of concern. Tommy had never been an easy man to love, but he'd also never been this self-destructive. And I hated to admit it, but I was worried about him. Worried about what he'd do if he kept going down this path. Worried he'd do something stupid and get himself killed. Worried he'd drag the rest of us down with him.

I grabbed the bottle from him, ignoring his protests, and poured him one last shot, sliding it across the bar to him. He gave me a wry look.

"I wasn't finished with that," he drawled.

I arched an eyebrow at him. "You are now. You need to slow down."

"Speaking of work," Grady interrupted even though nobody had mentioned a thing about work. "I've got a meeting set up with a new buyer tomorrow. Callum recommended them, so they should be good for business."

"Whatever," Tommy said dismissively, waving him off with one hand as he took another gulp of whiskey. "Do what you think is best."

Grady and I exchanged a glance. Tommy's indifference was becoming a real problem. Someone was going to fill the hole left by Lorenzo Moretti sooner or later, and if we didn't make a play for new inventory and territory, the clan would lose its grip.

"We need to talk about this," I said sharply. "This is your operation now, Tommy. Act like it."

Tommy looked up with a scowl, but for the first time I saw a flicker of his old self in his eyes. "You questioning my authority?" he rasped.

"Someone has to," I shot back. "Before you run the whole clan into the ground."

I watched as anger and pride flared in his eyes. He opened his mouth to reply, but just then, a voice cut loudly across our conversation.

"Hey, is that Tommy Quinn?" A couple of burly guys strode up to the bar, grinning like idiots. "Hell of a fight tonight, man."

"Yeah, that was savage," one of them said, slapping Tommy heartily on the back as they arrived beside us.

"Pure carnage," agreed the other, his eyes wide with a mix of admiration and awe.

"Thanks," Tommy replied, forcing a smile as he turned to greet them. "I aim to please."

"Are you kidding? That was some of the best action I've seen in years. You really put the hurt on that guy, man."

"Hey, what can I say? I'm good with my fists."

Tommy shot me a triumphant look as the two guys laughed. I rolled my eyes and turned back to the bar, ignoring him. If he wanted to get his ass kicked in a ring every other night, that was his business. But I wasn't going to sit back and watch him throw away everything we'd worked so hard for.

Tommy moved off with his new friends, and Grady and I fell into an uneasy silence. I busied myself wiping down the bar, trying to ignore the knot of anger and frustration building in my chest.

"He's just going through a rough patch," Grady said quietly, as if reading my mind.

"A rough patch?" I snorted. "It's been more than a year, Grady. He needs to pull his head out of his ass and start acting like the leader he's supposed to be. Or are we just going to sit back and let someone else take over North Boston? Because I can tell you right now, I won't let that happen without a fight."

Grady sighed. "I know, Sloane. But it's not that easy. You know how much Tommy looked up to Callum. And with Michael, the cancer..."

My face heated. I'd forgotten about Tommy's dad. I guess it was easy enough, being as removed as I was from the whole situation, but still. Having to watch not one but both of your parents die wasn't something one just shrugged off. I didn't think to ask how Tommy was doing with all that because he never spoke about it. Not once.

"Tommy visits him a couple times a week," Grady continued, "But it's hard for him to step into his shoes. Besides, things have been quiet lately. Maybe that's a good thing."

"You know what they say about the calm before the storm, right?" I retorted, polishing a glass with more force than was necessary. "If we don't make a play for new territory and inventory, the Russians or the Italians will. And then where will we be? We'll be right back where we started—on the defensive, fighting tooth and nail to survive."

I slammed the glass down on the counter harder than I intended, the noise drawing the heads of a couple patrons. Anger and frustration built inside me, threatening to boil over. Tommy needed to get his act together, or we were all going to be in trouble.

Grady watched me closely, concern written all over his face. "We're not on the defensive, Sloane. And we're not going to be. I promise."

I scoffed. "Sure doesn't seem that way to me."

"Hey, boss." Grady reached across the counter and put his hand over mine, giving it a gentle squeeze. "Give him some time. He'll come around. He just needs to work some things out."

"Yeah, well, he'd better do it soon," I muttered darkly, "or we're all going to be in a world of trouble."

2

Tommy

Gunshots are louder in movies than they are in real life. Pop. Pop. Pop. Inconsequential noises, really. Little things you almost don't notice, because maybe it's just a car backfiring or some kids shooting off fireworks. They certainly couldn't be coming from the people standing across the alley that your naive twenty-two-year-old mind trusted.

Aiden's eyes are so wide, it's almost comical. Or at least it would be under any other circumstances. He looks confused, almost, his hands brushing over his chest like he was shooing away an annoying insect. Standing one second, then he just drops, knees buckling, fast and clumsy like a bag of concrete to the ground, flat on his back. He's still brushing at his chest.

I'm not sure what's happening at first.

Then I see the gun.

They're shooting at us.

It's okay though. Aiden is wearing a vest. We both are. Bullets can't go through vests, that's why they're called bulletproof.

I am twenty-two years old when I find out that a high-powered rifle round can penetrate body armor.

Blood wells under Aiden's fingers. A dark stain spreads across his shirt.

So much blood.

I pull him into my arms. Rip off his vest. There's a small little hole in his shirt, right where his heart would be. It sucks wetly, pulsating crimson.

"No, no, no—"

"It's...okay," he coughs thickly, trying for a smile. "Just...got the...wind knocked out of me."

"Shh, don't talk, just breathe," I plead. My voice cracks. I press my hands over his, trying to stem the flow of blood. "You're gonna be fine. Just hold on, alright?"

Aiden tries to speak again but only manages a wet, choking sound. Blood trickles from both corners of his mouth.

"Somebody help! We need help!"

He looks so young. So damned scared.

"T-Tommy..."

I don't know what to do. I don't know what to say.

"I'm here," I hold him close. "I'm here, Aiden. Help's coming, just...just hang on, okay?"

"C-Can't...breathe..."

Aiden coughs again, choking. Blood bubbles past my fingers. His eyes are wide and filled with terror, but he's still trying to be brave. He's always been the brave one.

I hold him as tightly as I can, as if somehow that might keep him from slipping away. Tears prick my eyes and I swallow hard. "Just stay with me, okay? Stay with me, Aiden. Please."

Beneath my hands, I feel his heart slow. Stutter. I see the blood slow and his face relax. His hand loses its grip on my shirt.

I shake him, desperate, but his head rolls limply against my chest, his eyes half-open and glassy.

Someone is screaming.

I don't realize that it's me.

Nobody comes. I am alone on that dark street with my best friend dying in a pool of his own blood, but when I look back down, it's not Aiden's face anymore.

It's Connor's.

"Tommy, keep pressure on the wound!" My sister is by my side, shouting orders through gritted teeth as her body tenses with contractions. The van tilts beneath us. I scramble to shove my hands over Connor's abdomen.

"I'm trying Cass," I grunt, panic rising in my throat. The blood just keeps coming.

The stethoscope in Cassidy's hands shakes. It's the first time I'd ever seen her look so lost. "I can barely hear the heart. Blood pressure's dropping. W-We need to start an IV."

"Can you tell if he's bleeding internally?" Alfie rasps.

"I...I don't know."

Her voice breaks, and I break with it. Cassidy ducks her head, trying to hide the tears that threaten to fall. "I-I can't even think right now, I—"

Connor blinks sluggishly before focusing on me. He raises a bloodstained hand. "Promise..."

No, no, no. This is not happening again.

I can't—

"Don't do this shit, brother." I grip his hand back like I gripped Aiden's. "You are not dying. You're going to be fine, so don't start asking for promises—"

"Take...care...of them."

"You're gonna take care of them yourself. You're gonna see your son be born, okay? Don't be a fucking martyr. I can't lose you, too. I won't. Dammit, Connor, don't do this. Don't you dare do this to me again—"

But he is already gone.

I gasped awake, choking on the air like a drowning man as I fought against...something...where was I?

My bed.

My room.

My apartment.

Still gasping for air, I shoved at the suffocating sheets. I didn't want to get blood on them, because my hands...my hands...

Were trembling. But clean. Unmarked.

It was just a dream. That same fucking dream.

My heart was still racing, throwing itself violently against my sternum like it was trying to break out. I pressed my hand to my chest as if that would be enough to keep it where it belonged.

Jesus Christ.

I sat up and rubbed my hand over my face, sweaty and clammy. My head pounded in time with my heart. I pressed the heels of my hands against my eyes until starbursts exploded behind my lids, trying to banish the images seared into my mind. Even after all these years, they were still a knife to the gut.

The clock said it was almost noon. I had been asleep for only a few hours, but it felt like I hadn't slept in days. My skin was prickling, my senses on high alert as I listened to the sounds of the city drifting through the window.

I swung my legs over the side of the bed and dropped my head into my hands, elbows braced on my knees. My breath came in ragged gasps as tried to push through the foggy remnants of the dream. It was always the same.

No matter how many times I relived it, it never got any easier.

I peeled myself off the sweat-drenched sheets, my body a lead weight of aching hangover and restless demons. I made it to the bathroom just in time to empty the contents of my stomach into the toilet.

Charming.

Once the vomiting stopped, I pulled myself up to take a piss. The cold tiles under my feet were grounding in a way that reality wasn't right now, but I still felt like something that had been scraped off the bottom of a shoe, and the floor beneath my feet tilted ominously.

The fluorescent lights above the mirror were unforgiving, illuminating every flaw. I leaned on the sink and glared at my reflection. If it weren't for the tattoos and wilted fauxhawk, I wouldn't have recognized myself. Shadows clung to the hollows of my cheeks, eyes bloodshot, skin pale. My once hard, sculpted body had softened, and just below the ink scrawled across my chest, toned abs had given way to the beginnings of a gut. A tangible sign of decline.

"Gettin' old," I scoffed, turning away from the ghoulish sight of my own reflection. "And not like fine whiskey."

I dragged myself downstairs, bare feet slapping against the cold wood floor. The familiar ache behind my eyes had blossomed into a full-blown migraine, made worse by the whiskey sloshing in my stomach. Every step jarred until I made it to the kitchen and popped a handful of aspirin, chasing them down with a glass of water and a few deep breaths.

The kitchen was no kinder than the bathroom; the morning light streaming through the blinds was harsh, revealing last night's sins spread out on the counters. With a grimace, I poured some Cap'n Crunch into a bowl while I rummaged through the cupboards with the other. After a brief search, I found what I was looking for – a half-full bottle of whiskey. Hair 'o the dog. Downing two shots quickly, I winced at the burning sensation but welcomed the temporary relief from my headache. I chased it with a sigh, feeling somewhat human again.

"Alright," I said to the empty room, "let's get this shitshow started."

I flicked the coffee maker on, the familiar gurgle and aroma a small comfort in the chaos of my mind. As the dark brew filled my mug, I eyed the mess around me: scattered bottles, unwashed dishes, general disarray. The place used to be immaculate, all high-end furnishings, polished surfaces, and sleek electronics. Now, it looked like something out of a post-apocalyptic film.

Early frat boy meets wino, I thought acidly.

"Probably shouldn't have fired the maid," I chuckled, although laughter felt like a foreign concept. There was no one here to hear it anyway.

The coffee burned as I gulped it down, the bitterness somehow fitting. But it lacked kick, so I unscrewed the whiskey again, tipping the bottle over my mug. The amber swirls blended with the black, an intoxicating alchemy that promised to numb the loud fucking shit playing on repeat in my head—at least for a while.

My phone buzzed on the counter, the vibrations rattling across the laminate. I glanced down at the caller ID. Callum.

I stared at the screen for a moment, then let it ring. And ring. And ring.

I had nothing to say to him. Not now, maybe not ever.

What could he possibly have to say to me, anyway? Sorry I left you to pick up the pieces? Thanks for keeping everything together, kiddo?

Yeah, right.

I set down my coffee and headed out into the living room, my feet carrying me without conscious thought. That room was a mess, too, but I barely noticed. My eyes were fixed on the wall of photographs and memorabilia that I'd created in a vain attempt to reclaim some semblance of the past.

It was a shrine to my failure, a memorial to the life I once had, the family I'd lost. Connor? Gone. Alfie? Gone. Aiden...dead. And in the middle of it all, a single photograph of the man that I'd idolized my entire life, his steely blue eyes gazing out from beneath the brim of his hat.

Michael Quinn. My father. The former head of the Irish mob. The man whose shoes I was supposed to fill. The man whose legacy I was supposed to protect. The man whose expectations I could never seem to meet.

He'd be gone soon, too.

I stared at the picture of him, but all I saw was disappointment. In me, in the way I'd let things go. In the choices I'd made. The things I hadn't done.

He'd never say it to my face, but then again, he didn't have to. I already knew it.

My head was fuzzy, but not fuzzy enough to dull the anger that simmered beneath the surface. Anger at Connor and Alfie for finding love and abandoning me, leaving me to deal with the mess they'd made. Anger at Callum for checking out and leaving the reigns of the clan in my ill-equipped hands.

And anger at Sloane for judging me. She had no idea what it was like, what I was dealing with. How could she? She was just another person who'd left me. Another person I ultimately wasn't good enough for. Someone who I was obsessively, irrevocably in love with, someone I thought could be my happily ever after, but someone who would never care for me even a fraction of the way I cared for her.

But most of all, I was angry at myself. Disgusted by my own self-pity. And I was tired. So damn tired of being the one left behind. Tired of caring only to be kicked in the teeth.

Goddamnit, I needed to hit something.

I grabbed my gym bag from the floor and headed for the door. God help the poor shmuck who stepped into the ring with me today.

The heavy bag in front of me wasn't enough to absorb the piss and vinegar eating through my veins. Every strike hit harder than the last, each blow more vicious. My knuckles were split and bleeding, my breath ragged, but I couldn't stop. I needed to keep going, relishing the burn of pain in my muscles, the ache in my bones. It was the only way to quiet the voices in my head.

"Christ, Tommy, you're gonna tear that thing from the ceiling," Big Saul's voice cut through the haze of my exertion, his tone light but edged with concern.

I glanced at him, barely registering the peculiar sight of this small, scholarly man with the tweedly little mustache amidst the clanging weights and grunts of exertion. "It can handle it," I growled before turning back to the bag.

"Your hands, however, might not," he remarked dryly. I hadn't bothered to tape my knuckles.

It was ironic that the owner of this grungy fight club was such a tiny, bookish guy – but he knew his stuff and had helped turn the place around since I'd bought controlling shares a few years back. "You ready to let off some real steam?"

"Always."

"Good, 'cause we got a new guy who's been talking big game. Thinks he can take you on," Saul said, his eyes twinkling with mischief. "Figured you might enjoy showing him the ropes."

"Perfect."

"Hey, Quinn!" A cocky voice called from the other side of the gym, drawing my attention to a well-muscled man with a smirk plastered on his face. "Heard you're the one to beat around here."

"Something like that," I replied, stepping into the ring. "But you won't be the one to do it."

"Talk is cheap, old man," the guy taunted, already bouncing on his toes like he was itching for a fight. I read the arrogance in his eyes – he thought he had me pegged, but he had no idea what he was about to face.

I rolled my neck, working out the kinks and a smile curled my lips. I didn't even bother to get into a stance as I motioned for him to bring it on.

The kid was good, I'll give him that. Fast on his feet, light on his toes. But he telegraphed his punches like a neon sign, and it was all too easy to dodge and deflect his hits. I watched him dance around me, feinting and jabbing. He was playing with me, like a cat with a mouse. But I wasn't about to let him get the upper hand.

I waited for my moment, then struck. My fist connected with his jaw, snapping his head back. He reeled away from me, eyes rolling in his head. But I wasn't done yet. I followed up with another blow to the ribs, sending him staggering backwards.

The kid came at me again, swinging wildly. I blocked his blows with ease, then landed a solid punch to his stomach, doubling him over. I followed up with an uppercut that sent him sprawling to the ground.

He lay there, dazed and gasping for breath. I stood over him, my own chest heaving, then I reached a hand down and hauled him to his feet. "C'mon, you ain't done yet."

The kid glared at me. He was feisty, I'd give him that. He spat on the mat and launched himself at me again, determined to make me pay for humiliating him. I feinted a jab, then landed a vicious hook to the kid's side. A groan escaped his lips as he stumbled back, but I didn't give him time to recover. I dodged his clumsy assault and slammed a knee into his gut, knocking the wind out of him.

"Ease up, Tommy!" Saul warned, concern etched on his face. "That's out of line!"

I ignored him, focusing on the adrenaline coursing through my veins. I landed another blow, then another, until the kid was on the ground and barely able to move.

I stood over him, panting heavily.

"Alright, break it up!" Saul finally intervened, stepping between the kid and me. He shot me a stern look. "Tommy, you need to watch yourself. The ref would have to be blind not to call that, and I don't want to see you barred from the ring."

"Relax," I said with a dismissive wave of my hand as I helped the kid to his feet. "I've got it under control."

"Control? You call that control?" Saul shook his head. "You're supposed to be teaching this guy a lesson, not beating him into a coma."

"Then he'll know not to get into the ring with me next time." The look the kid shot me was withering but tinged with respect, and I watched as he gingerly made his way to the locker room, glad to see he wasn't too roughed up. I didn't mean to go that far with him.

Saul sighed and pinched the bridge of his nose. "Tommy, you're better than this. This isn't the way you used to fight. You need to find a way to channel your anger, this...this aggression into something positive. This is destructive, and I'm not just referring to the poor sap who steps into the ring with you."

I bristled. "Thank you, Dr. Phil. Am I going to be charged for these little words of wisdom, or is it on the house?"

"Don't be an asshole. You better not pull this shit at the fight tomorrow night."

"Look, I'm fine. Just leave me alone."

Saul studied me for a long moment before shaking his head and walking away. I peeled off my gloves. Aches and pains were starting to slip past the waning adrenaline, but it felt good in a way that always made me crave more.

As I headed toward the locker room, I spotted Saul's niece, Lizzy, waiting for me in the hallway. Her dark, curly hair was cut into a short bob, and her crooked little smile with one dimple peeking out had always reminded me of the way Sloane used to smile at me.

"Hey, you," she said, her voice soft and sweet.

I forced myself to smile back. "Hey."

She bit her bottom lip, looking up at me through thick lashes. "You looked good in there," she said, nodding towards the gym. "Real good."

"Thanks," I replied, winking. It was a move that usually worked with women, but this time, the gesture felt awkward and forced.

Her eyes traced over my body, lingering on my tattoos, and she smiled coyly. "You know, if you ever want a sparring partner outside the ring... I'm free tonight."

The offer was tempting. She was attractive, and I knew she'd be a handful in bed. But there was no spark, no connection, nothing that made my breath catch or my heart pound. And that was the problem.

I forced another smile. "I appreciate the offer, but I think I'm gonna call it a night."

She pouted, batting her lashes. "Are you sure? I know some moves that would leave you begging for more."

I chuckled dryly. "I'm sure you do, sweetheart. Another time, maybe."

Her hand reached out to touch my chest, but I pulled away, unable to bear the thought of anyone else touching me right now.

Lizzy's mouth tightened into a small pout, one that made her look like a bratty little kid. "You know, the guys all think you're losing your edge. They say you're playing too close to the line."

"Do they now?" I said with a scoff, turning away to hide the flash of anger. "They worry too much."

Lizzy moved closer, still trying for something I wasn't going to give her, her hand coming up to brush my shoulder. "If you ever need anything, Tommy..."

"Just go," I rasped.

"You're kind of a jerk, you know that?"

I turned and walked down the hall to the showers. "As much as this may surprise you, sweetheart, you are not the first person to tell me that today. And you won't be the last."

I stepped under the hot spray and let the water wash away the sweat and grime. Damn that cute little bob and dimpled smile. I tried to focus on the soothing spray of hot water against my tense muscles, but my thoughts kept returning to Sloane. Her laughter, her wit, her fierce loyalty – everything about her was intoxicating. I ached for her.

But she was never going to be mine.

I rested my forehead against the cool tile, cursing myself for falling in love with someone so unattainable. She'd made it clear that she didn't want me in that way, and I couldn't blame her. I was a mess, a ticking time bomb waiting to explode.

I should be over Sloane by now. It was pointless to dwell on what could never be, but I couldn't help myself. Images of her flashed through my mind – the curve of her smile, the flash of fire in her dark green eyes, the way she moved with such grace and confidence. The pert curve of her breasts beneath those too-tight tee shirts, riding up when she'd grab a glass off the high shelf to tease just the briefest hint of soft, lickable skin above her hips. That throaty, sensual voice of hers, the way she said my name even when she was exasperated with me...

My cock twitched. I looked down, surprised to see it standing painfully erect, the head swollen and glistening with a bead of cum just at the thought of her. Breathless and a little dizzy from the tension thrumming through me, I slid my hand down and palmed myself, squeezing until it almost hurt. My eyes closed on instinct. There was no harm in indulging the images that ran through my mind, and all I wanted was some goddamn release. Even if it came at the expense of the ghost of a woman I could never have.

I stroked slowly, teasingly, wishing it was Sloane's hand wrapped around my shaft. God, what I wouldn't give for one more kiss. Just once...I needed her so badly, I could almost hear her voice in my ear, her fingers touching my skin.

"You've always been such a hopeless case. Let me help you, Tommy."

I shuddered, my fantasy becoming more real than ever as a surge of need raced through me. I braced a hand against the tile wall, hot water sluicing over my back as I stroked myself roughly. I groaned. In my mind's eye, it was Sloane's clever fingers wrapped around my cock, her full lips curling into that crooked smile as she leaned in to nip at my throat, her dark hair slick with water as she moved with me.

"Sloane..."

I breathed her name like a prayer, rocking into my fist. I felt my balls tighten, tension coiling in the base of my spine. Her nipples were hardened into two perfect, pink buds, slick with water as I took one into my mouth, then the other, circling with my tongue and biting just hard enough to draw a pleasured gasp from her lips that sent fire straight to the base of my spine.

Her hand grabbed my ass possessively, nails digging in to pull me even closer. Deeper. Harder. My name tumbled from her lips as I pushed into her, lost to the feeling of her body wrapped around mine. I gripped her hip, pulling her against me until I was pressed tight to her, every inch of us touching, a litany of curses and prayers mingled with my name coming from those delicious lips of hers.

Her eyes were dark with lust, her pulse racing beneath my lips as I kissed down the column of her throat, tasting the salty sweetness of her. The goodness, the purity, tainted with a wicked, sinful streak that I loved beyond measure. I was intoxicated, drunk on her touch, her kiss, her body.

"Please, Tommy. Come for me."

She gasped my name, her release shuddering through her, an ecstatic trembling that drew mine from me like a lightning strike. My hand moved faster, driven by desire and desperation as I chased after her, my pleasure burning through me like a wildfire until I came with a ragged groan, spilling myself across my fist and onto the tile.

For a moment, I stood there, letting the spray of the water wash away the last vestiges of the dream. But when I opened my eyes, it was just reality.

Sloane wasn't there.

She had never been there, and she never would be. I was alone.

Panting and flushed, I leaned against the shower wall, the sting of humiliation burning through me. Even in the privacy of my own thoughts, Sloane remained out of reach, a cruel reminder of everything I couldn't have. I stood there for a moment longer, water sluicing down my body, mingling with the remnants of what should have been shared with someone who wanted me as much as I wanted them. But that was just a pipe dream—a fool's hope.

Disgust and self-loathing rose, swift and bitter. I was pathetic, mooning over a woman who wanted nothing to do with me like a lovesick teenager.

With a snarl, I turned off the water and yanked a towel off the rack, scrubbing it over my skin as I stalked out of the shower. After slinging the towel around my waist, I gathered my things and threw them in my gym bag. Work was waiting, and I couldn't afford to be late—not when there were whispers questioning my ability to lead. I couldn't let them see the cracks, the doubt. I had to be the boss, to be Michael Quinn's son, not this... mess.

I stepped out of the locker room, the noise of the gym fading into the background as I made my way to the door. Each step felt like a march toward a future I wasn't sure I wanted, but it was all I had. As I pushed open the door and stepped out into the brisk morning air, I steeled myself for another day in a life that was slowly spiraling beyond my control.

3

Sloane

Going to Tommy's boxing exhibition was a terrible idea. Bringing my friend Kat along was an even worse one.

Stale beer and sweat hit me as soon as I walked through the door of the IBEW hall. I wrinkled my nose but scanned the room for Tommy anyway. He was never going to let me live it down if he found out I'd come tonight. Still, I was curious.

"What are we doing here, Sloane?" Kat asked as she glanced around. "I didn't think you were into boxing."

"I'm not," I replied, still scanning the room. The place was packed with people, most of them from the neighborhood.

"Then why are we here?"

"Because I needed to get out of the apartment, and you said you were bored."

Kat rolled her eyes. "Liar. Try again."

"Just came to see a friend fight, is all."

Her grin widened. "A friend, huh? Is he cute?"

"It's not like that. We just work together." The lie slid off my tongue easy as breathing.

"Oh yeah?" She raised a skeptical eyebrow. "So if this guy is just a coworker, why did you put on those tight little jeans and that slutty top?"

"Hey!" I looked down at my tee shirt. I guess the rips were a little provocative, but so what? "This is my comfy shirt."

"Uh-huh. You keep telling yourself that, girly. I'm not buying it."

"Ugh, you're so annoying." I rolled my eyes and continued to scan the room.

"So, what's this guy like?" Kat asked as we pushed our way through the crowd.

"He's a jerk. Cocky, arrogant, thinks he's God's gift to women."

"Oh yeah?" Kat sounded intrigued. "Sounds like my kind of guy."

I elbowed her in the ribs. Kat grabbed my arm. "Come on, Sloane, lighten up," she said, looping her arm through mine. She and I looked like we could be sisters, both of us sporting short dark hair and a heavy Boston accent. The only difference was her curls. Kat was my friend from down the hall, completely unaware of my connections to the mob. We were both bartenders, and sometimes I'd spend my nights off at her bar when I needed a change of scenery.

"Easy for you to say," I muttered, scanning the crowd for any familiar faces. "You're not the one who has to put up with his shit."

She raised an eyebrow at me. "You sure you ain't got a thing for him?"

"Please," I scoffed, rolling my eyes. "I'd rather kiss a pissed-off porcupine. Come to think of it, actually, that's a pretty close comparison."

She laughed, the sound bright and carefree. "Your secret's safe with me," she teased, unaware of how close to the bone her words sliced.

The atmosphere inside the hall was electric; people shouted and cheered, placing bets and nursing beers as they eagerly awaited the next fight. The ring was set up in the center of the room, surrounded by a crowd of spectators. We found seats just as another match ended, and Kat's attention flitted away, caught by the adrenaline and raw energy pulsing through the hall. Me? I couldn't shake the gnawing sensation in my gut. Tommy was trouble, always had been. I didn't want to care, but there was no denying the pull, the infuriating tug of concern I felt for the man who could never seem to escape his own shadows.

Predictably, Kat was texting and bored after the first few bouts. So was I. I had seen better fights at Lady D's on a Saturday night.

"Hey," I said, tapping her on the shoulder, "I'm gonna grab us drinks."

“Thanks,” she waved me off, distracted by her phone. "I’ll save our seats."

I weaved my way through the crowd towards the concession stand. The line was long, but I was in no hurry to get back to my seat. I fiddled with the hem of my shirt, my thoughts still chasing themselves in circles. Scanning the room, I noticed the bookies tucked away in one corner, taking bets on the fights. None of them looked familiar, and my jaw clenched with frustration over yet another missed opportunity for the clan.

I ordered two beers, then leaned against the wall to people watch. The guys were all pumped up, laughing and slapping each other on the back. The women were just as loud and raucous, cheering and hollering obscenities at the fighters. The noise level was almost deafening, but I saw why Tommy loved it. Despite myself, I was starting to feel a little hyped up.

The announcer called out the next fight just as I got back to our seats.

"Alright folks, it's time for our next fight. Making his way to the ring, weighing in at 220 pounds, the Southie Scrapper, Tommy Quinn!"

The crowd went wild.

"Wow—who is that?" Kat leaned forward, eyes wide as they followed the figure emerging from the shadows. “Is that your guy?”

“He’s not my guy.” I glanced at the ring, my eyes widening as I spotted Tommy. He was stripped to the waist, his muscled torso on full display.

He looked good. Really good.

I couldn't tear my gaze away from him.

Tommy strode towards the ring with a predatory grace that belied his usual swaggering demeanor. I hadn't seen him shirtless since we were kids, but damn, he'd filled out. A canvas of densely inked skin stretched over a frame that had grown considerably since the last time I'd seen him bare-chested. Broad shoulders tapered down to muscular arms, evidence of countless hours spent honing his body into a weapon. His chest was a work of art, dusted with a tantalizing line of dark hair that trailed down to the waistband of his shorts. The black ink swirling over his chest and arms only accentuated how powerful he was.

His chest rose and fell with each breath, showcasing the beginnings of abs that hadn't quite given up their fight against the softness around his middle—a testament to his love affair with liquor. But despite the rough exterior, Tommy was still a formidable sight, radiating a raw, almost savage power as he climbed into the ring.

Dangerous.

"Holy shit," Kat breathed. "He's fucking hot."

I couldn't help but agree. The sight of him was enough to make my heart skip a beat, the butterflies in my stomach taking flight.

"Damn," I whispered under my breath.

"But seriously, is that him?" Kat asked, her eyes wide with interest.

"Yeah," I said weakly, my voice coming out softer than intended. My throat felt tight, and I swallowed hard, trying to ignore the flutter in my stomach. I hated how he could do this to me, how just the sight of him stirred something deep inside, something I'd sworn to keep buried.

"Did he always look like that?" Kat asked, not taking her eyes off him.

"Guess people change," I replied, but my eyes remained fixed on Tommy as he bounced on the balls of his feet, throwing a few shadow punches. He looked ready, dangerous, and for a fleeting moment, I was almost proud—until I remembered that he was about to beat the shit out of some poor sap.

"Ooh, he's cute, too." Kat cooed, eyeing Tommy as he settled into the corner of the ring closest to us. "He's got pretty eyes, and that bone structure... and the hawk is badass. Hell, if you don't want him, I'll take him. I bet a stud like that can go all night."

A jolt shot through me, not of jealousy—definitely not that—but of protectiveness, maybe? Or just plain irritation. "You don't want anything to do with him," I said, sharper than I'd intended. "He's a train wreck."

Kat laughed, the sound short and full of mischief. "Honey, the best ones in bed are."

My cheeks flamed, and I turned away to hide my reaction, but not before shooting her a glare that would've sent weaker souls running. "I don't know what you're talking about."

She snorted, shaking her head at me. "Whatever you say, Sloane. Just tell me one thing."

I sighed. "What?"

"Does he have a girlfriend?"

"No. He's too busy beating the shit out of people and chasing whiskey to find someone to settle down with."

She frowned. "So, you're saying he's a player?"

I rolled my eyes. "I'm saying he's Tommy Quinn. He doesn't date. He fucks around."

"Fine with me," she shrugged.

"Just leave him alone, Kat."

"Okay, okay," she relented, holding up her hands in surrender. "I'll back off. I can see when territory is staked."

I clenched my jaw. Territory staked? There was no territory, nothing between Tommy and me but a shared past and a tangled web of clan business.

And yet, as I watched Tommy bouncing lightly on his feet in the ring, the very image of controlled power and pent-up aggression, I couldn't shake the feeling that something deep within me struggled against the lies I kept telling myself. It wasn't just irritation that bubbled under my skin—it was something darker, more primal.

"Let's just watch the damn fight," I muttered, folding my arms tightly across my chest, as if I could physically hold back the unruly emotions threatening to spill out.

The bell rang, a sharp clang that cut through the din of the crowd like a razor. I leaned forward, elbows on my knees, as Tommy circled his opponent, his movements a fluid contradiction to the brutality of his intent. Graceful yet savage.

"Damn," Kat murmured from beside me, her eyes wide as we watched Tommy dodge a jab only to take a body shot that had the other fighter grinning. But Tommy's answering grin was feral; he absorbed the blow, shook it off, and moved in closer.

"Yeah, well, he's not exactly made of glass," I replied, unable to tear my gaze away from the spectacle unfolding before us. The way Tommy's muscles flexed under the spotlight, the sweat glistening on his skin, it stirred something within me that I didn't want to examine too closely.

The fight grew more intense, both fighters exchanging blows that made the crowd gasp and cheer in equal measure. But Tommy... Tommy was relentless. He pressed his opponent back, graceful and brutal all at once. He sacrificed body shots, knowing full well he could take the pain, and focused on getting close to his opponent, wearing him down one vicious hit after another. The crowd roared, their excitement palpable as they watched the raw display of power.

"Come on, Tommy, make him feel it!" someone shouted behind us, and the sentiment seemed to spread like wildfire, the crowd's energy pulsing with every strike landed.

"He's crazy," I heard someone say in front of me. "You gotta respect a man who can take a hit like that."

"Yeah, but he's taking too many," someone else argued. "He'll never be able to last at this rate."

Tommy danced away from his opponent, circling him like a shark. It was an effective strategy. His opponent was already getting sloppy, tired from throwing too many punches and not dodging enough. Tommy saw an opening and took it, landing a powerful right cross that sent the guy sprawling to the mat.

The crowd went wild, chanting Tommy's name as his opponent struggled to his feet. Tommy grinned, but it wasn't a pleasant sight. He looked primeval, his eyes burning with an intensity that sent a shiver down my spine.

The second round was almost as brutal as the first. Tommy's opponent was visibly tired, struggling to keep up with the pace set by Tommy. It was only a matter of time before Tommy took him down for good. He was toying with his opponent, letting him get in hit after hit, almost like he wanted it. Craved it.

Bloodlust thickened the air. Tommy spread his arms wide, beckoning, the message clear: bring it on.

The crowd's chants grew louder, more raucous, but my legs had turned to jelly and I couldn't seem to stand. The ref shouted something to Tommy, pulling him out of a clinch, but he didn't seem to be listening. Unease coiled in my gut at the ruthlessness in his eyes. This wasn't the Tommy I knew. This was a killer in action.

And then came the fouls. A low blow that had the ref stepping in, another warning issued that went unheeded by Tommy, who smirked and set his stance once more. Another foul, this time an elbow that connected too low. The crowd was rabid.

"Is he always this dirty in a fight?" Kat asked.

I didn't have an answer for her. All I could do was watch, my heart pounding in my chest as Tommy continued his relentless assault.

In the end, it took only one final, brutal blow for the knockout. As his opponent crumpled to the floor, a twisted mix of triumph and unease coursed through me. I knew Tommy was rough around the edges, but I'd never seen him like this – so unbridled, so ruthless. Tommy stood there breathing heavily, the crooked grin failing to reach his eyes. The ref spat out words at him, but Tommy just shrugged, dismissive, unconcerned.

I shuddered, sickened and thrilled all at once. He was dangerous, but damn if he wasn't hot as sin.

"God, Sloane, did you see that?"

"Yeah, I saw it," I managed to say, my voice hollow. Too late, the realization crashed over me like a wave—the man in the ring wasn't the boy I'd grown up with anymore. That Tommy had been replaced by something far more dangerous. A killer, wearing the same crooked smile, but stripped of any warmth I remembered.

I felt sick. Sick at the violence, sick at my own reaction to it, and sick at the undeniable truth that despite everything, some dark part of me was drawn to the very thing that should repel me most.

"Come on," I muttered. "Let's go."

She looked at me in surprise. "But the night's just getting started. Don't you wanna stick around and see who else fights?"

"I've seen enough," I said, pushing myself up from the sticky seat, my eyes scanning the crowd at the IBEW hall for an exit that wasn't choked with testosterone and sweat.

"Wait up!" Kat fumbled in her purse for her phone, her curls bobbing as she hurried to catch up.

As we weaved through the crowd, a familiar figure caught my eye, and I had to look twice. Tommy was leaned against the wall, his towering frame relaxed despite the intensity of the match he'd just dominated. But it was the man he was talking to who grabbed my attention—the Russian who had once been a temporary ally against Moretti. It took me a few tries to remember his name.

Misha.

I didn't know much about him. From what Connor told me, Misha had come on the scene last year, magically appearing when we needed an ally against the Italians. The extra manpower and weapons had come in clutch rescuing both Connor and Tommy from Moretti, despite a brief moment where it had looked like the Russians had sold us out. In reality, the Russians had been playing both sides, and they ended up opening fire on the Italians.

Yet, while Callum and Connor—an apparently Tommy—had conveniently forgotten our history with the Russians, I hadn't forgotten. Or forgiven. Misha might not have been the one to pull the trigger, but it was the Russian's betrayal that had killed Aiden all those years ago.

Historically, the Russians weren't our enemies...but I wasn't sure if we could call them our friends, either.

Misha and Tommy were speaking in hushed tones, their heads close together, and even from a distance, I sensed the gravity of their conversation.

"Who's that guy Tommy's with?" Kat asked, peering over my shoulder.

"Nobody good," I murmured, watching Misha's eyes flicker across the room. Clearly, he was used to having to watch his back. That unease from earlier twisted tighter inside me. What the hell were they up to?

As if sensing my gaze, Tommy looked up and caught my eye. First confusion, then surprise twisted his features before they settled out into glowing triumph.

Damn, now he knew I'd come to see him fight. I swallowed hard, my mouth suddenly dry as his gaze locked onto mine. There was something in his eyes that I couldn't quite place – a raw intensity that made my stomach clench. Something raw and primal.

"Come on, let's get out of here." I grabbed Kat's arm, pulling her away before my curiosity betrayed me and I ended up doing something stupid.

"Fine by me. I need a drink."

The bar next door was packed with people from the fight, competitors and spectators alike. We squeezed our way to the counter where the bartender already looked overwhelmed.

"Vodka tonic," Kat yelled over the din, flashing a sympathetic smile.

I ordered a double Jack and coke. Kat wasn't the only one who needed a drink after that fight. The bartender was quick and efficient, sliding our drinks over and moving on to the next order. Kat and I pushed our way through the crowd, trying to find somewhere to sit, but there was no space to be found.

Kat huffed in irritation. "I gotta pee, see if you can find us a spot."

I sighed and pushed my way back through the crowd. It was a sausage fest, packed with men and very few women. Post-fight testosterone surged throughout the room. Finally, I spotted an empty table at the back, and weaved through the crowd, snatching it up before anyone else could.

What the hell was I doing? Didn't I get enough of this scene at work? I wasn't sure what had possessed me to come down here tonight, but I had seen enough, my suspicions about Tommy's extracurricular activities confirmed. My already foul mood soured. Tommy had time to bash people in the skull, but he didn't have time to even attempt to put forth effort at work.

That's it, I decided. *I'm just going to have one drink and head home.*

I'd try to get Kat to go with me, but I doubted if she would. I just wasn't in the mood to deal with men tonight, especially not the douchey types who thought they could buy their way into a woman's pants with a few overpriced drinks.

A rough tap on my shoulder yanked me out of my thoughts. I whipped around, my hand already curling into a fist, but instead, I found Kat grinning at me and Tommy standing beside her with a smug smirk spread crookedly across his face. There was a glint in his eye, half mocking, half something else entirely—something that made my skin prickle with annoyance...and something else I refused to acknowledge.

"Look who I found," Kat chirped.

My cheeks flushed. Great. "What are you doing here?"

Tommy raised his eyebrows in mock-surprise. "You're the one who's following me, princess."

I bristled at the endearment, glaring at him. "I'm not following you, asshole. We were just leaving."

"You sure about that?" His grin widened, revealing that crooked dimple on his chin. "Because it sure looks like you came to see me fight."

I flushed again, cursing my traitorous body. "It was Kat's idea."

"Was not," she protested.

I shot her a glare, and she at least had the grace to look a little sheepish.

"Whatever," I muttered. "I've seen enough for tonight. I'm going home."

"Oh come on. The night's still young." Tommy's smirk only grew wider, his eyes gleaming with mischief. "You didn't think I'd miss the chance to celebrate my win with my favorite bartender, did you?"

His words slurred slightly, and I realized with a pang of annoyance that he was already drunk. "You should go home and sleep it off."

"Aw, Sloane," he drawled, his gaze flicking over me suggestively as he leaned close. "You offering to tuck me in?"

"Get away from me, Tommy," I hissed, pushing him back with as much force as I could muster. He stumbled slightly, but his infuriating grin never wavered.

"Whatever you say, princess," he murmured, raising his hands in mock surrender. "Just remember, you're the one who came to watch me fight."

Anger bubbled up from a well I thought had run dry long ago. "You're disgusting," I spat, meeting his gaze dead-on, my own eyes blazing with a fire I didn't want to admit was fueled by more than just disdain. "I wouldn't sleep with you if you were the last man on earth."

His expression flickered almost imperceptibly before the mask of nonchalance returned. But I caught it—the briefest moment where my words might have actually struck home. His grin faltered for a moment, but he quickly recovered, chuckling darkly as he leaned in closer.

"Your loss," he shrugged, but there was an edge to his voice, a jagged line cutting through the drunken haze in his eyes. "There's plenty who would."

"Then go find 'em," I threw back, not sure if I wanted to slap him or do something far less appropriate.

Tommy's crooked grin faltered again for just a fraction, and the raucous laughter around us seemed to dip into silence. Or maybe it was just the blood rushing in my ears. I caught the briefest glint of something in his eyes that flickered like a faulty neon sign before it was swiftly extinguished beneath his usual bravado.

His gaze slid over to Kat. "Maybe your friend will take me to bed then."

Tommy gestured with a lazy tilt of his head toward my friend, who had been observing our heated exchange with amused curiosity. Kat's gaze swung between us, her eyebrows arching as she read the tension that hummed like live wires in the air.

"Sloane? You sure?"

I knew that if I said no, Kat would leave it alone. But I saw how badly she wanted Tommy, and I wasn't about to be That Girl. I was a great wing-woman. I crossed my arms, feeling the weight of Tommy's stare, heavy and expectant.

"I couldn't care less," I said, the words sharp and brittle on my tongue, betraying none of the tightness that clenched in my chest.

Kat grinned at me, her eyes dancing with mischief. "Suit yourself. Come on, Tommy. Let's go."

For a second, Tommy's eyes locked with mine, and I saw something that looked suspiciously close to hurt flash across his eyes. God, when did they get so blue? But I must have imagined it, because to feel hurt, you have to have a heart first. And Tommy was most certainly lacking one of those.

I tossed back the rest of my drink and closed my eyes so I didn't have to watch them leave. I couldn't believe I had let him get to me like that, but the thought of him with my friend stirred something dark and ugly inside me that I didn't want to dwell on.

He's not worth it. Just take a deep breath, it's the come down from the fight. Tommy is not worth this heartache.

But even as I repeated those words over and over again in my head, I couldn't shake the feeling that they were nothing more than a lie.

4

Tommy

I STEERED KAT THROUGH the throng of bodies, her laughter spiking above the bass-heavy music thudding against my skull. The press of her side against mine was a warm, distracting line of heat, but it wasn't what I wanted.

It wasn't what I wanted at all.

I could admit to myself—at least to the darkest corners of my mind—that I had draped Kat's arm around my shoulders and angled my body just so all for the benefit of catching Sloane's gaze from across the bar. I wanted her to see me, to know that I was moving on with someone else.

Because when I caught the irritation in Sloane's face morph into hurt when I leaned down to whisper in Kat's ear, it wasn't smug satisfaction I felt.

It was shame.

Sloane's cheeks were a vibrant shade of crimson, not from the spill of neon signs, but pure, unadulterated anger. That look on her face, like she'd gladly throw me into a woodchipper and laugh while doing it, told me everything I needed to know. I'd hit a nerve tonight.

What the hell was I doing? I knew this was fucked up. I knew this was twisted, and I knew it would only lead to trouble. But I couldn't help myself. Like a little boy pulling his crush's pigtails, I craved Sloane's attention, her acknowledgment.

And a dark little sliver of me wanted Sloane to hurt just as much as I did. I wanted her to know how it felt.

I clenched my jaw. Who was I kidding? Sloane couldn't possibly understand what it was like to have your heart broken over and over again, to be so fucking unlovable that even the people who were supposed to care about you abandoned you. No, Sloane had the luxury of a normal life, a normal family, a normal heart.

And this little game I was playing?

You can't hurt someone who doesn't feel a thing for you.

Triumph evaporated and left me feeling like the lowest of assholes. Kat's laughter was too loud, her breath too warm on my skin, and the weight of Sloane's eyes on us a burden I didn't want to carry. I didn't want any of this. I wanted to numb my senses until I didn't feel anything at all. I didn't want to think about Sloane, or how she made me feel things that I had no business feeling.

"Are you always this much of an asshole, or is there something going on between you two I should know about?" Kat's question was a low murmur in my ear, but she sounded far more sober than she had a few minutes before.

I glanced down at her, my gaze sweeping over the curves of her body, the swell of her breasts, her short, dark curls bobbing softly against her shoulders. She was beautiful, there was no denying that. But she wasn't Sloane.

"Not a thing, sweetheart," I grunted, the word souring as it passed my lips. Another lie. A performance. My grip on Kat tightened ever so slightly, an unspoken apology for dragging her into this petty game of one-upmanship. "Just having a bit of fun."

"Good. So am I."

Kat leaned up on her tiptoes, lips seeking mine, and my stomach churned. I turned my head at the last second so her mouth landed on my cheek.

"Not here," I said gruffly, the ache in my chest spreading. Christ, I needed some air. I grabbed her hand and pulled her towards the door. "Come on."

Outside felt like walking into an oven, the asphalt trapping the heat of the day. Kat's hand was still wrapped around my arm, her grip possessive and all too eager. The rush of having Sloane's eyes on us moments ago faded fast, replaced by a gnawing hollowness in my gut. I should've felt like the king of the world after that fight, but instead, I just felt like a royal asshole.

Kat laughed throatily as she pulled me into the shadow of the building, just beyond the reach of the streetlights. "Come on, tough guy. Show me what you're made of."

Her lips found mine with a surprising ferocity. A warm, female body pressing against me in a way that was impossible to ignore. For an instant, her silhouette melded with Sloane's in my mind—the same dark hair, the same height—and my pulse thundered in my ears. Her fingers were bold, raking through my hair and down my back, gripping at my jacket with an urgency that bordered on desperation.

And for a moment, just a single, fleeting moment, I allowed myself to be swept up in the fantasy. Maybe this could work. Maybe...

"Tommy..."

I froze. Her voice. It wasn't laced with that biting wit and smoky undertones that drove me wild when Sloane spoke. Her voice was wrong. Her body was wrong. She...*goddamnit*, this was wrong. A flicker of disgust twisted in my gut. What the hell was I doing?

"Kat," I murmured between kisses, "slow down."

"But you wanted me to," she giggled, her hand slipping inside my jacket.

"That's not what I meant," I said, my words coming out sharper than I intended. I grabbed her wrist. Her hand stilled against my chest, and I felt her pulse thrumming wildly beneath my fingertips.

"Did I do something wrong?" Her voice was small, uncertain, and I immediately felt like a piece of shit for using her like this.

"No, sweetheart. It's not you," I sighed, pulling away from her. "It's me."

The old line rang hollow even to my own ears. Undaunted, Kat slipped her arms beneath my jacket.

"Tommy," she whispered against my skin, her hands wandering over my body. "You're so tense. Let me take your mind off things. Take me back to your place."

Screw it.

"First off, stop talking," I growled, pulling back just enough to look into her eyes, trying to find something there that might halt this reckless descent. "Second, this isn't going anywhere but tonight."

My voice was a warning, sharp as a knife's edge. "Third..."

I pulled away completely, looking down the street at the neon sign flickering above a nondescript hotel entrance. I never took women back to my apartment, and I wasn't about to start now. "There's a hotel a block down."

Her only response was a devilish grin, and she dragged me onwards without another word.

I woke with a kink in my neck and a skull-splitting headache. My mouth tasted like an ashtray. Blinking against the harsh morning light, I realized I was in a cheap hotel room, the thin walls barely muffling the sounds of the city outside.

I shifted, feeling the warmth of another person curled against me. For a fleeting second, my hazy mind tricked me into believing it was Sloane—the short, dark hair, the lithe, naked body pressed back into my chest. My heart kicked traitorously. Before reason could claw back control, my arms tightened around her and I hugged her closer, nuzzling into her neck, almost expecting to hear her soft, teasing laughter.

But as her body shifted in my arms, I caught a glimpse of her face and reality came crashing down on me.

And that's when last night came flooding back.

I sat up, blinked heavily, and looked down at the woman who was sprawled next to me. It wasn't Sloane; it was Kat. Her friend. Shame washed over me, and I untangled myself from her as gently as I could, careful not to wake her. I'd already used her enough. The least I could do was let her sleep.

The room spun around me as I tried to find my clothes. My shirt was crumpled on the floor, my jeans in a heap near the door. I had no memory of undressing or even what came after, only a vague recollection of how we ended up here in the first place.

I stumbled into the bathroom and splashed cold water on my face, trying to clear my head. What the hell had I been thinking? I couldn't even remember if we used a condom. A brief peek through the trash answered that question, and I exhaled shakily in relief.

Fuck.

I needed to get out of there. I needed to get home, take a shower, and wash away the shame that was creeping up my spine.

But first, I needed to find my keys.

I slipped out of the bathroom and padded across the room, careful not to disturb the sleeping figure on the bed. My wallet was on the dresser, but I didn't see my keys.

I checked the pockets of my jeans. Nothing. I searched the floor around the bed, but still no keys. I swore under my breath, running a hand through my hair in frustration. Where the hell could they be?

"Looking for these?"

Her voice startled me. I looked up to see Kat leaning against the doorway of the bathroom, a bed sheet wrapped loosely around her chest, and my keys dangling from her fingers.

I stared at her, my mouth going dry.

"Thanks," I managed to say, stepping forward to take them from her. But she pulled back, a mischievous glint in her eyes.

"What's the rush? Come back to bed." She held my keys hostage behind her back, a wicked grin curving her lips. "I think you owe me a few more hours."

She reached for my hand, pulling me back towards the bed, but I resisted. Her expression faltered. "Is something wrong?"

"No," I lied, pulling back, "but I gotta go."

"Fair enough."

She tossed me the keys. Surprisingly, I caught them, off balance from her sudden shift in mood.

"Thanks," I said again, feeling like a complete idiot.

She shrugged, her expression unreadable. "It's not like I expected anything else."

I didn't know what to say to that, so I said nothing at all.

Kat looked me up and down. "You know, I like a good time as much as the next girl. I was blessed with startlingly few morals. But in an effort to not be a complete bitch, I feel compelled to say that you and Sloane really need to get your shit together."

That caught me off guard. "What?"

"You heard me," Kat said, not missing a beat. "You're clearly into each other. Whatever happened between you two, you need to fix it. Because right now, you're just being a dick to her, and she doesn't deserve that."

"Yeah? And what makes you think you know anything about it?" I shot back, my temper flaring.

She raised an eyebrow. "I saw how you looked at her last night. You couldn't take your eyes off her. And I saw how she reacted to seeing you with me, even if she denied it. It's obvious there's something there."

I snorted. "She hates me, remember?"

"Yeah, well, hate's a fine line." Kat's gaze softened, and she sighed. "Look, Tommy, I'm not saying you have to marry her. Just don't fuck with her head if you're not serious. She's been through enough already."

I wanted to argue, to tell her she had no idea what she was talking about, but the words died on my tongue. I was too tired and hungover to fight.

"Whatever. I gotta go."

"Go home and take a shower, Tommy, then go fix things with Sloane," Kat said, not unkindly.

By the time I got to Lady D's, I found Grady nursing a cup of black coffee, his eyes bloodshot, clutching onto his coffee cup like his life depended on it. I slumped into the chair opposite him as he brought me up to speed on the current status of the clan, my mind still tangled in the hotel's rumpled sheets, and I found it hard to focus on his words. I nodded, trying to look like I knew what the hell he was talking about. But my thoughts were elsewhere—or, rather, with someone else.

"Tommy, this is serious," Grady's voice cut through the fog. "You need to listen."

"Sorry. Long night."

"Yeah, me too, but I need you to focus right now."

"Yeah, yeah, I got it."

Grady sighed, running a hand through what was left of his hair. "Look, I know things have been off with you lately. But we need you sharp. You're the leader here, whether you feel like it or not."

I scraped up what was left of my dignity. "Okay, I get it. Just tell me what's going on again. Please."

"Right. Since you asked me nicely." He straightened himself up in his chair. "I met with those new buyers yesterday. They seem solid enough. Shipment's coming in next Thursday, bigger than usual. New dockmaster down there, too. I sent Davie to sniff around to make sure he's not a liability."

"Sounds good."

"It's not good," Grady said, his expression souring. "The guys think the new dockmaster is skimming off the top, just like Unger did. And if that happens, we're fucked."

I frowned, trying to follow Grady's train of thought. "What are you saying?"

Grady leaned forward, lowering his voice. "I'm saying we need to make an example of him. If we let him get away with it, we'll be overrun with thieves. And that's the last thing we need."

"So have one of the guys do it."

His gaze wavered, just a fraction, as if he was measuring his words, choosing them carefully to avoid outright disrespect. I sensed it through the hangover and self-loathing, the edge of doubt in his tone that hinted at something more insidious: a lack of belief in me.

"I think...I mean, w-w think that we should send a message. You know, show them who's in charge here."

I sighed, rubbing my temples. "Look, I've had a rough night. Just say what you mean, Grady."

"You need to do it. You need to take care of the problem yourself."

Grady's voice was tight with concern, and I bristled, not wanting to hear any more of his lecture. "Fine."

Grady eyed me warily. "Are you sure? It's been a while since you've... well, you know."

"I said I'll handle it, okay? Jesus. What else?"

"Well, there's some good news too," he said, looking grateful for the change of topic. "That charity, Skip and Mary's Place, it's doing really well."

"Skip and Mary's?" I frowned. I didn't remember anything about a new charity. The old couple had been like saints to the neighborhood, until Moretti murdered them and used their deaths to paint a target on the clan's back. We'd been talking about doing something to give back, but that was about as far as we'd gotten.

"Yeah," Grady said, his voice softening. "After what happened last year... the community wanted to honor them. It's been a success."

"Whose idea was that?"

Grady hesitated, then shrugged. "It came together. A lot of folks pitched in."

“Who's idea, Grady?" I pressed, the intensity in my gaze pinning him like a butterfly.

"Look, Tommy, it doesn't—" He tried to deflect again, but I wasn't having any of it.

"Spit it out."

"Fine," he relented with a sigh. "It was Sloane's idea. She put in a lot of legwork to get it off the ground."

I clenched my jaw, the familiar mixture of anger and affection swelling in my chest. And pride. Damn that woman. Always pushing her way into places she didn't belong, including my goddamn head.

"Sloane's idea..." I echoed, swirling the glass in my hand, feeling the cool condensation against my palm.

"Yup. She's been putting a lot of effort into it. She's got a good heart, that one." He glanced at me before adding hesitantly, "In fact, she's been asking to take on a more active role in the organization."

"No."

The word was out before I could weigh it down with reason. Sloane couldn’t get involved in this. Not now, not ever. It was bad enough that her father had allowed her to worm her way into the organization this far, but there was no way in hell I was going to let her get her soil her hands the way mine were.

I couldn't allow her to get hurt. The idea of losing her was unbearable.

God there were so many ways. It could happen so quickly. A ricochet, a bullet to the head. A car bomb. A drive-by. My thoughts started spiraling.

Images of Sloane hurt—or worse—flashing through my mind. I couldn't lose her like I lost Aiden.

Grady cleared his throat, and I realized I hadn't said anything.

"Tommy, you should let her help. She's got skills that might be valuable to us," Grady persisted, clearly not understanding the gravity of what he was suggesting.

"No," I repeated, more firmly this time. "She's done enough already."

"Look, she's smart. Resourceful. She knows how to keep her mouth shut. And she's not afraid to get her hands dirty if need be," he pressed, but I was already shaking my head.

"Absolutely not. She's not getting involved in any more clan business."

"But—"

"No means no, Grady. End of discussion. Tell me when those buyers want to meet. Until then, keep Sloane out of it."

"Tommy—" Grady tried, but I was already halfway to the door, my mind racing, my chest tight.

"Out of it, Grady!" I tossed over my shoulder as I pushed through the heavy door of Lady D's and out into the warm night air. I needed space, clarity, and a goddamn drink.

I slammed my palm against the heavy metal door, and it groaned aside, revealing the dimly lit cavern of the storage garage. The air was tinged with the scent of motor oil and rubber, a perfume that always managed to calm me. I stalked through the rows of dormant vehicles until I reached her.

Diana.

There she was, bathed in the dim light, her midnight blue paint job as dark as the ocean at night. My fingers itched to feel the rumble of her 6.4L V8 HEMI engine—the one indulgence I allowed myself, my therapy, my salvation. I'd spent years fixing her up, every curve and chrome detail meticulously restored to perfection. And when I needed an escape, she was always there.

"Hello, beautiful," I murmured, running a hand over her sleek hood. "It has been too long."

With a flick of the keys, the garage echoed with the growling purr as Diana came to life, headlights cutting through the gloom like the eyes of a predator. Boston's city lights gave way to the open freeway, and I found myself thumbing the card Misha had slipped me, its edges already worn from the number of times I'd pulled it out just to shove it back into my pocket.

If you ever want to really let loose in the ring, let loose that darkness inside you. No rules, no refs...

Temping. Very tempting.

I gripped the steering wheel, white-knuckled, and pressed my foot down on the accelerator.

An hour sped by. Kennebunkport crept up on me, the quaint coastal town nestled into the rocky Maine shoreline. I eased off the gas as the summer house came into view. It was a sprawling, luxurious affair, perched on the edge of the cliffs overlooking the ocean. But tonight, the grandeur of the place was lost on me. I was here for one reason only.

The scent of crisp, ocean air and brine filled my lungs, mingling with the familiar aroma of fresh-cut grass. Despite my troubled thoughts, I felt a pang of nostalgia as I gazed at the sprawling beach house that had been our family's refuge for generations. The front door swung open before I even had a chance to knock, revealing a tall, lanky man with salt and pepper hair and a grin that was all teeth.

"Tommy!" Callum called out, intercepting me as he carried a tray of drinks down to the beach. "I didn't know you were coming up today."

"I didn't either. How's Dad?"

"Today's one of the good days." His weather-beaten face softened, and I read the unspoken 'thank you' in his eyes for making the trip. "He's down by the water. Let's not keep him waiting."

We made our way down the steep, sand covered steps leading to the rocky beach below. I spotted my father immediately. Perched on a chase lounge, blankets swaddled around him, they couldn't hide the ravages of disease. He looked so much frailer than the last time I'd seen him. The cancer had eaten away at the once-strong man I knew, reducing him to a fragile shell. His hair was nothing but whisps now, and his skin had taken on a papery, jaundiced hue. But when Michael Quinn saw me, his eyes lit up, and he beckoned me over.

"Hey, Pop," I said, my voice cracking like a teenager's.

His hand, more bone than flesh, patted the empty chair next to him—a throne of sorts for the heir apparent, though I felt anything but regal as I took my seat. The sea air was thick with salt, and the summer breeze cut through my tee shirt as I settled into the chair next to Dad's.

Was he warm enough? Christ, it looked like a stiff gust would blow him away.

"It's good to see you, son," he said, his voice thin and reedy.

I nodded, my throat tight. "Good to see you too."

"Cassidy was here yesterday...or was it..."

Callum's wife answered when he looked at her, floundering. "She was here on Tuesday, Mikey."

"That's right," he agreed. Then he frowned at me. "She says you've been busy. How are things with you?"

"Things are fine. I've been getting some more fights down at the club, Saul's got a big match for me next month. Work is good. You know, busy. The clan's never been stronger. We've got some new buyers, and—"

He waved me off. "I don't care about the clan. I asked about you. How are you?"

I shifted uncomfortably, not wanting to say anything that would worry him. "I'm alright."

"Are you sleeping? Eating okay?"

"Yes, *Dad*—"

"Because you look like shit."

"Gee, thanks. I'm fine, though. Great, actually."

His eyes narrowed, and I knew he didn't believe me. "You're a shit liar, Tommy. What's going on?"

I sighed, running a hand through my hair. I knew I couldn't hide anything from him. He knew me better than anyone, and he always seemed to have a sixth sense when it came to my moods.

"I'm just having a rough time lately," I admitted. "Work has been busy, and things with the clan are a little...tense."

He snorted, his expression grim. "They always are, Tommy. You can't let it get to you. You have to keep your head in the game. There will always be people who try to undermine you, people who want to take what's yours. But you can't let them. You have to be strong, Tommy. You have to be smart. You can't let your guard down."

"I know, Pop. I won't."

He glanced at me out of the corner of his eye. "Sloane still giving you hell behind the bar?"

"She's fine," I grunted. "She's a pain in my ass, mostly."

He laughed, a wheezy, rattle that made me wince. "That's because you let her. She's a smart girl, Tommy. She's got her head on straight. And besides, the best ones are always a pain in the ass. It's what makes life interesting."

5

Sloane

Next Thursday was my day off, so on a whim, I went down to the docks. The guys was supposed to be accepting the new shipment in today, and I needed to see for myself how bad things had gotten. Grady, bless his loyal heart, was out of his depth. I'd seen how the guys were starting to push him around at the bar. He was a good man, but he didn't have the fortitude that dealing with this stuff took.

The salty harbor air cut through the muggy night as my boots crunched on the gravel. I tugged my leather jacket tighter and glanced around the darkened dockyard, scanning for any signs of movement. The docks were eerily quiet at this hour, most of the workers having cleared out hours ago. Only the occasional slap of water against wooden piers broke the silence.

Until a shout rang out ahead, followed by the unmistakable click of a gun cocking.

I froze in my tracks, hands raised. Three figures emerged from behind a stack of crates, pistols trained on me.

"Easy, cowboy," I drawled, raising my hands just enough to show I wasn't a threat without dropping my nonchalance. "It's just me."

"Sloane?" the guy echoed, lowering the gun fractionally. He squinted at me through the dimness. "What are you doing here?"

"Taking in the sights," I replied with a smirk, stepping closer. The metal of the gun was still an ominous glint in the dark, but his arm was lowering, inch by reluctant inch.

"Shit—put your guns down!" Grady nearly keeled over when he realized who I was. He waved at the guys and glanced over my shoulder, scanning the area. "What are you doing sneaking around down here? Are you trying to give me a heart attack?"

"Sorry," I said, not sounding sorry at all. "I just wanted to see how things were going. My night off was too quiet for my taste."

"Tommy will have my head if he finds out you're down here."

What the hell. Tommy didn't want me down here? Where did he get off? I couldn't believe he had the balls to think he could exclude me from my father's own business like this.

"Then let's make sure he doesn't find out," I said, stepping past the still-shocked gunman. "Our little secret, yeah?"

Grady sighed, the sound heavy with resignation, as he motioned for the others to get back to work. "Fine. But if anything goes wrong, I'm blaming you. I don't know how you always manage to talk me into this shit."

We both knew I'd do as I pleased, regardless of what anyone said. And if Tommy had a problem with how I chose to spend my free time, he could take it up with me himself. Grady had enough problems of his own without Tommy picking on him.

The shipping yard was worse than I thought.

The whole operation was a mess. An unruly, disorganized mess. There weren't nearly enough guys to cover all the exits, let alone manage the transfer. Grady was trying his best, but he was out of his depth. There were only two other guys helping him, and they didn't look like they were cut out for the job either. The docks were in chaos, and it was clear that Grady had no idea what he was doing.

I sighed and tucked my hair behind my ear. This was bad. If we didn't get the shipments in order, there would be hell to pay on the other end. Our buyers weren't exactly the kinds of people to look the other way when inventory was missing or incorrect. I watched as the men unloaded the containers from the ship, the sweat on their brows reflecting the lights from above.

I frowned and stepped over to where Grady was huddled over the inventory list. "Have we vetted the unloading crew? Who's watching them to make sure they don't take a peek? And what about our exits? I only see one guy on overwatch."

"Um..." Grady paged through the inventory sheets like they held the answer. "I'm doing what I can, Sloane. But between you and me, I'm no ringleader."

"Clearly," I scoffed. Grady winced, and I immediately felt bad. "Sorry. It's not your fault. Where the hell is Tommy, anyway?"

"Uh..."

"Never mind. Forget I asked." I rolled my eyes, knowing Tommy was probably at the bar getting sloshed. Or sleeping off whatever piece of ass he'd brought home the night before. Not that it mattered. If he couldn't be bothered to show up to work, then I would just have to do it myself.

I hitched up my jacket and strode over to where the dockworkers were milling about, impatience etched into their features. Time to put on a show.

"Evening, gentlemen," I greeted them with a winning smile. "I know this isn't my usual hangout, but I'll be overseeing things tonight."

A few of them exchanged wary looks, clearly unsure about taking orders from me. But with Grady nodding approvingly at my side, they had little choice but to comply.

"First, we need more people covering the exits. Mickey, you're on lookout. Eyes sharp, yeah? Danny, check those crates—everything single one, cross-reference with Grady's inventory sheet. I don't want any surprises."

One of the new guys crossed his burly arms over his chest. "Since when do you call the shots?"

I walked over to an open crate of rifles and picked one up. In seconds, I had it field stripped. Working at a speed that would make a Marine drill instructor proud, I reassembled the weapon, aimed in on the sign above the shipping office door, a hundred yards away, and put a shot right through the 'O' in 'Office'. Just like Dad taught me.

"Since your asses needed saving," I shot back with a withering glare. "And unless you want Tommy tearing you a new one for screwing around tonight, you'll do as I say."

They exchanged wary looks, but after a moment, they got moving, following my orders. Grady gave me a grateful nod.

"Thanks, Sloane," Grady said as we watched the operation begin to take shape. "I didn't know what we were going to do."

I smirked at him. "Neither do I. But someone has to keep the wheels turning around here, especially when our fearless leader decides to take a powder."

"Tommy's got his reasons, I'm sure," Grady said quietly, though even he didn't sound convinced.

"Maybe. But right now, we've got a job to do, and I refuse to let everything fall apart just because he's not here to hold our hands."

I checked the cargo personally, test firing several weapons, even digging down to the bottom of the crate to make sure we weren't shorted. When I was satisfied, I ordered the dockworkers to load up the trucks, making sure to keep track of the numbers as they went. We'd have to reconcile them later, but at least everything seemed to be going smoothly for the moment.

"New dockmaster's green as spring grass," one of the more grizzled workers muttered to me as he passed by, muscling a crate. "Ain't sure he can keep his gob shut."

"Leave him to me," I replied, flashing a shark-like smile. I caught the dockmaster's eye, a lanky young guy sweating bullets under the scrutiny.

"How's it going?" I asked, approaching him. "First night on the job, huh? Must be stressful."

"Y-yes, ma'am," he stammered, looking like he'd rather be anywhere but here.

I gave him a sympathetic smile. "It'll get easier, trust me. But listen, I just want to make sure we're on the same page. You see, Tommy doesn't like it when people try to skim off the top. Or run their mouths. And

I don't like it either. You wouldn't want to make me unhappy, would you?"

I gave him a little pout and cocked my hip, making sure that he saw not only my curves, but the gun strapped in my shoulder holster, too. He swallowed thickly, eyes wide, and I knew I had him right where I wanted him.

"No, ma'am," he squeaked, his Adam's apple bobbing nervously.

I smiled sweetly at him, patting him on the arm. "Good boy. Now, you just keep quiet and do your job, and everything will be just fine. Alright?"

"Yes, ma'am."

I flashed him one last smile and turned back to the task at hand, a smug sense of satisfaction blooming. This was what I was meant for. Not simply slinging drinks behind a bar but making a real difference.

I could get used to this.

The rest of the operation moved quickly and efficiently, and within the hour, the trucks were loaded and ready to move out. With the last crate secured, the convoy of trucks rumbled toward the checkpoint. I trailed behind, my mind already racing ahead to the next potential hiccup. As we approached the guards, palms sufficiently greased to look the other way, I pulled Grady aside.

"Night watch at the warehouse: who's got eyes on it?" I asked.

"Ownership's changed hands recently," he replied hesitantly. "Haven't had time to grease the new gears, if you catch my drift."

I stepped back, waiting until the trucks had cleared the gates before turning to Grady with a frown. "New management, my ass. Until we know who's really in charge at the warehouse, divert the trucks to the old depot. We'll sort out where to store everything there."

"That's risky. Tommy won't like it."

"Tommy can suck it," I growled. "It's the only safe option we've got right now."

Grady sighed, shoulders slumping. "You're probably right."

"Damn right I am."

The docks were deserted now, the last truck rumbling away into the night. I looked around at the empty crates and felt a sense of accomplishment for the first time in weeks. For once, things had gone smoothly. And it felt good. Really good.

This was where I belonged.

Afterwards, Grady and I grabbed coffee at the 24-hour diner down the street, the only place open at this ungodly hour. We talked about his ex-wife and his kids, college funds and his lamentable golf game, and I realized that I had never spent any amount of time actually speaking to the man about anything that truly mattered to him. Grady was a pretty likable guy once you got to know him.

Cradling my mug between my hands, I inhaled the bitter aroma as my eyes drifted shut.

"Thanks, Sloane," Grady said again, for the tenth time.

"Don't mention it," I replied, waving him off. "Seriously. I'm glad I could help."

"Well, you did more than help. You saved our asses."

"It's nothing. I just did what needed to be done."

He sipped his coffee, his expression unreadable. "Listen, Sloane. About what you said before..."

"About what?"

"Doing more for the clan," he clarified, lowering his voice. "I know it's not my place to say, but I think you should talk to Tommy about it."

My jaw tightened. "Tommy doesn't want to listen to what I have to say."

"Well he doesn't listen to me, that's for sure. I tried telling Tommy we needed more hands. I told him you could handle it, but he refused."

It stung, hearing that confirmation. "Did he say why?"

"You know how he is. Stubborn as an ox."

I hummed, staring into the swirling depths of my coffee. Tommy's refusal to accept help had caused more headaches than I could count. But his reasons were his own. I'd long ago given up trying to figure them out.

"Anyway," Grady said, clearing his throat. "Thanks for stepping in. I know Tommy can be difficult. But it means a lot, you having my back like that."

"Speaking of Tommy," I swirled the coffee in my mug. "Where is he tonight? I think you know."

"Uh," Grady hesitated, shifting uncomfortably in his seat. "I shouldn't say this, but you helped me out tonight, so here goes. You didn't hear it from me, alright?"

"Spit it out, Grady."

"This was on his desk when I was tidying up the office," he blurted. He held up a worn, cream-colored business card. "It's for a parking garage downtown. I did some asking around. Word is, there's some kind of underground fight club operating out of that garage. Off and on, you know how these things move around. But..."

"But what?"

"The kind of fighting they do there, Sloane, it's...brutal. People have been killed." Grady trailed off, his brow furrowing. "I think Tommy went there tonight."

I stared at the card, a cold knot forming in my stomach. The garage's address seemed to glare up at me, as if confirming my worst fears. Tommy had always been one to run toward danger rather than away from it. And if what Grady said was true...

I pushed back from the table. "I have to go."

Grady rose with me. "Wait. Don't go by yourself, it's not safe."

"Oh, I'm sure it's not." I shrugged, sliding my jacket over my shoulders. "But I'm a big girl. I can take care of myself."

I stalked out of the diner and into the night, the card clutched tightly in my fist. I was going to find that idiot one way or another tonight, and when I did, a little bareknuckle boxing would look like a cakewalk compared to the beatdown I was going to give him.

“Aw, shit. Okay, who ratted me out?”

Tommy was sitting off to the side of the makeshift ring, getting his hands taped. His dark hair, shaped into that signature faux hawk, was damp with perspiration, and the scar across his chin seemed more pronounced in the harsh lighting. Three more fighters waited nearby, each one bigger than the last.

I scowled at him. "Give me a little credit—"

"Who?"

"Grady," I muttered.

"I knew it. Nosy old—What are you doing here, anyway?"

"Just taking an interest in your extracurriculars," I shot back, crossing my arms. "What the hell is this, Tommy?"

"What's it look like?" Tommy held up a taped hand. "I'm fightin'. Gonna mop the floor with this guy."

"That's the spirit, kid." The guy taping his hands clapped him on the back, and Tommy grinned up at him. All teeth.

The smile was a lie. I had seen that smile before, and I hated it.

Lately, I'd been seeing that smile more and more.

I looked over at the guy he was supposed to be fighting. "You are not."

"Come again?"

"Fighting him. Absolutely not." I reached for his arm. "Get your stuff, Tommy, you're going home."

He frowned at me. "I don't remember asking for your opinion."

"Well, you're getting it anyway. You're not doing this."

Tommy yanked his arm from my grasp, scowling. "You're not my ma, Sloane. Back off."

"I will not back off while you're pulling stunts like this!" I jabbed a finger at his face, still bruised from his previous fight. "When are you going to stop being so stupid and start taking care of yourself?"

"You don't get to tell me what to do," Tommy said, voice dropping to a dangerous growl. "Why don't you run back to the bar where you belong, *princess*, and let me handle my own business?"

I gaped at him, momentarily stunned into silence. I didn't know which part of that sentence pissed me off more—that he was willing to throw his life away, or that he thought he could dismiss me so easily.

"You're unbelievable," I hissed, my temper rising. I poked my finger into his chest. "Fine! Kill yourself for all I care. But don't come crawling back to me when this blows up in your face."

I turned on my heel and left him sitting there, my anger simmering over to boil. If Tommy wanted to be self-destructive, so be it. I was done trying to save him from himself.

I made it almost to my car before I turned back around.

I can't let him do this. I can't just leave him here.

"Tommy! Tommy, wait!"

I raced back toward the garage, but it was too late. Tommy was already in the middle of the ring, facing off with his opponent. His eyes shot to me, and a flicker of surprise and regret flashed across his face before he locked it down tight.

Or maybe I just imagined it.

The atmosphere was electric with testosterone and anticipation. The guy opposite Tommy was big—no, he was a goddamn titan, built like a fireplug and with a face that looked like thunder. He raised one giant paw, playing to the crowd and feeding into their frenzy. I stared at those dead shark eyes and almost missed Tommy's name being announced.

Everything was in Russian. Suddenly, Misha's involvement made sense. Tommy was smaller than his opponent, but there was no mistaking the lethality of his movements, sleek and lithe, the icy predatory stare of a wolf stalking his prey. It was at once both terrifying and beautiful.

And it also might have left me the slightest bit aroused.

The mismatch did nothing to diminish Tommy's presence in the ring, and the crowd worked itself into a rabid frenzy when they saw him. It felt like the countdown to an execution, both fighters never taking their eyes off each other, muscled gleaming in the overhead lights from the parking garage. No passion. Just a promise of violence.

No bell, just a guttural shout, and they were off. The crowd went wild, baying like dogs as the two men circled each other. Tommy ducked and weaved, using his agility to his advantage. But his opponent was a beast, a slab of meat with fists like sledgehammers. The same tactics Tommy used before weren't going to work this time. Tommy tried to dance under the next punch, swiveling under the man's arm to land a couple solid hits to the jaw, but the giant caught him over the eye with a counter that ripped his head to the side.

Tommy stumbled back, surprised.

The crowd surged forward, closing in on the ring.

Tommy was breathing hard, sweat dripping from his hair. Blood poured from the cut over his eyebrow, but the look in his eyes was fierce and defiant. He bared his teeth like a cornered animal and charged forward, ducking under the man's swing and landing a brutal uppercut to his chin. The man's head snapped back, and the crowd roared, pushing against the ropes.

The guy recovered quickly, and I winced as he managed to land a nasty blow to Tommy's ribs. I hoped the crunching sound was imagined. Incredibly, Tommy actually stepped into the punch, sacrificing a body shot in order to hit his opponent with an uppercut that rocked the bigger man back on his feet.

"Come on Tommy, protect yourself!"

I was on my feet, shouting with the rest of the crowd. Even though it must have hurt him, Tommy stayed within his opponent's reach, forcing him back against the ropes again before the man came to his senses and knocked him away. I kept looking for someone to signal the end of a round, but as time wore on, I realized that there were no rounds. They were just going to keep going until one of them dropped.

I knew Tommy well enough to see how much he was hurting. Blood poured down the side of his face, smudged along his cheek where he had tried to clear his eyes. He was favoring his left arm. I could barely look at the bruising that was already visible on his chest and sides. His opponent, meanwhile, looked barely winded.

The giant was playing with him.

I wanted to yell at him to stop, to get out of there while he still had the chance. But I knew that Tommy would never give up, not until he had nothing left to give. He was too proud, too stubborn to admit defeat, but even this went far beyond pride.

This was Tommy's darkness drawing him down. It almost looked like he was trying to get himself killed.

The big guy landed a blow to Tommy's jaw, and he went down hard. The crowd roared in approval, but Tommy wasn't finished yet. He rolled onto his side and pushed himself up, his legs trembling with the effort. Pulled a second wind from god-knows where. Sent a quick jab to the bigger man's kidneys to open him up, an uppercut that sent him reeling, swaying on his feet as Tommy went in to finish him off.

I was pushed up against the ropes with the rest of the crowd, both hands tented in prayer over my nose and mouth as Tommy swung a right cross at him and...

Missed.

His opponent ducked back at the last second. It was all the opening he needed.

The first blow connected with Tommy's temple, snapping his head to the side with an audible crack. The second knocked him in the opposite direction, sending blood spraying across the concrete as the third blow landed a spit-second later, and Tommy dropped like a stone.

I tried to push into the ring, but someone held me back.

The guy was still hitting Tommy.

Tommy wasn't moving, he...

Oh, God. Was he even breathing?

The arms tightened around my waist, caging my arms, and a voice with a faint Russian accent spoke in my ear. "Easy, *Ptichka*. Look. He is getting up."

Misha.

I looked, and sure enough, Tommy was getting to his feet, staggering under the weight of his own body. He shook his head like a dog, clearing it, then set his jaw and charged forward, throwing himself at his opponent with reckless abandon.

I wanted to scream, to tell him to stop, but the words wouldn't come. My eyes burned and the parking garage lights wavered. There was nothing I could do. Nothing at all. Helplessly, I watched as Tommy threw himself at the man, fists flying. Something had snapped in him. I watched in horror as he took hit after hit, each one landing with sickening precision. His face was a bloody mess, but still he kept going, well past the limits of what I thought a person could take.

"Tommy! Stop!" I yelled, but it was no use. He couldn't hear me over the roar of the crowd.

The crowd swelled, roaring now and me along with it. Tommy was a freight train. A maelstrom. Driving his opponent back, and it was all the other man could do just to keep his hands up, batting fruitlessly at Tommy as he continued his onslaught. The guy had been toying with him before, but Tommy wasn't playing games anymore. He was a man possessed. He fought like someone who had nothing left to lose.

And then, just like that, it was over. I didn't even see the last hit, but suddenly Tommy's opponent was sprawled across the concrete, unconscious.

The crowd erupted in a deafening roar. Tommy's arm was hauled aloft, money changed hands, and I tried my best not to throw up on Misha's shoes.

Tommy won.

But it felt like he'd lost something much more important.

He was barely conscious, slumped upright against a concrete pillar when I finally got to him. His face was a mess, his body raw and bleeding, but he grinned crookedly at me anyway.

"Aww, you stayed. Thought you were leaving me to my own devices," he said through split, swollen lips.

"You're a goddamn idiot, Tommy Quinn," I snapped, helping him to his feet.

He hissed as he tried to take a deep breath. "Fuuuck. That hurts."

"Does it? Good."

"So mean."

"Shut up." I kept my hand on his elbow to steady him. "Let's just get you home."

But before we could go anywhere, spectators descended on him, clapping him on the back, their faces split with grins as they recounted the fight like we all hadn't just watched it. But it was Misha's approach that set my teeth on edge, the Bratva soldier cutting through the crowd with the ease of a shark through water. He was all blond hair and cold blue eyes, his light accent tinged with amusement as he spoke loud enough to be heard over the din.

"You lasted longer than I thought you would," Misha said, the corner of his mouth quirked up.

"That's what...she said." Tommy wheezed out a laugh, the sound laced with pain.

Misha rolled his eyes, then they cut to me, looking me up and down, not missing a thing. He was perceptive. I didn't like it.

"Who's your friend?" he asked.

"I'm nobody's friend," I said coolly. "Certainly not yours. Do you think this was funny? He could have gotten himself killed, asshole!"

The laughter in Misha's eyes gave way to something sharper, more calculating. The crowd picked up on it, quieting enough to make me wonder if Misha was more than just a simple soldier.

Then he threw back his head and laughed. "I like this one, Quinn. You should keep her around."

Tommy tried to answer, but I was already dragging him away, muttering curses under my breath as I helped him limp toward the stairs.

Tommy's weight grew more and more substantial as I finally led him towards the couch in Lady D's infamous back room. One hand was wrapped protectively around his rib cage, and his head hung down until his chin was resting against his chest. He looked about thirty seconds from passing out.

"Sit," I ordered, pointing to a chair in the back room where first aid supplies were haphazardly stored. Tommy obeyed with a grunt, wincing as he lowered himself down.

"Jesus, Sloane, are you always this bossy?" he joked weakly, wincing.

"Only when I'm patching up stubborn idiots who think they're invincible," I shot back, my hands surprisingly steady as I began to clean the cuts on his face.

"Ow, watch it—"

"Stop being such a baby," I muttered, though my touch became gentler. My fingers worked meticulously, dabbing disinfectant onto a wad of gauze and applying it to the gash above his eyebrow. Tommy winced, his jaw clenching, but he didn't pull away.

"Does it hurt?" I asked, unable to keep the concern from my voice.

"Only when I breathe," he said, trying to smirk through the pain. "Or move."

I smiled and tilted his chin up to get a better look at the bruises blossoming across his cheek. His stubble rasped against my palm, and a spark of awareness shot through me.

“Thanks," he whispered, so low I barely caught it. His hand brushed against mine, a fleeting touch that sent an unexpected jolt through me. I looked up into his eyes, dark pools reflecting pain and something else—something raw and unguarded.

"Don't thank me yet," I replied, my voice steadier than I felt. "I've barely started."

"Lucky me."

I grabbed a clean cloth and wet it down, using it to wipe away the blood and grime. His skin was warm beneath my fingers, his muscles tensing reflexively as I traced the curve of his cheekbone, but he leaned into my touch.

"Why do you do this to yourself?" I asked, my voice barely a whisper.

His eyes fluttered shut as I ran the cloth along his jaw. "I don't know. It helps."

"Helps what?"

Tommy just shrugged. Despite his bulk, he seemed so fragile, so utterly breakable in that moment, his vulnerability cracked and splayed open in a way that cut off any sarcastic remark I might have made. The surprising intimacy swirled around us like a tangible haze. Tommy's breath was warm on my face, his eyes half-lidded, the shadows under them speaking to battles fought both within and without. With each shallow rise and fall of his chest against mine, the room seemed to shrink, pressing us closer.

I was painfully aware of the warmth of his skin and the closeness of our bodies, the scent of blood and sweat undercut with a rugged spice that went straight to my head. Tommy's eyes were impossibly dark, it must have been the light that made them look that way, want and desire and need so apparent even as the dipped down to my lips and back up, even as our bodies pressed together, the distance between our mouths becoming smaller and smaller until I could feel his breath, so warm and soft against my lips and I—

Tommy's phone rang, and I jumped back.

We both stared at the device where it lay on the table. My heart raced.

"You should get that," I said, my voice barely above a whisper.

Tommy nodded and reached stiffly for his phone, his expression unreadable.

I busied myself tidying up the table. I couldn't hear the conversation, just Tommy's monosyllabic grunts, but then he went rigid. "I'm on my way." He ended the call, looking noticeably paler.

"Everything okay?" I asked.

"No," he replied curtly, avoiding my gaze. "I—I gotta go."

"All right."

He stopped at the door, one hand braced for support, but he didn't turn around. "Thanks, Sloane. For, um..." He took a breath and tried again. "I'm sorry I..."

Tommy shook his head and left. He didn't finish what he had to say.

I wondered what would have happened if he had.

6

Tommy

"What happened?" The words were out of my mouth before I had made it all the way through the door to my father's room in the ICU at Boston Medical Center.

Connor and Cassidy were already there, standing vigil over a figure in the bed that looked nothing like my father. My gut clenched harder as Connor's light grey eyes met mine.

"Tommy," he said softly, his Irish brogue thicker under stress. He rose from his chair, the scrape of it against the tile overloud in the cramped room. "I'll give you two some space."

He gripped my shoulder tightly as he passed. I didn't like the look on his face.

"Cass." I stepped closer to the bed. My sister didn't look up. "What happened?"

She never took her eyes off Dad. "They're not exactly sure. We were all at dinner and he...he just collapsed. He'd been complaining of a headache earlier, so I got his meds, but then he said he felt fine.

"We went to dinner, at that favorite restaurant of his down by the water—you know the one. We ate, talked, Dad was laughing the whole time. It was almost like before." Cassidy sniffed. "Then we went to leave, and he collapsed. Like a puppet without strings. Unresponsive, pulse erratic. Connor called the ambulance and I tried to stabilize Dad, but he then he had a seizure—"

"A seizure?" I interrupted, starting to feel a little light-headed myself. How could this have happened so quickly?

Cassidy nodded, drawing herself up. "It was over by the time the paramedics arrived. After they transported him here, Jerome and I ran blood panels and a tox screen. It's...it's not good, Tommy. His liver is failing, which is causing a chain reaction in his other organs. His oxygen levels are dangerously low. He's been slipping downhill since he got here."

My father's chest rose fitfully, each breath a harsh, painful scrape despite the oxygen mask. The heart rate monitor beeped erratically, way too slow, and I knew he was slipping away before my eyes.

"But do they know what caused it?" I asked, hating how small and scared my voice sounded. "I mean, I just saw him a couple days ago. He was fine."

"This happens sometimes with cancer...at the end. The body is a complex mechanism, and sometimes it's just too much. Acute liver failure, fluid buildup, infection...his body is shutting down."

I hated that gentle, detached tone in my sister's voice. It was the one she used with patients who were dying. But this wasn't just another patient. This was our father.

Anger and resentment flared. "Then why aren't they helping him? Why are they just letting him suffer like this?"

Cassidy abruptly got up and walked up to me. I saw the unshed tears in her eyes, but she didn't close the distance, instead standing a foot away from me, her arms crossed in front of her chest defensively. "The doctors *are* doing everything they can, Tommy. They've given him medicine to help with the pain, but there's nothing else they can do now except make him comfortable."

"Make him comfortable?" I shook my head. "No. That can't be it. There has to be something else they can do."

She sighed, reaching up to tuck a stray lock of strawberry blond hair behind her ear. "Tommy, Dad has a DNR in place."

"A what?"

"Do Not Resuscitate," she explained softly. "He made his wishes clear. No extraordinary measures. Legally, we can't do anything. We talked about it, I tried to change his mind, but...we have to respect what Dad wanted."

Her words gutted me. Our old man, the indomitable Michael Quinn, had chosen his exit, and it was one I couldn't argue with. I felt the ghosts of past conversations haunting the edges of my mind, the ones where he lectured me about strength, legacy, and honor. I felt the sting of his words then, of all the times he had tried to instill the idea in me. The weight of responsibility on my shoulders seemed to grow heavier by the minute, and I swallowed hard.

"Is he..." I couldn't finish the sentence.

Cassidy took a deep breath, steeling herself. "He doesn't have long. Callum and Connor have already said their goodbyes. You should, too. I'm staying."

It was very clear to me that Cassidy did not expect me to stay, and the extra length of steel in her spine was her preparing for me to abandon her, yet again.

But hell, expectations never did sit well with me.

"Then I'm not going anywhere." The words came out gruff, my decision final. I slid my arm around her shoulders, pulling her into a tight embrace. She stiffened, her discomfort palpable, but she didn't shrug me off.

The air in the room was heavy with tension. I sat down next to her, my knees almost brushing against my father's bed. I sat there for a long time, numb and unmoving. Listening to each breathy rasp, the slow beep of the heart monitor. Trying to come to terms with the fact that this was the end. It was all happening too fast.

Cassidy fussed over him, adjusting his oxygen mask and IV lines, sitting rigid and prim in the hard plastic hospital chair. Despite everything we'd gone through the last two years, she still acted like I might bite her if she got too close. I had expected nothing less, but it still stung.

I hated how awkward it felt, that it took our father dying to get us in the same room together. I hated the fact that I was part of the reason for the distance between us.

I hated that I couldn't find the words to tell her that.

Taking Dad's hand in mine, I floundered a bit for the right words, disconcerted by the cool fragility of his skin beneath my rough touch. He'd been such a strong man, but now...I swallowed hard, blinking away the stinging sensation in my eyes.

"Hey, Pops, it's um, it's Tommy," I began, floundering. "I don't know if you can hear me, but I...I guess I do have some things I'd like to say to you."

I cleared my throat, hoping my voice wouldn't crack and realizing that it didn't matter if it did. "I'm sorry we didn't have more time. There's so much I wish I could have said. So many things I regret."

I paused, struggling for words. "You weren't always the best father, but you were the only one I had. And you tried, in your own way. You taught me what it meant to be strong, to fight for what's yours. You showed me how to survive."

"Growing up, we had our share of good times and bad," I continued, my voice halting. "We lost Mom, and that was hard on all of us. Cass and I, we were always fighting. I know she blamed you for it, even though it wasn't your fault. It was your lifestyle that got her killed, and there I was, praising you like a goddamn hero. Just chomping at the bit to go work for you and Callum. You could be a real bastard sometimes, you know? And despite everything, despite how hard I tried to be someone you were proud of, I was scared...scared that I'd end up like you."

On the other side of the bed, Cassidy had gone very still. I didn't care. Maybe my words were an explanation for her, too.

"But you turned it around, you know? You became someone I looked up to in the end. I just hope I can live up to your legacy." My heart clenched as I said the words hadn't been said nearly enough between us. "I love you, Dad."

Cassidy looked away, shoulders rigid. I took Michael's hand in both of mine, so much bigger now than his, and I pressed my lips against his knuckles. A peace offering to the man who had both saved and damned me.

Then, I let him go.

In the end, it happened peacefully. His breathing slowed, became softer, his chest rising and falling gently, and then not at all.

Cassidy moved toward the heart monitor, her trembling fingers reaching for the switch. She hesitated for a moment before turning it off, the silence that followed feeling far more oppressive than any alarm. Her hand lingered on the machine, gripping its side tightly. I realized she was crying.

I crossed the room in two strides and pulled her into my arms. Cassidy went stiff, resisting, but after a few moments she curled into my embrace. Her shoulders shook with sobs as she clung to me, and I held my sister close while she cried, stroking her hair and letting her grieve.

Cassidy rested her head against my chest. "I-I don't know why I'm acting this way. I hated him for so long."

"Because he was still our father," I murmured, trying to steady my own emotions. Our relationship with Michael had been far from perfect, but he was still our dad. We still loved him, even if we hadn't always liked him.

She nodded, wiping away more tears. "I just wish..."

"I know." I squeezed her shoulders, my voice soft. "I know."

"Thank you for staying."

I just held her tighter, knowing she needed me to be her rock right now, even if I didn't much feel like one.

Holding her like that hauled me back to another time, another hospital room, one year ago. Cassidy giving birth to her son while her husband fought for his life two floors down. The raw power, the pain. She was a force to be reckoned with. She always had been, even as a child. I couldn't help but think that my sister was the real strong one in our family.

Cassidy took a shuddering breath against my chest, then another, and she finally stood up straight to wipe her eyes with a little nod of her head as if to say, *all right that's enough.* I huffed a laugh and smoothed over a tear she'd missed.

Then her eyes lifted to mine, and the crease between her brows deepened. "Jesus, Tommy. What happened to you?"

Oh. That.

I shrugged, trying to play it off. "It's nothing, just a few scrapes. Don't worry about it."

"Don't worry about it?" She hesitantly touched a tender spot on my cheekbone, and I winced. "You look like you've been through a meat grinder."

I probably smelled like a bar floor, too. Whiskey, cigarettes, and sweat. It wasn't my best look.

"I'm fine, Cass. Really." I pulled back from her touch, hoping to hide my bruised knuckles and the pain that was starting to slowly seep back into my stream of consciousness. "Don't go all doctor-mode on me."

"Go home. Shower. Sleep." She spoke with the authority of her profession, but her eyes held the concern of a sister. "I've got this covered."

I looked at the sterile white bed where our father lay still. Then I looked back at Cassidy and saw the resolve in her posture, the faint tremor in her hands.

"I know you do, Cass. But if it's all the same to you, I'm staying."

7

SLOANE

THE INSISTENT NUDGING AT my cheek wasn't the wake-up call I was accustomed to. A sudden weight on my chest jolted me awake, and I found myself staring into the green eyes of my cat, Whiskey. He meowed loudly, demanding food.

"All right, all right," I muttered, rubbing my eyes. "In a minute, you little monster."

Whiskey arched his back and gave me an unimpressed glare before sauntering off the end of the bed. I chuckled to myself, rolling over and catching a glimpse of the clock. Most of the guys at the bar would probably shit themselves if they knew I was a cat lady.

I rolled back over in bed, stretching my toes and soaking in the last bit of comfort before I had to get up. Unbidden, my thoughts drifted, settling on the thorn in my side who had occupied all too much of my thoughts lately. Tommy.

That night after the fight—what was that all about? I tried to replay the sequence of events in my head, but they were fogged by something soft and sweet. The closeness of his body to mine, leaning closer. The hesitant vulnerability. The dark hunger. Tommy Quinn, that great, bombastic asshole, sitting in front of me, bleeding and more than half drunk, but all I could think of was how good his skin felt under my fingertips.

And how if he had leaned just a little bit further, he would have been kissing me.

I snorted at the thought. Kissing him. I had to admit, it had been a while, but I was not that desperate. A girl has standards.

No. It was nothing more than concern and maybe a little bit of protectiveness. I could admit that to myself, now. Tommy's actions were worrying, but it didn't go further than a friendly concern for his well-being. It couldn't. Tommy and I were friends at best, annoyances at worst. And that was all we would ever be.

Whiskey was getting insistent. With a sigh, I dragged myself out of bed and into the shower, letting the hot water wash away the lingering tension in my shoulders.

Afterwards, I threw on a pair of jeans and a tank top before padding barefoot into the kitchen. The sun streamed through the windows, bright and airy, flooding the apartment as I padded my way to the bathroom. The artsy, vintage vibe of the place was ever-present in the décor, with well-loved Red Sox memorabilia lining the shelves and colorful band posters plastered on the walls.

Whiskey was waiting for me in the kitchen, his tail flicking expectantly as I filled his bowl with kibble. He started eating immediately, ignoring my cooing and petting, the ungrateful asshole. Come to think of it, he and Tommy had a lot in common. I guess I had a type.

My stomach rumbled, and I took the stairs two at a time down to the coffee shop below my apartment. The scent of rich coffee and pastries had been the deciding factor in my choice of where to live, along with the free coffee and breakfast from the owners, an older couple who had been friends with Callum back in the day. I often wondered what sort of mischief he and Michael had gotten up to back then, but they were tight-lipped about the old days. I supposed they had their reasons.

The bell jingling overhead as I entered the shop. It was a quiet morning, which was typical for the late hour. A couple of regulars sat at tables near the window, nursing their cups of coffee while they read the morning paper. It was all very Norman Rockwell.

"Morning, Joan." I slid into my usual seat along the counter.

"Morning, love. The usual?"

"You know me so well." I smiled gratefully as she placed a steaming cup of coffee in front of me, along with a blueberry muffin.

I took a sip of coffee and sighed. "So, anything interesting going on this morning?"

Joan looked up from the cash register, shaking her head. "Not much, just the usual. Although, there was a bit of commotion last night."

"Oh?"

She nodded. "Harry and I heard it from upstairs. Some kind of fight, I think. A couple of young punks got into it, by the sound of it. They were gone before we could call the cops. Front of the shop was tagged this morning, though."

I must have missed that on my way in. "Do you know what they were fighting about?"

"No idea." Joan shrugged. "Harry thinks they might be dealing, though."

"Why didn't you call the boys?"

She waved her hand, looking uncomfortable. "I don't want to bother them, they've got enough on their plate. And besides, it was just a small scuffle. I'm sure it was nothing."

I hummed noncommittally and picked at my muffin. I knew Joan and Harry were wary of involving the clan, but they really shouldn't be. Yet another reason we needed to get back in the game.

"Can you describe them?" I asked.

Harry peaked around the door to the kitchen. "Two young guys, early twenties maybe. One had long, dark hair, and the other had a couple tattoos."

I frowned, taking mental notes of their description. "Don't worry, we'll take care of it."

"Thank you, Sloane, we really appreciate it," Joan said, relief evident in her voice. "It's just that, what happened with Skip and Mary...it really shook everybody up."

I could almost see the shadow of doubt in his eyes, the question he didn't dare to voice: Can we still hold our ground? It gnawed at me, this creeping uncertainty that slunk around the corners of our territory since last year. To be honest, I had been feeling some of that uncertainty myself, and I was more than ready to do something about it.

Instead, I offered a reassuring smile. "I'll make sure those punks understand that this neighborhood is off-limits. You have my word."

She nodded, her smile grateful. "Thank you, Sloane. That means a lot to us. And please, give the boys my regards."

I finished my coffee and muffin, then went to deal with the problem.

As soon as I got the bar, I found Grady at the bar going over receipts and nursing a cup of coffee. I approached him without hesitation. "Grady, we're going on rounds."

He looked up, startled, and sputtered, "What? Why? That's Tommy's job."

"Tommy's not here," I snapped. "People need to know they can still depend on us, even if he's gone AWOL. We can't afford to wait around for him to decide when he wants to do his job."

Grady frowned. "Listen Sloane, I get that you want to help. I really do. But the shipment the other day was one thing. This is another entirely. It could get dangerous."

"Don't worry, Grady." I winked at him. "You're safe with me."

“Ha, very funny," he grumbled, but I saw the corner of his mouth twitch upwards. It was fleeting, but it was there. "If we're doing this, let's do it right. Come on."

Grady led the way out to the car, opening the door for me before sliding behind the wheel. As he drove, I noticed him glancing in the rear-view mirror every so often, checking to make sure we weren't being followed. I wondered what exactly I'd gotten myself into.

The first stop was a small bodega on the corner of Broadway and Maple Street. It was owned by an elderly couple named Mr. and Mrs. Patel, who were good friends with my parents. Grady held the door open for me as I stepped inside, the scent of spices and fresh produce greeting us. The interior was brightly lit and well-stocked, shelves lined with fresh produce and spices from all over the world.

Mrs. Patel was behind the counter, her gray hair pulled back into a tight bun. Her eyes lit up when she saw us. "Oh! Hello there, Sloane! It is good to see you again."

I smiled back. "It's good to see you too, Mrs. Patel. How are you and Mr. Patel?"

"We're doing well, thank you for asking," she said, beaming at me. "How is your father?"

"Good, he wishes he could be here himself. But he sends his regards."

"Ah, tell him we miss seeing him around here."

"I will."

I chatted with her for a few minutes, catching up on the latest gossip. It was what people wanted to see, what my father excelled at. Making people believe that the clan wasn't just an uncomfortable necessity, it was a lifeline if they needed it. It was about more than just collecting dues. It was about trust.

It seemed I was good at it too, even if I didn't always believe the words that came out of my mouth.

"Not bad," Grady said, impressed.

"Bartending is the art of bullshitting people just enough to hand over their money for something they don't really need. Band-Aids on bullet wounds. Gasoline on bonfires. This isn't too far from that. Our presence in this neighborhood is about cohabitation, first and foremost. The people are the currency we need to survive."

It was one of the first things my father had taught my brother Aiden about this job, a lesson I'd learned listening in at the doorway. He said if you can make people feel safe, you can do almost anything. Once you had them in your pocket, you were king.

"Let's go visit Mrs. O'Leary, she just had her hip surgery. And after that, we should swing by that new club on Broadway. The owner still owes us $30K."

Grady glanced at me. "How do you know all this? I thought Callum kept you out of clan business for the most part."

“Barstools are better than confessional booths for spilling secrets. You'd be surprised what you hear on the other side of a bar."

"Well, I don't care what Tommy thinks. You're not half bad at this."

"Only half?" I shot back, arching an eyebrow. The corner of his mouth ticked upward again.

"You still need to keep your head down. Stay out of trouble. You're Callum's daughter, and you don't have any protection. But...you're good with people."

"I can take care of myself, Grady, I'm not some ditzy damsel in distress."

He held his hands up in surrender. "I didn't mean to imply that you were. I've just seen a lot of people get hurt because of this life, and I don't want that happening to you. Neither does Tommy."

"I'm pretty sure he could care less. He just wants to boss me around."

"That's not true," he replied, shaking his head. "Tommy cares about you, Sloane. More than you realize."

I snorted. "Yeah, well, he has a funny way of showing it. Besides, Tommy doesn't do feelings. I'm pretty sure he wouldn't know a genuine emotion if it jumped up and bit him in the ass."

Grady looked over at me, frowning. "You know, he's been through a lot. Not just recently."

"That excuse his behavior."

"No, it doesn't," Grady agreed. "But he's deeper than you think. And he's capable of hurting just like anyone else, so maybe you should lay off his case, okay?"

I straightened up, a little surprised by Grady's fierce defense of his boss. "Fine. I'll be nice to the knuckle dragging caveman. But only because you asked so nicely."

Grady smiled. "Thanks, Sloane."

It took a little asking around, and it was late in the day when we found the two guys who had been harassing the neighborhood. Grady and I pulled up to the curb in front of a rundown apartment building and got out of the car. The sun was setting, casting long shadows across the street.

The building looked abandoned from the outside, but when we got closer, I heard the faint thud of music coming from inside. Two younger men leaned up against the bricks. It was clear as day that they were Moretti's men, low-level runners trying to make a name for themselves by causing trouble in our territory.

"Let's have a chat with these gentlemen, shall we?" I muttered to Grady, my pulse quickening.

"Are you out of your mind, Sloane?" Grady hissed, his eyes darting nervously between me and the drug dealers. "We don't know what they're capable of!"

"Relax, Grady," I said, my voice laced with confidence. "I've handled worse than these two at the bar."

Taking a deep breath, I strode forward, my boots clicking loudly on the pavement as I approached the unsuspecting duo. They looked up at the sound, their smirks widening as they saw me approach.

"Hey, there, boys."

The taller of the two stepped forward, leering down at me. "What can we do for you, sweetheart?"

"You can start by telling me why you're here," I replied coolly. "Seems you're lost. This isn't Moretti territory."

"Who's gonna stop us? You?" one sneered, his eyes brazenly raking over me, misunderstanding the danger he was in.

"Among others," I replied calmly, though my heart pounded fiercely against my ribcage. "But I'll be your first problem. And trust me, you don't want to find out about the rest."

His friend spoke up, his voice low and menacing. "We don't answer to you, bitch. So fuck off."

Grady's hand fell on my shoulder, and I shrugged it off. "Don't worry, Grady. I've got this."

I stepped closer to the two men, staring them down. "You're trespassing. That makes you mine. Now, I'm going to ask nicely one more time, and then we're going to get ugly. What are you doing here?"

They hesitated, exchanging looks before the taller one spoke again. "We're just here to deliver a message."

"And what message would that be?"

"Tell your boss that the Moretti family wants what's theirs," he said, his eyes gleaming with malice. "And if he doesn't give it to us, we'll take it anyway."

"Well, you can tell your boss that he can shove his threats right up his ass," I replied evenly. "Because the McTiernan Clan doesn't take orders from anyone. Especially not some half-rate thugs like you two."

"Bitch!" the second guy roared, lunging at me. I dodged out of the way, grabbing his arm and using his momentum to throw him into the ground. He landed hard, groaning as the air left his lungs.

His friend went for me too, but Grady stepped in, throwing a punch that caught him on the jaw. I caught him on the rebound with a tap to the balls, then hauled him up by his shirtfront, growling in his ear.

“The name McTiernan mean anything to you?”

He just wheezed.

I smirked.

"I'll take that as a yes," I said, tightening my grip on his shirt. The asshole was heavy. "I'm Sloane McTiernan, and this is my neighborhood. Now, I don't know what you're thinking, coming in here and trying to make trouble, but I can promise you this: it's not gonna end well for you. So I suggest you go back to your bosses and tell them to stay out of our territory. Unless, of course, he wants another war."

The thug glared up at me, but there was a hint of fear in his eyes now. I released him and shoved him back towards his friend. “Go. And if we catch you again on these streets, a busted face isn’t the only thing you’ll be bringing back from South Boston.”

I turned on my heels, ignoring their muttered curses and threats as I walked away. Grady fell in step beside me, shaking his head in amazement.

"Holy shit, Sloane! Remind me never to get on your bad side," Grady joked, a hint of awe in his voice.

I laughed. "Let's just say I've been around long enough to learn a thing or two about dealing with assholes."

Grady glanced at me. "You sure you're okay?"

"Never better," I answered truthfully. I felt better than I had in a long time, actually. The thrill of the fight still lingered, along with the satisfaction of putting those thugs in their place.

"Hey, Sloane." Grady's voice interrupted my thoughts.

I turned to him. "Yeah?"

"Thanks."

I arched an eyebrow. "For what?"

"For proving Tommy wrong. For being willing to stick your neck out for the clan."

"I wouldn't go that far," I said, though I appreciated his praise. "But you're welcome. I care about this place, just like everyone else."

He smiled, looking relieved. "So, you're sticking around then?"

"For now."

Grady clapped me on the shoulder. "Well, I'm glad to hear it. You're good for this place."

Tell that to Tommy.

I slid behind the bar, the familiar scent of whiskey and wood polish wrapping around me like a worn leather jacket. My hands moved automatically, pulling pints and mixing cocktails while I kept one ear tuned to the gruff murmurs around me. The regulars were a tough crowd, but I caught the undertones of respect in their nods and the way they made room for me to pass. I had earned my place here, and they knew it.

I lost myself in the rhythm of the bar, the soothing monotony of pouring drinks and taking orders, the constant hum of conversation a pleasant buzz in the background. It was only after my shift was over that I realized how late it had gotten. The bar was mostly empty, save for a few stragglers finishing off their pints.

I was just about to pack things up when my phone buzzed in my back pocket. I frowned, checking the caller ID.

"Dad?" I said, startled. He almost never called me directly. "Where are you? Are you okay? Is—"

"I'm fine, Sloane," he interrupted, his voice gruff.

"Then what—"

"Michael's gone."

The words hit like a sucker punch, knocking the air from my lungs. *Oh, Tommy.* I gripped the counter for support, my knees suddenly weak. "What? When? I thought he was doing okay."

"It happened fast. Last night."

That must have been the phone call Tommy got. His face...

"Is Tommy with you?"

"Yes. He's here. Got here just in time for...you know. Both him and Cassidy." He cleared his throat loudly. "We're taking care of everything on our end up here, but I need you to pass the word: the funeral is set for this Friday. Tell the boys. Grady will know what to do."

Thanks for the vote of confidence, Dad.

"Friday," I repeated numbly. "Yeah, I'll take care of it."

"Good. That's my girl."

My hand gripped the phone tighter. "Dad, how is Tommy? Really?"

A pause. "Tommy? He's good. Fine, actually. He's been a real rock for Cassidy—"

"Okay, because lately—"

"Don't worry about him, Sloane. He's got a good head on his shoulders, he knows what needs to be done. See that you do, too. Friday, remember."

I clenched my teeth. "Yeah, Dad. I've got it."

I ended the call before I could say something I might regret later.

Typical.

Don't worry about it, Sloane, we've got it covered, Sloane. Just serve us our drinks, keep our secrets, clean up our messes, listen to our bullshit. Funeral's on Friday.

Fuck that. I was done playing housewife to a bunch of knuckle draggers stuck in the 1950's. The clan needed me. Tommy needed me.

And if the past few days were any indication, Tommy was very, very far from fine.

8

Tommy

I DON'T BELIEVE IN souls. Or the afterlife. I don't believe that getting enough gold stars in this life will get you some kind of VIP access through a pair of pearly gates, and I sure as hell don't believe that there's some higher power out there watching over us. We are far to petty and uninteresting to spend that kind of time and energy on.

Once, I asked my dad what he wanted after he was gone. I think it was shortly after my mother's funeral.

"Just chuck me in the ground, throw some dirt on me, and get on with it," he'd grunted. "No point in making a big to-do over it. I sure as hell won't care by that point. Take care of your sister, though. Even if she won't let you."

Michael's casket was dark mahogany, with silver trim. The lid was shut, something both Cassidy and I insisted on. No viewing. She let me take the burden of the funeral details from her, which I was grateful for. I knew she actually believed in this stuff. Maybe that made it easier for me to do, but it still sucked.

Dad and I might not have believed in much, but we did believe in the finality of death. We'd seen enough of it. And while he might not have believed or even cared about his own funeral, I knew it wasn't really for him, anyway. It was for the rest of us left behind.

That still didn't mean I hated funerals any less.

My head pounded as I stood in front of the sea of black. The church was sweltering, stuffed to the gills with friends and enemies alike, all come to pay their respects to Dad—a funeral for a man as infamous as Michael Quinn invariably turned into a who's who of organized crime. On the left, I saw the Bratva contingent, including Misha, who nodded solemnly in my direction. Towards the back of the church, the Italians—Sal Giordano was the only one I recognized, now, the only one of the original family we hadn't killed off.

It was a wonder nothing untoward ever happened during things like this, but I guess there were some lines even men like us wouldn't cross.

I looked around for Alfie's pseudo-friend Luca, who had sided with us under the table from time to time, but I didn't see him. I wasn't surprised. Luca didn't make it out much anymore, not since he'd gotten half his face blown away helping us last year.

I tugged at my tie, my bruised ribs throbbing under the stiff shirt. The collar of my black suit felt like a vice around my neck, and my head pounded with yet another hangover. I knew I looked like hell. The room was stifling, the air thick and cloying with the scent of flowers. My gaze swept the crowd, settling on Cassidy, baby Aiden gurgling in her arms. Connor's arm was wrapped protectively around my sister's shoulders, and I felt a surge of gratitude. I'd had my doubts about them in the beginning, but Connor had proven again and again that he would move heaven and earth for Cassidy. I couldn't ask for anything more for her.

Callum sat a few pews behind them with his wife, his wrinkled face set in a grim line. Grady and the boys filled out several more rows, some of them so new they'd never even met Michael. So many new faces.

And there, next to Callum, was Sloane. Her hair was swept up, tendrils curling around her neck. The cut of her black pantsuit hugged every curve. No dresses for my little spitfire. She looked regal, poised, and utterly in control. The irony that it pissed me off as much as it turned me on was not lost on me.

Why the hell did she have to look so perfect, so untouchable, when I was falling apart at the seams? I had to force myself to look away before the urge to punch a hole through the wall overwhelmed me.

Instead, I turned and faced the packed church. There were so many people here—friends, family, and enemies alike. Michael had touched the lives of many during his time as head of the clan, and while not all of those relationships had been positive, it seemed like everyone had come out to pay their respects. It was a sobering reminder of just how much influence Michael had wielded and how many people he had impacted during his life.

I took a deep breath, trying to calm my nerves. I hadn't prepared a speech. My father didn't believe in sentimentality or grandiose gestures. But he had always believed in the importance of legacy, so here I stood.

"Today is a hard day for our family," I began, my voice echoing in the cavernous church. "We've lost a husband, a father, and a friend. But more importantly, we've lost a mentor, a leader, and a brother."

I took a deep breath, trying to compose myself. I felt the eyes of the crowd boring into me, their hushed whispers and murmurs echoing in the quiet space.

"Michael Quinn was a complicated man. He was...he was a tough old bastard right up until the end..."

The priest glared at me. Probably shouldn't say bastard in a church.

I cleared my throat. "He, uh...he made mistakes..."

What the hell was I supposed to say? My voice cracked, and I paused, swallowing the lump that threatened to choke me. My fingers drummed against the wooden podium, the rhythm erratic, matching the hammering of my heart. The room swelled with silence, expectant, heavy.

Fuck, I couldn't do this.

My eyes somehow found Sloane through the sea of faces. Her gaze met mine, steady and calm. A lifeline. A sharp, clean clarity lanced through the haze of alcohol still lingering in my system. Her chin lifted in that defiant way of hers that said she knew I was better than this, stronger than this. She nodded, and I gripped the edges of the podium.

"Michael was a lot of things. He was hard. He was stubborn. But most of all, he was loyal. Loyal to his family and loyal to his friends. He may have had his faults, but he always did what he believed was right, no matter the cost. And that's more than most people can say.

"I mean, who hasn't made mistakes? Who the hell doesn't have regrets?" Next to me, the priest coughed disapprovingly, but I didn't care. I loosened my tie a bit. "If it's one thing that my father taught me is that it's never too late to say you're sorry. It's never too late to make amends. To reconcile with those we've hurt. He may not have been perfect, but he did the best he could do with what he was given, and in the end, he left on his own terms and surrounded by the family who loved him.

"Michael Quinn was a grumpy bastard, but he was a good man. He was my father." I looked over at the photograph on the casket. My eyes were starting to sting a little. Must be the hangover. "I'm going to miss you, Dad."

I left the podium, my throat thick. The priest stood, his expression stern.

"Let us pray," he began, his voice booming through the church.

I made my way back to my seat, my limbs heavy, matching the ache building in the back of my head. I was not going to cry goddamnit.

As I settled into the wooden pew, my gaze drifted instinctively toward the back of the church, searching for Sloane. Instead, my attention was drawn as a shadow detached itself from the wall and slipped out the door near where the Moretti family was sitting, not really bothering to be discrete. Tall and powerful, familiar in a way that I struggled to place.

I blinked, and the figure was gone. Just a trick of the light and too much whiskey playing havoc with my mind. Cassidy took my hand as I sat and squeezed it tightly, and I filed the sighting away for later. I knew better than to let it go completely. In our world, the devil was always in the details.

Later, at the gravesite, I stood next to my sister as a few last words were said. Connor had his arm around her, offering what comfort he could, but she leaned into me as well.

"Thank you," Connor mouthed to me as I put an arm around Cassidy's waist, pulling her close.

I nodded, tightening my grip on her.

As the service drew to a close, I scanned the crowd of mourners. My eyes locked onto a small group standing off to the side—Misha and a few of the Bratva contingent. I wondered which one, if any, was Aleksandr Volkov. The Russian leader was as mysterious as he was elusive, and Misha hadn't exactly volunteered up any information. Our friendship, if you could call it that, existed mostly outside our professions.

Further down were the Italians. Their presence was more of a surprise, given everything that had gone down last year, but still not that much of a shock, given the tenuous truce that existed between our families and the tradition of honoring the passing of a patriarch. I finally saw Luca, his hair longer now and falling forward over the ruined left side of his face, and he gave me a stiff nod. Beside him was Sofia and a tall man who looked enough like her to be her brother, and finally Sal Giordano, the defacto head of the house since we'd killed off the rest of the Moretti family. His expression was carefully neutral, but his eyes were cold and hard. I felt my hackles raise, but I forced myself to remain calm. The last thing we needed was another war with the Italians.

As the mourners began to disperse, Cassidy pulled me aside, her brow furrowed.

"Tommy, look at you," she chided softly, her pale fingers lightly tracing a yet-to-heal cut above my brow. "You're a mess."

I pulled back and shrugged. "What's a few more scars on this ugly mug? Chick's aren't exactly lining up for my looks."

She ignored me, clicking her tongue as she turned my face to inspect the bruise on my jaw. Aiden squirmed in her arms.

"Here. Let me hold him," I said.

Cassidy hesitated, then relented, handing him over. I cradled him against my chest, feeling his solid warmth in my arms. Aiden gurgled happily, reaching for my face with his tiny hands. There was something about holding that kid, born on the eve of much loss, which felt like the only real thing left in this world. I would never forget the miracle of seeing him brought into the world as long as I lived.

"Hey there, little man," I murmured, marveling at the innocence in his blue gaze. He was so small. So damn perfect, his little body warm and solid nestled against my heart. Something so tiny and fragile held in my big, scarred hands. My vision blurred, and I swallowed the lump in my throat.

"Aiden likes you." Cassidy's voice was soft, her eyes glistening with unshed tears. "He likes your voice."

I cleared my throat, fighting back the emotions that threatened to overwhelm me. "Yeah, well, he's got good taste, then."

Cassidy reached up and smoothed Aiden's hair, jet black like his daddy's. Like his namesake's. Cassidy's breath hitched, her mouth opening and closing like she was working up to saying something, so I just waited. We Quinns took a little longer when it came to the emotional stuff, but we'd get there eventually.

"I don't think I ever thanked you for that night, Tommy. In the hospital with Aiden." My sister's voice cracked, and she cleared it fiercely. "I don't think I would've gotten through it without you. Without knowing Connor's condition, if he was even..."

"Aw, hell," I started, then looked down at the baby in my arms. "Sorry, *heck*. Cass, you're one of the strongest women I've ever known, and that night proved it. You didn't need me. You never have."

"I've needed you more than you realize. Especially the last two years." She smiled, but it didn't reach her eyes. "I'm worried about you, Tommy. You look exhausted."

"It's nothing I can't handle," I assured her, trying to sound confident. "I'll be fine."

"Will you?"

Before I could prepare a comeback because I was truly sick and tired of people sticking their noses in my business, Cassidy was called away by one of our distant relatives. I kept ahold of little Aiden, not ready to give him up quite yet.

"Looks like it's just you and me, buddy." I bounced him gently in my arms, and he nuzzled into my shirtfront.

It felt good to hold him. It felt right.

I looked up to see Sloane approaching. Her black pantsuit hugged her curves perfectly, and the light breeze played with tendrils of her hair. She looked dangerous and sleek, dressed to kill. No. She looked like a fucking goddess, and my mouth went dry at the sight of her.

"Never took you for the nurturing type," she teased, the corner of her mouth twitching upwards.

"I'm full of surprises," I winked at her, my heart skipping a beat when her smile widened. It was rare to catch Sloane off guard, even rarer to share a moment that didn't end in some verbal sparring match.

"Clearly," she said, smiling as she looked down at Aiden. "You're good with him."

"Thanks," I replied, unable to resist a small grin of pride. We fell into an awkward silence, the air between us heavy with things left unsaid.

"Tommy, I..." Sloane hesitated before continuing. "I'm really sorry about Michael."

I sighed, my shoulders slumping. "Yeah, well, it's not exactly unexpected, is it? We all knew it was coming. We've been preparing for this for months. I just...I just didn't think it would happen so fast."

Sloane nodded, her expression sympathetic. "Still, it must have been hard for you."

"Michael was like family to you, too," I said softly.

She nodded, her voice barely above a whisper. "Yes, he was."

There was a beat of silence, then she cleared her throat. "Look, Tommy, I know we've had our differences. I know you didn't ask for my advice, and you probably don't want it, but...I'm here for you. If you ever need anything, all you have to do is ask."

I stared at her, surprised. I knew Sloane cared about me, but this was unexpected. I wasn't used to her being so direct, and I wasn't sure how to respond.

Aiden stirred in my arms, and I cupped the back of his tiny head in my hand. His weight was grounding. "I guess I've uh...not been the easiest to be around, lately."

I sounded like an idiot. Shit. I really wasn't good at this kind of thing.

Sloane smirked. "No, not really."

"I'm sorry," I said, meaning it. "You didn't deserve that."

"No, I didn't." There was no anger in her tone, just honesty. I shifted uncomfortably. "But I get it, Tommy. I know you're hurting, and I know you're trying to deal with it the best way you know how. You're allowed to make mistakes. You're only human."

My lips twitched into a smile, but there was little humor in it. "You know, my dad said the same thing a few weeks ago. He was always telling me to get my head out of my ass where you were concerned."

"Oh?" One dark brow arched. "And have you?"

"Trying to." The admission slipped out before I could stop it.

Sloane's lips parted, her eyes searching mine. For one wild, impossible second, I thought she might actually give in to the heat simmering between us.

Then she stepped forward, wrapping her arms around me. I froze, heart pounding as she pressed close. "You're my friend, Tommy," she murmured against my chest. "I don't know what I'd do without you."

Friend.

The word was a knife to my ribs, sharp and twisting. I closed my eyes, clinging to her for just a moment longer, wishing for something she would never give.

When she finally pulled back, I forced a smile. "You're my friend too, Sloane."

Liar.

Her eyes searched mine, as if looking for a sign of the jokester or the tough guy she was used to sparring with. But in that instant, I couldn't muster up the bravado; I could only offer her a nod, a brittle facsimile of my usual grin etched onto my face.

"Good," she said, stepping back and smoothing down her black pantsuit. "Remember that, okay? Friends are there for each other."

"Got it," I replied, the words sticking in my throat. It was a dance we'd done a thousand times before—me reaching out, her stepping back. Only this time, the music had stopped, and we were left standing awkwardly in the wake of its silence.

She gave me one last look, then turned and walked away. I watched her go, my heart heavy. I knew what I was doing to myself, but I didn't know how to stop.

Sloane was right. I was a mess.

I stood there for a moment, the weight of everything settling around me like a heavy blanket. Aiden squirmed in my arms, breaking me out of my daze. I shifted him to my other arm, so lost in my own thoughts that I barely noticed Connor's approach until his hand landed heavily on my shoulder.

It was hard to rectify Connor McTiernan with the man who'd been locked up in that slaughterhouse along with me a year ago. A memory, one of many, that I tried and failed to forget. Tensions with the Italians had reached an all-time high, first with my sister's abduction at the hands of that bastard turncoat Teagan, and then Alfie and Emilia's illicit romance, all of which had culminated in Connor and I being tortured at the hands of Lorenzo Moretti's two sons, Angelo and Dominic.

Dominic had taken a special shine to me that night. I wasn't sure if he had a bully complex and I was just the bigger of the two of us, or if he'd taken special exception to me running my mouth, but Dominic had used me, making Connor watch while he tortured me. Too bad Dominic didn't realize who he was dealing with—Connor would sooner cut off his left hand than sell out his brothers. Even if it meant losing a pound of flesh to Dominic's knife.

I was usually a devil-may-care kind of guy, but for a minute there, it had gotten pretty dark. We were going to die in that hellhole, and sometimes I think the thought of getting Connor back to his pregnant wife was the only motivation that made me get back up on my feet and keep fighting. Connor was my brother in all but blood, and I would do anything for him. Including pretending to be happy while he got to walk away and live his happily ever after with the woman he loved.

The past year almost looked like it hadn't happened to him. After the surgery to repair the extensive damage done by Angel's bullet, Connor had lost weight, but he'd since gained it back, his usually pale skin glowing with good health. Even the haunted look that I'd seen since he'd first come to live over here was gone, replaced with the look of a man who had gotten everything he'd ever hoped for.

Although now, looking at me, his lips thinned into a disapproving frown that I unfortunately knew all too well.

"Tommy, we need to talk," he said.

"Sure, man," I replied, smoothly handing Aiden back into his father's arms. "What's up?"

"Not here." Connor glanced around at the mourners still milling about. "Let's take a walk."

We walked down the path in silence, the cemetery's quiet broken only by the occasional rustle of leaves in the trees overhead. It was peaceful here, tucked away from the city's noise and bustle. I saw why Cassidy had picked it.

We stopped next to one of the old oak trees, the trunk's gnarled branches providing shade from the sun overhead. Connor took a deep breath, turning to face me.

"Tommy, we need to talk about this," he said quietly, his brow furrowed.

"About what?" I asked, trying to keep my tone neutral. But deep down, I knew that Connor wasn't here for small talk or condolences.

"Your life, or what's left of it," he replied bluntly, his gaze unwavering. "You're killing yourself."

"What are you talking about? I'm fine."

"Really?" Connor arched an eyebrow. "Because from where I'm standing, it looks like you're about two steps away from going over the edge. You look like shit, man. And your drinking? The fighting? That's not healthy."

I scowled. "I said I'm fine. Stop mothering me, Connor, I can handle myself."

"Don't lie to me." His eyes flashed. "I know darkness. I lived in it for a long time, remember? What you're doing...it's going to end bloody. And I don't want to see you get hurt because of it."

I swallowed hard, feeling the sting of his words. They weren't new, these accusations, but coming from Connor, they hit different. "I'm holding up just fine," I lied.

Connor shook his head, a rueful smile briefly touching his lips before his expression darkened. "I've been where you are, Tommy. I've stared into that abyss and let it swallow me whole."

He paused, his gaze turning distant as if he could see the past playing out before him. "I remember lying in the back of that van, dying. Bleeding out while my wife tried to save me. That's when it hits you—the darkness, the self-destruction, the goddamn martyrdom. You think it's just about you, but it's not. You're hurting more people than just yourself."

His eyes snapped back to mine, sharp and piercing. Without another word, he glanced over at Cassidy, her red hair a bright flame even in the somberness of the day. Then, his gaze drifted to Sloane, standing a little apart, her posture all grace and strength wrapped in sorrow.

"Your actions," he continued, "they ripple out, Tommy. They hurt everyone around you."

"Stop."

He ignored me. "You can't keep going on like this, Tommy. You have to find a way to let go of the past. Otherwise, you're going to destroy yourself and everyone else in the process."

Connor pointedly looked over at my sister, and then at Sloane.

"I said stop." My hands clenched into fists at my sides. I felt the raw edge in Connor's words scrape against my insides, harsh and unyielding. He was right, but that didn't make his truth any less bitter to swallow.

"Take your head out of your arse, Tommy," he growled. "Look at yourself, man. You're half the person you used to be, and it's not just you who's paying for it."

The sting of his admonishment felt like a punch to the gut, rattling through my bruised body. I wanted to lash out, to tell him to mind his own damn business, but the fight in me was as drained as the last dregs of whiskey from yesterday's bottle.

"Start with taking care of yourself," Connor said. "If that's too much for you to handle, then start taking care of the people around you. You owe them that much."

I swallowed hard and nodded. There were no words to give, nothing that would ease the rawness in my chest. Connor clasped the back of my neck briefly, pressing his forehead to mine, and then walked away, joining Cassidy. They leaned into each other, her head on his shoulder, his arm around her waist. The picture of love and comfort I'd craved for so long.

What the hell was wrong with me? Why did everything I touch turn to ashes?

Sloane. The thought of her was a knife in my gut, twisting deeper with each breath. No wonder she wanted nothing to do with me beyond friendship. I was lucky to have that. She deserved better than the wreck I'd become. Better than a man haunted by his own demons, drowning under the weight of a duty he couldn't escape.

I turned away from the happy couple and walked to my car, fingers curling into fists inside my pockets. Connor was right - I was killing myself, inch by inch, day after day. The alcohol-fueled benders, the reckless fights, the hollow nights—they hadn't brought me any closer to peace or redemption. Just more scars, more regrets. The path I was on ended in a dark, bloody place, but I didn't know if there was any other way out. Any escape from the cage I'd built around myself.

Maybe it was time to stop wallowing in self-pity, to stop letting the ghosts of my mistakes dictate my present. Maybe it was time to start pulling myself out of this pit I'd dug, to claim something other than sorrow and anger for myself.

I glanced back at Sloane one last time, her black bob swaying gently as she spoke to someone offering condolences. There was a grace to her, even in mourning, which made my chest ache. Pining for a woman who saw me as nothing more than a friend was another chain I needed to break. If anyone deserved to be happy, it was her.

Maybe someday I would deserve to be happy too.

But maybe Connor was right. I could start by taking care of the people around me.

I unlocked my car and took one last look back at the dispersing crowd. The Italian and Russian contingents were already gone, but there was still a figure standing at the edge of the tree line, too far away to make out but with a stance that looked eerily familiar. I thought about the person I'd seen leaving the service earlier, the one I couldn't quite place.

As I squinted, trying to discern who it was, they raised a hand, pointing it at me like a gun. My heart pounded in my ears as they mimed pulling the trigger, then vanished into the woods before I could react.

"Who the fuck..." I muttered, adrenaline coursing through my veins.

"Tommy?" Sloane's voice drew me back to reality, and I turned to find her standing behind me. "What's going on?"

"Nothing," I lied. "Just a shadow."

"Are you sure you're okay?"

"Positive. Let's get out of here." I glanced at her. Might as well start now with the old olive-branch routine. "You, uh...need a ride back to Lady D's?"

Her eyes widened, surprise flickering across her face, but then she smiled. "Sure."

9

Sloane

The Saturday night after the funeral was trivia night, so the bar was packed. Normally, this would be a good thing—I could stomach a few rowdy trivia fans if it meant extra tips—but I'd gone on another run with Grady the night before, and my hand was a little worse for wear.

Although it did look a lot better than the guy's face I'd bounced it off.

I didn't think it was broken, but it sure felt like it. I'd been icing it all day, hoping I could keep down the swelling enough to maintain mobility. A handful of Ibuprofen and a long-sleeved tee with thumbholes to cover the obvious, and I was in business, or so I thought until the rush started.

Can a girl get a break?

I should have called Kat in for help. I didn't really like other people behind my bar; things were just where I wanted them, and it took so long to establish flow with a second body behind the bar that it was easier just to do it myself. At least the tips were good.

I looked up at the sound of a low voice, ready to smile my way through the next customer, but I froze when I saw Tommy sliding behind the bar.

"Shove over, Spitfire," he growled, his tone more playful than usual.

"What are you doing?"

"What's it look like I'm doing? Pouring drinks."

"You're not supposed to be back here."

He shot me a look that was all too self-assured as he rolled up his sleeves and grabbed a glass to fill with ice. "You're slammed. I'm gonna help."

"Did you hit your head or something?" I teased, watching Tommy fumble with a shaker, his brow furrowed in concentration.

"I've spent enough time on the other side of this bar to know my way around it."

I arched a brow, watching as he worked with an ease that surprised me. "You're sure about that?"

"Would I be back here if I wasn't?" His lips quirked up at the corners. "Relax, Sloane. I won't break anything...important."

"Comforting," I said dryly.

Honestly, I couldn't believe my eyes. Tommy was the very last person I expected to offer help. But there he was, ready to jump into action. A small part of me wondered if this was just another way for him to try to get closer to me, but I quickly dismissed the thought. The bar was drowning in orders, and I needed help.

I watched him for a moment, impressed by his skill and surprised by his sudden change in demeanor. Tommy might be a pain in the ass, but he held his own behind the bar.

I studied Tommy out of the corner of my eye, wondering what had gotten into him. He'd been acting strange all week, ever since the funeral. I'd seen him and Connor talking, and something Connor said had clearly pissed Tommy off. After that, Tommy had just stared off into the woods behind the cemetery, eyes distant and haunted, like he'd seen a ghost. Whatever was going on in that thick skull of his, he wasn't sharing.

Typical.

Still, his behavior nagged at me as we worked side by side behind the bar. Try as I might, I couldn't figure out what had changed. The old Tommy would never have volunteered to help me here, not without an ulterior motive.

But if there was another reason for him stepping in tonight, I couldn't see it. Maybe Connor had knocked some sense into him back at the funeral. Stranger things had happened.

I glanced at Tommy again, but his expression gave nothing away. The mystery deepened.

"See something you like?" Tommy's voice cut into my thoughts, a hint of amusement coloring his tone.

"Just wondering if you're planning to rob me blind when my back is turned."

"Honey, if I wanted to rob you, I wouldn't need to wait until your back was turned." His lips curled into a teasing smirk, the old familiar glint in his eyes. "But lucky for you, I'm just here to help."

I snorted. "How noble of you."

"I have my moments."

We fell into an easy rhythm, handing out drinks and trading banter. To my surprise, Tommy was good at this, although his people skills left something to be desired.

“Our wine list?" Tommy was scowling across the bar. "Look lady, we’ve got...uh...some red stuff. And some white.”

I barely contained my giggle. He was waiting on a posh older couple, clearly bemused by their bartender's lack of knowledge about wine.

"A Cosmo-what? Get outta here! Order something else."

I slid down to his end of the bar. "I'll get it."

Tommy blocked me. "Just show me how to make whatever the hell she wants."

"I thought being a borderline alcoholic was the only job qualification for a bartender," I cocked an eyebrow in challenge as I poured ingredients into a cocktail shaker.

The smile he gave me was boyish and crooked, and it made my stomach flip.

"Guess there's still a few things you can teach me. I'm finding that out more and more."

Tommy was a quick student. I found myself watching him work, noticing little details—the way his forearms flexed as he poured shots, the quick, charming smile flashed at anyone who caught his eye, the low timbre of laughter when someone landed a good joke.

Heat crept into my cheeks again as I realized I was staring. *Get a grip, Sloane.*

The truth was, I enjoyed working with him like this. We'd always had a spark, for better or worse, and tonight it felt like we were finally on the same wavelength.

The thought should have alarmed me more than it did. Tommy was trouble, through and through, and getting close to him was a surefire way to end up with a broken heart. Or a bullet. But for the first time, I felt like I could breathe around him. The usual tension that crackled between us had morphed into something else. Something more playful, more comfortable. It was...nice.

We worked well together, moving around each other like a well-oiled machine. Tommy was quick with a joke and a smile, and I found myself laughing more than I had in a long time. It was refreshing to see this side of him, to see him let his guard down a bit.

"So, you're actually a pretty good bartender," I teased, wiping down the countertop.

"Like I said, I've got a lot of hidden talents." He waggled his eyebrows suggestively.

I rolled my eyes. "Humble, too."

Tommy just shrugged. "What can I say? I'm a man of many mysteries."

"I guess so."

We continued working in silence for a while, but I found myself sneaking glances at Tommy. There was something about him, something I couldn't put my finger on, that drew me in. He was trouble. No doubt about that. But tonight, the dark, dangerous energy he usually radiated was tempered by a lightness I hadn't seen from him in a very long time.

"Keg's tapped," I said. "You got this for a sec?"

Tommy nodded. "Sure."

As I squeezed by him, I felt his hand brush my lower back, lingering for the briefest moment. I froze, my pulse racing. Tommy's touch sent a jolt through me, and I felt the heat of his fingertips through the thin fabric of my shirt. It was nothing, a simple brush of skin on skin, but it was enough to make my heart beat a little faster.

What the hell was wrong with me?

In the back room, I tried to take my frustration out on the keg. Not the greatest choice when your hand feels like a swollen meat sack. My grip slipped on the handle and the keg clanged on the floor. I cursed loudly.

"Hey what's taking so long back there?" Tommy called from the front. "We're drowning out here."

"Dammit," I muttered under my breath. Using my body as leverage, I tried to roll the keg forward, hoping to get it into position before—

"Need some help?" Tommy's voice came from behind me, making me startle. I hadn't noticed him slip away from the bar, but there he was, his broad shoulders filling the doorway.

"Uh, no, I've got it," I lied, trying to shield my injured hand from his view. But Tommy's sharp eyes had already caught sight of it and narrowed in concern.

"Hey." Tommy rounded the corner, his eyes dropping to my hand that I instinctively tucked against my chest. "Your hand. What happened?"

"Nothing. Just a little mishap with the last delivery. It's fine."

"Like hell it is. Let me see." The protective edge in his voice was unmistakable. His dark hair seemed to bristle with his mood, the scar across his chin more pronounced as he frowned.

"Nothing, I just...banged it up is all," I replied, attempting to shove him out of the way. My shoulder brushed against the solid wall of his chest, and I ignored the electric tingle that followed. "We can't leave the bar untended."

"Fine, but we're going to talk about this later."

"Whatever you say, *boss*," I replied, the hint of sarcasm failing to mask the undercurrent of tension between us. It wasn't often that Tommy showed genuine concern for anyone, let alone me. I brushed by him, catching a whiff of his cologne mixed with the scent of whiskey and spice—an intoxicating blend that screamed Tommy Quinn.

I felt him watching me as I left the room. I forced myself to keep walking. He was bad news, a hot mess just waiting to implode, and the last thing I needed was to get caught up in his self-destructive orbit.

The night wore on, the bar teeming with life and laughter as I poured drinks and exchanged banter with the regulars. I couldn't help but notice that Tommy's eyes lingered on me more than usual, his protectiveness sending a warm thrill through my body. It was strange, feeling this way about him, infuriating, even. But there was no denying the growing affection in my heart.

"Hey, gorgeous," a customer slurred, leaning against the bar. His glassy-eyed gaze fell upon my bruised hand as he reached for it. "Ouch! What happened to you?"

Tommy answered for me. "She bounced it off the face of the last guy who talked smart to her." He pronounced it *smaht*.

An older lady sitting next to the drunken lecher looked between Tommy and me, clearly noting his bruised jaw and making an assumption. She smirked approvingly and raised her glass to me. "Good for you, honey."

Tommy chuckled and continued mixing drinks. I couldn't help but smile back, a genuine one that crinkled the corners of my eyes. The customer backed off, hands raised in mock surrender, and I turned to Tommy with a smirk.

"I'm pretty sure she thought I punched you in the face."

“You’d have to get in line to do it.” His smile faded as quickly as it appeared, the deep crease between his brows making him look a lot more like his old self. "You shouldn't have to put up with guys like that."

"Thanks, but I can handle myself."

"Never doubted it for a minute," Tommy shot back, but his eyes softened for a moment before he busied himself with the next order.

The rest of the night went smoothly, and I found myself enjoying Tommy's company more than I expected. At closing time, after the lights had been turned up and the last of the patrons had stumbled out, I began wiping down the bar, determined not to let him know how much he'd impressed me tonight. I hadn't expected any offer of help, but Tommy surprised me yet again, sweeping the floor and stacking chairs like it was the most natural thing in the world.

"You don't have to do that."

"I know," he said, the corner of his mouth twitching into a small smile. "But I want to."

"Since when do you do cleanup?" I laughed. I had this image in my head of his apartment, dirty dishes piled high and beer cans scattered on every available surface. Tommy barely kept himself looking presentable, and most days, that was using the term loosely.

He started unloading the dishwasher. "Since your stubborn ass won't hire help. And I'll have you know, I am generally a pretty clean guy."

"Is that so?"

"Housebroken and everything," he winked at me, and I stifled a grin.

With the bar finally spotless and the door locked, Tommy glanced at my bruised hand. His eyes narrowed, and before I could protest, he gripped my arm and pulled me into the backroom.

"What are you doing?" I hissed, trying to pull away.

He nudged me towards the worn leather couch. "Sit."

"This isn't necessary."

He ignored me, dug through the cabinet for the first aid kit, and crouched down beside me. "I'm not going to bite you, princess. Well, not unless you ask me really nice."

"Jerk."

"Yes, but I'm your jerk."

I tried to keep the scowl on my face for the sake of appearances, but I couldn't help the flutter in my stomach. I'd always found it difficult to stay mad at Tommy for long. He had a way of getting under my skin that was equal parts infuriating and endearing.

His hands were surprisingly gentle as he examined my bruised hand. "Last time we were here, you were patching me up," he noted, his voice dry. "Now, what's the story here?"

I pulled my hand back instinctively, wary of how close he was leaning in. "The kegs shifted when we were unloading them. Got my hand caught between two of them," I lied smoothly, avoiding his gaze.

"Sounds painful," he muttered, though I caught the skepticism in his tone. A part of me wanted to confess everything, but I didn't think that would go over well. Tommy may have changed, but he hadn't changed that much.

"It's nothing. I've had worse."

"Still, you should be more careful," he murmured, his voice low and gravelly. His breath was warm against my skin, sending shivers down my spine. My body reacted to his proximity, my heart fluttering as he held my hand in his.

Tommy's silence filled the room as he concentrated on dabbing ointment onto my busted knuckles. He was so...gentle. Large hands, roughened by countless fights and hard work, cradled mine as if it were a fragile blossom.

"I can take care of this myself," I tried to protest, but he silenced me with a stern look.

"Stop fussing', Sloane. Just let me do this."

"Yes, Dr. Quinn."

He didn't smile at my attempt at humor. Instead, his focus remained unwavering on bandaging my hand. The intensity of his care was disarming, and I felt a warmth creeping up from where his skin met mine, spreading through me like spilled whiskey—hot and heady.

I found myself studying him, really looking at Tommy Quinn as he was now, not the explosive mob leader or the smartass with a sharp tongue, but the man who was so close I could count the dark lashes framing his deep blue eyes. His closeness stirred something within me; an attraction that both surprised and terrified me. The faint scent of his cologne mixed with the natural musk of his body, causing a shiver to run down my spine.

Tommy's tongue flickered out, wetting his bottom lip before pulling it between his teeth in concentration. Heat bloomed low in my belly. His Adam's apple bobbed with a swallow, the pulse in the hollow of his throat beating faster than it should be. Was he as affected by our proximity as I was?

"Done," he announced, securing the bandage. He didn't release my hand right away, instead holding it between his own for a moment longer than necessary. Our eyes locked, and I found myself wondering what he would taste like, what he would feel like pressed against me.

The silence stretched out between us, dense and charged, and I felt my own heart race to match his. I tried to steady my breathing, but the harder I tried, the more erratic it became.

"Everything okay?" Tommy asked, his voice soft and low, a far cry from the usual gruffness that accompanied his words.

"Y-yeah," I stammered, cursing myself for sounding so flustered. "Why wouldn't it be?"

He raised an eyebrow, his blue eyes searching mine, and for once, I couldn't tell what was going on inside his head. Instead, he continued to cradle my hand, the rough pads of his fingers tracing over the bandage, his touch feather-light. It sent a shiver up my spine, and a swarm of butterflies took flight in my stomach.

"Tommy..." I breathed, not sure what I was even going to say. But his name on my lips was enough to break the spell.

He released my hand, clearing his throat as he stood and took a step back. "I should go."

"Okay," I said, unable to hide the disappointment in my voice.

"Yeah." Tommy ran a hand through his hawk, a gesture that I knew meant he was wrestling with something. He seemed to make a decision, and he turned to me again, his eyes intense. "Sloane, I just wanted..." He paused, searching for the right words.

"What?" I prompted, my heart hammering.

Tommy hesitated for a moment, then reached up to brush a stray lock of hair out of my face.

"Nothing," he murmured, his voice rough and strained. "Goodnight."

With that, he turned and left, the door swinging shut behind him.

10

Tommy

SWEAT TRICKLED DOWN THE side of my face, stinging my eyes as I bobbed and weaved, my fists up and ready. Misha's shadow danced across the gym floor across from me, his movements light and fluid, his technique perfect. After hours at Big Saul's, it was just the two of us, the clock long ticked past midnight, but here we were, throwing punches instead of downing shots.

"Is that all you've got?" Misha taunted, a smirk on his lips. "To be honest, I expected more out of you."

"You talk too much," I shot back, throwing a quick combination that he easily blocked.

Misha chuckled. "And you hit like a girl. Where's all that rage? Your fire?"

I shook my head, circling him, trying to anticipate his next move. "I'm done with that shit."

He arched a skeptical brow. "You are? Really?"

I grunted, dodging one of his jabs and countering with a hook that barely grazed his chin. Surprisingly, I'd been feeling pretty good lately. Weeks of foregoing booze and cigarettes had been paying off in the gym. I already saw results. I wasn't gasping for breath after a few minutes in the ring, and my feet moved quicker than they had in years. It was surprising how good it felt—like I'd been walking around half-dead and hadn't even realized it.

I shrugged, throwing a few jabs to keep him on his toes. "Figured it was time to get my shit together."

"And the drinking? The cigarettes?"

I smirked, throwing a hard punch that connected with his stomach. "What are you, my fucking sponsor now?"

He grunted, retaliating with a sharp kick that knocked me back a step. "Just curious to see what's motivated the change."

"Maybe I just got tired of feeling like shit all the time." It was the truth, mostly. I'd looked in the mirror one day and saw what a waste of space I'd become. But that wasn't the only reason.

"Or maybe it was a certain dark-haired woman with a smart mouth," Misha said, his eyes glinting with amusement.

Connor had been right. Of course, I'd never admit that to him. Not that he'd need to hear it. He'd have that smug, self-righteous look on his face for the next decade.

At the time, I wasn't actively thinking about Connor's advice. In fact, I wasn't sure what made me jump back behind the bar to help Sloane out that night, only that she was struggling and her stubborn ass was too proud to admit it. Something primitive kicked off inside me, some insane caveman gene flipping a switch in my brain to jump in and help. Just helping Sloane out when she was sinking and the way she'd responded made me want to be better. To try harder.

I'm no hero. Damsels in distress were never my thing. Mouthy brunettes who acted like they wanted to kick my ass were.

But Connor was right.

Damn it.

Sloane would rather eat glass than admit she couldn't handle things by herself. She'd been that way as long as I'd known her, always taking the world on her shoulders. That stubbornness and loyalty were part of what made her so damn irresistible. I wasn't a fool. She could handle herself. I knew that better than most.

But I wanted to be there for her, too.

It was the strangest feeling, this pull to take care of her. Like a thread tugging at my heart. But it was there, and it was strong. So strong that I found myself daydreaming increasingly violent ways to dismember whoever had done that to her hand. Whoever had pissed her off to the point where Sloane felt the need to hit back. The bruises. The torn, split skin across her knuckles. Sloane had lied to me, which stung, but I'd been in enough fights to know the result from decking a guy.

If anyone dared to lay a finger on her, I'll—

Misha caught me with a sucker punch that knocked the thought clean out of my head.

"Sloppy," he said, cocking his head to the side. "What is wrong with you tonight? I see you standing across from me, but your head is a million miles away, *tovarish*."

I shook my head to clear it and spat blood into the towel at my side. "Nothing. Just got a lot on my mind."

"Like what?" He danced on the balls of his feet, waiting for an opening. "Or should I say whom?"

I ignored him and tried to cave his face in. It didn't work.

"Women are trouble," he continued, sidestepping me. Slippery bastard. "One bat of the eyelashes and men forget everything. Their pride, their duty, even their honor. They are deadly. It is why women make the best assassins."

"Speaking from experience?"

Misha chuckled, dodging another jab along with the question. "My experience with women has always been brief but enjoyable. Purely physical. Once you let them in your head, you're done for."

"And here I thought it was because you've got a face like the ass end of a bulldog."

Misha grinned at me, dazzling white teeth in a face that looked like it belonged on the cover of European GQ. "I use women when it suits me and let them use me. We both walk away satisfied. I thought you were the same way."

"I am."

Liar. I wasn't like that at all. Not anymore.

As I focused my attention back on Misha, I couldn't help but admire him as a fighter. Lean, compact, and well-muscled, he was a bit shorter than me, but like in real life, he played his cards close to his chest, revealing nothing. He was quick and calculated in his movements, which made him a formidable opponent.

It also meant he saw straight through my bullshit.

"This girl works for you, right?" The way he said it didn't sound like a question. "You have known each other for a long time."

"How the hell do you know that?"

Misha just shrugged in that funny way of his, a quick slouch of the shoulder. "It's my job to know things."

"A finger in every pot, huh?"

"Something like that." Misha waved us to a halt and reached over for his water bottle. "May I offer you a piece of advice? You Americans have a delightfully vulgar little phrase, I believe—'don't shit where you eat'? Yes, that's the one."

I chuckled.

"Be careful with this girl, Tommy."

I took a swig of my own water bottle, wiping my mouth with the back of my hand. "Sloane's not some chick from the bar I picked up for the night. She's different."

Misha laughed, a full-throated, genuine laugh. "Ah, so she is the one who has twisted you up. My friend, you are in deeper than I thought."

"Look, this stays between us, alright?" I warned him, my voice low and serious. He nodded in agreement, and I continued, "There's history between me and Sloane. She secretly loved my friend even though he didn't love her back. When I tried to do something about my own feelings for her, she shut me down hard. She barely gives me the time of day, but there are these moments...where I think that it might be something more. But she always shuts me down."

Misha muttered something in Russian.

"Yeah, well..." I trailed off, trying to keep the bitterness out of my voice. "Anyways, I've been doing a lot of thinking lately. About myself, my life. The things I've done. My friend knocked some sense into me, and Sloane took care of the rest."

"She sounds like a smart woman," Misha observed, his blue eyes twinkling with amusement.

I couldn't help but smile at that. "Yeah. She is. Smart and stubborn as hell. She doesn't take shit from anyone, and she doesn't let me get away with anything, either."

Misha chuckled. "Sounds like you are in love. Be careful, my friend. The loss of a good woman has killed many a good man."

I opened my mouth. Shut it again. In love? My obsession with Sloane, my constant need for her had always been something undefinable, but actual, true love?

I had never thought of myself as capable of loving someone else. Wanting, yes. Needing, yes. But I was too selfish to love someone, to offer up myself to someone like that. Not that kind of sacrifice. Whatever it was that a person had inside them that allowed it, whatever organ responsible for that kind of vulnerability, I didn't have it. My heart was nothing more than an inanimate lump of muscle, existing solely for the purpose of pumping blood throughout my body. Love did not factor anywhere into its function.

I forced myself into a laugh I didn't feel. "You've gotta be kidding me. Save the Hallmark bullshit and get your mitts up. I'm not done yet."

"I think you are," Misha chuckled and ducked under the ropes. "Besides, we haven't talked about the true reason you invited me down here tonight."

"You mean, it wasn't just for your personality?"

Misha laughed once, loud and sharp. "You're a charmer when you want to be, but I'm not one to be charmed. By anyone. Not even your friendship comes without strings attached."

"You wound me."

"I doubt that very much." Misha's smile faded. "You wanted to talk. So talk."

Misha and I didn't talk business. Ever. It was one of the reasons we got along so well...or, at least, as well as anyone could with Misha. The guy was a closed book. I wasn't foolish enough to think that what we had was anything close to resembling friendship, but Misha knew that. It was more of a begrudging respect, shadowboxing with each other even when we weren't in the ring. Not for the first time, I wondered just where Misha placed in the Bratva hierarchy.

All right. Cut to the chase. No bullshit.

"I want to get out of guns," I said.

Misha didn't even bat an eye. "And why do you think I care?"

"Because there might be something in it for your boss, if he's interested. Guns are good money, but they bring heat. The overhead alone is a bitch, and you need a lot of manpower to push them. A big organization. Something like what you've got."

A faint smile twitched at the corner of Misha's mouth. "I am amused you presume to know the breadth of Volkov's reach."

"It's bigger than ours, at any rate." I waved my hand dismissively. I wasn't looking to start a pissing match. "Look, Misha, it's not a secret that we've been hurting the past couple years. You're a big part of why we're even still standing here."

"I am glad our contribution has not been forgotten."

"It hasn't. Which is why I'm coming to you."

Misha stared at me with that impenetrable gaze of his, a faint, amused smile still on his lips, although it didn't reach his eyes. For all his good natured, dour Russian humor, he was still a very dangerous man. "So, you are proposing to give us your arms trade—"

"A cut," I corrected. "Not the whole operation."

"Fine, a cut. And what will be left for you, my friend?"

Actually, the thought had come to me at the bar. Fitting, I know. I'd been looking at all the old photographs up on the wall at Lady D's and wishing we could go back to the days where everything didn't seem like we were just treading water. Back to our roots. I had stared down at the glass in my hand, and the seed of an idea began to sprout. After a deep dive on the ol' Google machine, I knew I had a viable plan.

"Liquor," I said. "It's cleaner. Less blood, steady profit."

Less heartache is what I hoped. My family had suffered enough. Connor and Cassidy almost died for our way of life. Aiden had. Nearly every one of us had felt the impact at some point. Times were changing. Guns just weren't the smart move anymore, not with the heat the last few years had brought down upon us.

The other reason was that we simply didn't have the manpower to enforce our holdings and protect our backs anymore, but I wasn't about to tell Misha that.

"And where would we come in? Surely you would want something in exchange for handing us your operation." Misha tugged on his shirt, a study in nonchalance, but I saw he was interested."

"Connections for a start, maybe more if Volkov is interested."

"A partnership?"

"Of sorts."

You didn't just partner up with Aleksandr Volkov. This wasn't some kiddie handshake deal on the playground. The man was ruthless and had zero qualms about turning on anyone fool enough to let their guard down, but if you kept your wits about you and played the game, he could be an ally. Lorenzo Moretti had learned that lesson the hard way.

"It's a bold move, but it makes sense," Misha conceded. "It's what I would do, in your position."

I tossed my gym bag over my shoulder. "So is that a yes?"

"I'll see what I can do." Misha paused, but I knew there was more to come. I saw it in his eyes, the slight narrowing that meant he was sizing me up.

"Be careful, Tommy," he warned. "I don't have to tell you that these are dangerous times. Trust no one. Even those closest to you might betray you in the end."

"I'm touched by your concern," I said dryly. That was a lesson the McTiernan Clan had learned all too well two years ago when one of our own had turned against us as an informant for the Italians, and the fallout had nearly killed my sister.

I wouldn't be making that mistake again.

Misha's parting words continued to ring in my ears as I made my way down to the docks. A storm front rolled a heavy fog in off the harbor, the kind that seeps into your pores, so thick it feels like you feel like you're breathing water. I hadn't been keeping as close an eye on things as I should have lately. It was time to change that, especially if I wanted to make the changes I was proposing.

"Tommy Quinn, as I live and breathe!" Grady's voice rang out before his meaty hand clapped on my shoulder. "What—did you get lost?"

"Fuck off, Grady. How're things?"

"Oh, you know, same old same old," he said, lighting up a cigarette. "You finally decided to grace us with your presence?"

"I've been busy. Figured it was time to get my hands dirty again."

"No shit?" Grady blew a puff of smoke into the night air. "I was wondering if you'd decided to retire. Office is over here, if you want to get the lay of the land."

I nodded, scanning the area. I was impressed. This was a far cry from how we had been operating before. Crates were being unloaded from a cargo ship, the men moving with brisk efficiency. Numbers and cargo checked and double checked, like a well-oiled machine. Lookouts placed at the exit points, trucks manned and ready to go.

"Smooth as silk, see?" Grady said. He seemed a little tense all of a sudden, and I wondered why. "Come on into the office and I can show you—"

Then I saw her.

Sloane was directing traffic, her hands on her hips as she issued orders. She looked in her element, totally focused. Competent. In control.

Suddenly, the pieces clicked into place. Her new apparent understanding with Grady. Absent from the bar on her nights off, when she used to hang around. The new fire in her eyes, and...the bruises on her hand that night.

"The kegs shifted when we were unloading them. Got my hand caught between two of them."

She'd lied so smoothly that night, but I'd seen through it. I just hadn't known why until now.

Sloane had been running things behind my back. While I moped and drank and got my ass beat, she had stepped in to handle the day-to-day operations. Kept the whole machine running.

That beautiful, infuriating woman had gone behind my back this entire time to run jobs with Grady. The real work, the reason everything was running so smoothly, it was because of her. I stared at Sloane, a mix of emotions churning in my gut. Anger that she'd gone over my head. Impressed at how well she'd handled it. And underneath it all, a surge of desire so strong it nearly overwhelmed me.

"Since when has Sloane been part of this?" I asked Grady, my jaw clenched as I tried to keep my emotions in check.

"Uh, she's been helping out for a while now," Grady replied nervously. "She's got a knack for this stuff, Tommy."

"Apparently," I muttered, watching her, jealous and angry and betrayed.

Fuck it. And aroused. Competence was a huge turn on for me.

Sloane must have felt the weight of my stare because she turned, locking eyes with me for just a moment. Her face blanched, and she jutted her jaw out defiantly. Without breaking eye contact, I cocked my head towards the shipping office.

Sloane had the audacity to turn her back on me, dismissing me as she bent over another crate.

Something snapped inside me. The sounds of the docks faded away – the creaking ropes, the calls of the night shift, the lap of water against the hulls – until there was only the rush of blood in my ears. In three long strides, I closed the distance between us.

"Oi!" I barked, grabbing her arm and spinning her around. She let out a grunt of surprise as I hauled her towards the squat building that housed the shipping office.

"Get your fucking hands off me," Sloane hissed, struggling against my grip. Her cheeks were flushed, and her eyes flashed with anger and defiance. Fuck, she was beautiful when she was pissed off.

She tried to take a swing at me, but I batted it away, pushed her through the door of the office, and slammed it shut behind us. The room was cramped, papers scattered across the desk, and the single window looked out onto the docks, a voyeur to our little drama.

Sloane didn't waste a second; she swung at me again, this time aiming for my jaw. I captured her wrist and forced her back against the peeling paint on the wall. The feel of her body, tight and warm against mine, sent all my blood south in a rush that left me dizzily clutching at the wall with my free hand.

"Been a busy little beaver, haven't you?" I growled.

"Someone had to step up, Tommy. You sure as hell weren't doing it," she spat back, her fierce green eyes blazing.

I leaned in, pinning her with my body and my gaze. "Don't pretend this is about stepping up, Sloane. This is about you and your unending need to stick it to me."

"Get off me," she hissed, but there was no room to maneuver, no space between her body and mine. I felt her heart hammering against my chest, her breath coming in short, angry gasps.

"You like this, don't you, Sloane? You like pushing my buttons, making me crazy. You've always had that power over me. But I'm still the boss here, in case you've forgotten."

I leaned in close, our faces inches apart. I felt the heat of her body, smell her familiar scent. It only fueled my anger—and my desire. I wanted to hurt her, kiss her, fuck her. All at the same time.

"Some boss you've been," she spat. "When's the last time you came by the docks? Checked in on operations? Showed any interest in the business at all?"

I opened my mouth, then closed it again. She had a point. One I didn't want to admit.

Sloane's eyes narrowed. "Let go of me, Tommy."

"Why?" I asked softly. "Does this bother you?" I pressed into her, letting her feel exactly how much she bothered me.

Her eyes widened, and a flush crept up her neck. "Let go of me right now, or you'll regret it."

"Oh, I doubt that." The words came out as a growl. My grip tightened on her wrist. "I think you like it when I take control."

Her green eyes flashed, and she pressed her hips into mine, hard. "You have no fucking clue what I like."

I choked. The sudden movement sent a jolt of electricity through my body. My cock throbbed, and I fought the urge to pin her wrists above her head, press her into the wall, and kiss her senseless.

I wanted her. Badly.

Sloane glared up at me, her breathing ragged, lips parted. I wanted this little spitfire beneath me more than anything in the world, her body pinned between mine and the wall. Her scent filled my senses, intoxicating me, making it impossible to think about anything other than how good it would feel to take her right there on the desk, her wildcat claws in my hair, marking up my back, my cock buried so deep inside her she'd feel me for days.

I wanted to make her beg for it. To scream my name so the whole world would know she was mine. My eyes flicked down to her breasts, still heaving against my chest, then up to her eyes, dark with anger.

Her lips. Millimeters from mine...

My heart gave a painful thump against my sternum like it wanted her too, and that's ultimately what stopped me. That, and Misha's words.

Sounds like you are in love. Be careful, my friend.

For all her stubbornness, that tough girl act, Sloane was a romantic at heart. She wanted her happily ever after. She wanted love, and that wasn't something I could give her.

"Tommy?"

It took every ounce of strength I had to pull away from her, and I felt the loss of her immediately. Confusion flickered across her face, followed by something close to hurt, but it was gone before I could really study it, replaced by the frustration I was accustomed to.

"What the hell is your problem?" She shoved me back, and I let her. I even took the punch she aimed at me, catching it on my shoulder.

I held up my hands in surrender. "Look, I'm not trying to pick a fight with you."

"You could have fooled me. What the hell was that, just now?"

I frowned at her. Surely she understood how I felt about her by now, how much I wanted her. Did she really need me to spell it out? I already had, and she'd shot me down. *Just friends*.

"I don't know what you're talking about."

"Don't play games with me, Tommy. You can't just make me leave."

Oh. That. I'd been so tangled up in my own messy feelings for Sloane that I'd forgotten what I was angry about in the first place. Although when I thought about it, my anger was more of a product of fear that she'd gone behind my back to do something dangerous that I couldn't protect her from because I hadn't known it was happening in the first place. I never wanted to take away her autonomy. I just wanted to make sure she was safe.

Sloane was more than capable of taking care of herself. But I was still going to watch her back.

"Why the hell would I want to do that?" I shot back. "You've obviously been running the show, Sloane. And you're damn good at it."

Her anger seemed to falter for a moment, replaced by shock. Sloane blinked, clearly taken aback by my compliment. It felt strange, praising her when moments ago we were inches away from crossing a line neither of us would come back from.

"Wh-what?" she stammered, her dark eyes searching mine for any trace of sarcasm or deceit.

"Look at all you've done here," I said, gesturing to the bustling docks outside the office window. "Everything's running smoothly because of *your* hard work, and I'm not too proud to admit it."

Her eyes narrowed suspiciously. "What are you getting at, Quinn?"

"Look," I started again, taking a deliberate step toward her. I extended my hand, palm open and facing her. A peace offering, a new start. "I'm asking you to be my partner."

"You want me to be your partner?" she repeated slowly, her brow furrowing as she stared down at my hand.

"Yes. Why does that surprise you?"

"Because I assumed you'd want me out of your hair. I thought you'd be furious about this." Sloane waved her hand around the shipping office. "But instead, you want to work together?

"I'm not thrilled that you went behind my back," I said honestly. "But you've got a head for this. You're good at it. I need you."

"And that's it?" she asked carefully.

"That's it. Partners," I confirmed, the word feeling strange yet somehow right as it left my lips. "In every sense. No more secrets, no more going behind each other's backs. We run this thing together, side by side. Equal."

The corner of her mouth twitched, the barest hint of a smile threatening to break through her stony exterior. It was a dance we did well—push and pull, fight and relent—but this was a new step, one neither of us had anticipated. I could see the conflicting emotions warring in her eyes, and I knew what she was going to say before she even opened her mouth.

"You've got yourself a deal," she said, her voice steady as she reached out to shake my hand.

11

Sloane

PARTNERS. I'D HAD MY doubts at first, but for once, Tommy stuck to his word. The guys already looked to me for direction, so not much changed there, especially where Grady was concerned. The only thing that really changed was I wasn't hiding anymore. It was unprecedented. Borderline revolutionary. And I loved every minute of it.

Unfortunately, it also meant I had to suck it up and hire some help at the bar. A gal can only spread herself so thin. But luckily for me, Kat had developed an unhealthy obsession with designer shoes, and practically begged me to pick up some extra shifts.

"You sure you've got this?" I asked her as Kat poked behind the bar, familiarizing herself with the layout.

She sprayed me with seltzer from the soda fountain in response. "Get outta here. I know this is your baby and all, but I swear, I'll treat her like my own. "

"So, dumpster baby left on a curb. Fantastic."

"Fuck you very much."

"Seriously though, Kat, the clientele here isn't exactly what you're used to dealing with." I rapped on the bar top. Kat's usual gig was at an upscale wine bar near the Harborwalk. "This is just a hole-in-the wall joint, nothing fancy. Dockworkers and blue collars from the neighborhood. They want their drinks fast, cheap, and cold, and they won't be afraid to let you know about it."

Never mind that a good percentage of them were also mob associates. Kat still had no idea about that side of my life, and I intended to keep it that way.

Kat grinned from behind the bar. "Don't worry, I left my pearls at home. I'm looking forward to a change of pace, actually. How long are you going to need me for? Not that I mind, of course. Those Choos aren't going to earn themselves."

"I don't know, actually. Let's just start with the weekend, and if it goes longer than that I'll look at hiring some more help."

"Are you going to tell me what this mystery project is that's got you working side-by-side with Slugger McGee?"

"Dad's trying to bring him into the back end of things here, show him the ropes." I lied smoothly. "You know, distributers, licensing..."

"You two seem to be spending an awful lot of time together lately."

"We're partners, Kat. What do you expect?"

"Partners, huh?" Kat smirked, waggling her eyebrows. "Is that what the kids are calling it these days?"

"Shut up," I snapped, heat rising in my cheeks. "It's not like that."

Kat held up her hands. "Hey, I was just teasing. If you like him, you like him."

I glowered at her. "I don't like him."

"Yeah, but he likes you," she teased, polishing a glass with more vigor than necessary. "It's not like everyone hasn't seen the way Tall, Dark, and Broody looks at you."

"Ancient history. We're friends, nothing else."

"Tell that to his dick."

"Gross."

"Liar. Don't tell me you haven't thought about it." Kat sobered and looked at me seriously. "But answer me one thing honestly, Sloane. Are you upset about me and Tommy that one time?"

"I told you that night to go ahead."

"Answer my question. I've barely seen you at all since then."

"I've been busy." Not exactly a lie, but I also hadn't made an effort to talk to her, either.

My stomach knotted at the thought of them together. Tommy's hands on Kat's body, his lips tasting hers, their bodies moving as one. That old, unwelcome tightening in my chest flared up, but I shoved it down deep where it belonged. I shook my head hard, trying to dispel the image. It was none of my business who Tommy fucked.

I forced a laugh and hoped it sounded genuine. "Upset? Please. If I were upset about that, I'd have to be mad at half of Boston's female population. Tommy's been dutifully working his way through Southie since he first discovered boobs."

"Good," she breathed out, relief flooding her features. "Because, you know, girl code and all that."

"Girl code doesn't apply to trainwrecks," I quipped, flashing her a grin that didn't quite reach my eyes. "Besides, we've got bigger fish to fry. And thanks, Kat. You're a lifesaver."

"Anytime, hon," she replied, tossing the towel over her shoulder. "Just remember, if you want to talk about it, I'm here."

My phone buzzed in my pocket, and I quickly checked the screen. It was a text from Tommy asking me to meet him downtown at his gym.

"Hey, I've got to run. Thanks again for covering my shifts. Try not to burn the place down while I'm gone." I grabbed my jacket off the hook, throwing it on as I headed for the door.

"Never a dull moment with you, McTiernan," Kat called after me, her laughter trailing me out into the warm Boston evening.

Stepping into the dimly lit gym, I paused for a moment, allowing my eyes to adjust. The familiar sounds of grunts and the thuds of fists against punching bags filled the air. My eyes scanned the room, past the heavy bags and the scattered free weights, and then they landed on him.

Tommy was across the room, sans shirt, working out on one of the weight machines with an intensity that seemed almost primal.

I stood there, mesmerized by the sight of his shirtless body glistening with sweat. His muscular arms flexed as he pushed through each repetition, veins popping with effort. I couldn't help but notice the way his broad shoulders now tapered down to a narrow waist, droplets of perspiration rolling down the valleys of his defined abs. His entire body radiated raw power and masculinity, and I found myself suddenly short of breath.

"Jesus," I murmured.

He didn't notice me, too focused on his form, on the extension and retraction of his arms as he powered through another set. The tattoos, once just a part of who Tommy was, now told a story of change, of a man shedding his past like snakeskin. I watched the muscles in his back ripple and tried not to drool.

This wasn't the same disheveled, hungover Tommy I had become accustomed to seeing over the years. No, this man before me was something else entirely. I felt a flush crawl up my neck, heat blooming in my cheeks and somewhere much, much lower as I took in the sight of him.

Tommy was... hot.

It wasn't a word I'd ever associated with him before. For a moment, I allowed myself the luxury of just watching him, taking in the way his biceps bulged, how his chest rose and fell with heavy breaths. He'd moved on to the speed bag, now, and I watched as he pivoted, fists still flying, and I got a glimpse of his taught ass. A dark trail of hair disappeared into the waistband of his sweatpants, my gaze following it down to—

Nope. Nope, nope, nope. Definitely not thinking about his dick.

I jerked my eyes up, face flaming. What the hell was I doing? This was Tommy, for God's sake. The same arrogant jackass who'd made my life a living hell for years.

So he looked good. Like, really, really good.

That didn't change anything.

Tommy glanced up and caught sight of me standing in the doorway. A slow, delighted smile spread across his face, brightening his sea-blue eyes. He dropped the weights with a resounding crash and jogged over, an unfamiliar apology shaping his features in a way that made him look almost boyishly handsome.

"Sorry, Sloane," he said, out of breath but grinning. "Didn't expect you to get down here so quick."

Dimples. The man had dimples. Why hadn't I noticed them before?

I shrugged, struggling to look as casual as possible. "I had some time to kill. Hope I'm not interrupting."

"Not at all."

Tommy wiped his face with a towel, and I tried not to ogle his perfect washboard abs. Where did those come from? Up close, his freshly shaven jaw emphasized the strong lines of his face - high cheekbones, a square jaw and a mouth made for kissing. Or other things.

I shoved that thought away, too. What the hell was wrong with me today?

Trying to look anywhere but his mouth, my gaze traveled up to his hair, and I had to blink twice to make sure that I wasn't seeing things.

The once unmistakable faux hawk that had crowned his head for years was gone. Instead, his dark locks were now close-cropped on the sides, slightly longer on top, and artfully mussed as if he had just rolled out of bed. It was so unbelievably sexy, I was pretty sure my ovaries just imploded.

"Your hawk flew the coop," I remarked casually, trying to keep my voice nonchalant despite the fluttering in my chest.

Tommy ran a hand through his hair, tousling it and somehow making it even more sexy.

"Yeah, figured it was time to grow up," he said with a wink that knocked the breath from me. There was a lightness to his tone that I wasn't used to, a playfulness that seemed at odds with the Tommy Quinn who always kept the world at arm's length.

"Grow up, huh?" I quirked my brow, folding my arms over my chest. "Does this mean no more underground brawls and drinking until four in the morning?"

"Can't promise anything." His smirk was infuriatingly charming. "But I'll try to keep it classy. For your sake."

"Don't do me any favors." I rolled my eyes but couldn't quite suppress the smile tugging at my lips.

"Give me a sec to shower, will you?" he said, gesturing toward the locker room. "Don't want to discuss business smelling like I've been mucking stables."

"Sure, go ahead."

I watched, unabashed, as he jogged away, his muscles flexing beneath the sheen of sweat that coated his skin. Despite myself, my gaze dropped to his ass, which was... well, it was something to behold. I fanned myself with my hand, the image seared into my brain, and cursed under my breath.

"Get your shit together, Sloane," I muttered, leaning against the wall for support. I couldn't afford to be weak-kneed over Tommy freaking Quinn. Not when there was so much at stake: the business, our precarious alliances...

My own sanity.

He might have cleaned up nice, that trainwreck of a man, but a haircut didn't erase the chaos he dragged around like an anchor. He was still the same old Tommy underneath, a ticking timebomb of sarcasm and bad decisions wrapped up in a new, devastatingly attractive package.

I needed to be careful here. We were partners. Friends at the most.

Nothing else could happen.

I was in so much trouble.

The neon lights of Shawmut's trendy Thai restaurant cast a warm glow on the bustling street, and I couldn't help but feel surprised as Tommy led me inside. I'd never told him that Thai food was my favorite; it seemed he'd done his research.

"Thai, huh?" I asked as he held the door open, a gentlemanly move that seemed at odds with the rough edges I knew all too well.

"Grady mentioned it."

Damn you, Grady. "Since when do you recon my food preferences?" I tried for a teasing tone, but there was an undercurrent of suspicion that I couldn't quite shake.

He just grinned, that lopsided smirk that had charmed more than its fair share of Boston's female population. "Just trying to keep my partner happy."

We slid into the booth, both instinctively choosing the side that allowed us a clear view of the entrance. My stomach dipped, not from hunger, but from the strange tension that crackled in the air between us as we sat down together.

This felt suspiciously like a date.

Tommy handed me a menu. "You go ahead and order for both of us. I don't know what the hell I'm looking at."

"You've never had Thai?" I raised an eyebrow.

"I'm a Thai food virgin," he winked. "I guess you'll be the one to pop my cherry."

I hid my creeping blush behind a menu and ordered ribeye pho for myself and just about one of everything for Tommy. The man looked like he could put away half the menu just as an appetizer. The waiter came and left, and Tommy lightly touched my wrist.

"You okay?"

I nearly jumped out of my chair. "Yeah. Yeah, I'm just...long day."

"We can save this for—"

"No." I sat up straighter and forced myself to look at him. I was a professional, goddamnit. "We came here to discuss business, so let's discuss business."

Tommy stared at me for a beat, and for once, I couldn't tell what was going on behind those blue eyes.

"Okay," he said finally. "Why don't you give me a rundown of our current operations and your evaluation."

"What do you want to know?"

"The truth. Grady only tells me what I want to hear."

I laughed. He had a point.

Tommy's focus was laser-sharp now, the playfulness replaced with an unprecedented sincerity. "I meant to tell you, skipping out on the new warehouse—that was a good call."

I hesitated for a moment, surprised by the approval in his tone. Tommy wasn't one to hand out compliments freely, especially not to me.

"Thanks," I said gruffly, taking a deep breath before diving into the intricacies of our less-than-legal endeavors. "The docks are running smoothly, payments are up..."

As I spoke, Tommy listened intently, nodding along and interjecting with pointed questions that showed he was more than just muscle and mayhem; he had a mind for strategy too. And as much as I hated to admit it, his attention made something warm unfurl within me, a dangerous spark that I quickly tamped down.

Our food came, the fragrance of lemongrass and basil making my stomach growl. I glanced up from the array of colorful Thai cuisine to find Tommy watching me, an unreadable expression in his eyes. For a moment, I forgot about the undercurrent of tension between us, the unspoken words that hung heavy like the humid Boston summer outside.

"Dig in," he said with a casual nod, reaching for the chicken satay and handing me a pair of chopsticks.

"Thanks." My fingers closed around the utensils, and I speared a piece of papaya salad. "You know, this is actually nice."

Tommy beamed.

"Thought you'd appreciate a change of scenery from backroom deals and smoke-filled bars." He popped a piece of satay into his mouth, his attention momentarily diverted. “Wow. This is pretty good.”

Tommy abandoned his chopsticks in favor of a fork and efficiency, and I smothered a laugh.

"Speaking of which," I started, "our informants are saying something's brewing with the Italians again. It looks like Sal Giordano, Lorenzo's number two, has emerged on top—or been appointed to it, at least. He's got ties to Providence."

"What're they up to? Any idea?"

I shook my head. "Nothing, so far, but there's unrest. We might want to check in with Luca. He was pretty tight with Alfie for a while, wasn't he?"

"Yeah, until he got his face blown off trying to save that Alfie's ass. Nobody's heard much from him since," Tommy frowned. "I can reach out to Alfie and see if he's or Emilia have been in contact."

"That would be helpful. We need to keep an eye on that. Can't have them thinking they can encroach on our territory without consequences. We should focus on strengthening our own operations first. Make sure we're ready for whatever comes our way."

Tommy nodded his head, agreeing. "What else?"

As we continued to dissect strategies and discuss the delicate balance of alliances and rivalries, I found myself inching closer to him, drawn by the gravity of his presence. Tommy's leg was now so close to mine I felt the warmth radiating from him through my jeans.

Without fully realizing it, my knee brushed against his under the table. A casual, almost innocent touch that sent a jolt of awareness through me. When I dared to sneak a glance at him, I saw the faintest hint of red creeping up his neck.

"Everything okay?" I asked, feigning innocence.

"Fine," he muttered, though the flush spreading under his collar betrayed his cool demeanor. "Just hot in here, is all."

I couldn't help but feel a thrill at the subtle color that climbed up Tommy's neck. It was like a silent admission of something he'd never say out loud, and for a moment, I reveled in the reaction I'd drawn from him. From the corner of my eye, I observed his ruggedly handsome features, the way his jaw tensed when he tried to maintain control.

But then, I mentally shook myself. What the hell was I doing? This was Tommy—brash, infuriating, impossible Tommy.

"Something on your mind?" His gravelly voice pulled me out of my thoughts.

"Other than the usual dilemmas?" I quipped, trying to deflect. "Nope, just enjoying the conversation."

"Good," he said, and after a pregnant pause, he surprised me by steering the conversation in an unexpected direction. "Sloane, where do you see the clan heading?"

I hesitated before answering. "We need to diversify. Guns are too risky these days, too much heat from the cops. Dangerous and risky with not enough cash flow. We need to modernize, change things up, maybe even go back to our roots."

"Go on," he urged, leaning back and giving me space to elaborate.

"We need to adapt and get ahead of the game." I leaned forward, excitement igniting within me at the prospect of real change. "Maybe even go back to our roots. Look at the bookies—we could start shifting gears there, distancing ourselves from guns."

"Bookies, huh?" He mulled over the idea, his expression unreadable. "It's risky, changing up the playbook."

"Less risky than another Feds' investigation or gang war over shipments. We have to evolve, Tommy. It's the only way to survive."

He nodded slowly, absorbing my words, and I saw the gears turning behind those piercing blue eyes. Tommy leaned back in his chair, considering my words with a thoughtful expression. I held my breath, waiting for his response. Would he shoot down my idea, or would he see the potential in it?

Tommy's face was a mask as he stared down at the table. "You want to change the way we've been doing things," he echoed, his voice betraying no emotion. "Everything."

"Damn right, I do." My voice came out more forceful than I'd intended, but I couldn't back down now. We had suffered enough at the hands of a business that only ever paid in blood and tears. "It's brought nothing but heartache, Tommy. You know that better than anyone."

He remained silent, his gaze still fixed on the table. I felt the tension building in the air between us, and as the seconds ticked by, I prepared for him to disagree with me. When he didn't say anything, I couldn't hold it in any longer.

"Look, Tommy," I began, anger flaring. "You wanted me for a partner. You wanted my opinions. I'm trying to help us, to help the clan. So don't just sit there and—"

"Let's go for a walk," he cut me off, pushed back from the table, and stood up abruptly.

It wasn't a suggestion. It was an order. Tommy threw more bills than necessary on the table and walked out the door.

I followed him through the winding streets, the echo of our footsteps a staccato rhythm against the old cobblestones. Past the bars spilling laughter into the night, past the yellowed streetlights that painted shadows across Tommy's blank face.

We reached the public garden at Beacon Hill, and for a while, we walked in silence under the canopy of trees. Tommy's hands were buried deep in his pockets, shoulders held stiff like he was bracing himself for a fight. With every step, my anger simmered, ready to boil over once again.

"Tommy, if you dragged me out here just to ignore me—"

Tommy stopped so suddenly I nearly crashed into him. He spun and faced me.

"I want to get us out of guns," he blurted. "Entirely."

12

Tommy

Sloane's anger evaporated, replaced by shock. "What?"

"I want the clan out of guns," I repeated, my eyes searching hers. "I've been thinking about it for a while now, but hearing your ideas tonight solidified things for me. You're right. Guns have brought us nothing but bloodshed and misery. I can't do it anymore."

It was no small thing, admitting that I couldn't hack it anymore. That I wanted out of guns. To anyone else, admitting such a thing would have been impossible, but with Sloane, it was a no-brainer. If anyone understood the high price we'd paid running guns, it was her.

Sloane looked over her shoulder, scanning the area like she was afraid of someone overhearing. Then she stepped closer to me, and I tried to silence the triumphant purr in my chest.

"Where is this coming from, Tommy?" she frowned. "For a year, you've barely been here. A ghost. You couldn't care less about the clan, and it's showed."

"I'm trying to change that."

"How? This is huge, Tommy. You can't just decide one day to change up the whole playbook without a plan. What're our suppliers going to say? What about the current inventory? Who's going to fill the gaps?"

She shook her head. "And if not guns, then what else? The bookies will only make us so much, and you know we can't run in the red for long. I'm not saying I'm against it, but you can't simply throw something out there like this and expect Grady and I to figure it out."

"I'm not asking you to figure it out." I crossed my arms, defensively, I realized, and I forced myself to relax, shoving my hands in my pockets, instead. "Look, I know I haven't given you much of a reason to have any faith in me—"

"—you got that right."

I held up my hand. "But I've been thinking about this for a long time. I just didn't have a way to see it through until now."

"How?"

"The Russians."

Sloane went still for so long, I was about to poke her to make sure she wasn't having a stroke or something. Then she cursed, loudly and creatively, taking a step back and looking at me like I'd lost my mind.

Oh, I knew how it sounded. The Russians didn't exactly have a reputation for trustworthiness. They didn't get where they were by putting anyone's interest but their own first, and they had zero scruples about turning coat to preserve the bottom line. Unlike our own organization—and even the Italians'—they didn't operate as a family. The Russians operated as a business. A cutthroat, ruthless business, and anyone who was preparing to get in bed with them would do good to remember that.

Fortunately, I was no stranger to betrayal. We learned the hard way with Teagan. One of our own selling us out to the Italians, a shitshow that nearly took my sister's life. As it was, that bastard had left his mark on her, physically and mentally. My blood still raged when I thought about what she'd gone through, and my greatest regret, even more than my failure to protect her, was that Connor had killed Teagan before I could.

No, I knew better than to trust anyone completely. Letting someone in was no better than handing them the knife. Your heart, or your head—either way, they had the potential to destroy you.

Especially Sloane.

Tonight had been almost more than I could handle, and I mentally kicked myself for falling into that same old trap with her. It was just so goddamn easy. Throw me a treat, just a little bit of attention, and I rolled right over on my back, panting and begging for more. It was so pathetic. I knew better than that. We'd been down this road before.

The truth was, Sloane just wasn't interested in me. She never had been. It was a hard pill to swallow, especially when every beat of my heart since I was seventeen years old had pulsed to the rhythm of her name. It wasn't infatuation, lust, or even love, like Misha had said. It was something far more visceral, down to my bones. To my very soul, if I even had one.

Sloane was it for me.

But I couldn't give her what she wanted, and even if I could, she didn't want it from me.

So where did that leave me? Begging for scraps at the door? Pining after something I would never have? I wasn't sure. And to be honest, I didn't care. I would give Sloane everything I could, every piece of me. Until my heart pumped its last beat and her name spilled from my last breath. It was the only love letter I was capable of giving her.

If Sloane wanted a partner, a *friend*, then I was going to be the best goddamn friend she ever had.

"I know what you're going to say," I said. "And for the record, I don't trust Misha as far as I could throw him. He's helped us in the past, but he's also fucked us over."

"That's putting it mildly." Sloane's expression shuttered.

"Which is why I negotiated an equal trade. A partnership, where both of us stand to lose if the deal falls apart."

Sloane leaned closer. I had her attention now. I took her by the arm and we started walking back towards the T station.

"The Feds have been all over guns and narcotics since the late nineties," I explained. "What used to be a headache for our fathers has turned into a royal pain in the ass for us. Yeah, the money is good, but the overhead is a bitch and the risk is quickly outweighing the benefits. I agree that gambling can be profitable, but you'll never match the income. We need something big. Something drastic."

"And where do you propose to find this proverbial cash cow?" Sloane smirked.

"Alcohol. Specifically 192-proof grain alcohol."

"Bootlegging." Sloane laughed. "When you said you wanted to get back to our roots, I didn't think you meant literally. It'll never work, Tommy. You can't swing a dead cat without hitting a distillery in the US. There are over a dozen here in Boston alone."

I grinned. "And you have contacts at every single one of them."

She shook her head. "There's no market for bootlegged spirits anymore. Strictly novelty. The return would be less than anything we'd make running bookies. Importing would be a non-starter, too. The Feds are all over anything that comes into the US."

"Which is why I'm not looking to import. I'm looking to export."

"Where?"

"Eastern Europe." I paused a moment to let that sink in. "Look, I know it sound crazy, but I had Grady run the numbers. It's much cheaper for Eastern European countries to import US made alcohol than it is for them to produce it themselves. The barriers, of course, are the heavy tariffs imposed by the Russian government. The black market is booming with the stuff—over half of the liquor over there is illegal."

Sloane blinked. "But how are you going to smuggle it out?"

I grinned. "That's the beauty of it. Grain alcohol is odorless and colorless. We disguise it with dye and ship it out as windshield-wiper fluid...cleaning solvent...mouthwash..."

Sloane barked a laugh, rubbing at her temples. "Tommy, this is crazy."

"It's not unprecedented," I said. "Operations like this have been popping up for years. But it's small scale. They don't have the contacts or the shipping manpower. We do. Lady D's already has contracts in place with half the distilleries in Boston—"

"And let me guess, Misha has contacts in Eastern Europe," Sloane finished.

I shrugged. "He says after you remove the dye and dilute the grain alcohol the stuff isn't half bad, by Russian standards."

Sloane shook her head, but she was grinning. "And here I thought you were done with liquor."

"It's what we know, babe." I put my arm around her shoulders, pulled her to my side, and indulged myself with a kiss to her temple. She smelled like citrus and vanilla. "We can make this work."

"It's a very Tommy-esque plan," Sloane said. "I've got loads of questions, but I have to admit, it is kind of genius in its own way. Where do we go from here?"

"Manpower and logistics. Throw out some feelers at the distilleries and lock down the docks—we're shipping out, not in this time. Maybe contact a chemist for a non-toxic dye we can use. We've got our work cut out for us."

"I don't mind a little hard work," Sloane grinned at me. "It feels good to be doing something, especially if it means less risk for us."

Sloane didn't pull away the entire walk back to the T station. In fact, she wrapped her arm around my waist, and it took every ounce of control I had not to push her up against the wall and kiss her until she couldn't remember her own name.

There was a new feel to the atmosphere between us. Not uncomfortable or antagonistic, like it had been; nor electric, like I knew it had the potential to be. No, this was something far more comfortable, like someone had taken a giant broom and swept away all the shit between us, leaving nothing but an empty, clean space to work.

The T wasn't crowded, so we both took our seats as the doors closed. Throughout the car, everyone mostly just kept to themselves, staring at their phones. A few people, though, chatted back and forth, small talk and friendly conversation.

She wants a friend? I'm going to be the best friend she ever had.

Small talk. Yeah. I could do that.

"So," I began, scrabbling for a topic, "you got any plans for the weekend?"

I cringed at my own awkwardness. *Got any plans for the weekend? Could I sound any lamer?*

If Sloane noticed the fumbling conversation starter, she didn't react. "I'm off, so I thought I'd catch the game on Saturday."

"The game?"

This time, she looked at me like I'd grown a second head. "The Sox. Baseball."

What a dumbass. "Oh yeah. Right." I smiled depreciatingly. "I'm more of a boxing and UFC fan myself. Football sometimes, when the Pats are doing decent."

"Which hasn't been often, lately," Sloane said. "So, not much of a baseball fan, then?"

"Never could make it all the way through a game. Too slow for me."

Sloane turned to face me fully. "Wait. So, you're telling me that you've never been to Fenway?"

"Nope."

"How can you even call yourself a Bostonian? Uh uh. Nope. This is something we're going to have to fix." Sloane shook her head. Her eyes were bright with excitement, that little flush coloring her cheeks prettily that only happened when she had the bit between her teeth. "You're coming with me to the game this weekend."

"Is that right?" I said, amused.

Sloane was not joking. "Sox vs. Yankees, 7:00pm. Don't be late."

I held up my hands in surrender. "Okay, okay, spitfire. I'll be there. It better be worth it."

I was teasing, of course. I could give two shits about baseball, but the prospect of spending the afternoon with Sloane was doing things to my insides that made me feel like I'd chugged a bottle of champagne. Fizzy and effervescent.

Not a date. It is not a date. Just two friends hanging out.

"You're going to love it." Sloane nodded her head once like that settled things, then sat back in her seat.

She'd been ramrod straight and facing me while we'd talked, but when she settled back in the hard plastic chair, Sloane melted into my side. Pressed up against my shoulder in an awkward way, shifting a little like she was trying to get comfortable.

It was just a reflex. That was all. Sloane's shoulder was digging into my shoulder with every lurch of the subway car, so I raised my arm and settled it behind her on the back of the chair. Skirting the edges of her jacket, her raven hair pillowed on my arm. I let my hand dangle limply, my fingers inches from her body.

It would only take an inch or two. I could have moved my arm until it was wrapped protectively around her shoulders. I could have touched her if I wanted to.

I could have. But I didn't.

The train pulled up at Broadway Station. This was where we parted ways. Sloane got up first, and I followed, one hand behind her back as we stepped from the car, close enough to feel her heat but not to touch.

Sloane turned to me, fidgeting adorably, and she tucked her hair behind her ear. "Thank you for tonight. It was...nice."

I chuckled. "You say that like it's surprising."

"With you, Tommy, it is."

"Guess I had that coming, huh. I know I've been kind of an asshat."

Sloane smirked. "Yeah, maybe, but not lately. Whatever you're doing," she made a sweeping gesture up and down my body, "it's working. I'm glad you're doing better."

"Aww, Sloane, if I didn't know better, I'd think you were worried about me."

"Don't push your luck Tommy." Sloane tried to scowl at me, but she couldn't stop her grin. "I don't worry about you. I don't have to. There isn't an obstacle you've met that you haven't been able to punch or headbutt your way through, and I don't expect that to change anytime soon. I just like that I don't have to deal with the side of jackass that usually went with it."

I snorted a laugh, but I didn't try to correct her. I'd made a name for myself being hard-headed, and it wouldn't do me any good for her—or anyone else—to see me as anything different.

Sloane, honey, if you only knew.

She turned and started down the street, but she turned back at the last minute. "I'll see you tomorrow, yeah?"

"I'll be there," I said as I shoved my hands in my pockets and watched her walk away.

Blearily, I watched as the clock ticked over from three to four a.m. Scrubbed a hand down my face.

I had thought that laying off the booze would help me sleep better, and while what little sleep I was getting seemed to be better quality, I had unfortunately taken away the one thing that stopped my overactive imagination from coming up with new and interesting ways of torturing me in the middle of the night.

Alcohol-fueled oblivion never sounded so good.

Tonight, the nightmare had been the same as it always was, except for a new starring role—Sloane. Wisps of fire and smoke. Her blood on my hands. Feeling like a hand was fisted around my heart until I couldn't breathe, squeezing and tearing and ripping the organ clean from my chest as I watched her breaths get slower and shallower. Cradling her in my arms, begging her to stay. The terrible finality of the light fading from eyes that held nothing but hatred and blame.

You couldn't save them. And you couldn't save me.

I shuddered and lurched to my feet. I was so tired it felt like I was swimming through a thick fog, limbs heavy, joints protesting like a wind-up tin soldier on its last revolution before shutting down. I stumbled into the kitchen. It was harder to find things now, after I'd hired my cleaning service back and endured their withering glares when they'd caught sight of the state of the place, but some things were still right where I left them.

I reached up behind the cereal and pulled down my emergency bottle of Jameson. Took a shot straight, then another, and put the bottle carefully back in its spot. Purely medicinal. I sat at the kitchen island with my head in my hands and waited for the shots to kick in.

As I waited, my mind wandered to the last time we had all been together. Cassidy and Connor, Alfie and Emilia, Callum, Dad, and, of course, Sloane. It had been nearly a year ago at Alfie's wedding. Such a strange little interlude, Spanish moss and warm sand beaches on a little island I still couldn't pronounce in South Carolina. If anyone had told me that Alfie Doyle—a man who had grown up in the worst of Southie's greying, dilapidated projects and practically bled Boston pride—would end up kicking back running charter boats on an island paradise, I'd have said they were crazy.

The wedding was the capstone to one of the hardest points in my life. For six months, none of us had hardly had time to breathe. Teagan's betrayal hit us all hard, but even harder was the fallout from Cassidy's abduction. She's been tortured and nearly raped, and it was only through her own ingenuity and Connor's timely arrival that she'd survived at all.

I swallowed back bile. Even now, I could barely stomach the thought of what she'd endured in that room. And then, later in the hospital, to find out she'd been pregnant the entire time with Connor's child? I shook my head. My sister had a quiet kind of strength that sometimes terrified me.

My thoughts drifted to another moment, later, in the back of our getaway van as we fled the slaughterhouse where Connor and I had been held hostage. Another moment the byproduct of hubris and belief in our own invincibility.

Alfie, shot in the shoulder, barely conscious.

Connor, bleeding out on the floor of the van. Dying.

And Cassidy, struggling against contractions from a baby coming far too soon, while she tried desperately to save her husband's life.

One single moment where I thought I was about to lose nearly everything I loved.

Sloane was behind the wheel that night. We found out later that she'd hit two cars, a bicycle rack, and had driven last half of the route to the hospital up on the curb. Still, she had somehow gotten us there in time to both save Connor and welcome baby Aiden into the world, everyone safe and alive at the end of the day. A miracle by the skin of our teeth.

All of that had come back to me, standing there with my toes in the cooling sand during Alfie and Emilia's wedding. I think that was the moment I decided that I would do whatever it took to change the way things were. To make sure we could endure in relative peace and safety.

But how much of that was just a gamble? Getting out of guns was one thing, but would our new set-up be any better? How long would I have to wait, how hard would I have to work to ensure the sins of our past wouldn't come back to bite us on the ass in the end?

Really, there was only one way.

Connor did it. So did Alfie. They got out. They kept their family safe.

Besides Cassidy, the only person I really had left was Sloane. She was here, she loved the work, and she wasn't leaving anytime soon.

She also wasn't mine, and she never would be.

I shuddered again as the retreating wisps of my dream came back to me. As long as Sloane was here, I would be too.

I could do this.

I would keep her safe and build an empire that would make my father proud.

Stretching, I looked at the clock. Nearly four. The whiskey had given me a pleasant, warm feeling that made me think that I just might be able to get some sleep after all. I stood and started to pad back to my bedroom, but I stopped when I saw something lying on the floor next to the front door. I walked over, bent down, and picked it up.

It was an envelope of photographs.

Instantly, I was jolted awake as I thumbed through them. My stomach churned. Pictures of me and Cassidy at the hospital outside Dad's room. One of Dad in his hospital bed; it must've been taken a few hours before I'd gotten there. Pictures of Connor and Cassidy in the pew at the funeral service. Callum.

Sloane.

I swallowed thickly, my heart rabbit-fast in my chest. The last picture was of me and Cassidy standing by the grave marker. My arm was around her, and our heads were together, bowed. To get a shot like that, the photographer either used one hell of a telescopic lens, or they'd been practically on top of us.

I flipped the photograph over.

TOO BAD ABOUT YOUR OLD MAN

Adrenaline flooded my veins, ice shot gunning through my system. My head spun. I staggered back to the kitchen and slammed down the photos, but I didn't reach for my emergency stash of whiskey. I'd never felt less like having a drink.

Had someone done something to Dad? Poison, or an overdose? That would explain his collapse and his sudden decline. I remember Cassidy talking to Jerome about tox screens at one point, but I didn't remember what they'd said. Had they been abnormal? I couldn't remember.

My heart, already pumping madly away, ratcheted up a notch.

This was a warning. A taunt. Someone had gotten to us, and they might have even had something to do with my father's death. But who?

More importantly, if they could get to him...

Who else could they get to?

13

Sloane

Lady Devine's was quiet. After hours. I was alone behind the worn oak bar, cash register, shots, and taps forgotten in the wake of the 250 pounds of male that was pressed against me, caging me against the bar.

Both of his arms bracket me, the heat of him seeping into my thighs as I stared up at him, frozen in place, my skin tingling where he touched me. He was so close I could see the flecks of gold sparking through the green in his eyes and count each of his long, dark lashes.

"Tommy, what—"

But I never got to finish. His hand slid around to the back of my neck, pulling me up against him, and then his mouth was on mine and I was lost. I kissed him back without thinking, my hands curling into the front of his shirt. He tasted of whiskey and chocolate and something uniquely Tommy that I'd always craved but never dared admit, even to myself.

Tommy's arms wrapped around me, crushing me close, one hand tangling in my hair to angle my head back. I gasped, and his tongue swept into my mouth. Heat flooded through me, pooling low in my belly. I pressed closer, craving more, but then Tommy growled low in his throat, something visceral and primal that shot straight to my belly. He pulled back, breathing hard. I felt his heart pounding against my chest.

"I shouldn't have done that," he said roughly.

"Why not?"

Tommy's eyes darkened, his gaze dropping to my mouth. "Because if I kiss you again, I won't stop there."

A delicious shiver ran down my spine at the dark promise in his voice. "So don't stop."

With a muffled curse, Tommy's mouth claimed mine again. He swept me up in his arms and backed me up against the wall of the bar, pinning me in place with his body. I wrapped a leg around his hip, tangling my hands in his hair and kissing him fiercely. The solid length of him pressed against me, and I rocked my hips forward with a gasp. Tommy groaned, his hands sliding down to grip my ass and grind me harder against him.

"Back room," I panted against his mouth. "Now."

Tommy didn't need to be told twice. He scooped me up and carried me to the back entrance of the bar. I nibbled at his neck, reveling in the shudder it elicited as he fumbled with the door handle.

The door swung open. Tommy kicked it shut behind us and set me on my feet, already stripping off his shirt. My nipples hardened painfully at the sight of perfect washboard abs narrowing to a vee, the thin, dark dusting of hair ducking teasingly beneath the waistband of his jeans. I followed suit, tossing my top aside and reaching for his belt buckle.

A slow, wicked grin spread across Tommy's face. He released my hands, wrapping his arms around me instead and lifting me off my feet.

Tommy lowered me onto the couch, bracing his hands on either side of my head as he settled between my thighs. The weight of him pressed me into the cushions, solid and warm, and I arched up against him with a soft moan.

His mouth found the sensitive spot below my ear, teeth grazing skin, and I tangled my hands in his hair to keep him there. Tommy obliged, sucking a mark into my neck that was sure to bruise. I arched into him. I wanted him to mark me...to make me his...

I hitched my legs higher, hooking him closer, and rolled my hips up to meet his. His cock, rock hard and straining at the seam of his jeans, pulsed against me through our clothes, sparking pleasure that rolled down my spine in waves.

Tommy groaned, his lips drifting lower to close around one nipple. I gasped, back arching, and he soothed the sting with his tongue before moving to the other breast. By the time he kissed his way down my stomach, I was writhing beneath him, desperate for more. He paused at my waistband and glanced up at me through dark lashes, eyes glinting with mischief.

"Tell me what you want," he said, his breath hot against my skin. He ran one finger under the edge of my jeans, teasing. "Or I might just stop right here."

I fisted a hand in his hair and tugged in warning. "Don't you dare."

He quirked a brow, waiting, and I growled in frustration.

"You. I want you," I said. "All of you. Now get these fucking pants off before I do it myself."

Tommy barked out a laugh but made quick work of my jeans and underwear. I was bare before him, heart racing, and the way he looked at me—like I was a feast he planned to devour inch by inch—nearly undid me right then.

Fingers on his belt buckle, zipper undone, jeans and boxer briefs pushed down past perfect hips and delicious thighs to reveal just how aroused he was for me, his swollen cock thick and needy and pulsing with desire.

For me.

I looked up at Tommy, and his gaze darkened. No joking, now. No teasing. Tommy lowered himself over me again, calloused hands sliding up my inner thighs. I gasped as he gripped my hips, tilting them up, and then he was sliding into me with one hard thrust.

Pleasure, sharp and sweet, lanced through me. I cried out, digging my nails into his back, and Tommy began to thrust faster. Harder. Driving deeper into me with every angle of his hips, penetrating past all my well-constructed defenses and safety nets until there wasn't anything separating us anymore.

Blissful. Beautiful. Powerful.

My mind blanked. My eyes rolled back. I couldn't breathe, or maybe I was breathing too fast, pleasure and need building faster than I could comprehend until sparks began to fire behind my closed eyelids. Tommy roared my name as I felt him spasm, filling me, and I tumbled off the edge of oblivion with him.

Tommy stilled inside me with a groan. We were still for a long moment, two halves of a whole, and when Tommy met my gaze his eyes were soft. Vulnerable.

"Christ, Sloane," he said, his voice rough. "What have you done to me?"

Gradually, the dream dissolved around me. For a long moment, I just lay there, breathing heavily. My eyes were still closed and the room still spun, but I begrudgingly forced them open. I didn't want to wake up yet. I couldn't get enough of him, the way he looked at me...

Nothing. I was alone in bed with the sheets tangled around my body.

Shit.

Horror mounting, my fingers crept between my legs. Yep. I was drenched.

Fuck. I'd had a sex dream about Tommy.

And it was hot.

Growling, I pushed up from the bed. Whiskey yowled in protest—creepy cat—and I glanced at the clock. Four in the morning.

I buried my face in my hands and rubbed my temples. This could not be happening. I could *not* be having sex dreams about Tommy. Especially ones that ended so sweetly, that made me think that my subconscious was interested in more than just Tommy's new sexy body. His rock-hard muscles...miles of lickable skin...the way I still felt phantom aches just from the absence of him...

"No. Nope, we are not going there, Sloane, so you better...you better just find yourself somebody else to fantasize about. Not that I was fantasizing about Tommy Quinn. Ugh!"

God, I needed to get laid. That was all this was. Yes, Tommy was hot—I'd have to be dead not to appreciate that body—but it ended there. Just a primal bodily urge when confronted with a powerful male specimen. A reflex. Subconscious.

The hint of vulnerability I'd witnessed in the park had been imagined. The boyish charm. Tommy didn't have a sensitive bone in his body. He was a freight train of toxic masculinity, and the only reason he was being so nice to me now was because he needed my help to un-fuck the clan and pull him out of the hole he'd dug.

And then there was his dating history. Or lack thereof. Alfie had been quite the ladies' man as well, but he hadn't been as celebratory about it. Before he met Emilia, Alfie had enjoyed women and made no qualms about it. With Tommy, conquests between the sheets were just that. Another notch on the bedpost. There was no way I was going to become such a cliché.

Thinking of Alfie caused a pang of regret. I envied what he had with Emilia. The little looks, the gestures, a language all their own. They truly seemed two halves of a whole. I'd seen the look on Alfie's face last year when he'd thought Emilia was dead. Devastated wasn't the word for it. And then, later at the hospital, he looked at her like she was the air he needed to breathe, like she'd hung the moon and the stars. Two planets, orbiting each other.

I wanted that.

I wanted to be romanced. I wanted to be someone's gravity. Call it sentimental, call it a girly fantasy, but I wanted to be *loved* by someone. Not lusted over.

Tommy was incapable of love. In order to love someone, you have to care about more than yourself, and Tommy cared about one person and one person only. Oh, I hadn't forgotten all the suggestive glances from Cassidy—why she was determined to get us together I have no idea—nor had I forgotten Tommy's ham-handed confession of his feelings last year. Spectacularly ill-timed, it had been adorable in an almost juvenile way, but I'd seen it for what it was.

For Tommy, I was the one who got away; the notch on his bedpost he hadn't been able to score, and it ate at him.

This latest "new leaf" was just another tactic. A charming one, admittedly, seeing as I was now *having sex dreams about Tommy!*

"You just need to get laid," I said to myself. "That's all this is. A good old flush of the pipes, and all this will go away."

Whiskey watched me from her perch on my dresser, head cocked in feline judgement. I flopped back onto the bed and pulled the comforter over my head. Great. Now I was talking to myself.

Needless to say, I did not go back to sleep, and as a result, a very grouchy Sloane showed up at Lady D's on Saturday morning. There was an astonishing amount of work to be done, but after a herculean sized cup of coffee and delegation of tasks to Grady and Kat, I was able to settle in and start running logistics for Tommy's new plan.

Dressed professionally in my light grey pantsuit and heels and feeling like a candidate on *Shark Tank*, I met with my contacts at the distilleries, the ones who supplied Lady Devine's. To the few that knew of our less-than-legal dealings, I bluntly offered them a role in the new operation, and I carefully threw out feelers to the rest.

By the end of the day, I had four suppliers on the hook. Another two were interested, but they wanted the operation up and running first. All-in-all, a pretty successful day.

Now, to see how Tommy had done with the enigmatic Misha.

That was the only part of the plan that didn't sit well with me. When Tommy first mentioned the Russian, my first instinct was to refuse outright. I hadn't forgotten the way Volkov's men had turned tail on the Italians, or how his predecessor's betrayal had cost my brother his life. Misha was a slippery bastard, and I hoped Tommy had been serious when he said he didn't trust him completely.

Tommy and Misha looked quite at ease when I met them at Dooley's Pub, an innocuous little gastropub down by the waterfront. Leaned back in the seat, arms spread on the back of the book like he owned the joint, Tommy looked far too good in his black tee shirt and denim jacket, artfully ripped in a way that looked like it was intentional, but I knew it wasn't. The engine grease stains and worn cuffs were all hard earned. He'd had that jacket almost as long as I'd known him, but I'd never noticed how good he looked in it until today.

Misha said something to Tommy, and Tommy's head swiveled towards me. For a second it looked like he paled, his lips thinning out into a frown. It must've been the lighting, though, because he straightened and turned his million-watt smile on me.

"Sloane. Hey. Grab a seat."

"What did I miss?" I asked, sliding into the booth. The waiter immediately brought over a Shipyard Summer Ale, from one of my favorite breweries in Maine. Apparently, Tommy had ordered for me, and the gesture did not go unnoticed.

"You haven't missed much," Tommy said. "How did it go with the suppliers?"

Misha was watching me with that carefully composed way of his, faint permasmile etched on his lips, giving away nothing. I hadn't noticed until now how attractive his bold, Eastern European features were: strong jaw, prominent cheekbones divided by a wide, aquiline nose. He'd almost be considered handsome, if it weren't for the eyes. Irises of the palest blue I'd ever seen, intelligent and sharp, missing nothing.

And as cold as the Russian winter.

"We've got four on deck with another possible two," I said, turning my focus solely to Tommy. I wasn't going to let Misha rattle me. "We should be able to start production as soon as next month."

Tommy nodded. "Were you able to negotiate a cut?"

"70/30." I smirked at his raised eyebrows. "Blarney Mark wanted 40, and Black Dog was ready to walk, but I talked them both off the ledge since we'll be taking all of the risk."

"Nice," Tommy said. "Let's circle back around next week and pay them a visit in person. Make sure that they're ready to get with the program."

"I already told them to expect us once we get going."

"That's my girl." Tommy turned to Misha. He rapped on the table and pointed his finger like a gun. "Sloane's been running Lady Devine's since she was old enough to pour a shot. She's got the connections when it comes to product."

Misha smiled and turned his gaze on me. "It's hard to say no to a beautiful woman."

My eyes narrowed. "I think I'm a bit more than just a pretty face."

Misha didn't blink an eye. Instead, he held up his glass in salute. "No offense intended, *ptichka.* Russia is much more modernized than she used to be, but we have never forgotten the value of our female comrades. Intelligent. Calculating. Masters of the long game. And behind every beautiful smile is a she-wolf ready to pounce. Tommy is lucky to have you. I keep telling him this."

"She-wolf, huh?" I swirled my beer and took a sip, smirking. "I suppose I have been known to be quite the bitch from time to time"

Misha laughed and shook his finger at me. "I knew I liked you. Come, let's celebrate. Good Russian vodka—"

"Hold on a minute," Tommy said. During the back-and-forth between Misha and me, he'd grown increasingly restless, almost as if he were a little jealous of Misha's attention towards me. "What did your boss Volkov say?"

Misha shrugged. "He agrees. We will facilitate communication with our contacts in Moscow, and in turn, you will introduce us to your contacts here...along with giving us access to the seaport."

"Woah, woah, woah. That wasn't the deal, Misha." Tommy scowled. "Nobody said anything about the seaport."

The seaport was our bread and butter. South Boston wasn't the most lucrative of locations, but the seaport alone made up for any shortcomings. Losing control of the waterfront would be devastating to our bottom line; even letting the Russians have a sliver of it would affect us.

And once they had a toe hold in our territory, there was no telling where they would stop.

Misha held up his hands. "I am just the messenger. Volkov is interested in obtaining a piece of your rather massive pie. A sliver, really."

"I don't care if he only wants a crumb," Tommy said, "he's not getting it."

"If Volkov wants to do business on the waterfront, he's going to have to do it through us," I added.

"Fair enough," Misha shrugged. "I will bring this back to Volkov, and we will see what he says. He is very interested in our partnership, so I don't imagine it will be much of an obstacle."

Tommy sat back. "I hope it won't be. We want to make this work, Misha, but we're not going to budge on the seaport."

"Understood. Now, about that vodka..."

Tommy's mood improved as the afternoon wore on, though whether it was the vodka or Misha's unflappable charisma, I wasn't sure. I remained wary of our Russian friend, but even he managed to wear me down a little bit, and by the time we were ready to leave, I was pleasantly buzzed and my cheeks hurt from laughing.

Misha said his goodbyes and left, but Tommy hooked my arm as I was ready to turn towards the T station. "We still up for the game tonight? Because I'm holding you to it."

"Of course! I've been looking forward to it all day."

It wasn't a lie. The past few weeks had been stressful, to say the least, and I was ready to forget it all for a little bit. Even better, it was going to be Tommy's first game. It was one thing to go with my friends or some of the guys, but I couldn't help that little seed of excitement blooming in my chest at the thought of sharing one of my favorite things with him.

Tommy bought us both Fenway Franks and beers, refusing to let me pay. He even bought a Sox baseball cap, which made me double over in laughter when I saw him in it. I'd never seen him in a ball cap in my life. The old Tommy never would've let anything mess with the integrity of his hawk, but it seemed this new Tommy was more cavalier about his hair.

The night was perfect for it. A warm summer breeze kept the stands cool as we picked our way down to our seats on the first base line. The season tickets had been a birthday gift from my dad last year, and the seats were primo. I explained the positions and the basic rules to Tommy as the team warmed up—he really was clueless about baseball—and he surprised me yet again by asking questions like he really cared.

By the first pitch, Tommy was eagerly watching the game. I think he was a little disappointed by the lack of physical contact. Not surprising, coming from a boxing fan. A fight broke out in the third inning, though, and that perked him up a bit.

Personally, I was having a hard time paying attention. For the first time in my life, my attention was zeroed in on the person next to me instead of the game. In a gentlemanly gesture, Tommy had relinquished the armrest between us, but his hand was on his knee, inches from mine. His long legs were no match for the cramped stadium seating, and I could feel the heat of him next to me.

Brayan Bello was pitching in the bottom of the seventh when I felt Tommy's leg brush up against mine. Tommy stared straight ahead, but it hadn't been an accident.

Without thinking, I reached out and hooked my pinky finger around his. Tommy visibly flinched, looked down at our entwined fingers, and back up at me. The smile that bloomed on his face was so boyishly pure it took my breath away.

Tommy folded my hand in his and held it for the rest of the game.

It was the first Sox game I'd ever been to where I wouldn't have been able to recount a single play at gunpoint. Tommy was beginning to have that worrying effect on me. By the time the game was over I felt tipsy and unstable, a feeling that had nothing to do with the heat or the beer I'd drank and everything to do with the guy sitting next to me.

Still holding my hand.

Tommy was chattering a mile a minute as we walked out the game. Clearly, I'd made a convert out of him. If he noticed my unsteadiness he didn't show it; he simply guided me through the crowd, clearing the way with one hand placed protectively at the small of my back.

"Well, I guess this is it," he said. Dazedly, I realized we were at the T station. "I really had a good time tonight, Sloane. I had my doubts, but you delivered."

"Told you you'd like it," I grinned up at him.

"The company wasn't bad, either."

Tommy reluctantly released my hand, and I smoothed my palm down the thigh of my jeans, the skin tingling like it already missed the contact. I didn't want him to go. Not yet. Maybe not ever. I liked this new side of him, and I wasn't ready to give it up yet.

"You know, I shared something I love with you," I began hesitantly, folding my arms across my chest in what I knew was a defensive gesture, yet I was unable to stop myself. "It's only fair you return the favor."

Tommy blinked, momentarily lost. "What do you mean?"

"What I mean is, you and I are kind of similar. We're both hardheaded—"

"You've got that right."

"Don't interrupt. We both live for work, and we don't have much else going on." I narrowed my eyes at him "You're a mystery to me, Tommy. I shared something with you, I think you should share something with me. What is it you love? What do you—I don't know—what do you like to do to let loose?"

Tommy leaned against the building's brick façade and shoved his hands in his pockets. His eyes sparkled at me, such a dark shade of blue in the streetlight, a pretty shade of indigo shot through with gold. How had I never noticed them before?

"You want me to share something I love with you," he repeated. "Something that I like to do to let loose."

I immediately realized how it had sounded. "Don't be gross."

Tommy laughed out loud, a great big clap of laughter that had me giggling, too. He took off his ball cap, smoothed back his hair, and looked at me like I was going to be the death of him.

"All right, spitfire. If you want to find out what I like to do to let loose, meet me at Lady D's tomorrow morning at ten."

He started to walk away, and I hustled after him, curious. "What is it?"

"That," he winked, "is the surprise."

14

Tommy

My phone rang as I was heading out the door to meet Sloane at Lady D's. Irritated and already running behind because I'd spent way more time than I should have getting ready, I swiped at the screen and barked into the phone. "Tommy here."

"Mr. Quinn, I've got some news for you," Jerome said on the other end of the line. I set my jacket back on the kitchen counter, my haste forgotten.

I had spent the day I'd found the photographs stuffed under my door scouring the building's security footage, but all I'd turned up was a big, fat zilch. Whoever had done it was a professional. It was hard to spot, but I knew my way around security cameras, and for a thirty-minute period between two and three in the morning, the cameras all fell into a hiccupping loop showing nothing but an empty hallway. The photographs were clean, no prints. Cheap home printer photo paper, available in any drugstore in Boston. A dead end.

Reluctantly, I turned to Cassidy's boss, Jerome. I didn't want to believe my dad had been murdered, but I had to know. I had to know how deep this thing went and who else could be in danger.

And if it were true, I wanted to be the one to find the bastard myself.

The last thing I wanted was for Cass to get involved with this. She had enough on her plate. Jerome knew about our line of work already—he'd done us a solid last year when Alfie was on the run—and I knew he could be trusted to keep his mouth shut, especially if my sister's welfare was at stake. Getting in touch with Jerome was another problem, which involved a complicated series of side-steps in order to get him alone at work without Cassidy witnessing.

I didn't pull my punches. I showed Jerome the photographs and asked him about my dad's tox panels. Jerome shook his head and said that there were several readings which had been abnormal, but nothing unexpected for late-stage cancer and organ failure. The threatening message on the back of the photos made him pause, though, and he promised he'd do some digging and get back with me.

The phone creaked in my hand as I gripped it hard. "What did you find out?" There was a pause on the line. "Dr. Carter?"

"It might be nothing," he began. "You must understand, in cases like your father's, where the pathology clearly indicates complications resulting from the cancer, it's an open and shut case. Autopsies are expensive and are rarely performed, only if foul play is suspected."

"I know that," I snapped, impatient. "They asked us if we wanted one anyway, but Cass and I didn't want to put him through that. Didn't see the need. Now I wish we had."

"Exactly. These cases never even make it to the ME's desk. In Massachusetts, a death certificate can be completed by any physician. So all we can go on now is the blood panels that were pulled when your father was admitted."

"Cut to the chase, Jerome."

"I just want you to understand the nature of this, Tommy, and why I can only offer you so much under the circumstances."

"Noted. Get on with it."

A heavy expulsion of air on the end of the line. "At the time your father was admitted, the official diagnosis was acute liver failure. This caused a domino effect in his remaining organs, and they began shutting down one by one. Not uncommon in end-stage cancer. The admitting physician didn't question it, and neither did I.

"Michael's blood panel was all over the road. Again, not uncommon in a case like his, so we didn't question it. Just a brief check to see if there was anything glaring, and there wasn't. But you asked me to treat this like a homicide, so I took another look.

"Based on the original diagnosis, I took a look at his liver enzymes. They were low. Dangerously so. This could have been a by-product of his body shutting down, but what if it were the cause? Low liver enzymes, loss of consciousness, seizures. That sounds a lot like Debrancher Enzyme Deficiency, which is usually found only in children, but it can be caused by misuse of prescription drugs in elderly adults."

I was gritting my teeth so hard they hurt. "What kind of prescription drugs?"

"Well, I took a look," Jerome said. "Your father was taking azathioprine for his arthritis. Azathioprine is an immunosuppressive drug, and one of the side effects is the lowering of liver enzymes. In your father's case, it was carefully administered and monitored, but a misuse of the drug—"

"You mean, if someone overdosed him," I interrupted.

"Yes. An overdose could have caused your father's symptoms. In his already overtaxed body, the effects would have been irreversible."

"I see."

"Now, Tommy, please take this with a grain of salt, I don't have all the information and—"

"Thanks, Jerome. I've got what I needed."

I hung up on him. Heavily, I sat down in the chair, my hands and face numb.

Someone killed my father.

God—who could have done such a thing? A tired, washed-up old man, trying to live out the rest of his preciously few days in peace and quiet with whatever dignity he could hold on to. He was already dying, but they'd taken that from him as well.

It was too much of a coincidence. Those pictures had been sent to taunt me. To warn me. Sloane, Cassidy, Connor, Michael—pictures of my family. My friends. Someone knew how to get to me, how to hurt me. The message was clear.

I wasn't untouchable.

Anger, my old friend, surfaced hot and fast, and I swung at the wall with a roar, putting my fist through the drywall. Again. And again. Until I hit a stud, but I kept hitting until my knuckles were bloody and swollen and the red haze over my eyes began to retreat a little. Just a little to start thinking clearly.

One: Cassidy could never know.

We'd already lost Mom that way, and Cassidy had a front row seat that day. A car bomb meant for Michael that ended up killing not only Mom, but nearly Cassidy as well. She still struggled with it. Cassidy's relationship with Dad had been complicated, but to find out that he'd been murdered as well? That would break her.

Two: Sloane couldn't know, either. She'd take the bit between her teeth and end up doing something rash. I couldn't tell her until I knew more.

I had to keep this quiet for now. Do some digging on my own. And once I found the son of a bitch who killed my father, I'd make him wish he'd never been born.

I tried to muster up enthusiasm for my date-not-a-date with Sloane, but it was hard. I had too much on my mind. Sloane, of course, saw right through me.

"You look like shit," she smirked, trying to keep it light. "Again."

"Didn't sleep well."

"Want to talk about it?"

I sighed. Rubbed a hand over my mouth. "Not really. What I really want is to get the hell out of here."

Sloane was frowning at me, her eyes evaluating every shadow and line in my face. "We don't have to do this today, Tommy."

"That's just the thing," I said, mustering up a smirk. "You wanted to know what I did to blow off steam? Well, follow me."

I took off down the sidewalk, and Sloane trotted to keep up with me. "Where are we going?"

"To get our ticket out of here."

Diana was housed in a storage garage a couple blocks down from the bar. Not a far walk, but Sloane peppered me with questions non-stop. Her curiosity was adorable, and despite the black mood I was in, even I couldn't ignore the way my heart skipped and stuttered at the sudden attention from her.

"Here she is," I announced proudly, sweeping the dust cover off her. Two tons of gleaming Detroit steel winked back at us in the bright lights, low and mean and looking like sex on wheels.

"It's...your car." Sloane said, nonplussed.

"Yep."

"But it's just a car."

I snorted. "Not just any car, it's *Diana*."

"Okay...is there something I'm missing, here?"

"We're going for a drive."

Sloane backed away. "Uh, uh. Nope. I've seen the way you drive that thing. I like all my body parts where they're currently located, thank you."

"Hey." I stepped up to her and grabbed her forearm, sliding my hand down until I could lace my fingers through hers. "Do you trust me?"

Sloane stared at me, green eyes flicking back and forth between mine. As I watched, her pupils dilated and she squeezed my hand. "Yes."

It took everything I had not to roar in triumph. To pull her in my arms just then and tell her she's mine, that she would never have to be afraid again. That I would gladly throw myself in front of any bullet, that I would protect her until my last breath.

That I loved her.

But I couldn't tell her that, so I just winked at her and told her to get in.

Sloane slid into the passenger seat, and I walked around to the driver's side. My heart stopped as I reached for the door handle.

Photographs were stuffed underneath the windshield wiper.

I hadn't seen them in the glare from the overhead lights. Hastily, with shaking hands, I snatched up the photographs and rifled through them as I felt the blood drain from my face.

Connor and Cassidy in the park walking Aiden. Sloane and me at the ballgame. At Lady D's. The restaurant. Big Saul's...

"Tommy? Are you okay?"

Sloane was still standing by the car, staring at me with a worried look on her face. I quickly shoved the pictures in my back pocket. "Just the garage floor attendant messing with me. Come on, let's go."

She gave me a funny look, but she got in.

I waited until we were out of the city to really open her up. The horses screamed, churning up mile after mile of backwoods highway, and I felt my fears shrink along with the Boston city skyline in the rearview mirror.

"So, why Diana?" Sloane asked, holding onto the door handle. She hadn't let go once. "You've never told me the story behind the name?"

I bit back a smirk. "No story."

"Oh, come on. It's such a random name."

"No, it's not."

"Yes, it is. There's got to be a story behind it."

"Diana Prince, okay?" I blurted. Sloane looked at me, confused, and my face heated. "Wonder Woman? I used to watch the tv show as a kid, and I always thought she was...ah..."

Sloane was struggling not to laugh. "Yeah?"

"I thought she was hot, okay?" I said sheepishly. Nobody had ever asked me about the car's name before, and now that I'd said it out loud, it sounded stupid.

Sloane gasped theatrically. "Tommy Quinn, are you...a nerd?"

"No, I'm not."

"Yes, you are! You're secretly a nerd!"

"You are having way too much fun with this."

"Tommy likes Wonder Woman. Tommy likes Wonder Woman," she sang, clapping her hands.

"I regret everything." I grumbled. "I am never telling you anything again."

"How kinky does this get? Have you ever done it with a girl in a Wonder Woman costume?" She had a shit-eating grin on her face. "Oh! Do you go to conventions? You know, the whole dress-up thing? You would make a sexy Thor."

"Stop it. And that's Marvel, not DC."

"Grow the hair out..."

"Sloane!"

She laughed, the sound low and husky and shooting straight to my crotch. I tried to maintain my scowl for her benefit, but it was becoming more difficult by the minute.

"It's stupid," I said.

"It's not." Sloane reached over, took my hand, and interlaced her fingers with mine. "I think it's cute."

"Perfect. Exactly what I was going for. Cute."

I glanced down at our interlocked hands resting on the center console. She'd done it again. Held my hand. The first time she'd done it, at the baseball game, my heart had started to beat so hard and so fast I felt like she'd be able to hear it from where she was sitting. But now, while it still gave me that unsteadily giddy sensation, it was starting to feel almost normal.

As if someone like her could ever be my normal. My constant.

The rest of the ride passed uneventfully, aside from eliciting a few squeals from Sloane when I took the long, curvy road up to the beach too fast. Before I knew it, we were pulling into the drive of Callum's summer house and parking next to Connor and Cassidy's car.

"What is this?" Sloane asked as she got out. "Dad didn't mention anything..."

"Spur of the moment," I said. "We haven't seen each other since the funeral, and I figured it was time."

That was only partially true. In reality, I wanted to double check Callum's security system for myself and make sure that he and Connor were keeping their defenses up. The photographs burning a hole in my back pocket were never far from my mind.

The house seemed empty without Michael. Callum looked like he'd aged five years overnight, but watching your best friend go before you would do that to a man. I surreptitiously checked through the security system while the girls were preparing dinner, and Callum and Connor were occupied watching Aiden toddle back and forth across the living room. Nothing glaring there. Security was tight and functioning properly. I'd installed it myself a few years ago, and made sure Callum kept up with the maintenance.

After I was satisfied, I took a moment to look at the newest photographs again. No message this time; at least, not a written one. The intended message was clear. Somebody had my number, and none of my family was safe.

I cornered Connor after dinner. "Hey, man, got a second?"

"Yeah, what's up?"

I cocked my head towards the patio. "Let's take a walk."

Connor followed me outside, his hands in his pockets. His entire demeanor had changed, a complete one-eighty from the man at dinner. "Nothing good ever begins with 'Let's take a walk.' What's going on, Tommy?"

"How's the security at your new place?" I asked, not mincing any words.

"A dozen cameras with a silent alarm, monitored by a third party. Redundant feeds, backup power. And I always carry when we're out of the home." His pale eyes regarded me evenly. "Is there a threat?"

"Yes."

"Against the clan?"

"No. Me." I tilted my chin up. "And the family by proxy."

Connor nodded. "What do you need?"

I shook my head. "I'm handling it for now, but I wanted to give you a heads up."

"Thanks." He smiled grimly. "I knew there was another reason you came all the way up here tonight."

"Not true. Well, not completely true. I wanted to see you guys."

"You should come around more often. Cassidy would love for you to have a more active role in Aiden's life." Connor leaned back against the railing, and I felt his stare bore into me. "Cherish the time you do have with the ones you love, Tommy. You never know when it's going to be the last time."

I was beginning to understand that. Connor clapped me on the shoulder, giving it a squeeze, and started to head back inside. I caught his arm just before he was out of reach.

"Connor? Let's just keep this between us for now. Cassidy and Callum don't need to know. They've been through too much."

Connor nodded solemnly. "I agree. Let me know if you need anything. Anything at all."

"Will do, brother."

I stood at the railing and watched the ocean for a long time after he left, lost in thought. The crashing surf against the rocky beach matched the surging blood in my ears. I sat heavily on the porch swing.

I didn't know what I'd do if I lost anyone else. Another death might just break me. Strip away my humanity until I became the animal everyone knew me to be, feral and deadly. Or maybe I'd just disintegrate, a thousand pieces of Tommy floating away into the ether.

"Hey, you. I was wondering where you'd escaped to." Sloane walked up and sat on the porch swing next to me, the length of her body brushing mine. "What's going on? You've been off all day."

"It's nothing, Sloane," I began, but she cut me off.

"If it's something to do with work, you need to tell me," she said. "We're supposed to be partners. No more hiding shit you think I can't handle, no more carrying the load by yourself."

"It's not that," I said quickly. "It's just...Dad. I guess it's all hitting me now."

"Oh."

"Yeah."

"I'm sorry."

"Don't be," I said. "It's the way these things go, I guess. I'll be all right."

Sloane looked up at me, her eyes glittering in the starlight. "It's okay if you're not. You know that, don't you?"

My throat felt thick and my eyes stung. Nobody had ever told me that before. Least of all myself.

Without thinking, I wrapped my arm around her. Sloane didn't brush me off or make a cheeky comment. Instead, she melted into my side with a smile, and I angled my body in the seat so she could rest against my shoulder. "I do now," I said quietly, murmuring the words into the crown of her head.

Together we watched the stars until Sloane's eyes started to get heavy, her breathing evening out in sleep. I gently tugged her further into my arms, cradling her head against my heart.

Carefully, oh so carefully so I wouldn't wake her, I kissed Sloane's temple. Pressed my lips against her silky hair, murmuring things I could never say to her in the light of day. My thoughts, my fears. The deepest reaches of my heart laid bare to her in the dark. What I wouldn't give to hold her like that forever. Or even for a day. Just one more minute...

I wasn't that lucky.

My phone buzzed, and I swiped up to view the incoming text. It might be Jerome with more information.

It was not.

Is this Tommy Quinn?

Who's asking? I texted back.

Luca Mariano. I got your number from Emilia, who got it from Alfie. Alfie says to tell you that you still owe him 2G from the last Super Bowl.

Okay, so it was legit, at least. But why would Luca be texting me now? *What do you want?* I asked.

We need to talk. Where can I meet you?

Four hours later, I walked into Big Saul's Gym to meet Luca. It was about as neutral of a territory as we were going to get. I'd bundled a sleepy Sloane into the car and dropped her off at her place before parking Diana for the night and taking the T downtown.

Luca was waiting for me when I arrived.

His hair was longer than I remembered it from the wedding, curling down past his chin and laying thickly over the left side of his face. It was greasy and stringy. A week's worth of growth covered his chin, broken up by tendrils of scar tissue from his left eye. With his worn blue jeans and faded flannel shirt handing over his shockingly thin frame, he could have passed for any one of Boston's homeless.

Jesus Christ. The guy I remembered had been built like a brick shit-house, with an easy smile and witty remark, primed to unravel tensions and put everyone at ease. Luca's appearance hit me like a punch in the gut. Life had chewed him up and spat him out, and it looked like he was barely hanging on by his fingernails.

"What can I do for you, Luca?" I was well aware of what he'd sacrificed for Alfie, and I took pains to temper my impatience.

"It's what I can d-do for you." The words were slow, gummy. Luca jerked his head, and I saw that the left corner of his mouth was pulled back in a grimace from scar tissue that stretched up to his cheekbone. "I hear you've...got yourself an admirer."

The photographs in my back pocket felt like they weighed a hundred pounds. I pulled them out and held them aloft. "You could say that."

"D-Dominic sends his regards."

Ice flooded my veins. Christ, why hadn't I seen it before? Dominic Moretti's body hadn't been found at the slaughterhouse with his father and brother, and if anyone held a grudge against me, it was him.

I thought back to the funeral. At the shadowy figure I'd seen at the back of the church and in the woods overlooking the cemetery. Dominic had been there.

"Dom's out of his mind," Luca said. "B-Blames you for everything. Lorenzo. Angel. *Everything*. I kept quiet because it was just hot air at first, but now he's getting serious. Wants to hurt you...the people you love. Take from you. Your family. Your friends. Even E...E..."

"Emilia," I finished. I'd heard from Alfie that Luca had a thing for her, even though he'd given her up so she could be happy with Alfie; Luca even helped them escape, and it had nearly cost him his life.

"Yes," he hissed through his teeth. "Even her. I'm out of the Family. A h-has been. Broken." He gestured to his face. His body. "I can't protect her now. Can't do...a damned thing about it. But you can."

Fucking right, I would do something about it. Dominic murdered my father. He threatened my family. He threatened *Sloane*. I was not going to let that slide.

God—Sloane. Now she was all wrapped up in this. Before, the bar provided her a thin veneer of insulation from what we did, but now she was in the thick of it. Our job was inherently dangerous enough without that bastard painting a big 'ol target on her back. Until I took care of Dom, I was going to have to double down on protection. Sloane was going to hate me for it, but I didn't see any other way around it.

I took a step towards Luca, clenching my fists. "Where is he? I'll end this right fucking now."

"You can't. Not unless you want to start another war. Sal's keeping Dominic under his thumb at the compound...for now. But I'll let you know if he makes a move."

I nodded. I didn't like it, but at least I had a name, now. It was as good as I was going to get. "Thanks, Luca. I owe you one."

Luca shrugged and turned towards the exit. "Just watch your back, Quinn."

15

Sloane

It's always a shitshow in Boston around the Fourth of July, but never more so when the Fourth is on a Saturday *and* it's the first day it hasn't rained all week *and* you work in a bar downtown. The only worse day to be slinging drinks in my opinion is St. Patrick's Day.

The Fourth of July was fun when I was younger. We'd usually escape up north to the summer house to avoid the tourist-swollen metro area for a couple days of sun, swimming, hotdogs, and fireworks on the beach. After high school, I went straight to work at the bar and had worked every Fourth since. Tonight was no exception.

Kat and I were behind the bar, and I'd even hired a barback in anticipation of the surge of customers our newfound "neighborhood bar" status had earned us. I hadn't been wrong. Lady D's was packed to the gills, and I'd barely had a second to breathe since noon.

Tommy, inexplicably, was nowhere to be seen. I even asked Grady, who had been down at the warehouse all day before picking up his kids from the ex-wife, but he hadn't seen Tommy all day. The fact irked me more than I wanted to admit. After our little interlude up at the summer house, I had thought that we'd turned a corner and he was actually treating me like a capable human being. A friend. But now, he was acting dodgy.

Was it something I did? I barely remembered falling asleep on the porch swing with Tommy. Exhaustion, good food, and one more glass of wine than I was used to having added up. Tommy had looked upset, I remembered, his face pinched while he spoke in angry, hushed tones with Connor on the patio. I meant to ask him about it, but the next thing I knew, I was being bundled into the car by Tommy for the ride home.

Come to think of it, Tommy had been off all day, even before the drive up. Whatever he'd found—and tried to hide—pinned beneath his windshield wiper had darkened his mood, but he'd already been on edge that morning.

Not much had changed between us since that night, but Tommy had been noticeably distant. Constantly busy, even though the new operation was on hold until we heard from Misha. Was he going behind my back? Was there something I didn't know?

Needless to say, I wasn't feeling very festive tonight. Kat was in fine form, flirting her way through drink orders and racking up a healthy tip jar. It was all I could do to muster up a smile and keep the orders straight. Tommy was in my head, right where I didn't want him to be.

Glancing at the clock to see what time it was, I spied Kat talking to a tall blond man leaning lazily against the bar top. Misha.

He was holding court at the other end of the bar, and Kat was hanging off his every word. I could practically see the hearts in her eyes as he turned the full force of his European charm on her, pale eyes sparking and a surprising dimple popping up at the corner of his mouth when he smiled at her. Kat was eating it up. I motioned to the barback to cover my section, and I made my way over to them.

"Misha," I said to catch his attention as I slid next to Kat, but his eyes had been following me since I left my post.

He brightened. "Sloane! Just the woman I was looking for."

"I've been here all night."

"Yes, but I was detained by the lovely serving staff you have here. What was your name again, my dear?" He smiled again at Kat, who practically swooned.

"Cut the crap, Misha," I snapped. "Why are you here?"

He pouted. "Is that any way to treat an old friend?"

"No, a new one who is walking on a very thin line," I said. "Back room. Now."

Misha whispered something to Kat that made her giggle, and he grinned wickedly as he tucked the number she scrawled on a bar napkin into his back pocket. I rolled my eyes. Not waiting for him to follow, I left the main floor and let myself into the back room.

Misha was right behind me, and he closed the door. "You do not like me."

"I don't trust you," I said. "I haven't made up my mind whether I like you or not."

"Then there is hope for us yet, *ptichka.* And no, you shouldn't trust me."

I narrowed my eyes. "Oh, really?"

"No." Misha tapped his temple. "Trust yourself, and no one else. Less heartache that way."

"A cynical viewpoint, but one I can get behind," I agreed. "So, Misha, now that we've established our relationship, what do you want? Tommy isn't here."

He frowned. "So I have noticed. He's not been around much, yes?"

"He's been busy."

"Has he told you what with?"

I shrugged. Misha looked serious, but I didn't like the way his eyes danced as if he knew something I didn't.

"I'm not his keeper," I said, crossing my arms defensively. "Tommy can do as he likes."

"Yes, he's been very good at that. Doing what he likes, regardless of the consequences. One can only hope they won't end up stabbing him in the back."

That felt like a warning. "What do you mean?"

"I make it my business to know things about the people I work with. Even the people I don't. It's best to look several miles down the track to avoid any...unpleasantness."

"Or manipulate people."

"Or that." Misha spread his hands. "I look out for Misha, first and foremost. I have always been up front about that. But I may have heard whispers...and Tommy may have also mentioned something."

"Quit playing games." I took a step towards him, feeling my blood pressure rise. "Is something going on with Tommy? Is he in trouble?"

Misha shrugged. "You will have to ask him, he would be upset if I told you. But you should warn him to watch his back. Sins of the past, and all that."

I wasn't sure what he meant by that. It could be anything, it could be nothing. It could just be Misha playing games. But I couldn't stop the feeling of dread that began to pool in my gut.

Oh, I would be asking Tommy, all right. Especially about why he chose to confide in Misha and not me.

I clenched my jaw. "Did you have anything useful to say, or did you just come to gloat and hit on my staff?"

Misha chuckled. He looked disdainfully at the worn leather couch pushed up against the wall and settled for the straight-backed wooden chair next to it. He pulled out a cigarette, lit it, and leaned back, crossing his arms over his chest.

"Aleksandr Volkov has agreed to your terms."

I blinked, floored. "All of them?"

"Yes. If you agree, he will set up a meet in a few days to finalize the details of our arrangement."

"I thought he wanted access to the seaport? What happened with that?"

Misha just shrugged and took a drag of his cigarette. He stood and dusted a speck of ash from his jeans. "Talk it over with Tommy and give me your answer, the sooner the better. Volkov is eager to get started. Until then, Sloane."

He left me standing in the back room, half elated that Volkov had agreed to the deal and half stewing over this new development with Tommy.

Tommy. My stomach clenched at the thought that he might be in trouble. It wasn't exactly surprising—the man seemed to invite it in spades—but things had changed, now. I wasn't foolish enough to deny it. Somehow, in the tangle of everything, our friendship had morphed into something more.

Curled up next to him on the porch swing, enveloped in his massive arms, I'd never felt so safe. I didn't make a habit of letting my vulnerability slip, but with Tommy, it was almost too easy. Even something as simple as holding hands had become second nature. Grounding. Us against the world, side by side.

Until now.

Tommy was keeping something from me. Something he'd trusted Misha with, apparently, and something that could put him in danger. I paced across the back room as images of him beaten bloody in the ring resurfaced. Collapsing to the floor. Gritting his teeth on the couch in this very room while Cassidy dug a bullet out of his side.

I didn't want to lose him. I couldn't. Tommy was reckless, always had been, but in the past year his reckless streak had taken on a darker undertone. Sure, the past few weeks had been better, but how long would that last? How long until he fell off the edge and did something that couldn't be undone?

Huffing out an angry breath, I pulled out my phone and texted him. *Need u at Lady D's asap.*

I tried to be nonchalant about it as I pushed through the door and went back to work. Tommy would either answer, or he wouldn't.

So it was to my surprise that Tommy burst through the door a mere thirty minutes later looking out of breath and ready to fight. I nearly dropped the draft I was pouring, and I quickly set it down on the bar before turning to Kat.

"Hey, I need a minute, can you cover for me?"

She grinned while she poured two beers at once. "Go—more tips for me. I'm making more tonight than I did all last week."

"I won't be long."

Kat looked over at Tommy and gave a knowing grin. "Take as long as you need, hon."

I ripped off my bar apron and tossed it on the shelf behind me. I was just about to come around the bar when Tommy grabbed my arm and pulled me aside. "Is everything all right? Your text—"

"Not here." Glancing around at the packed floor, I ducked back behind the bar and led us through the storage room and out into the alley behind Lady D's. I needed some air.

I kept walking down the alley, gathering my thoughts. I hadn't expected Tommy to show up so soon, and I especially hadn't expected him to come ready to put down a fight. Misha's warning was making more and more sense.

"Sloane, slow down." Tommy jogged up behind me. "Did something happen?"

A big, meaty hand grabbed me by the arm and spun me around. Tommy's eyes were wide, frantic. Visually he scanned down my body, his hands running down my arms like he was looking for damage. "Are you okay?"

I jerked out of his grip. "I'm fine, no thanks to you. Where have you been all night?"

Tommy pulled back, scowling at my tone. "I was down at the warehouse with Grady."

"Liar. Grady said he hasn't seen you all day. Try again."

"I don't have to explain every move I make to you, Sloane," he growled.

"You do when we're about to launch a new operation and you're being shady as fuck." I shot back. "Where the hell were you tonight, Tommy? Why weren't you answering your phone—until I sent you the 9-1-1 text, that is. What is going on?"

Tommy's features blanked out. "It's nothing to do with you or the clan. You don't need to worry about it."

"Oh, I don't need to worry about it, but you can tell Misha, is that it?" I shoved his chest, but Tommy barely moved. "We're supposed to be partners, you ass."

"Where is this coming from? Wait—Misha was here?"

"Oh, he was here all right," I scoffed. "Looking for you. Saying some cryptic shit about consequences coming back to bite you in the ass and how you need to watch your back. But when I asked him what he meant, he just said I needed to ask you. Because, apparently, he's the one you go to now when you're in trouble."

Tommy sighed and scrubbed a hand across his mouth. "Sloane, it's not like that."

"Then what is it like, exactly? Because it sounds like my *partner*, my *friend*, is holding out on me."

Tommy flinched at the word friend. It was small, but it was there. "I'm not in trouble, Sloane. I've got it under control."

"Sounds like it."

"Don't be like that."

I crossed my arms and glared at him, and he glared right back. My chest heaved with unspent anger and frustration. Tommy's eyes dipped down to my mouth, my breasts, and back up, and I almost slugged him. Instead, I took a step back.

"You still don't trust me. All that bullshit about being partners, it was all just lip service. Wasn't it?" I shook my head. "I'll always be that little girl on the beach with the daisies in her hair to you, won't I, Tommy? Poor little Sloane wants to play with the big boys. Let's take pity on her, throw her a bone, and maybe she'll go away."

"Sloane—"

"Fuck you, Tommy." I started to walk away, but then I whirled back at him. "You know what? You can keep your fucking partnership and shove it up your ass. I don't need handouts from you. You were running this clan into the ground before I came along and pulled us out of the hole you'd dug. I did that. Not you.

"And the thing is, you're capable of so much more than you realize. The only reason we were falling apart was because of your selfishness and your absolute refusal to let anyone help you. But you had me fooled, didn't you? I thought you'd changed. I thought we were friends. I thought—"

I broke off, my voice catching in my throat. Tommy continued to stare stonily at me like he was facing down a firing squad.

"I thought that you actually valued my contributions," I continued, "I thought you valued me as a *person*, but that was just another fucking lie to placate me, wasn't it? Because at the end of the day, you're holding out on me and I'm left holding the bag. You confide in Misha, someone who self-admittedly has only his own interests at heart, but you can't show me the same respect. It hurts, Tommy. It really hurts. And I am so goddamn sick and tired of being nothing more than a nuisance around here."

Tommy exhaled heavily. "Sloane, that's not true. I don't think of you that way."

"Oh, come off it, Tommy," I spat. "The only way you think of me is on my back, legs spread. Some things never change, I guess."

Tommy paled. He looked like I'd just stabbed him in the heart. He opened his mouth, closed it, and stared at the ground.

I'd had enough. I turned and walked back towards the bar. Tommy didn't stop me.

Just before I was out of earshot, I turned my head and said over my shoulder, "Oh, and by the way. Volkov accepted the deal. Congrats, *partner*."

I worked the rest of my shift and sent Kat home when the bar closed down at one in the morning. I was exhausted. Mentally, physically, and emotionally. Tommy hadn't come back to Lady D's. I didn't know where he was, and for the first time, I didn't care.

Across the city, the fireworks and cannons had been fired from Hatch Memorial Shell as the festivities ended, and the city settled down to sleep off the hangover. Only this time, the relative quiet of the early morning hours were underscored with unease. Maybe it was the inevitable wind-down after a raucous party, or maybe it was our own version of fireworks that had been set off in the alley between Tommy and me.

I felt bad. Don't get me wrong—Tommy had it coming—but I'd been pretty harsh with him. The look on his face had been unexpected. I thought he'd throw it right back at me like he used to, tease me and taunt me and push every single one of my buttons, but instead, he just stood there and took it. Like he expected it. Deserved it, even.

I shook my head. Whatever. I was still pissed, and I'd drawn a line in the sand. I was done being treated with anything less than equality by any member of this clan, Tommy included. And if he didn't like how that sounded on paper, he could kiss my ass.

Taking my time, I didn't end up locking the front doors until nearly two, but I still didn't go home. Instead, I walked upstairs to my father's old office. Scratch that; it was Tommy's office, now.

Not much had changed. The same worn, leather wing chairs bracketed the desk, and the same dingy window looked out over D Street. I wondered when the last time the window was opened. The room still stank of cigarettes.

Absently, I pawed through the desk drawers, but I didn't find anything interesting. Nothing in the bookshelf or the safe. I didn't know what I expected to find. Whatever Tommy was hiding, he was keeping it locked down tight.

"What is going on with you, Tommy?" I sighed and sank down on the low settee against the wall. I remembered napping on it when I was a kid.

Tommy was giving me whiplash. One second, he was his same, douchebag self, misogynistic and arrogant. The next, he was sweet and vulnerable and looking at me like I hung the moon and the stars. Like I was someone he respected.

Someone he could even love.

I stood abruptly, poured myself a bourbon from the stash in the desk, and plopped back down on the settee. After a second thought, I took the bottle with me. "Oh, get over yourself," I said aloud. "Do you even hear how you sound right now?"

I downed my drink in one gulp and poured another. Downed that one, too. I was a hopeless romantic, but I was okay with that. God only knew where I got it from. My father was about as romantic as a Saturday Night Special, but I'd always held out hope for my own happily ever after. Not the Disneyesque princess-singing-from-a-hilltop version, but one where I found someone who not only loved me for who I was, but who also respected me.

The feelings I had for Tommy were dangerous. I liked Tommy a lot, and today had been such a bitter disappointment. I really thought he was changing, but today just proved that Tommy was incapable of truly loving someone.

Other than himself, that is. That had always been apparent.

Feeling broken hearted and sullen, I finished my drink. I'd had just enough to make me sleepy, and the settee was far too comfortable to even consider making the effort to get up and take the T back to my sad little apartment. I'd get a few hours of sleep, then go home in the morning. Hopefully I wouldn't see Tommy for the rest of the weekend.

I curled up on the couch and pulled my jacket over me like a blanket. I was asleep almost before my head hit the pillow.

I was sleeping so soundly, I didn't even wake when smoke began to seep under the office door two hours later.

16

Tommy

"What the hell, man?" I shoved Misha.

He slammed back against the double row of lockers. After Sloane's verbal evisceration behind Lady D's, I called Misha and demanded to meet him at Big Saul's.

"If you want a fight, I suggest we step into the ring," he winced.

"Here is fine. What I wasn't to know is what in God's name possessed you to tell her that."

"Tell her what?"

I grabbed his shirt collar and pressed him against the lockers. "Don't be smart. I ain't in the mood."

Misha was quiet, looking at me with that cool, appraising way of his like I didn't have him hoisted six inches off the ground. Then he spoke. "Your girlfriend—"

"She's not my girlfriend."

"Would you like me to continue, or not? *Da?* Well then. Your not-girlfriend was smart enough to notice that you have not been around much. She was concerned. So I voiced some concerns of my own."

I let Misha's feet return to the floor, but I didn't release him completely. "I want to know what you said to her. Exact words, Misha."

He let out a long-suffering breath and muttered something in Russian. "I told Sloane that you needed to watch your back because there are some people in this town that do not forgive old wounds so easily. That was all the information I gave her. Beyond that, I said she would have to ask you."

"Oh, she warned me all right. She was fucking pissed that I went to you instead of her."

"Why didn't you?"

"Because I'm trying to keep her safe!" I slammed my fist into the locker next to Misha's head, and it gave a satisfying *boom!* Misha, to his credit, didn't even flinch. "If I told Sloane about Dominic, then she would make it her personal mission to hunt him down."

"Just like you are doing?"

"Yes—I mean, no." I released him and stepped back, scrubbing a hand down my face. "Look, I trust Sloane with my life. She's wicked smart, she's better with a gun than half the guys, and she can hold her own in the fight. But Dominic is fucking crazy. And that was before we killed his father and his brother. Now..."

Sloane hadn't been in that room with him like I had. She hadn't seen the pure enjoyment he took at taking someone apart and making them suffer. Just an overgrown bully ripping the wings off butterflies. Sloane would go in there hard-charging like she always did, but if Dominic ever got his hands on her, the fallout would be biblical.

I clutched at my hair. What a mess. I'd hurt Sloane. Badly. She thought I didn't trust her. Didn't respect her. She filed me away with the rest of the assholes who for her entire life had told her that the only thing she was worthy of was slinging drinks from behind a bar.

"You don't trust her." There was Misha, cutting right to the heart of things as always.

"I do, but—"

"But not with this." He shook his head. "Sloane is a strong woman. Prideful. But she is not stupid. Perhaps you should have trusted her with this, no?"

I sighed heavily. "Maybe."

I left him standing by the lockers and walked over to the ring. Leaned my forearms on the ropes and tried to parse a way out of this mess that didn't involve pissing off Sloane more than I already had.

"Have you heard anything from the Italians?" The only reason I'd told Misha was because the man had one ear to the ground and a finger in every pot in Boston. If anything was brewing, he'd know.

"I don't hear much from the North End these days," he said, smoothing out the wrinkles in his shirt. "They are still quite upset over what happened last summer."

"Where you showed up and saved our bacon."

Misha grunted and suppressed a smile at the pun. The last shoot-out had been in a slaughterhouse.

I turned back to him and shoved my hands in my pockets, my anger at Misha dissolving. It wasn't like I'd told him about the photographs and my suspicions about my father's death in confidence. He'd just been looking out for me.

“Sloane also said that Volkov accepted the deal,” I said. “Even without the seaport? Just like that?”

“Just like that. It is how we negotiate in Russia. Demand the moon and see what happens.”

“You mean, I called his bluff.”

He shrugged. “Volkov knew he’d never get access to the seaport. It was worth a try, anyway.”

I nodded. I could respect that, I guess. “When does he want to meet?”

“Volkov has a house outside the city. We can drive up there tomorrow.”

My cell phone rang, cutting him off. Thinking it might be Sloane, I checked the caller ID, but it was only Grady. I almost didn’t answer it, but at the last second, I swiped up.

“This better be earth-shattering, Grady—”

My master-at-arms interrupted me, breathless. “Where are you?”

“At Big Saul’s, why?”

“Is Sloane with you?”

Unease clenched my gut. “No.”

“Have you seen her at all tonight?”

“Just earlier at the bar.” I gripped the phone tightly. “Grady, what the hell is going on?”

“Someone set the bar on fire. The new alarm system notified me, but the sprinkler’s never went off. I just got down here, and it’s...oh, God, Tommy, it’s bad, and nobody can find Sloane—”

“What do you mean, you can’t find her?” I became aware of noise in the background behind Grady’s tinny voice: shouts, sirens, and a dull, crackling roar.

"She won't answer her phone. I sent some guys to her apartment, but there was no answer, and the fire department is having a hard time gaining access to the bar." Grady was nearly sobbing, now. "Oh, Christ, Tommy, was she still in there?"

I didn't answer. I wasn't sure if I even hung up. I shoved the phone in my pocket and was out the front doors before my feet even registered what they were doing, my mind a static blank of blind fear.

"Tommy!" Misha was on my heels. "What happened?"

"Somebody set the bar on fire, and Sloane is missing."

He paled. "I'm coming with you. We'll take my car."

The flames could be seen from three blocks away. Two fire engines and a ladder truck from City Point EMS blocked the street around Lady Devine's, and a cordon had been set up around the entire block to keep the crowd back.

The bar was gutted. Great gouts of flame spewed from the ground floor despite the hoses trying to battle them back, and smoke poured from the first and second floors. Even from where I stood, the heat was hellish, the smoke making my eyes water and my throat tight.

Sloane could be in there.

Misha went one way, and I went the other, searching the crowd. Blood roared in my ears, my heart beating way too fast, drowning out the inferno. Every call I'd placed to Sloane had gone to voicemail. Just like Grady had said.

She couldn't still be in there. She couldn't.

Oh, God, Sloane. Where are you?

"Sloane!" I choked on the smoke and my own fear, shoving civilians out of the way as I pushed towards the safety cordon. "Sloane!"

Hands pushed me back, professional and firm. "Sir, you can't go past the line."

"That's my bar! That's—Sloane might still be in there!"

"Hey, pal, you need to calm down."

"Why isn't anyone checking the building?" I panted, forcing my way through the dense knot of hands trying to hold me back. "Send somebody in there—"

"Let him through." A stout, grizzled man in turnout gear grabbed me by the arm and hauled me towards one of the engine trucks. His helmet said Captain on it. "This your bar, son?"

"Yes, and you need to send someone in. My friend's still in there."

His face fell. "I'm sorry, but the building's unstable. It's not safe to send my guys in there."

I felt like I was going to throw up. I couldn't breathe. "But—"

"Ladder Company 12 hauled someone out earlier, though, and so if you just sit tight for a minute, I'll go check for you."

The compassion in his voice was nearly killing me. Weakly, I nodded, and let hands guide me to a seat on the fire engine's rear bumper.

She has to be okay. She has to be. Please, God, if there is anyone up there, please let her be okay. I can't live without her. I won't survive—

Through the smoke, I saw the Fire Captain jogging back to me. His eyes looked tired, but he had a smile on his face. "Your friend's name is Sloane? Sloane McTiernan?"

"Y-Yes." I shot to my feet.

He pointed down the block. "She's about fifty yards that way with EMS. A little smoke inhalation, but she's going to be okay, son."

I blurted out a hasty thanks and sprinted in the direction he pointed. An ambulance was parked at the curb.

"Sloane! *Sloane!*"

There were too many figures crowded around the back of the ambulance to see who was inside. I probably looked like a crazed maniac, charging down the street like a raging bull and yelling my head off, but I didn't care. She was all that mattered.

"Woah, there." A paramedic stepped in front of me, his hands raised. He was a pretty big guy, but I was bigger. Judging by how wide his eyes were, he didn't have a prayer of holding me back, and he knew it. "Are you Tommy?"

"Yeah. Is Sloane—"

"We've got her. She's been asking for you."

"How bad is she?" I side-stepped him, but he kept pace.

"We're about to transport her, but she's going to be okay. Just take a deep breath and calm down, okay, big guy?"

I growled at him, and he backed off. Like hell was he going to keep me from Sloane.

I finally pushed past the last few medics congregating around the back of the ambulance, and I saw her.

Sloane was laying on a gurney in the back with an oxygen mask over her nose and mouth, and her eyes were closed. Her skin was smudged with soot. Blood spattered her right arm and down her shirt.

"Sloane!" At the sound of my voice, her eyes fluttered open, searching, unfocused, before landing on me. Beneath the clear mask, I saw her lips twitch up in a faint smile, and she stretched her fingers towards me.

Before anyone could object, I bulled my way into the back of the ambulance and took her hand, grasping it tightly. "I'm here, honey. I'm here. You're going to be okay."

Her eyes were already drifting shut again. I pulled her hand to my lips and kissed her knuckles.

"How bad is she?" I asked the paramedic in the back with me, a young woman with blond hair pulled back into a ponytail.

"Ms. McTiernan has moderate smoke inhalation, her oxygen count's a little low, so we're going to take her to Boston Medical Center to get checked out. They're probably keep her overnight to monitor her, but she's young and healthy. She'll be back on her feet before you know it."

The paramedic placed a sympathetic hand on my shoulder, and I closed my eyes in relief. "What happened to her arm?"

"She was trapped on the second floor, in an office. The fire started fast and was out of control before we arrived; the fire suppression system malfunctioned. The window was jammed shut, so Ms. McTiernan broke the windowpane so she could signal to fire and rescue, and the glass cut her arm up. Nothing too serious, maybe worth a stitch or two. She's a brave woman."

I nodded blindly, brushed her bangs back, and kissed Sloane's sooty forehead. "You did good, baby. You're going to be okay."

"Sir, we need to transport her," a paramedic at my elbow was asking. "You can follow the ambulance to Boston Medical Center, but we need to leave now."

"I'm not leaving her."

"There's not enough room," the paramedic protested.

I felt my anger start to rise. I was about to go nuclear, but then Misha appeared out of nowhere, gently tugging me out of the back of the ambulance and away from Sloane with quietly murmured Russian.

"Let them work, my friend. You will only get in the way."

"Sloane—"

"Needs them more than she needs you right now, Tommy. Let her go."

His words were harsh, but they were what I needed to hear. I let Misha pull me back onto the sidewalk as the paramedics buttoned up the back of the ambulance and it pulled away from the curb, lights flashing.

I turned back towards Lady Devine's. Flames were now licking up the second floor and onto the third.

"Are you all right?" Misha asked gently.

"No." I swallowed thickly. "I'm not."

"The firefighters said it looks like arson."

"Looks like."

"Was this your boy Dominic's handiwork, do you think?"

I nodded. Now the terror and adrenaline were beginning to recede, leaving me with a black hole of rage in the center of my chest. "This was Dom's handiwork. I know it was."

The entire night seemed surreal. First that blowout with Sloane, and now this. God—what if that had been our last words? What if I never got the chance to explain, to apologize? What if Sloane hadn't woken up in time, what if she hadn't been able to break the window...

What if, what if, what if.

This had been close. Too close. As it was, irreparable damage had been done.

My father had been murdered. Lady Devine's was gone. Sloane had almost been killed.

But revenge would have to take a back seat for the moment. Sloane was hurt, and that was my fault. Right now, she needed me.

"I need to go the hospital," I said.

"I know." Misha held up his keys. "I'll drive."

17

Sloane

I've never been admitted to the hospital before. Never had to go to the emergency room, not even urgent care. With how wild my childhood had been, that was a minor miracle. No broken bones, sickness, not even an ear infection. I'd always been the one visiting others in the hospital, plastering on a face of sympathetic understanding while secretly glad it wasn't me.

I did not like being on this end of things. Poking, prodding, one million repetitive questions—loads of fun when you can barely breathe, let alone talk—and all I wanted to do was sleep and forget the horrible look on Tommy's face when he found me in the back of the ambulance.

Hours after the three-ring circus that was the emergency room triage center, I was finally admitted up to a general room. By some minor miracle, I'd somehow missed seeing Cassidy or Jerome. I wasn't sure if they were working tonight, but I was glad to avoid them all the same. I never would have heard the end of it. Cassidy meant well, but I didn't think my frayed nerves would've been able to withstand her fussing. Connor was a saint to put up with it.

The oxygen mask had been changed out for a length of tubing beneath my nose. IV, monitors, and a dozen beeping, whining things that were going to make it impossible to get any sleep. Despite my protests, they had admitted me overnight for observation, which was ridiculous. I was perfectly fine, other than a bone rattling cough and a dozen stiches in my arm. I told the nurse that much, but she just patted my hand patronizingly and told me to get some rest. How anyone was supposed to sleep with this much racket was beyond me.

But despite my foul mood, I ended up falling asleep quickly. I was exhausted. The last thing I remembered was contemplating how far I'd get if I made a break for it, and I was out.

I awoke several hours later to the grey dawn filtering through the blinds and Cassidy frowning at me from the foot of the bed.

I quickly shut my eyes, but it was too late.

"I know you're awake, Sloane, so you can stop faking."

I cracked open an eyelid. "I was hoping you'd go away."

"Fat chance," she smirked. "I heard you've been giving the nurses a hard time. How are you feeling?"

"I'm perfectly fine," I said, struggling to sit up straighter in bed. The movement loosened a rasping cough from deep in my chest, betraying me. Damnit.

Cassidy cocked an eyebrow. "Oh, yeah. You sound great. You're lucky to be alive, you know."

"I know," I scowled at her and picked at the scratchy hospital blanket. "How did you find out I was here, anyway?"

"There's a pissed off Irishman down in the waiting area right now, giving the staff hell for not letting him up to see you."

"Tommy?"

Cassidy nodded. She lowered herself into a nearby chair, sighing gratefully and kicking her feet up onto my bed. With a faint smile, I noticed that she was just beginning to show.

"How long has Tommy been down there?"

"All night. I didn't let him up because I wasn't sure where things stood between you two."

Where things stood. It should have been a simple enough question, but it wasn't. Our relationship had always been undefinable and had rarely been simple. An on again, off again friendship. Coworkers. Rivals. Partners. An unrequited crush and brief, lust-filled thoughts. There wasn't any firm foundation to be had, nothing I could hold onto and name. Even now, after that blowout of a fight—which I was still angry about—the thought that Tommy had spent the entire night in the waiting room was more than I cared to think about. I was afraid to see what was down that rabbit hole, or how far I'd fall if I looked too deeply.

"He was really here all night?" I asked quietly.

Cassidy nodded, looking at me levelly. "He refused to leave, even after they told him you were all right. Visiting hours were over, and they said you were resting, but he's been parked down there ever since, glowering at the nurses like an overgrown kid throwing a tantrum. It would be funny if it wasn't so..."

She looked down at her lap. Cassidy seemed to be deciding whether to tell me something. Finally, she raised her head and looked me square in the eyes. "Tommy's not doing great. He is not okay, and I don't think he has been for a long time."

I nodded. I had thought as much myself, but hearing it from his sister was sobering.

“This thing with you seems to have pushed him over the edge. I’ve never seen him like this. He was frantic when he found you, and now that he can't see you, it's worse."

"Cassidy, I—"

"He loves you, Sloane. Don’t you see that? That man loves you more than anything in this world. He would do anything for you. But he just doesn’t know how to show it. I know, because I can be the same way. The way we were raised, after Mom died...let’s just say we weren’t encouraged to share our feelings. Tommy’s a byproduct of that."

I was stunned. Stunned into silence, because I didn’t know what to say. Because I was pretty sure she was right, and that terrified me.

"I know it’s not an excuse for past behavior,” she continued. “Tommy is an ass, but he's my brother . He has a good heart somewhere underneath all the bravado and ego, but he keeps it locked up tight. Sometimes I’m not even convinced he thinks he has a heart at all. If you feel even a fraction of what he does for you, then you need to talk to him. He needs to know."

"He doesn't trust me—"

"That's bullshit, and you know it," she snapped. "You know what happened last summer, what Dominic did to him. What he’s lost. You know why he's like this, and if you're going to sit here and give me some bullshit excuse about why you can’t even talk to him about this, then you aren't the person I thought you were."

"Tommy is incapable of loving anyone except himself. He thinks with his dick, not his heart. Always has. Whatever he feels from me isn't love, it's lust. I need more than that. I'm not afraid to admit it, Cassidy. I'm not you."

She let that barb slide and said nothing, her face pensive. She stared at her feet, which were propped up on the bed. "That's an excuse, and you know it. Your infatuation with Alfie wasn't about love—"

"That was different."

"Let me finish. Alfie was your distraction. It was convenient and easy. You knew you two could never work out. You weren't in love with him, but he was there. He was familiar. Comfortable. Safe."

"That's not—"

"Tommy's not safe, Sloane. You and I both know it. He's everything you shouldn't want, but you do anyway. You're so busy worrying about what everyone else will think of you that you're making excuses not to see what's right in front of your face." She sighed heavily and got to her feet. "Look. Ultimately, I don't care what you do. It's your heart, and I have no right to tell you who to open it up to. But for better or worse, Tommy is my brother, and I've got to look out for him. Talk to him or not, it's up to you. Just don't lead him on. Don't give him hope where there isn't any."

She walked over to the door, pausing when she got there. "I'm glad you're okay, Sloane. I'm also sorry about the bar."

I snorted. "You hated that place."

"Maybe, but it meant something to you, and I'm sorry you had to lose it like that. What are you going to do?"

"Rebuild, I guess," I shrugged. I hadn't given it much thought.

Cassidy shook her head. "That's not what I meant."

I knew that wasn't what she meant. I was stalling. I took a deep breath. "You can send him in."

Cassidy smiled faintly and nodded. "Thank you."

She slipped out the door, and I closed my eyes, steadying myself for the confrontation that was about to happen.

Seconds later, the door opened again. I kept my eyes shut, giving Tommy the chance to see me without having to deal with my reaction. I heard him hesitate by the door, then he crept across the room to my bedside. I felt the warmth of his body, smelled the spice of his cologne, and I knew he was inches away.

I cracked open an eyelid and looked up at him.

He looked like hell. His dark hair was mussed, and his eyes were bloodshot, the skin around them tight. A heavy growth of stubble darkened his jawline, and he looked like he hadn't slept in a week. His clothes were rumpled, and there was a coffee stain on the front of his shirt.

"Sloane." The relief in his voice was palpable. He dropped into the chair Cassidy had vacated and reached for me. His hands fluttered for a second, unsure, then aborted course to settle in his lap, knuckles white and clenched.

"Hey." My voice came out rough, barely more than a croak. I cleared my throat and tried again. "Hey, Tommy."

Tommy's eyes carefully skirted mine, flitting up to the monitors like a trapped animal, wild and skittish. Carefully taking in every number, every line and tube like he was filing information away for later. His fists tightened, and he nodded to himself, a muscle ticking in his jaw.

"You scared the shit out of me," he breathed. "Don't you ever do that again, you hear me?"

"It wasn't exactly my idea of a fun time, either," I said dryly.

The corner of his mouth quirked up in a faint smile, but it disappeared as quickly as it had come. He shifted in his seat, his body language tense and uncertain.

"How are you feeling?" he asked quietly.

"I'm fine."

"You almost weren't."

I sighed. I didn't have the energy to fight with Tommy. Not here. Not now. Not with everything else going on.

"The bar is gone," I said instead.

Tommy looked away, his gaze distant. "Yeah."

"Any idea what happened?"

"We've got some ideas."

"Are you going to tell me?"

"Not right now."

"Why not?"

"Because I don't want you to get involved."

That old anger flared in me, white hot. "I think I'm involved at this point, Tommy. My bar just burned down, and you're sitting there acting all cagey—"

"That's because I know what happened, and I'm trying to keep you out of it!" he snapped, body tense. "Why can't you understand that? This is serious. It's not just a game anymore. Don't you get that?"

"No, I don't get it! All I've done is try to help you, Tommy. I've always tried to help you, and you keep pushing me away. Why won't you let me in?"

"Because I can't protect you if you're in the middle of it!"

"I'm already in the middle of it, you moron! You can't keep me locked away in a tower somewhere, Tommy. I'm not a damsel in distress."

"I know that!"

"Then why—" I broke off into a coughing fit. Tommy paled and reached for me.

“Sloane, honey, breathe. Just breathe.” Gently, he pushed me back into the bed and fussed with the oxygen line, his hand gripping the bed rail in distress. “Something's wrong. I'm calling the nurse—”

“Don't...do that,” I wheezed, trying to calm myself down. “I'll be okay in a minute.”

“Nothing about this is okay. You can't even breathe—”

I took his hand in mine and brought it to my chest so he could feel my heart beating. That seemed to calm us both, and after a moment, the tightness in my chest eased. Tommy matched his breathing to mine, his eyes latched on my face like he was afraid I was about to disappear.

"I can't lose you, Sloane," he said miserably.

My mouth snapped shut. Tommy closed his eyes and sank back into the chair, rubbing a hand over his face. "I can't lose you like I lost Aiden. Like I almost lost Connor. And Cassidy. I can't lose another person I—"

He broke off, swallowing thickly. He sat quietly for a moment, his gaze fixed on the linoleum floor. Then he raised his head to look at me. The expression on his face was devastating. "I need you, Sloane. I've always needed you. You're the one good thing left in my life, and if something were to happen to you..." He took a shuddering breath. "I wouldn't be able to live with myself."

My anger evaporated. The admission seemed to take a physical toll on him. He was exhausted, mentally and physically. Defeated. And I hadn't even noticed. Or maybe I had, and I just didn't want to see it. I had been so angry at him, so hurt. "Tommy..."

"I don't know what I'm supposed to do," he said, his voice low and full of pain. "I don't know how to protect you, and I don't know how to keep you safe. You're too independent for that. I love that about you, but it's driving me crazy. I don't want to do this without you. Please, Sloane."

I laced our fingers together. I felt the tension in his body, his desperation. "Then trust me. Stop shutting me out."

I chose to ignore his confession. Cassidy was wrong. Tommy was just in shock. He was hurting, and I had a feeling that whatever he felt for me, it wasn't love. It was an attachment, a dependency. He wanted someone who made him feel less alone, but he didn't know how to show it. Cassidy had gotten that right, at least.

Tommy leaned forward in his chair, his eyes bright with emotion. He brushed the hair back from my forehead, his fingertips gentle on my skin. His gaze was soft and full of longing. "I do trust you, Sloane. More than I trust myself." He laughed depreciatingly. "I've made such a mess out of things."

I squeezed his hand. "It's not too late to fix it."

Tommy went quiet, staring at the bank of monitors by the bed. Down the lines and tubes attached to my body, his expression growing somber and cold. He was withdrawing again, putting that wall back up.

I nudged him with my foot. "Hey. Where'd you go?"

He shook his head. "I'm right here. I just—I need to tell you something."

"Okay."

Tommy took a deep breath and looked me square in the eyes. "My father was murdered. He didn't die of pancreatic cancer."

I blinked. I was too tired to process that bombshell. "Wait, what?"

"The night my dad died. It wasn't cancer that killed him."

"But Cassidy said he—"

"I know what she said. She thinks he died from complications related to the cancer. But he didn't. Dominic Moretti killed him."

Silence settled over the room, thick and viscous enough to choke on. "Dominic is dead, Tommy," I whispered.

"They never found the body."

I struggled to sit upright in bed. The monitor by the bed beeped in protest, and Tommy pushed be back down, stopping me. "Why are you telling me this now? Why didn't you tell me before?"

"I told you. I didn't want to drag you into it. You're already in danger."

Quickly, he told me about the photographs he'd received. The threats. Luca's warning. Tommy's words spilled out faster and faster as he spoke, his anger and fear taking shape. "Dominic is trying to send me a message,

Sloane. He wants me to suffer. He wants to make me feel what he felt. If he can get to my family, he can get to you."

I gaped at him. "Did you tell Cassidy?"

"Not yet."

"You need to tell her. She and Connor aren't safe, either, if Dominic's after them, too."

"I know."

I stared at the rumpled sheets. Everything was happening so fast.

"What are you going to do?" I asked.

"I'm going to kill him." There was no hesitation, no doubt. Just cold, hard determination.

"That's not a plan, Tommy," I said quietly. "That's revenge. There's a difference."

"Yeah, well, I don't much care right now. He burned down your bar, Sloane. He almost killed you. He killed my father. He's going to pay for that."

"And what will that get you? Revenge never solves anything."

"It's not just for me. It's for you. For Connor and Cassidy and everyone else that son of a bitch has hurt."

"Killing him won't bring back my bar or your father."

His mouth tightened. "Maybe not. But it'll make me feel better."

I knew Tommy well enough to know there would be no arguing with him. He was on a mission, and he wasn't going to listen to reason. "Then at least let me help you."

He shook his head. "I told you—"

"You're going to need help," I cut him off. "You can't take down Dominic and his men alone."

"I've got Misha."

"Misha is one man," I said gently. "It's not enough."

Tommy's eyes narrowed. "I don't want you in the middle of this, Sloane. I've already lost so much, and I won't lose you, too."

I could see the worry in his eyes, the fear, but I couldn't back down. Not when he needed me. Not when I needed him. "And I don't want lose you. You're my friend, Tommy. So please, let me help you."

Tommy flinched at the word friend, but he took my hand in his own and nodded. "Fine. But you have to promise me you'll do what I say. That you will listen to me, even if you don't agree. I can't keep you safe if we're not on the same page, understand?"

"I can't promise I'll like it."

That got a smile out of him, boyishly adorable and igniting a bloom of warmth in my belly. "I'd expect nothing less."

I looked at our joined hands. I was still angry about the way he'd treated me, but I couldn't keep running away from it. From him. If he needed my help, then I was going to give it. And if I had to put up with his bullheaded stubbornness to do it, then so be it. "Friends?"

Tommy's eyes softened, and he raised my hand to his lips. "Friends."

He reached into his pocket, rooting around for something, and when he found it, a blush of color darkened his cheeks.

He pulled out a single daisy and laid it in my palm.

My heart gave a painful squeeze. The flower was slightly crushed and worse for wear, but it was perfect all the same.

"Peace offering," he said.

Daisy chains on the beach, sand between our toes. The sea at our backs and his hand in mine.

"See? We're friends now. I'm Sloane."

"I'm Tommy."

"You remembered," I murmured.

Tommy smiled crookedly, and my heart somersaulted. "How could I ever forget?"

I reached over and wrapped my arms around his neck, hugging him tightly. Tommy stiffened in surprise, then relaxed. His arms came up and held me against him. I buried my face in his neck and took a deep breath, inhaling his scent. Spice, soap, the lingering traces of smoke in his clothes. His body heat seeped into me, chasing away the chill that had crept into my bones. Tommy tightened his arms, pulling me closer. I could feel his heart beating under my cheek, steady and strong. Safe.

"Thank you," I whispered.

"For what?"

"Trusting me. And for staying tonight to check on me."

Tommy pulled back so he could look at me. He smiled, the expression in his eyes soft and tender, and brushed the hair back from my forehead. "Anytime, Sloane."

He leaned forward, and for a second, I thought he was going to kiss me. But at the last moment, he tilted his chin up, his lips landing on my forehead, instead. The touch of his lips sent sparks through my body, but it was different than what I'd felt before. It was something more. Something deeper.

He kissed my forehead again, then pulled away. I tried not to show my disappointment, or how even a chaste kiss like that had affected me. Instead, I held up the daisy.

"Where did you get this, anyway?" I asked.

Tommy looked sheepish. "There was a bunch of flowers at the end of the hall. I saw the daisy and thought of you."

"You stole it?" I tried not to laugh.

"Don't call the cops on me, okay?"

I smiled and tucked the daisy behind my ear. "You know, you're a lot sweeter than people give you credit for. They see the tattoos and the attitude and the bad boy persona, but underneath it all, you're just a big marshmallow."

Tommy grinned wickedly and leaned back in his chair, stretching out his long legs and crossing his ankles. He propped his hands behind his head and looked at me with a glint in his eye. "And you're my little spitfire."

I smiled back, but it quickly morphed into a yawn. Tommy saw it and got to his feet, tugging the sheets and blankets up around me. "You should try to get some more sleep."

"You should, too."

Tommy hesitated, then dropped another kiss on my forehead. "I'll be back later. Get some rest."

He slipped out of the room and shut the door behind him, leaving me alone with my thoughts. My hand crept up to my temple, my fingers brushing against the soft petals of Tommy's daisy.

18

Tommy

THREE DAYS LATER, SLOANE and I stood at the ruins of Lady Devine's and watched the fire investigator coil up his crime scene tape so the insurance adjuster could do his thing. The entire block was a mess. A couple of cars had been burned, the bar, and the two shops next door. It looked like a war zone, all charred bricks and broken glass.

So far we had been able to keep the police out of it. The fire was ruled arson, not that it took the investigator much to figure that out. Starting in the keg room with clear pour patterns out into the bar and up the stairs, the fire had burned hot and fast, designed to being about maximum destruction as quickly as possible. An inspection of the fire suppression system showed the relay for the sprinklers had been cut. Someone wanted to make sure Lady D's burned to the ground.

Less clear was if the arsonist had known that Sloane had been upstairs in her father's old office. She said she'd fallen asleep on the couch and hadn't woken until smoke had begun to seep in beneath the closed door. The audible alarm never went off. Sloane had tried the door, which hadn't been locked, but the wood was hot to the touch so she didn't open it. Smart girl. The investigator said that decision probably saved her life.

For the millionth time today, I felt a dizzying wave of relief wash over me, followed quickly by terror. If Sloane hadn't been such a light sleeper...if she had opened the door...if she hadn't thought to break the window to signal to the ladder truck...

That night might have ended differently.

Sloane stood next to me with her hands stuffed into her jean pockets, watching the proceedings solemnly. Bandages peeked out from beneath her tee shirt. She had gotten lucky, but the look on her face told me she wasn't feeling very lucky at the moment.

I took a step closer and let our arms brush. It was still almost a shock to see her standing next to me. I kept having flashbacks to finding her in the back of the ambulance, thinking she might be dead, and my heart squeezed painfully.

The thought of losing Sloane was unfathomable.

She leaned into my touch and sighed heavily. "I can't believe it's gone."

"It's just a building."

"Not to me, it wasn't."

"You're more important." I put my arm around her shoulders and tugged her to my side, holding her tightly against me. I wanted to keep her safe, protected, hidden away somewhere so nothing could touch her. But that was impossible, so I'd settle for second best. "We'll rebuild. Better than before, this time. A new bar for a new era, right? Just like we talked about."

Sloane nodded. I knew it was a lot to take in. Her world had changed so quickly. She'd lost her home away from home, the bar her grandfather had built. Her livelihood. And now we had a madman to hunt down. It wasn't the ending either of us had expected, but at least we were together.

"Come on." I steered Sloane down the sidewalk towards my car. "Let's get you out of here. You need to go home and rest, and I have a few things to take care of."

Sloane frowned, digging in her heels. "I don't want to rest. There's so much to do."

She started back towards the bar and was about to duck inside, but I grabbed her arm, stopping her. "Don't. It's not safe. There's still pieces falling from the ceiling, broken glass and fallen bricks to trip you up, and that smoke won't be good for your lungs. The doctor said—"

"I know what he said," Sloane snapped. She looked away from me, her mouth a thin line, her eyes shiny. Her throat worked as she swallowed, trying to regain control of her emotions.

Christ. I had never seen Sloane cry a day in my life, and seeing her look like she was about to now made my chest ache. I wanted to pull her into my arms and tell her that everything would be okay, but I knew she wouldn't appreciate that. Hell, she'd probably sock me in the mouth.

"Sloane..."

She shook her head and started walking back down the sidewalk. I followed her, keeping pace easily with my longer stride. I didn't reach for her, didn't touch her. I knew she needed space. Sloane was a fighter, a survivor. She wouldn't let something like this knock her down. She'd be back on her feet soon enough, and I'd be there to support her when she did.

But only as a friend, I thought, that taunting voice laughing at me inside my head.

I pushed that voice aside. We *were* friends. That was what mattered. I'd told her as much in the hospital. She'd made it clear how she felt, and I respected that. I wasn't going to push her or try to convince her to change her mind. I didn't deserve her, and I knew it. If she could be happy without me, then I would have to be happy for her, even if I wasn't.

Because I knew one thing: Sloane was it for me. There would never be anyone else. I was doomed to chase her for the rest of my life. It was just the way things were. I couldn't be with her, but I would do everything I could to protect her, to keep her safe. It was the least I could do.

"Hey," I said as we got to the car. I unlocked the door for her, but she hesitated, her hand resting on the frame. She was staring at the bar, her eyes distant. "Talk to me."

"I can't stand this, Tommy. Being stagnant like this. I have to do something."

"We'll find him, Sloane. I promise."

She signed heavily. "I'm not talking about Dominic. This violence for violence—that's exactly what got us into this mess. We need to be focused on rebuilding. Yes, we got dealt a hard blow, but we can't go scrapping for a fight."

"Fighting is all I know how to do, Sloane," I said.

"Then maybe it's time you learned something new."

I took a deep breath. Revenge had always been my driving force, my motivation. You take a good one on the chin and you hit the bastard right back even harder. It was the way things had always been, generation after generation.

But it had also been what had gotten us into trouble so many times before.

"I'm not letting Dominic get away with this. He has to pay for what he's done. The bar. My father. You."

Sloane shook her head. "That's not enough. We have to show him that he's not going to win. He's not going to break us. We're better than that. Better than him. We've still got the plans for the new operation underway, so let's use them. Let's focus on something positive."

I looked down at her, my arms crossed over my chest. She was right, and I knew it. But it was a hell of a lot easier said than done. I'd been gunning for revenge for so long, it felt wrong to suddenly let it go.

"You're right." I said. "I know you are. But I can't just sit around and wait, either. Misha and I are going to meet with Volkov tonight, and I'm going to see what he knows about Dominic. I don't think he's going to tell me much, but it's worth a shot."

"Just be careful," Sloane said. "I don't trust him."

"I know. But he's pulled through for us so far, and we need his contacts in Moscow if we're going to make this work. Speaking of which, are you still up for tackling the suppliers today?"

Sloane nodded. "Absolutely."

I looked at her sternly. "You need to take it easy. I mean it."

"I know, I know." Sloane rolled her eyes. "I'll make Grady do all the heavy lifting, I promise."

"Good. Now go home. You need to rest."

"Fine." She climbed inside and slammed the door shut, looking mutinous.

"And Sloane?"

She leaned out the window and glared at me. "What?"

I gave her a small, crooked smile. "Be careful tonight, okay? I need you to stay safe."

She softened slightly and reached through the open window, resting her hand on my arm. "I promise."

I watched her drive away, then turned back to look at the remains of the bar. Smoke still curled up from the roofline, the acrid smell of burning chemicals stinging my nostrils. It was a loss, that was for sure. But we would rebuild. The McTiernan Clan would survive, and we would do it on our own terms.

Twin headlights cut through the gloom hovering over the rain slicked freeway. At the last minute, I'd offered to drive us up to Volkov's estate in Diana, a decision I was now regretting as the rain choked traffic put a serious damper on things.

I eased my foot off the accelerator as traffic slowed again, signaling a construction crew or a fender bender ahead.

Misha glanced up from his phone, where he'd been texting. "What is this?"

I leaned forward over the steering wheel, trying to see what was going on. "No idea. Friday night and everybody is trying to leave town at once. You know how it is."

We crawled forward a few more feet, then came to a complete stop. The car idled, the wipers sweeping back and forth on the windshield. Rain splashed down in thin sheets, turning everything grey and hazy.

"Maybe we should take a different route," Misha said. "Volkov does not like to be kept waiting."

"Yeah, well, we'll get there when we get there."

The traffic began moving again. I put the car into gear and inched forward. Up ahead, I saw the exit ramp to the next highway and made a split-second decision to take it, cutting off a minivan. The driver laid on the horn and flipped me the bird, but I ignored him. The ramp curved up onto the highway, and I eased us onto the roadway. Traffic was moving faster here, so I pressed down on the accelerator and began to pick up speed.

Volkov owned a large estate in the countryside on the outskirts of Quincy. It was secluded and heavily guarded, a good place for us to have this discussion. Volkov had always been a valuable ally, but lately I was starting to wonder if he was becoming an albatross around our necks. As far as I knew, nobody had ever seen the guy. So far, all our dealings with him had been conducted through Misha, and even then, he was slippery as an eel. Something felt off. I just didn't know what, yet.

The road curved through the woods, taking us away from the city. Here, the rain was lighter, so I cracked the windows to let some air in. I fiddled with the radio, trying to find a station that wasn't just commercials, then gave up. The silence stretched out, broken only by the wipers scraping across the windshield.

Finally, I couldn't stand it any longer.

"All right, so tell me about Volkov."

Misha looked at me, his expression bland. "What do you mean?"

"You know what I mean. Where did you meet him? What's he like? Does he ever leave that fucking mansion of his?"

Misha shook his head with a faint smile. "No, he does not."

"Then how does he run an organization like this? Doesn't he have to talk to people?"

"He has people to deal with the day-to-day operations, and he has me."

"And what, exactly, are you to him?"

Misha paused, thinking about it. "I suppose you could call me his right hand. Volkov is a private man, and he values his privacy above all else."

"Including his own men?"

Misha shrugged. "That is a price he is willing to pay for the way of life he has created. Many people want him dead. It is better this way."

I was quiet for a moment, processing that. I guess holing yourself up in a fortress was one way to dodge assassination attempts, but that was no way to live. I looked over at Misha, who was still staring out the window and watching the countryside flash by. I realized I knew next to nothing about his life. He was always around, but he didn't really exist outside the work we did together. "How long have you known Volkov?"

Misha turned to face me. His blue eyes were piercing and clear. "A very long time."

"Do you trust him?"

Misha thought about that for a moment. "Not always. But in the end, Volkov does what is best for Volkov. He is smart and cunning, but he will not betray us if it does not benefit him to do so."

"That's not much of an endorsement," I said dryly.

"No, but it is honest. That is more than many people can say."

I didn't like the sound of that, but it wasn't like I had any other options. "What about you? Any family over here? Friends? I mean, you basically know my entire life story by now."

Misha chuckled and shook his head. "I have a brother in Moscow. We speak sometimes, but we are not close. My parents are gone. There is no one else."

I frowned. "So what brought you here, then?"

Misha was silent for so long I thought he wasn't going to answer. He stared out the passenger side window, watching the trees go by.

"My father was a good man," he said finally. "He was honorable. Loyal to a fault. He always did what he thought was right, no matter what the consequences were. But there were some who were not so noble, and they took advantage of him. They used his honor against him and got him killed. The rest of my family was destroyed. My mother could not bear it, and my brother turned to drugs. I swore I would never be like them, and so I came here."

"Why here, though? Why come to America? Why work with Volkov?"

"I did not want to work for Volkov at first," he admitted. "But he offered me a chance to be something more than a soldier. He gave me purpose. He saved my life."

I didn't want to insult Misha, but I still didn't understand. "Why do you need someone else to give you purpose? You seem pretty capable of figuring that out on your own."

Misha smiled faintly. "When you have lived a life like mine, you begin to wonder what the point is. You become jaded, cynical. Life loses its meaning. But Aleksandr showed me that there is always another path. That even if you do not start out with a clear direction, there is always a way to find one. To be more than you are, to do more with your life than simply survive."

I thought about that for a moment, trying to relate. I'd never felt the need to look outside of myself, to rely on someone else. The Irish mob was my life, my family. I'd never needed anyone else. But then, I'd never had someone like Sloane in my life. We had been surviving for years, our families, but nothing more than that. Treading water. What Sloane was offering was more than that. It was a chance to live again, to really live. A chance at something more, something better.

"He gave you hope," I said.

"Yes. And a future."

We fell silent again. I knew what Sloane wanted, what she dreamed of. She wanted to make a difference. To help people, to build something good and lasting. And I wanted to give that to her.

But how could I, when there was still someone from my past who threatened to take it all away?

My jaw clenched, my knuckles going white on the steering wheel. Dominic had to be stopped. He was a threat to us all, but especially to Sloane. He wanted me to suffer, and he was willing to go to extreme lengths to get his revenge. I couldn't move forward with Sloane until he was dead.

The road curved ahead of us, sleek and shining as the moon broke through the low hanging clouds. I slowed down, easing around the bend, then accelerated again.

Over the roar of Diana's engine, I heard a high-pitched whine. I looked in the rearview mirror just in time to see a Ducati fly by, passing us, the rider's helmet gleaming in the moonlight. Their headlight was out, which is why I hadn't spotted them earlier. As they passed us, their taillight illuminated the rider's slender, feminine build.

Misha was still staring down at his phone. "You're going to make a left up ahead—"

"Shit!"

The wheel tried to jerk its way out of my hands. In the milliseconds before the front tire blew and I lost control of the car, a muzzle flash illuminated the back of the motorcycle. I feathered the brakes, trying to keep her on the road, but the car was going too fast, the road too wet. We started to fishtail, left, right, then left again, my knuckles white on the steering wheel. The ditch was coming up fast. I braced for impact.

Diana left the road without a sound, everything strangely muted as the world flipped upside down. Once. Twice. I shut my eyes and curled my arms around my head. The windshield exploded, glass flying everywhere. The car rolled once more, then slammed to an upright stop against a tree.

For a moment, all I could hear was my own rasping breaths sawing in and out of my chest, my heart beating way too fast. Something dripped down my face. I lifted a hand to wipe it away, but it came away slick with blood. My head was pounding.

I tried to turn towards Misha, but pain exploded across my chest. I gasped, spots swimming across my vision, and collapsed back into my seat. My left shoulder was on fire, the arm below it numb. I took a deep breath and tried again, slowly. Misha was slumped over in the seat next to me, his face covered in blood and broken glass.

Sound whooshed back into the picture. The ticking of cooling metal, a hiss of steam from the engine compartment. Cracked radiator, most likely. My own breathing, still too loud and harsh. I swallowed thickly and reached for the door handle, fumbling with my good arm, but the door was jammed. I don't even know why I tried.

"Misha. Hey." Blinking back the blood dripping into my eyes, I reached over with my right hand and touched his neck, checking for a pulse. It was there, slow and steady. I shook him gently. "Misha, wake up. *Wake up.*"

Slowly, he began to stir. His eyelids fluttered, then snapped open as he gasped in pain. He groaned and pressed a hand to his head, cursing loudly in Russian.

"Easy," I said. "You're okay, just breathe. Slow and deep."

Misha nodded and took a few steadying breaths. I kept a close eye on him, but he didn't look like he was about to pass out anymore.

"You good?" I asked.

Misha tried to shrug, but he grimaced and through better of it. "I am alive."

"Good. Let's keep it that way. We need to get out of here."

I was already looking around. The road was dark and quiet. The trees looming over us, their branches heavy with rainwater. No sign of the motorcyclist, although I was beginning to doubt what I'd seen. Already, the seconds before the crash were insubstantial and hard to hold on to.

"Can you get out?" I asked.

Misha nodded, bracing himself against the dashboard. He groaned and pressed a hand to his ribs, breathing heavily. I reached over to help him, but he batted my hands away. "I am fine."

"Okay, okay."

Misha unbuckled his seatbelt and pushed on his door, which thankfully opened when he tried it. He slid out of the car, grimacing as he bent over. Pulling my bulk over the center console proved to be more of a challenge than I was up for, though, and I tumbled out and landed on my hands and knees, the world tilting crazily around me. I dry-heaved, my stomach roiling, and I struggled to stay conscious.

A moment later, Misha's strong hand gripped my arm, and he hauled me to my feet.

"Thanks," I muttered. I still felt like a newborn calf trying to figure out how to use my legs.

Misha said nothing. He kept his hand on my arm to steady me as I got my bearings. It felt like a knife was stabbing into my shoulder, and my head was spinning.

Misha frowned. "Are you all right?"

"Fine," I said, wiping the blood from my face.

"We're lucky to be alive."

Diana was totaled. Front end crushed, every single body panel bent and crumpled, the engine compartment smoking slightly. I patted the roll cage and said a silent word of thanks to what was left of my car.

"Luck had nothing to do with it. That roll cage saved our life," I said, hobbling to the front of the car. "But it wasn't for someone's lack of trying."

Misha followed me. "What do you mean?"

Swallowing a groan, I leaned down by the driver's side front tire. It was shredded, any proof of what caused the blowout long gone. Carefully, I ran my fingers over the rim until I found what I was looking for, and I smiled bitterly. Maybe the proof wasn't gone after all.

"Look at this."

I held up the flattened bullet, letting it glint in the moonlight. It was mangled and unidentifiable, but it was proof enough of what I had seen. "That motorcycle rider shot out our tire. They tried to kill us."

Misha solemnly took the bullet. "You think this could be your man's work? Dominic?"

I stared at the dull metal gleaming in the moonlight. An assassin's bullet that almost found its mark.

"I'm sure of it."

19

Sloane

I WAVED OFF THE last of the guys as they exited the warehouse, then I closed the roll-down overhead door behind them. Slumping against the building's corrugated wall, I tried to negotiate the distance to the shabby shipping office with my overworked, fried brain. It was close to three AM, and I hadn't taken a breather all day long.

My footsteps echoed in the cavernous space as I crossed the floor. The open bottle of Jameson that Grady kept stashed in the desk was calling to me. I closed the door to the office, poured myself a congratulatory drink, and settled myself in the chair, propping my feet up on the desk.

Today had been a good day, despite how it had started. If anything, seeing the ruins of my bar had propelled me beyond what my stamina and the doctor's orders had allowed. Everything had been set up with the suppliers. I had worked my ass off all day, running back and forth across South Boston to meet with each one of the distilleries on our list in order to make sure that the first delivery would be ready to go off without a hitch.

After a few hours in the warehouse with Grady and the boys, we were ready for business. Everything now hinged on how Tommy and Misha had faired with the elusive Aleksandr Volkov.

The whiskey burned all the way down, warming my stomach and bringing a much-needed smile to my lips. It felt good to be back in action, to be moving forward instead of wallowing in despair over what we'd lost. The pain and loss was still there, but for the first time since I'd woken up in the hospital, I felt like I was doing something about it. I was making a difference rather than sitting around to wait for someone else to handle things. I was a doer, a fixer. That's who I was.

I was also tired as hell.

I sighed and let my head fall back against the chair, closing my eyes. I had tried Tommy's phone a couple of times, just to check in, but it had gone to voicemail every time. No doubt he and Misha were swimming in Russian vodka by now, which meant that the meeting was going well. I probably wouldn't see him until morning.

I opened my eyes, feeling a pang of loneliness and worry. It was ridiculous, of course, to be missing Tommy already. We had just gotten back to normal after our fight, and now he was gone again. But I couldn't help it. I wanted him here with me.

Somewhere along the line, I had grown accustomed to his presence.

There was also this thing with Dominic. The idea of Tommy being out there without me watching his back made me nervous. Tommy was a force to be reckoned with, sure, but he was also reckless and stubborn, and it would only take one wrong move on his part for something to go horribly wrong.

I had downplayed the threat from Dominic not because I wasn't worried about it, but because I didn't want Tommy to do anything rash. He tended to go off half-cocked when he thought I was in danger. I had seen it before, and I didn't want him doing something stupid that would get him hurt.

Still, I had to admit that I was worried about him.

I looked at the clock on the wall and sighed. It was late. I should go home, but I was too comfy to even consider moving right now. Instead, I pulled out my phone and checked my email. There was one from my insurance agent, a form to fill out with questions about the fire. I quickly sent it back to him, then scrolled through some missed texts from Kat, asking how I was doing. She had gone back to work at her old bar now that Lady D's was closed for the foreseeable future. I quickly sent her a reply, letting her know I was okay, then closed my eyes for just a moment.

I must have fallen asleep because the next thing I knew, I was startled awake by the sound of the warehouse door shutting.

I jerked upright in the chair and stared at the office door in alarm. Nobody should be here this late. The boys had left hours ago, and Tommy wasn't likely to be back until morning.

Heavy footsteps approached. I reached into the drawer, pulled out the Glock hidden there, and ducked next to the closed office door, my back to the wall. The footsteps paused. Whoever was out there had heard me move, but I wasn't giving them anything else.

Slowly, the door opened. The figure who entered was backlit by the warehouse lights, but they paused when I cocked the gun, the muzzle inches from their temple. "Surprise, asshole."

"Sloane?"

"Tommy?" I lowered the gun, heart hammering.

"It's just me."

"What are you doing here?"

We spoke at the same time, and I shoved the gun in my waistband. "Christ, Tommy. You scared the shit out of me. Why are you lurking around like that?"

"A slow lurk is about all I can manage right now, honey," he grunted as he shut the door.

The light was still dim in the office, but now that he'd stepped closer, I was able to get a better look at him. Tommy looked like hell. His head was bandaged and he was covered in blood. He held himself stiffly, like every movement caused him pain. His left arm was immobilized in a sling. He looked like he'd been run over by a truck.

"Tommy," I breathed. "What happened? Did Volkov do this?"

"We never made it." He leaned against the wall tiredly.

"What?"

"Someone tried to kill me. Us. On the way to meet with Volkov. It was a hit."

My eyes widened, and I reached for him. "Oh my god, are you okay?"

Tommy shook his head, his face grim. "I'm fine. Just a few bumps and bruises. I'll live."

"And your arm?"

"Dislocated. Misha popped it back in for me."

“Your car?”

He grunted. “Totaled.”

“I’m sorry.”

“I am too. I liked that car.”

"Jesus, Tommy." My hands fluttered uselessly around him, wanting to help but not sure how. "Sit down."

I pulled him towards the chair, but he shook his head. "I'll never get up again."

"Fine, then stay here." I poured a healthy drought of whiskey into my glass and handed it to him. "Where's Misha? Is he okay?"

Tommy drained the whiskey and grimaced. "A little banged up, but he's all right. He's calling our guys to clean up the mess and tow the car. He also wanted to do a sweep of the area to make sure no one followed us."

"Do you think this was Dominic?" I didn't want to ask, but I had to know.

"I'm sure of it."

In between sips of whiskey, Tommy told me how a blacked-out motorcycle had passed them seconds before the front tire blew out on his car, sending them into an uncontrolled spin. Tommy hadn't gotten a good look at the rider or the motorcycle, but he was confident that it had been a woman. The evidence had been right there for him to find when he'd finally managed to climb out of the wrecked car and locate the remains of the bullet lodged in the wheel rim.

I grabbed a hand towel from the sink in the kitchenette, wet it, and began dabbing at the dried blood on Tommy's face, frowning. "If you think you saw a woman rider, how could it have been Dominic?"

"I don't know," Tommy admitted. "But I can't think of anyone else who would be after us. This has his signature all over it."

I finished cleaning the blood off his face in silence. Tommy closed his eyes, leaning into my touch. My fingers trembled slightly as I ran my thumb across his cheekbone, wiping away the last of the blood.

How many times had I done this very thing? Patching him up after he got hurt, cleaning the blood from his skin, comforting him. I wondered how many more times I'd be able to do it, how many times before the violence came for him, for both of us, and took him away from me forever.

"Hey." Tommy's voice was soft, his blue eyes dark and warm, looking at me with a tenderness that made my heart ache. He reached up and cupped my cheek with his good hand, his thumb tracing the line of my bottom lip. "I'm okay, honey."

I nodded, fighting back tears. I leaned into his touch, reveling in the feeling of his calloused palm against my skin, his breath warm across my lips. For a moment, we just stayed like that, frozen in time.

Then I kissed him.

As kisses go, it wasn't spectacular, yet at the same time, it was perfect. Slow and sweet and just a bit hesitant, the tentative press of my mouth against his. Warmth, soft skin, and the scent of him. I inhaled deeply, drawing him into me. Both our eyes were still open, and I watched as Tommy's pupils swallowed the blue of his iris. He stood frozen, shocked, not moving, not even breathing, until a faint shiver ran through his limbs, and he inhaled sharply and pulled away.

“You don’t want this,” he grated.

I shook my head. “I don’t.”

“Then why did you kiss me?”

"I wanted to see what it was like."

Tommy hummed. "And what did you decide?"

"I'm going to do it again."

My hands slid up his neck and into his hair, my fingers twisting in the strands as I pulled him close. I could feel his heart pounding, pounding against my chest. Tommy groaned low in his throat, his eyes fluttering shut as I kissed him again. This time he responded, his lips moving against mine. His hand found my hip and slid up my side, his fingers leaving a trail of fire in their wake.

I let out a little gasp as he deepened the kiss, his tongue pressing against mine. I opened to him, tasting the whiskey on his tongue, letting it burn me all the way down. I kissed him again, feeling his mouth curve into a smile beneath my lips.

His good hand tightened on my hip, hard enough to bruise as his erection pressed against my belly. The feeling of him ignited something primal in me, something raw and urgent and demanding. I pushed closer, mewling, my hands roving over his body. I couldn't get enough of him, couldn't get close enough.

I kissed him harder, deeper, letting my tongue explore his mouth, my fingers tangling in his hair. Panting breaths mingled in the stale office air, hands searching, tugging at clothes. Tommy nudged my head aside and kissed down my throat, nipping at my jaw, my thundering pulse, my collarbone, until he sank his teeth into my shoulder. My gasp turned into a feral growl, and I dug my hands into his ass through his jeans, grinding his cock against my hip.

It was like a switch flipped in Tommy. One moment we were kissing, and the next, he was lifting me up one-armed and slamming my back into the wall, his body pinning mine. The kiss turned into something wild and ferocious, all teeth and tongues and hot, wet lips. With one good hand, he hoisted me onto the desk, sending the lamp crashing to the floor.

I didn't care. I wrapped my legs around his hips and pulled him closer, grinding against the bulge in his jeans. Tommy hissed, his hand tightening on my thigh. I felt him tremble, fighting for control.

I didn't want control. I didn't want safe.

Not here. Not now.

Not with him.

I bit his lower lip hard enough to draw blood, then licked away the red smear. Tommy growled and slipped his hand under my shirt. His palm was hot against my skin, his fingers rough and calloused, up, up my ribcage to the swell of my breast while his lips mapped the column of my throat. When his surprisingly nimble fingers dipped beneath my bra, I arched my back and groaned, my nails digging into his shoulders. The pad of his thumb kneaded at my nipple, teasing it to a hard point, pinching it and rolling it mercilessly.

I hissed, pleasure shooting through me, my legs tightening around his hips. I was so close already, my entire body wound tight as a bowstring. I could feel the tension building inside me, the pressure coiling deep in my core. I needed more. I needed everything.

Tommy knew it. He could feel it in the way my body responded to him, the way I pressed myself against him, my hips moving of their own accord, searching for friction, riding him. With a start, I realized I was about to come, fully clothed, on his thigh.

The idea of it sent me over the edge. I bit back a cry, my nails digging into Tommy's shoulders, my head thrown back as my orgasm rolled through me in waves. Tommy never stopped kissing me, his mouth hot and demanding on mine, swallowing every one of my moans, drinking down my pleasure.

With a jerk, Tommy's hand clamped down on my hip, pulling me close. His breath hitched in his throat and stopped. A tremor rocked his body before he stilled, his face still buried against my neck.

For a moment, neither of us moved. Our ragged breathing echoed in the tiny office, the only sound in the warehouse besides the ticking of the clock on the wall.

"Sloane."

I froze. My name sounded like it had been ripped from his gut with barbed wire, destroying me in a single breath. It was anguish, it was hope. It was everything he couldn't say and could never promise, but I understood.

This is why we would never work out. There was too much fire between us. Too much heat. Tonight had been nothing more than pent up frustrations and desperation, all tied up with a neat little bow of exhaustion.

I took a deep breath, steadying myself. "I'm sorry, Tommy."

"Don't be." He shook his head, his voice rough. "This is my fault. I should have never—"

I cut him off with a kiss, my hands framing his face. I kissed him softly, sweetly, trying to put everything into it that I couldn't say. Tommy made a low sound in his throat and pulled me into his arms, and I rested my head against his chest, listening to his heartbeat. It was still racing.

Tommy cleared his throat. "Are you okay?"

I nodded, not trusting myself to speak. I felt raw and vulnerable, exposed. I wasn't used to feeling that way around him.

Tommy brushed my hair away from my face, his fingers trailing across my cheekbone, and then he let them fall away to hang awkwardly at his side. He stepped back. "It's late. We should go."

I nodded again, feeling a lump forming in my throat. Tommy was right. It was late, and we needed to rest. But I couldn't shake the feeling that something had shifted between us tonight. Something fundamental and irreversible.

We didn't have time for this. Even though I had started...whatever this was tonight, I was going to have to be the one to shut it down.

I straightened my shirt and smoothed my hair, then grabbed my jacket off the back of the chair. "Let's go."

Tommy waited for me to pass him, then followed me out into the warehouse.

20

Tommy

I came in my pants like a goddamn teenager.

My fists sunk into the heavy bag like they could turn back time. But I couldn't do anything about what had happened. It was too late. I had crossed a line with Sloane, and there was no going back.

The bad hook with my left sent a shockwave of pain through my arm. My shoulder was still healing, but I couldn't wait. I needed to be able to fight. I needed to get back in the ring. But if I was being honest with myself, I just needed to get my mind off her.

That night in the office with Sloane had been every wet dream and fantasy rolled into one. The way she'd looked at me with those green eyes liquid with worry, with unshed tears *for me.* I had felt myself cracking, splitting open with the need to hold her, to comfort her, to make her feel safe. Sloane cared about me, more than she would ever let herself admit. I saw that in her eyes that night. Maybe it wasn't love and could never be, but it was more than just concern for a friend.

Then, she kissed me.

She. Kissed. Me.

Never in my wildest dreams would I have allowed myself to imagine Sloane initiating a kiss, but she did, and wow, what a kiss it was. Toe curling, sweet and smoldering, literally stealing the breath from my body the moment her lips met mine. I knew then that I was utterly and completely fucked.

What happened next was a blur. Dizziness, exhaustion, and my own disbelief colored the memory until I wasn't sure what had been real and what had been fantasy. All I could remember was the feeling of her body pressed against mine, her hips grinding against mine, the heat of her mouth on mine. I had been hard as a rock in moments, my body reacting to hers without any input from my brain. And when she came crying out into my mouth, it was all I could do not to rip her clothes off and take her right there on the desk.

I had barely managed to restrain myself. I had wanted to bury myself inside her, to feel her clenching around me, to make her mine. And when I felt her come on my thigh with my name on her lips, my body reacted before my brain could shut it down, and I came in my fucking pants like a kid with his first case of blue balls.

It was humiliating. God, what had I done? All Sloane had done was kiss me, and I reacted like some kind of animal. Exactly like the kind of man she didn't want, and exactly how she thought I was. I thought it was over, any shred of friendship gone, but then she just apologized and kissed me so sweetly I felt like my heart was being ripped through my sternum.

And now we were back to pretending like nothing had happened. Great.

My phone rang, pulling me from my thoughts. I stopped beating up the bag and grabbed my phone off the bench where it was charging. It was Connor.

"Hey." Silence on the line. I checked to make sure the call was still connected. "Connor? Is everything okay?"

"No," he said tightly. "Everything is not okay."

I hear Cassidy in the background, demanding to be put on the phone with me. "Connor, what happened?"

"Hold on."

Through the line, I heard muffled conversation that flared into a brief argument, and then Connor was back. "Someone broke into our flat tonight."

My blood froze. "What?"

"The front door lock was broken when we got home tonight. They didn't take anything, but they left a message for us. A photograph of Cassidy and Aiden, taken at the park. It was pinned to the cabinet with a knife. I was able to get rid of it without Cassidy seeing it, but she's pretty shaken up."

Fuck. This was Dominic. It had to be.

"What about the tapes," I asked, even though I already knew the answer.

"The security tapes had been set to loop. Professional job. Someone wanted us to know they could break in any time they wanted. This was a message." Connor paused. "Tom, do you know anything about this? Is my family in danger?"

I wanted to laugh and tell him that we were always in danger, but Connor didn't want to hear that. He'd left this life to protect his family, and I had to make him believe I had this under control. Cassidy would never forgive me if I let Connor get himself tangled up in this life again.

"The clan's heading in a new direction, and it's ruffled some feathers," I lied. "Give me a couple days to smooth things over, I'll send some guys over to watch the house. It's under control, Connor."

"Are you sure? Because this is my family the bastards went after."

"And you're my family, Connor. I'll take care of it. You have my word."

I heard Connor sigh. "All right. Anything you need, let me know. I've got your back. Always."

I hated lying to Connor, but I needed to keep him out of this, and the only way to do that was by lying to him. Connor and I were one in the same mind when it came to protecting our families.

"Thanks," I said. "I'll call you if anything changes. Take care of yourself."

I ended the call and tossed my phone back onto the bench. This had to end. Regardless of what Sloane thought, I was going to go after Dominic. I couldn't ignore these threats anymore.

A sharp pain shot through my shoulder again as my fist connected with the bag. I cursed and stepped back, rubbing at the joint.

"You going to be ready for tonight, Tommy?" I turned around to see Saul leaning his forearms against the ropes. "Because you're favoring that arm, and Donnelly ain't gonna let that slide."

"Yeah, I'll be fine," I grunted, resuming my assault on the punching bag. "Just need to loosen it up."

"You sure? You seem a bit off tonight."

"I'm fine," I snapped.

Saul held up his hands in surrender. "Alright, man. I'm just checking in."

I let out a slow breath, trying to calm my frayed nerves. Saul was just looking out for me, like always. And he was right. I did need to get my head in the game tonight. It had been weeks since my last match—official match, that is. I'd long since given up Misha's underground ring. I told myself I didn't need the money, and I didn't need the pain. But the truth was, I had started to enjoy it too much. The violence, the adrenaline, the risk. The control.

I didn't want to be that man anymore.

Saul clapped a hand on my back, and I winced as the motion sent shock-waves through my shoulder. It felt like my arm wasn't even attached to my body anymore.

"We'll get him next time, Tommy," he said sympathetically. "Get that arm of yours healed up, and I can see about a rematch."

I lost the fight. First time in years.

I should have been angry, but I wasn't. I was disappointed, but more in myself than anything else. I had brought my emotions into the ring with me, and this time, it had cost me.

Up ahead, I saw a lean figure with pale hair leaning against the wall by the locker room's entrance, lighting a cigarette. Misha. Just the guy I wanted to talk to.

He jerked his head in my direction as acknowledgement. "Not your best fight, my friend."

"I had a lot on my mind."

He hummed thoughtfully. "Yes, about that. Walk with me. Even here, the wall have ears."

We started towards the exit, moving slowly through the crowd of people leaving the stadium.

"Volkov sends his condolences," Misha began. "He also gave the green light to go ahead without the meet." He palmed a flash drive into my hand. "The contacts. Everything has been set up on our end, all you have to do is call."

"Thanks." I pocketed the flash drive and looked at him expectantly.

Misha sighed. "You're not going to like what I have to say next."

"My day's already shit. Hit me."

"You need to get this thing with the Italian under control." Misha took a long drag on his cigarette. "It is bad for business."

"I couldn't agree more. That's why I'm going to have a little chat with Sal."

Misha frowned. "You are aware that this is a terrible idea."

I crossed my arms. Meeting problems head on was what I did. I didn't know anything else. "What do you suggest?"

"I know people. Say the word, and I can get you in a room with him. Alone."

Anger and unease shot through me. "If you had access to him all this time, why didn't you say so, Misha? You were in the car when his crony tried to kill me, you could've been killed too."

Misha stared at me, his pale eyes giving away nothing. "Volkov does not want to take direct action against the Italians. Any assistance I provide must be under the table. Nothing can trace back to us. *Nothing.*"

I knew where he was going with this. "Are you saying you want to set him up?"

Misha shrugged. "Dominic is a dangerous man. If he went missing, the world would be a better place."

I thought about it for a moment, but only for a moment. The truth was, I wanted to hurt Dominic. I wanted to make him bleed. I wanted to see him suffer. I wanted him to feel every ounce of pain and fear that he'd put my family through, and then some. I wanted to make sure he never threatened us again.

But still, I had to be cautious. "Let me sleep on it," I said. "We'll be in touch."

"You know where to find me."

I made my way home. Alone, since nobody wants to be around a sad sack loser licking their wounds, but that was okay. I wasn't in the mood for company. Once I got home, I showered, threw on some sweats and an old Patriots tee, and poured myself a whiskey.

It had been a long night. The only silver lining was that I had managed to keep my opponent from landing any serious blows to my already injured shoulder. Saul had told me to ice it, but for now, the whiskey was working just fine.

If only it could get rid of the ache in the center of my chest.

I sipped my drink and stared out the window. The city stretched out before me, a glittering sea of lights and humanity, each one a story of struggle and hope. Violence and death. Love and loss. All that wealth and power right alongside the suffering, but none of it mattered when you were alone.

I sighed and tipped my glass back, draining the last of the whiskey. My thoughts drifted to Sloane. I wondered what she was doing. Was she asleep yet? What did she dream about at night? Did she dream about me?

I shook my head. This was stupid. I needed to get a grip. So what if she kissed me? We were both emotional that night at the warehouse, and I barely survived an assassination attempt. I hadn't been in my right mind. Obviously. It had been a long day. I knew how Sloane felt about me, and she wasn't going to change her mind overnight.

She was stubborn, but so was I. And I had nothing but time to convince her otherwise. I could undo this. Show her that what happened that night was no big deal, that I could handle it. I could be the guy she needed me to be, not the one I was.

My phone was out and I was dialing her number almost before I knew what I was doing.

"Hello?" Her voice was warm and sleepy. I swallowed and closed my eyes, picturing her curled up in bed, her hair spread out across the pillows.

"Hey. It's me."

There was a pause, and then I heard Sloane shift on the other end of the line. "Tommy? Is everything okay?"

"Yeah, everything's fine. Sorry if I woke you."

"No, it's okay. I wasn't asleep. Just watching TV."

I smiled. "What are you watching?"

"Just some dumb action movie. I was going to fall asleep in front of it anyway."

"Well, then I'll let you go." I felt stupid for even calling. What the hell was I doing?

"No, it's okay," she said quickly. "I can talk."

"Are you sure? It's late."

"I'm sure," she said. "I'd like the company."

"Okay."

The silence stretched between us as I tried to think of what to say next. "Volkov came through with the contacts. We're good to go."

"You met with him?"

"Well, no. Misha gave them to me. Everything has been arranged, all we have to do is call."

"Oh. That...that's good."

"Yeah." I gripped the phone as we lapsed into another uncomfortable silence. I didn't want to talk about Volkov. I didn't want to talk about the business. I wanted to talk about what was going on between us. Where we stood. What she was feeling. What I was feeling.

But I couldn't ask her that.

"How's your shoulder?" she asked finally.

"Better. It's still sore, but it's getting there."

Sloane latched onto the topic like I'd thrown her a life ring. "How was your fight?"

I winced. "I lost."

"What? Are you okay? You didn't reinjure yourself, did you?"

"No, no. I'm fine. It was just a bad night."

"Bad night," she repeated.

"It happens."

"Not to you."

No, it didn't. But it had been happening more and more lately, and I knew the reason.

"I'm sorry, Tommy," she said quietly.

I shrugged, even though she couldn't see it. "It happens. Saul thinks I'll be able to get a rematch if I get my shoulder healed up."

"That wasn't what I was talking about." Sloane paused, and I heard rustling in the background. "Tommy...do you want to come over?"

The question caught me off guard. "What?"

"I mean, I know it's late, and you're probably tired, but I thought maybe you could use some company. If you want."

I couldn't believe what I was hearing. Sloane wanted to see me.

"Um...yeah, sure. I can do that. Give me twenty minutes?"

"Sounds good."

"Okay, see you soon."

I hung up the phone and stared at it for a moment, trying to figure out what had just happened. Did Sloane really want to see me? Or was this some kind of pity invite?

I decided I didn't care.

In a record time, I dressed and was on my way out the door. I was halfway to her apartment before I remembered to text her and let her know I was on my way.

I was nervous. I couldn't remember the last time I had felt like this, but my stomach was in knots, and I couldn't stop fidgeting. I didn't know what Sloane wanted. Was she going to talk to me about what happened, or ignore it? Was she going to let me in, or shut me out? I didn't know what to expect.

I paused outside her building and took a moment to compose myself. Then I took the stairs two at a time and knocked on her door.

Sloane answered almost immediately, as if she'd been standing by the door waiting for me. She was dressed in leggings and an oversized tee that hung off one shoulder, one of Aiden's old shirts, I realized with a start. It was the first time I'd seen her in anything other than her usual work attire, and she looked completely different. Younger. Less guarded. I couldn't help but notice that her feet were bare and that she had painted her toenails bright red, a small, feminine touch that tied my stomach in knots. I was overcome with the image of her wearing nothing but one of my shirts, wrapped around her curves, my scent marking her, and I felt a surge of possessiveness unlike anything I'd ever felt before.

"Hi," she said softly.

I cleared my throat. "Hi."

We stood there awkwardly for a moment, neither of us sure what to say.

"Come on in." Sloane stepped back to let me inside, closing the door behind me. "Can I get you anything to drink? I think I have some beer in the fridge."

"No, thanks. I'm good." I followed her into the living room, taking in the sight of her apartment. It was small, but neat and cozy. The walls were painted a warm sage green, and the hardwood floors had been stained dark and polished to a high shine. A black leather couch was positioned in front of the television, and a coffee table scattered with magazines and books sat in the middle of the room. A large, framed map of Ireland hung on the wall next to the window, and the smell of cinnamon and cloves hung in the air from a candle perched on the windowsill.

It was a space that felt lived in, that felt like a home, and the realization made me ache with longing, the brief image of a place we might have built together there and gone in a second.

I followed Sloane to the couch, and we sat down beside each other. For a moment, we just sat there, neither of us speaking. The tension grew between us, but I didn't know what to say or what to do.

Then a mangy little ball of black fur jumped up on my lap.

"What the hell is that?" I yelped.

Sloane laughed. "It's my cat, Whiskey."

The little thing curled up on my lap, purring contentedly. I raised an eyebrow at Sloane. "I didn't know you had a cat."

"Yeah, he's a bit of a loner, he's not always friendly. But he seems to like you."

"Well, I'm honored." I ran my hand over the cat's back, and it arched into my touch. "He's very soft."

Sloane smiled. "Yeah, he's a little spoiled brat."

We lapsed into silence again.

"So," she began, "do you want to tell me what's going on?"

I sighed. "I told you, I lost my fight."

"No, that's not what I mean." She shook her head. "You sounded off on the phone, too. What's going on with you?"

I sighed and scrubbed a hand through my hair, clutching at the locks. Whiskey took the hint and sauntered over to Sloane's lap, abandoning me. "Connor called. Someone broke into their place."

"What?"

"It was Dominic, I'm sure of it. He left them a picture of Cassidy and Aiden from the park. It was a threat."

"Jesus, Tommy."

I nodded, staring unseeingly at the blank television. I wasn't going to tell her about Misha's offer. I already knew what she'd say.

The fundamental difference between Sloane and me was that she believed the strength of the clan would be enough to protect us. A unified front. I didn't. If you wanted justice, you had to take it. Revenge. I believed in taking out the trash, and Dominic Moretti was exactly that. He was a threat, and I couldn't let it stand. I had to stop him, or he would keep coming until he had destroyed us.

It had been that way for years, a hardscrabble fight against a world that saw us as nothing more than gangsters and criminals, violent men with no place in their world. We fought tooth and nail for every inch we gained, and we paid for it in blood. Aiden's blood. Connor's. Cassidy's. Every one of us paid the price at some point or another, and a few of us ultimately paid with our lives.

Their blood was on my hands.

"Tommy?" Sloane's warm fingers touched my shoulder, and I jumped. "Are you okay?"

"Yeah. Yeah, I'm fine. It's just—"

"You are not fine." Sloane scooted closer to me on the sofa. "You lost your fight. It's two in the morning, and you're sitting here staring at the wall like it holds the secrets of the universe. Why aren't you asleep right now?"

I sighed. "I don't sleep much these days."

"Tommy..." Sloane's voice was soft, concerned.

Fuck it. She already thought I was a train wreck, what's one more thing piled on the heap?

"I have nightmares," I shut my eyes. "About Aiden."

"Oh, Tommy." Sloane's voice was full of sympathy.

"I see his face every time I close my eyes. I can't stop it."

I took a shuddering breath. "It all happened so fast. The gunshot. And then he fell, Aiden...he looked so damn surprised, I thought it had hit his vest at first. I thought he was going to be okay. I was so relieved. Then I saw the blood."

The words started coming out in a rush, faster than I could stop them. "I-I tried to keep pressure on it. I tried to keep him calm. I told him he was going to be okay, he just had to hold on for a little bit longer, but it was a lie. He knew it. I saw it in his eyes. Eighteen years old, and when he looked up at me, I could see in his eyes that he knew he was dying. I couldn't stop it.

"I didn't know what to do. So I held him. I held him in my arms and I lied to him, keeping pressure on the wound and hoping for a miracle. I held him until I felt his heart stop beating. There was no miracle, not in that alley. Aiden wasn't going to be okay. Nothing was ever going to be okay again."

I swallowed, my throat suddenly thick. I felt Sloane's hand on my shoulder, warm and comforting, but it was too much. I stiffened under her touch, clenching my fists.

"His eyes...they're the same as yours. You both looked so much alike. Sometimes the dream changes and it's you there in my arms, and sometimes it's him. Sometimes it shifts, and it's Connor bleeding out in the back of the van, or Cassidy. I can't fucking sleep, Sloane. I can't close my eyes without seeing them. Seeing you."

Sloane wrapped her arms around me, pulling me into a tight hug. My head fell onto her shoulder, and I buried my face in the crook of her neck. I breathed in the scent of her hair, her skin, and let myself feel her warmth, her strength. It felt so good to be held, to have someone else take the weight for a moment, to have someone who knew my pain.

I felt the tears coming, but this time I did nothing to stop them. I let them fall, hot and silent down my cheeks, soaking into the soft fabric of Sloane's shirt. My hands came up to grasp at her, to hold onto her, to anchor myself in this moment, in this feeling. I clung to her like a lifeline, and she didn't pull away.

We sat there for a long time, neither of us speaking nor moving. I couldn't bring myself to let go of her. Not yet. Not when it felt like she was the only thing holding me together.

Sloane's hand came up and stroked my hair, her fingers gentle and soothing. The tenderness of the gesture nearly broke me. She didn't say anything, didn't offer any meaningless platitudes. She just held me, and that was enough.

Finally, I took a deep breath and pulled away, scrubbing at my eyes with the heel of my palm. "Sorry, I..."

"Don't apologize. You have nothing to be sorry for." Sloane cradled my face in her hands. Her eyes were bright with tears. "How long have you been carrying this alone? Aiden was my brother, too."

"The Quinn men aren't exactly known for their emotional depth," I said. "I learned that when mom died."

"That doesn't mean you don't have feelings, Tommy. This weight...it's been crushing you. It's been crushing both of us. We've all lost so much, and it's never going to be okay, but we don't have to carry it alone."

Sloane's hands dropped to my shoulders, and she squeezed them gently. "It's okay, Tommy. Let go."

My breath hitched in my throat as her fingers dug into my muscles, releasing tension I hadn't even known I'd been carrying. The physical touch was almost too much for me to bear, and I had to close my eyes and focus on my breathing to keep from losing it again. She moved her hands up to the base of my skull, her fingertips digging into the tense muscles there. I groaned as she worked out the knots, her touch firm and sure.

I couldn't remember the last time someone had touched me like this. Without expectations, without ulterior motives. Just...touched me.

My entire body felt like it was melting beneath her, the tension and stress bleeding out of me with each press of her hands. I leaned forward and rested my forehead against her shoulder, breathing in her scent. Sloane's breath hitched, and I felt her lips ghost over my temple, pressing a soft kiss there.

I turned my head, nuzzling against her neck. "Sloane..."

She sighed softly. "Yes?"

"I want to kiss you again. But I'm not sure if I should."

Sloane's hands stilled on my back. "Tommy, I..."

"Please," I whispered. "Just one night. Give me that. Give us that. Just let me hold you in my arms..."

...and pretend you are mine.

I couldn't bring myself to say the words. Instead, I just buried my face in her neck and inhaled her scent, letting it wash over me.

Sloane's hands came up to cradle my face. "Tommy..."

Her voice was so soft, so full of emotion, that I couldn't help but look up at her. I searched her eyes for any sign of doubt, any hint that she didn't want this. That she didn't want me. But I didn't see any of that. All I saw was the same pain and longing I felt, the same desire to be close to someone else who knew what it was like to lose the ones we loved. The ones we needed.

"Just for tonight," she whispered.

21

SLOANE

THIS WAS EITHER GOING to be a very good idea, or a very, very bad one.

I wasn't sure which yet.

All I knew was that the look on Tommy's face was killing me. He was so vulnerable, so raw it made my heart ache. I wanted to take away his pain, to make him feel safe and cared for. I wanted to show him that he wasn't alone, that I was here for him, no matter what.

I stroked his hair, my fingers running through the soft, dark strands.

"Just tonight," I whispered. It couldn't go any further, no matter how good it was. I wouldn't allow it. I pressed my hand to Tommy's chest and felt the steady rhythm beating beneath my palm. "You have a good heart, Tommy, despite everything that's happened, the person you've forced yourself to be. Let it feel, just for tonight. Be here with me."

"Just for tonight," he repeated, his voice a soft rasp.

My heart broke a little at the resignation in his voice, the way he gave in so easily. It wasn't right. Not for him. He deserved so much more than a one-night stand with someone he couldn't have, but I couldn't turn him away.

Tommy nodded, then leaned forward and captured my lips with his. He kissed me slowly, deeply, as if he were trying to memorize the taste of me. A first true kiss and a last kiss, everything that we were and everything we could be, wrapped up in a single breath.

His tongue brushed against mine, coaxing me to open for him. I moaned into his mouth as he deepened the kiss, his hands tangling in my hair. He tasted like whiskey and something darker, more primal.

I felt myself losing control, my body responding to his touch, to his scent, to him. I wanted to drown in this feeling, to lose myself in him.

Tommy's hand trailed down my side, caressing my curves before sliding around to cup my ass. Gently, he pushed me back on the couch before covering me with his body. I gasped at the sensation of his hardness pressing against my core. I could feel him through his jeans, hot and heavy and thick, and I couldn't help but grind against him, needing more.

I felt his lips curve up in a smile, and I pulled away, panting. "Tomm y..."

He kissed me harder, his tongue plunging into my mouth, claiming me. I whimpered against him as he pressed his hips against mine, his cock grinding against me through our clothes. The friction was delicious, but it wasn't enough. I needed to feel him against me, skin on skin, no barriers. I reached down and tugged at the hem of his shirt, trying to get it off him.

Tommy sat up and quickly removed his shirt, tossing it aside. My eyes raked over his bare torso, taking in every inch of him. He was solid muscle, his skin tanned and covered with tattoos. There was a large scar across his chest, and another just above his hip where he'd been shot.

I traced the scars with my fingertips, my touch feather-light. Tommy shivered under my touch, his muscles tensing as he held himself back.

"Sloane..." he said, his voice strained.

"I want you," I whispered. "All of you."

Slowly, he shook his head, his dark eyes boring into mine. "Not here. You deserve better than I quick fuck on a couch."

Tommy bent and pressed his mouth to mine, nipping at my bottom lip. He slowly worked his way down my throat and onto my chest until his mouth hovered over my breast. The heat of his mouth through the barrier of my shirt made my nipple harden and my back arch. I pushed myself against him, needing more, but he pulled back. Grinding into me with a firm thrust, he whispered in my ear.

"When I make love to you, Sloane, it will be in a bed. I'm going to worship every inch of your body with my hands, my mouth, my cock." He punctuated each word with a thrust of his hips. "You're going to come so hard you'll see stars, and then I'm going to start all over again. I am going to love you all night long."

I shivered as the words rolled over me.

He pulled back and looked at me, his expression serious. "But one word from you, and I'll stop. Even if it kills me. I'll never hurt you. *Never.*"

His words sent a rush of emotion through me. No one had ever been this gentle with me, this careful. No one had ever put my needs above their own. And I knew that if I asked him to, Tommy would stop. He would leave, and never speak of this again.

"I don't want you to stop." It was all I could manage to say, my breath coming in ragged gasps.

Tommy nodded, his dark eyes filled with desire. "Then let me take you to bed, Sloane."

I nodded, too overwhelmed to speak.

With one final press against me, he pulled away and stood up. My body was aching with need, and I could feel my wetness soaking through my panties, just from the want of him. Tommy reached out and helped me to my feet, his hands steadying me. Then, he swept me up into his arms and carried me into the bedroom.

My heart was pounding as he laid me down on the bed, the mattress dipping with our combined weight. He knelt above me, his dark eyes raking over my body. I felt exposed, vulnerable, but it didn't matter. I wanted him to see me, all of me.

Slotting his legs between mine, he leaned forward and kissed me, his tongue teasing my mouth as he pressed his hips against mine. I moaned, the sensation of him hard and thick against me sending waves of pleasure through my body.

Tommy broke the kiss, his lips moving along my jaw and down my neck, his stubble scratching at my skin. He trailed kisses down my chest, his mouth hot against my skin. He paused at the hem of my shirt and looked up at me, his eyes asking permission.

I nodded, my breath catching in my throat.

In one swift move, Tommy pulled my shirt over my head and tossed it aside. Me leggings were next. I lifted my hips as he slid them down my legs, taking my panties with them until I was bare before him, completely exposed.

Tommy sat back and looked at me, a curious expression on his face. It was more than lust or want, more than desire. It was a look of reverence, of awe. Pupils blown black, he looked at me, barely breathing. Slowly, he reached out a trembling hand and placed it on the flat of my stomach, heat seeping from his skin into mine until I was seconds away from immolation. Tommy slid his hand up, up, up between my breasts, and his fingers twitched, feeling the pounding of my heart beneath his hand. Heat painted my chest pink, up my throat to my cheeks as I realized how naked I truly was before him, physically and emotionally. Reaching up, I placed my hand over Tommy's, holding his hand against my heart.

Tommy let out a shaky breath. "You are the most beautiful woman I have ever known."

His words sent a shockwave through me, and tears pricked the corners of my eyes. No one had ever made me feel like this, like I was the center of their world. Like I was everything.

Tommy's other hand came up, cupping my face and tilting my chin up to meet his gaze. The emotion in his dark eyes was nearly overwhelming, and I found myself unable to look away. He leaned down and captured my lips in a kiss, soft and tender. His hands trailed down my body, leaving a trail of fire in their wake. Every touch was deliberate, every movement filled with intent. He mapped my body, learning it, committing to memory every touch, every moan.

I arched into his touch, my body craving more. I needed to feel him against me, inside me, filling me up until there was nothing left but him.

I reached for his jeans, tugging at the button. Tommy broke the kiss, his lips trailing along my jaw, his breath hot against my skin.

"Not yet, spitfire," he whispered, his voice low and husky. "I haven't even started yet."

I moaned as he nipped at my earlobe, his tongue tracing the shell of my ear. I felt his hand slide down my stomach, lower, lower, until he found the spot that made my body tremble with need. His fingers slid through my wetness, teasing my clit with slow, deliberate circles. I gasped, arching into his touch, needing more. Tommy chuckled, his clever fingers working faster, drawing pleasure from my body.

He kissed his way down my neck, his mouth hot against my skin. He paused at my breast, his tongue flicking out to taste me, sending waves of pleasure through my body. His teeth grazed my nipple, and I let out a breathy moan, my fingers tangling in his hair as I held him against me. He nipped and licked at my breast, his hand never stopping the delicious torture between my thighs.

I was so close. My body was trembling with pleasure, my breathing ragged and uneven. I could feel the orgasm building inside me, threatening to consume me. Tommy's fingers worked faster, his thumb rubbing against my clit, the sensation driving me mad.

"Come for me, Sloane," he whispered, his voice rough and husky. "Let go."

I couldn't hold back anymore. I cried out, my body shuddering as the orgasm ripped through me, sending waves of pleasure coursing through my body as Tommy kissed me, swallowing my cries.

Slowly, the orgasm subsided, and I collapsed back against the pillows, my body spent. Tommy grinned at me, his eyes full of desire. He kissed his way down my body, his mouth hot against my skin, and I moaned his name.

"Hush," he whispered. "I'm not done with you yet."

Down, down, down. He continued lower, kissing my stomach, my hips, the inside of my thighs. My legs trembled as his mouth hovered over my aching core. Teeth nipped at the sensitive skin of my inner thigh, then soothed it with a gentle kiss. My body was on fire, my need for him so acute, I felt as if I might combust.

"Please..."

Tommy smiled, his eyes full of desire. "Patience, spitfire."

He kissed the crease where my leg met my hip, then moved lower, his mouth hot against my skin. He nuzzled against me, his stubble scratching at my thighs. I could feel his breath against my wetness, and I shivered in anticipation. Slowly, he parted me with his fingers, exposing my throbbing clit to the cool air. He flicked his tongue against it, teasing me. I arched into him, needing more.

Tommy chuckled and wrapped his lips around my clit, sucking and licking, driving me mad with pleasure. My fluttering hands scrabbled at his shoulders as he pinned my legs down, the muscles in his back contracting as he held me in place. I cried out as he lapped at me, pushing me towards another orgasm.

In the dim bedroom, Tommy's eyes were nearly black as he looked up at me, his mouth never stopping. One nimble finger teased at my entrance before pushing in, curling and stroking me from the inside.

Then two. His tongue danced across my clit in time with his fingers, and I felt myself hurtling towards another orgasm.

"Tommy, I'm..." My hips bucked, eliciting a long groan from him that resonated through me. Tommy buried his face between my legs, devouring me with a passion and intensity that surprised me. The wet sounds of his mouth on me were erotic and obscene, and my moan built up into a scream as he drove me closer to the edge.

My hands tangled in his hair, pulling mercilessly, and he groaned louder, the pain spurring him on. I felt him growl against me, the vibration of it sending a shockwave of pleasure through my body. He worked me relentlessly, his fingers and mouth never stopping their delicious torture.

"I'm so close...oh, god, please don't stop..." I gasped, my back arching as he brought me closer and closer to release.

Tommy's mouth was relentless, his fingers working in and out of me in time with his tongue. He growled against me again, the vibration sending me over the edge. I cried out, my body shuddering as another orgasm crashed over me. I arched against him, my body wracked with pleasure as he licked me clean.

As my orgasm subsided, Tommy pulled back, his face glistening with my wetness. He looked up at me, his eyes dark with desire. He leaned forward and captured my lips in a kiss, his tongue swirling around mine, tasting me. His hardness pressed against me, and I reached for his jeans, desperate to feel him inside me.

This time, he let me.

I pushed his jeans down, revealing his thick cock. He was big, bigger than I'd realized, and my breath caught in my throat at the sight of it, painfully erect, throbbing veins leading up to a dark purple head suffused with blood, dripping precum. Ready for me.

"Touch me," he breathed. "Please."

I wrapped my hand around his length, feeling the hot, heavy weight of him in my hand. Tommy shuddered and growled, his eyes fluttering closed as I stroked him. I rubbed my thumb across the tip of his cock, spreading the wetness that leaked from him over the entire head.

"Fuck, Sloane," he groaned.

"You like that?" I teased.

Tommy didn't reply, just pulled me into another deep kiss as I continued to stroke him, his hips bucking into my touch. I could feel the tension in his body as he fought to control himself, but I wanted to see him lose control. I wanted to watch him come apart for me.

I swiped my thumb over the head of his cock again, this time spreading his precum over the entire shaft. Tommy groaned, his hips bucking against me. I worked his cock with my hand, stroking him faster, feeling the tension in his body grow. His breathing was ragged, and his fingers dug into my hips as he pulled me closer, grinding his hips against me.

"I need to be inside you," he growled. “Right now.”

"Yes," I breathed.

Tommy fumbled in his jeans for a condom, but I stilled his hand. “I'm on the pill.”

“I just got tested last week,” he said breathlessly.

I grinned. “Wishful thinking?”

“I thought, after the near miss at the shipping office...” Tommy shook his head, his expression pained. “Fuck, Sloane, are you sure? Because if I’m not in you within the next three seconds, it just might kill me.”

I released him long enough to spread my legs, and he settled between them. He positioned his cock at my entrance, and I gasped as he slowly pushed into me, inch by glorious inch. I let out a shuddering breath as he filled me, stretching me, the feeling of him inside me sending waves of pleasure through my body. I moaned, arching against him as he began to move, slowly at first, then picking up speed.

The feeling of him moving inside me, the sound of his breath mingling with my own, his hands gripping my hips as he thrust into me—it was all too much. I could feel the pleasure building inside me, threatening to overwhelm me.

"Oh, god, Tommy," I moaned. "Don't stop."

Tommy groaned, his hips slamming into me as he drove me closer and closer to the edge. I could feel my orgasm building, the pressure and pleasure coiling deep in my belly. I clung to him, my fingers digging into his back as he fucked me, harder and faster. I cried out as he buried himself deep inside me, the sensation of him filling me up pushing me over the edge. My body clenched around him as I came, my orgasm sending shockwaves of pleasure coursing through me.

Tommy's rhythm faltered. He made a low, feral sound ripped from the back of his throat and his cock pulsed as he came, spilling himself deep inside me. I felt his body shudder with his release, and he collapsed against me, burying his face in my neck. I held him close, our bodies entwined, our breathing ragged.

We stayed like that for a moment, both of us lost in the afterglow.

Finally, Tommy pulled away, looking down at me. He smiled a soft, almost shy smile that made my heart flutter in my chest, and he kissed me softly, his lips brushing against mine.

"Are you okay?" he asked quietly, his voice husky.

I nodded, my throat suddenly thick with emotion. "Yes."

Tommy pulled me into his arms, and I laid my head on his chest, listening to the steady beat of his heart. I felt safe and protected, wrapped up in his embrace. I closed my eyes, letting myself get lost in the moment.

Slowly, Tommy rolled me over onto my back. He tucked a strand of hair behind my ear, and I looked up at him. His dark eyes were filled with emotion, and he traced the curve of my cheek with his thumb.

Outside my window, life moved on. The city lights twinkled, the world was spinning, but here in this room, time stopped. Everything felt perfect. Just lying here in Tommy Quinn's arms as he kissed me softly and stroked my hair, every touch so loving and gentle that I felt the last piece of my walls crumble. Where has this man been? Where has he been hiding this gentle heart of his?

The thought made my chest ache. I couldn't be falling in love with him. It was too soon. It was too dangerous. Tommy was a fighter and a liar and a son of a bitch. But as he held me in his arms and kissed me, I couldn't help but think that maybe, just maybe, I was falling for him.

And it was terrifying.

As if he sensed the turmoil in my thoughts, Tommy pulled away. His dark eyes searched mine, and I wondered what he was thinking. His fingers traced the line of my jaw, his touch feather-light, and I leaned into him.

Tommy's touches stayed gentle and sweet, but despite myself, I felt myself growing aroused again. I knew that I shouldn't. I knew that it would only lead to heartbreak. But I couldn't resist the pull of him, the feeling of his body against mine. Tommy smiled shyly, but when he pulled me on top of him, I realized that he was hard again already.

He looked at me with such intensity in his eyes, such hunger, that I felt my heart skip a beat. I knew that I should stop this, that I should pull away. But I couldn't. I wanted him. I needed him.

I lowered myself onto him, taking him inside me. We both gasped as he filled me, our bodies fitting together perfectly. It felt so right, so perfect. I began to move, riding him slowly, savoring the feeling of him inside me. Tommy's hands gripped my hips, guiding my movements. Slower. Deeper. Meeting me thrust for thrust with a strength that terrified me, as if he was pushing his soul into my body. I could feel another orgasm building inside me, and I knew that I wouldn't last long.

Tommy's fingers dug into my hips, and he let out a low groan as he thrust up into me, strength and power, his body straining against mine. I clung to him, my fingers digging into his shoulders as I rode him, pleasure coursing through my body.

I moaned his name. "Tommy..."

"I'm yours," he panted. "I'm yours, baby."

The words sent a shiver down my spine, and I cried out, my body shuddering with pleasure. Tommy's lips met mine in a bruising kiss as his hips bucked, his cock pulsing inside me as he came, filling me again.

Locked in the aftershocks, Tommy gathered me into his arms, still inside me. He pressed his forehead to mine, breathing hard. Our sweat-slicked skin pressed together, and I felt his heartbeat thumping against my chest, matching the stuttering rhythm of my own.

"I love you, Sloane," he said, his voice a ragged whisper. "I'm in love you. I always have been, and I think I always will be."

No. No, no, no. Oh, God, his face. It was too much, too intense, and I couldn't hold back the tears. I buried my face in his neck, breathing in his scent as the tears rolled down my cheeks. Tommy held me close, his strong arms wrapping around me, holding me tight.

Tommy didn't mean it. He couldn't. He was physically incapable of love, of giving himself to someone on a deeper level. Everything was superficial to him. Immediate gratification. Those words were the byproduct of exhaustion and pent-up sexual frustration that had been building since that first, abortive kiss of his in the alley behind Lady Devine's. Love would never be a factor in our relationship, no matter how much he deluded himself.

God. Tommy. I wanted to give him what he needed. I wanted to tell him that I loved him, too.

But the words wouldn't come, because the words would be a lie.

I didn't love him.

Those words were locked inside my heart for someone else, and no matter how hard I tried, I couldn't bring myself to say them out loud.

I had to let him go.

So, instead of answering Tommy, I held onto him, knowing that it would be the last time. As I drifted off to sleep in his arms, I told myself

I was doing the right thing, that we both deserved better. I told myself it was for the best, and that it was the only way to protect us from getting hurt.

This was Tommy, and this was just supposed to be one night.

And that was all.

22

Tommy

I opened my eyes, and for a moment, I couldn't remember where I was. The room was unfamiliar, the light streaming through the window a different angle. The soft sheets and plush pillows were too comfortable, the silence too quiet.

The cat sitting on my chest. That was different, too.

With a start, I realized where I was: Sloane's bed.

We spent the night together.

Sloane. Where is she?

A brief moment of panic had me halfway out of bed, my heart in my throat as I kicked at the sheets. That was all it took for me to register the sounds coming from the kitchen and the scent of freshly brewed coffee. The cat shot me an annoyed look. He hopped off the bed and sauntered out of the bedroom.

Sloane hadn't left. She was in the kitchen, making breakfast.

I lay back in bed, my mind reeling. Last night had been...intense. It had been more than I ever could have imagined. We'd connected on a deeper level, in a way I'd never experienced before. I'd felt closer to her than I'd ever felt to anyone. I'd opened myself up to her, exposed my deepest, darkest parts. I'd let her in. I'd told her I loved her.

But she hadn't said it back.

That thought sent a jolt of pain through me. I'd known it was a risk, but I'd been willing to take it. I'd wanted her to know how I felt, even if she couldn't say it back, yet. I knew how she felt. I saw it in her eyes when she looked at me, heard it in the way she moaned my name. I felt it in her kiss, the beat of her heart against mine, the squeeze of her around me as she came apart in my arms. Sloane loved me, in every way that mattered. I didn't have to hear it to know it.

She loved me.

A slow smile spread across my lips. I couldn't have fought it if I tried. Suddenly I felt lighter than I had in years, like I could take on the world. Sloane loved me back.

God, I usually wasn't such a sap when it came to sex. Last night was different, though. It had been so much more than sex. It had been two people connecting on a deeper level, sharing a part of themselves that they'd never shared with anyone else. It had been two people who understood each other in a way that no one else ever would.

Last night was incredible. Sloane had been incredible. She'd been so responsive, so passionate. I'd never felt a connection like that with anyone before.

I was in love with Sloane, and last night had just solidified that fact. I wasn't going to hide it anymore. I was going to show her how I felt and make sure that she knew how much she meant to me. I would do everything in my power to make her feel loved, because she deserved it.

I was going to love her every day for the rest of my life.

The sound of clanking dishes broke me out of my thoughts. I threw off the covers and got out of bed and stretched, feeling the satisfying ache of muscles I hadn't used in a while. My body felt sated and relaxed, ready to take on the world. I felt like I could face anything, as long as Sloane was by my side.

Hunting around for my jeans, I finally found them on the floor. I tugged them on, then looked around briefly for my shirt before I remembered Sloane nearly ripping it from my body last night on the couch. Maybe she put it on this morning. The thought of her wearing my shirt made my chest puff out with pride, and I grinned to myself as I ran my fingers through my hair and walked out of the bedroom, following the scent of coffee and bacon.

Sloane looked so beautiful in the morning light, I couldn't help but stare. She must have showered while I was still sleeping, because she was already fully dressed, standing with her back to me as she filled two mugs with coffee. Her dark hair shone with dark auburn highlights in the morning sun, and the curve of her ass was mouthwatering in her tight jeans. She was the most beautiful thing I'd ever seen.

"Good morning," I said, my voice still rough from sleep. I picked up my tee shirt, laying forlornly on the floor by the sofa, walked up behind her, and tenderly kissed the nape of her neck. "You're up early."

Sloane nearly jumped out of her skin. She shied away from my touch, nearly spilling the coffee. "Tommy! I didn't hear you get up."

Her reaction surprised me. She was usually so tough, so resilient, but she seemed almost skittish. "Are you okay?"

"Yeah, I'm fine." She handed me one of the mugs of coffee. "Here, this should help wake you up. Busy day today."

I took a sip of the coffee, feeling the hot liquid slide down my throat. It was good, but it wasn't enough to distract me from Sloane's unusual behavior. "You're sure you're okay? I didn't hurt you last night, did I?"

"No, no, I'm fine," she insisted.

"Okay," I said, drawing out the word. I set down my cup. "Then what is it?"

Sloane looked at me with those big green eyes of hers, and I felt something inside me shift. The air between us was suddenly heavy with tension, and I knew that I needed to break it.

"Talk to me, spitfire," I said, my voice low and soft. I reached out and tucked a strand of hair behind her ear, letting my fingers linger on her cheek. "Tell me what's wrong."

Slowly, Sloane stepped back and put several feet between us, emotions warring on her face.

"Tommy..." she said, her voice barely above a whisper. "Last night...it was incredible. But let's not make it into anything more than what it was. It was just sex."

Just sex. The words hit me like a punch to the gut. I took a step back, as if the physical distance between us could lessen the impact. I couldn't believe it. I shook my head. "No...no, it was more than that. You know it was more than that."

"I'm sorry," she said sharply as she turned back to the counter. "But it's just sex, Tommy. It can't be anything else. You know that. You agreed to that."

I wanted to grab her by the shoulders and shake her. I wanted to yell at her. I wanted to kiss her. I wanted to do everything I could to change her mind, to make her see that what we had was real. That what we had between us was special.

But I didn't do any of those things. I just stood there, watching her, feeling the weight of her words pressing down on my shoulders. I'd been so sure, so certain, last night had meant something to her. But maybe I was wrong. Maybe it hadn't.

Maybe she didn't love me, after all.

I felt the last vestiges of hope draining away. Anguish flooded my veins, tempered sharply by anger. "I know what I felt last night, Sloane. I know what you felt. Don't tell me it didn't mean anything to you. Don't lie to me."

She spun around, her eyes blazing. "I'm not lying. Just because you can't rectify what happened last night with this...this ridiculous fantasy you have of me. Of us. It's all in your head, Tommy. There is nothing between us, and there never will be."

Sloane turned her back to me, and her words hit me like a punch to the gut. My anger simmered. She couldn't be serious. She had to be lying.

"Then look me in the eyes," I spun her around and pinned her to the counter, bracketing her with my arms and letting my bulk dwarf her. "Look at me and tell me last night meant nothing to you. That you didn't feel a single thing. Tell me I imagined the way you looked at me, the way you touched me."

Sloane's eyes were wide, her cheeks flushed, and I could tell she was struggling to control her emotions. But she met my gaze head-on, and there was no doubt in my mind that she meant every word.

"It meant nothing, Tommy. Nothing. We fucked. It's that simple. Just scratching an itch," she added cruelly. "And if this is how you're going to react, then maybe it never should have happened at all."

I felt like I'd been punched in the gut. I couldn't breathe. I couldn't believe it. Sloane couldn't be so cold, so heartless after what we'd shared last night. How could she deny it? How could she pretend last night had meant nothing to her?

I'd opened myself up to her, exposed my deepest, darkest parts.

I'd let her in.

I'd told her I loved her.

She doesn't love you back, asshole. When are you going to get it through your thick skull? Sloane will never love you.

I was such a fucking idiot.

I'd been so sure of myself. So sure of her. I'd let my guard down, let myself believe that she felt the same way. But I was wrong.

The realization hit me like a ton of bricks, and I felt the anger drain away, only to be replaced by a crushing sense of loss. Less than five seconds was all that it had taken for her to rip out my heart, and it was still beating on the floor at Sloane's feet where she'd dropped it. I was such a goddamn fool. I took a deep breath, trying to steady myself, but it didn't help. There wasn't enough air in the room.

"I'm sorry," she said, her voice quiet. She looked embarrassed. Hell, I would be too, if I had to tell off some schmuck declaring his unrequited love. "I know this isn't what you wanted to hear, but it's the truth. We're not meant to be together, Tommy. You know that as well as I do."

I couldn't look at her. I couldn't bear to see the pity written on her face.

I should leave. I should get the fuck out of here before I make a bigger fool of myself.

I just couldn't seem to remember how my legs worked.

Sloane peeked at me out of the corner of her eye. "Do you...want some breakfast? I made enough..."

I let out a sharp bark of laughter tinged at the edges with insanity. "Breakfast?"

Her brow furrowed in confusion.

"No," I said, shaking my head. "No, I don't want breakfast. I'm, um...I have to go."

If Sloane answered me, I didn't hear it. I was already out the door, grabbing my jacket from where I'd left it on the couch and heading for the stairs. I needed to get out of there, away from her. Away from this place.

I need a drink.

No, I needed to hit something.

And, just my luck, I knew a guy who would fit the bill perfectly.

Misha met me at a dive bar a few blocks down from where Lady D's used to be. At two in the afternoon, it was nearly deserted. Misha answered his phone on the second ring, almost as if he'd been waiting for my call.

I guess, in a way, Misha had quite a bit at stake in this fight. After all, Dominic had tried to kill him, too.

I'd downed a couple shots before Misha arrived, and I could already feel the warmth of the alcohol in my belly, spreading through my veins. It was a pleasant sensation, dulling the pain, making it more bearable. Purely medicinal, but when he offered to buy another round, I waved him off. I needed to keep my head clear.

Misha looked at me for a long time before he spoke. I can only guess how I must have looked, because he ordered another round anyway.

"We have a saying in Russia," he said at last. "The flame of love will warm you, but hold it too close, and it will consume you."

I laughed, a hollow, bitter sound. "How poetic."

"She broke your heart." It wasn't a question.

I drained the rest of my shot, feeling the liquid burn its way down my throat. I needed to stop while I still had feelings in my extremities. I set down the glass, the sound too loud in the quiet of the bar. "Something like that."

"*Govno.*" Misha grimaced, as if he'd been expecting my answer. He sat back in his chair and looked at me for a long moment, his dark eyes inscrutable. "I warned you about her, remember? I told you not to get involved."

I bristled at his words. "I knew the risks. I knew what I was getting into."

"You didn't know a thing about it," Misha said. "But you fell in love with her, anyway."

"I've been in love with her since I was seventeen years old," I snapped. But just as quickly as it flared, the fight went out of me. I sighed and ran a hand through my hair, suddenly feeling bone tired. "It doesn't matter."

Misha leaned forward, his dark eyes intense. "You need something to take your mind off it. A distraction. Something to work out your anger on."

I snorted. "Yeah, I have someone in mind."

"Good. That's why I am here."

"And that's why I called you. You said you could produce Dominic? Then do it. Tell him I'm ready. Just him and me. Tonight, at the parking garage where the underground fights were. I'm sure you remember the place."

He smiled flatly. "Of course. Give me a few hours to set everything up, and I will call you."

Misha clapped me on the back as he stood to leave, gripping my shoulder with one strong hand. "Don't do anything stupid until then, alright? I need you alive to take care of this problem. We are in this together."

"Don't worry, I can take care of myself," I said, not bothering to mask my annoyance. "Just make sure he's there."

"*Da.* Yes. It is already done." Misha continued to mutter in Russian as he left the bar.

Alone again, I stared down at the empty glass in front of me. Absently, I wondered what Sloane was doing right now. If she was still at work with Grady. If she wondered where I was. I laughed bitterly to myself and shook my head. No. I was pretty sure Sloane saw the depths of my humiliation this morning and had probably washed her hands of me completely. I didn't blame her.

Still, it would've been nice to see her once last time.

Just in case.

I briefly considered calling Connor, or at least Grady, but I banished the thought almost as soon as it appeared. They didn't need to know about this. I could handle Dominic myself. This was between him and me.

The last thing I needed was to drag my friends into my shit, especially when I knew they'd try to talk me out of it. Because one way or another, it would be over. Tonight I would step into that ring with a bitter opponent, and only one of us was going to come out.

And for the first time in my life, I really didn't care which one of us that would be.

23

Sloane

BOUNCING MY LEG, I checked the shipping office's wall clock for the five millionth time. Nearly eight o'clock, and still no sign of Tommy.

What did you expect, after you broke his heart like that?

I shoved that voice aside. I didn't break his heart. I couldn't break his heart. Not when he didn't have one.

Liar.

Oh, I heard what he'd said last night. Pretty words from a pretty mouth. But that's all they were, empty words, caught up in the heat of the moment. Passion on the tongue of a lifelong playboy. I had no doubt he thought he meant them in that moment—what, two seconds after he came in me for the second time that night? That wasn't love. That was lust, pure and simple, the only thing Tommy was capable of.

Then how do you explain the look on his face this morning? You couldn't have gotten a more visceral reaction if you'd taken a steak knife from the counter and stabbed him in the heart.

My breath caught in my chest as I remembered the hurt on Tommy's face, the pain in his dark eyes. He'd looked so broken, so betrayed. And I was the one who'd put that look on his face.

I hated it.

But it had been necessary. It was better this way, for both of us. I couldn't risk getting my heart broken again. I couldn't risk falling for him only to watch him chase the next skirt that passed by.

It's easier to hurt someone before they hurt you, than to pick up the pieces once they do.

Coward. Cold-hearted bitch.

"Shut up!" Angrily, I pushed back from the desk. My chair squeaked on its wheels as it rolled across the room and crashed into the wall. I took a deep breath and tried to calm myself. The last thing I needed right now was to lose it.

I paced back and forth across the tiny office space, eyes carefully avoiding the desk where I'd first kissed Tommy. Each time felt like a sucker punch to the gut. I'd been so stupid, letting him into my life. Letting him into my heart. I should have known better. I should have kept my distance. But I couldn't. I'd been drawn to him, like a moth to a flame. And I'd gotten burned.

It was better this way. Better to end it now, before either of us got hurt.

Then why did it hurt so much already? Why did I keep seeing the shell-shocked look on his face in my mind, the pain in his eyes? Why couldn't I stop thinking about him? About the way he made me feel, the way he made me laugh, the way he made me come?

Because you're in love with him, and you pushed him away.

A niggling seed of doubt began to worm its way into my mind. I'd seen the way he'd looked at me, the way he'd touched me, the way he'd held me. It had been so tender, so loving, so intimate. It had felt so real.

But it wasn't real, was it? It was just sex.

Wasn't it?

The memory of Tommy's face, his touch, the words he'd whispered in my ear...they were burned into my brain, haunting me. I wasn't usually one for self-doubt. Callum had raised me that way. Once I made a decision, I stuck to it, no matter what.

But what if, this time, the decision had been wrong?

This wasn't some business deal or bar fight. This was Tommy. This was my heart and his. This was everything. And I'd thrown it away, without a second thought.

Because I was scared.

I stopped in my tracks, feeling the truth of it wash over me. I'd been so terrified of getting hurt that I hadn't even given him a chance. I hadn't even tried to make it work. I'd just assumed the worst and run away, like a coward.

But now it was too late. I'd burned that bridge. I'd hurt Tommy, and he would never forgive me.

Fumbling for my phone, I dialed the number before I even thought about what I was doing. It rang once, twice, three times, before a familiar voice answered. "Hey girl, I was just getting ready to call you!"

I could barely hear Kat over the roar of the crowd in the background. "Kat? What's going on?"

"Oh, nothing. I just had to pick up an extra shift tonight at the bar. One of the bartenders called out sick, and we're short-staffed. How about returning that favor? I know it's probably too soon after Lady D's..."

"Kat, I think I fucked up."

"What? Wait, hold on." I heard the muffled sound of fabric shifting as Kat put a hand over the phone. The crowd noise dimmed as she stepped outside. "Say that again?"

"I...I messed up, Kat," I said. My voice sounded small and weak, even to me. "I think I made a mistake."

"Oh, sweetie, it's okay," Kat said, her voice soothing. "Everyone makes mistakes. Even you, although I can't remember you ever admitting to one." She laughed weakly, then her voice sobered. "What happened?"

I hesitated, not sure how to even begin to explain it. "It's...it's hard to explain."

"It's Tommy, isn't it?"

I winced, hating that Kat knew me so well. "Yes."

"I called it," she hooted triumphantly. "Didn't I tell you that you were perfect for each other? All that sexual tension? Come on, I saw it from a mile away!"

I frowned. "Yeah...tension might be one way of putting it. It's complicated. But I don't know what to do, Kat. I think I've screwed things up beyond repair."

"I'm sure it's not that bad," Kat said, her voice sympathetic.

"He told me he loved me and I basically slammed the door in his face."

I could practically see her wince through the phone. "Ouch."

"I told him it was just meaningless sex," I blurted out. "I told him that it meant nothing to me, that it was just an itch to be scratched. I broke his heart. And now I think I've broken mine in the process."

There was a long pause, then Kat sighed. "Well, shit."

"I know," I groaned, burying my head in my hands. "I know. I'm a terrible person. I told myself I didn't mean any of it, I was just trying to protect myself, but...but..."

"But you fell for him anyway," Kat finished.

I laughed bitterly. "Yeah. Pretty fucking hard. I never saw it coming. I just panicked. I was so sure he was going to break my heart, so I broke his first. But I was wrong, Kat. I was so wrong."

"Do you love him?" she asked quietly.

"I...I don't know. Maybe?" My throat felt thick, and I swallowed hard. "All I know is that it's not a no. It wouldn't hurt this bad if I didn't."

Kat sighed again, and I could hear the sympathy in her voice. "No, you're not. You're just scared. You've been hurt before, and you don't want to get hurt again."

"I'm not scared," I said automatically.

"Yes, you are," Kat said. "But it's okay. Love is scary, Sloane. It's supposed to be. And ugly and messy and unexpected. But it's also worth it, if you let it be. If you're willing to take a chance on it."

I felt my heart clench at her words. I'd been so focused on protecting myself, on protecting my heart, that I hadn't even considered the possibility that I could have it all. That I could be happy with Tommy, if I just let myself.

I'd made a mistake. I knew that now. But it wasn't too late to fix it.

"I've got to go, Kat," I said quickly. "Sorry about the backup tonight."

"Girl, I'd be pissed if you tried to come down here right now. Go get your man and tell him how you feel!"

I laughed as I hung up the phone, feeling lighter than I had in months. I had to tell Tommy. I had to tell him the truth, that I was falling for him, that I'd been wrong.

But first, I had to find him.

Grabbing my jacket, I rushed out of the shipping office, my heart pounding. I had no idea where to start, but I couldn't wait for Tommy to show up. I needed to find him. I needed to tell him.

Thunder rumbled overhead, shaking the rafters of the warehouse. It looked like the storm that had been brewing for the past few days was about to break. I hurried outside, letting the heavy metal door slam behind me. The air was heavy with moisture, and I could smell the rain in the air. I'd try Saul's first, and then Tommy's apartment. If he wasn't there, I'd hit all his regular haunts. I didn't care how long it took; I'd search the whole damn city if I had to.

Not wanting to waste a second, I hailed a cab, but just as I was about to get in, my phone rang. I pulled it out of my pocket and stared at the screen. The caller ID said Unknown Number. Frowning, I answered it.

"Hello?"

"Is this Sloane?" A deep voice with a New York accent I didn't recognize.

"Who is this?"

"It's Luca...Luca Mariano. T-Tommy gave me your number," he said slowly, as if speaking were difficult for him. "Said if I ever needed anything and he couldn't be reached, I should call you."

I pinched the bridge of my nose. Inside the cab, the driver threw up his hands and gave me a questioning glance, and I held up a finger to ask him to wait. I didn't have time for this. "Luca, I'm sorry, but this isn't the best time. Is there something I can do for you?"

"That's the thing...I'm calling about Tommy. I think Dominic's going after him."

"We already know. He's been sending threats, and he—"

"No. Tonight." Luca cut me off. "D-Dom's going after him tonight."

The blood drained from my face. "Tell me."

"I...I heard it. From the guys," he said, his speech halting. "I said I'd keep an eye on him for Tommy, but now Dom's gone...something big is happening. Sal took off with half the men, and Dom was with them."

I took off down the block, the cab forgotten. I didn't know where I was going. I just needed to move. "Why now? What makes tonight so different? First the fire, and then the car—if Dom wanted to kill Tommy, he could've done it already."

"Woah...w-what're you talking about? What fire? What car?"

Quickly, I filled him in on everything that had happened so far. Everything Tommy had told me about, at least. The photographs, the threats to Connor and Cassidy. Tommy's father. The fire at Lady D's and the assassin on the road. Luca was silent as I spoke, barely making a noise on the other end of the phone. When I finished, he let out a long breath.

"That wasn't Dominic. Not all of it."

"What do you mean?"

"Dominic doesn't have the kind of reach to kill Michael Quinn, and even if he did, he wouldn't make it look like a natural death. I don't know anything about a fire, but...the assassin couldn't have been ours. I know our guy personally, and that isn't his style."

"What do you mean, you know him? How can you be sure it wasn't him?" I asked.

Luca paused for a long moment, and when he spoke, his voice was grim. "Because I've seen his work. If it was him, Tommy would already be dead."

That stopped me in my tracks. My heart pounding, I took a deep breath, trying to calm my nerves. "Luca...what do you mean, him? Tommy said he saw a woman on the road that night."

Another long pause. When Luca spoke again, I had to press the phone against my ear to hear him. "There is only one female assassin I know of in the area...and she isn't ours. They call her *Chernaya Gadyuka*. The Black Viper. Nobody knows real name, because anyone who's ever g-gotten close enough to see her is dead."

Muttering on the other end of the line, Luca talking to someone. "Her...last known a-alias was Natalia Andreyev."

"Russian?"

"Yeah. Listen...is Tommy still working with that Russian? What was his name?"

“Misha.”

“That’s him. Look, I had my friend do a little digging...”

I listened as Luca told me everything he’d found out about Misha. My mind spun. It felt like there were pieces of a puzzle swirling around in my head, and I was only now starting to get a glimpse of the whole picture. But before I could ask Luca anything else, my phone vibrated with an incoming call. It was Grady.

"Luca, I'm getting another call. I've got to go."

"Good luck—"

I hung up on him before he could say anything else, swiping up to answer the incoming call. "Grady?"

"Sloane, thank God." Grady's voice sounded strained.

"Grady, what's wrong? What's going on?"

"I-I'm not really sure. I just got this weird text message from Tommy."

"Tommy? What did he say?"

"I don't know...he just texted me an address and said to meet him there. He said bring the guys with me."

An icy finger of dread trailed down my spine. "What's the address?"

"It's the same one on that business card I found in his pocket. The parking garage."

"The fights," I whispered. "Grady, read that text message back to me, exactly how he wrote it."

Grady did, and the pieces clicked into place. It didn't sound like him at all. My throat felt dry. I forced myself to swallow. "When was this?"

"About ten minutes ago," Grady said. "We were getting ready to head down there, but—"

"Go. Go now. Take as many of the guys as you can find, but make sure they're carrying and wearing vests."

"What? Sloane, why, what's happening?"

"Just do it, Grady. I'll meet you there." I ended the call and took off sprinting in the direction I came as the first fat raindrops began to pelt the sidewalk.

I only hoped I wasn't already too late.

24

Tommy

UNSPENT ADRENALINE COURSED THROUGH my veins as I waited beneath the flickering sodium bulb for Dominic to show. Outside, the storm had finally arrived. A crack of thunder sounded, followed by a flash of lightning. Rain pelted the abandoned parking garage, coming in sideways, dripping from long cracks in the cement overhead. The air was heavy with humidity, and I felt sweat bead on the back of my neck.

Misha stood beside me, his dark eyes alert, his body tense. I'd already given him my cell, keys, and jacket for safekeeping. I told him he didn't need to stay, but he insisted on playing lookout. If he wanted to see the show, more power to him; I doubted he'd be sticking around once the blood started flying.

The slam of a car door broke the silence. A few minutes later, Sal emerged from the shadows. He was wearing a dark suit and a long coat, and he was holding an umbrella. A handful of Dominic's goons filed out of the vehicle and surrounded him. Dominic stepped forward, his face yellowed and wan in the dim glow from the overhead lights. He was grinning, his teeth a slash of white in the gloom. Behind him, his men formed up, not even trying to conceal the weapons they were carrying.

Okay. So it was going to be like that.

I looked to my left, where Misha was also watching the Italians assemble, his face expressionless. He'd been duped, just like I had.

Looks like you're not walking away from this one.

Some part of me had been expecting this. I wasn't as surprised as I should have been. The anger I felt hardened into something more visceral, carving down into the depths of my soul and reaching the place where I'd stored away my last precious memories of Sloane. They were all I had, now. I had already said my goodbyes to her. I just hadn't realized it at the time.

I felt oddly calm. I knew I was about to die. There was no way I could take on the group of guys Dominic had brought with him with only the single gun I was carrying. Even with Misha, it was no contest, and I wasn't about to let him die for me.

"Misha, clear out. Now," I said quietly, not taking my eyes off Dominic. "You don't need to be a part of this."

Misha snorted. "Do not insult me. I will stay."

I risked a glance at him, and he gave me a slight nod. His hand was hidden by in darkness, but I knew he had a gun. I couldn't say what his angle was, but I was grateful for the backup.

I looked back at Dominic. He was still grinning.

"What are your boys doing here, Dominic?" I called out. "I thought we were meeting alone."

Dominic laughed, and the sound echoed off the concrete walls. "Don't be stupid. You know how this goes. You knew I'd come with a few friends. I just didn't think you'd be dumb enough to trust my integrity and not bring your own. You must have some kind of death wish, Quinn."

I didn't trust you, I trusted—

But Dominic was already speaking again, cutting off that thought at the pass. "Looks like I'll get one more crack at you before I send you to meet your old man. Shame how he died, by the way."

I didn't say anything. My pulse was racing, but my head was clear. I'd made my decision. I'd known this was a possibility when I agreed to meet him here, and I'd accepted that. I was ready to face whatever fate awaited me, as long as I got to face it head-on.

I'm sorry, Sloane. I love you, baby.

Dominic smiled again, but this time there was a hard edge to it. "What's the matter? Cat got your tongue?"

"No," I said slowly, stepping into the light. "I'm just tired of talking. Let's get this over with."

"With pleasure," Dominic growled.

The assembled men formed a loose ring around us as I tossed my sidearm to Misha. I wasn't going to be needing it. Misha pocketed my gun and stepped back to lean against the wall, the picture of nonchalance, as if he saw fights like this every day.

Dominic threw his jacket aside and took a fighting stance. We circled each other, neither of us making a move. I knew this would be different from the fight at the club. There, I'd been trying to keep him alive. Here, I had no such compunction. Dominic wouldn't be pulling any punches, either.

Suddenly, Dominic lunged forward, catching me off guard. He was faster than I'd expected. His fist connected with my jaw, and pain exploded across my face. I stumbled back, trying to regain my balance. He followed up with a punch to my stomach, driving the air from my lungs. I staggered back, struggling to breathe.

Dominic didn't waste any time. He pressed his advantage, raining blows on my face and body. I blocked as many as I could, but I was still off-balance from his first hit.

I lashed out with a punch of my own, catching him in the side. I felt something give beneath my fist. Dominic grunted, but he didn't slow down. He kept coming at me, hitting me with everything he had.

I ducked another punch, then stepped in and slammed my knee into his chest. I felt the crunch of bone, and Dominic let out a howl of pain. But he didn't go down. From the two different times I'd fought him, I had been able to get a glimpse of his fighting style. Back-alley brawler at best. Dominic was still all fury and no finesse, but something had changed in him. Snapped. He was like a machine, relentless in his pursuit of vengeance.

He caught me with a vicious uppercut that sent me reeling. I stumbled backward, but Dominic didn't give me any time to recover. He surged forward and slammed his shoulder into my chest. The force of the impact drove the breath from my lungs, and I gasped as I hit the ground.

Blood poured down the side of my face, obscuring my field of vision. I'd landed on my bad shoulder, hard. I was still sucking air into my spasming lungs when he came at me again, and I scrambled to my feet as Dominic closed in, his eyes wild. He was like a rabid animal, determined to tear me apart. I raised my fists, ready to take him on, but Dominic surprised me. He lashed out with a vicious kick that connected with my knee. I went down hard, the pain causing stars to explode across my vision.

Dominic pounced on me, landing blow after blow on my face and body. I struggled to get my hands up to protect myself, but he was relentless. His fist connected with my jaw. Pain exploded across my face, and I felt my lip split open. Blood filled my mouth. I tried to spit it out, but my mouth wouldn't work right.

I was losing. Badly.

Dominic didn't let up. He hit me again, and again, and again. I could barely get my hands up to cover my face anymore. Dimly, I realized that somewhere along the way, I'd quit. I wasn't even trying anymore. I didn't have the fight left in me. My heart was shattered beyond repair.

His hands closed around my throat. Dominic's face was twisted in rage as he squeezed, cutting off my air supply.

"I'm going to enjoy watching you die," he growled. His face was a mask of blood, and I could see the hatred burning in his eyes. I tried to push him off me, but he was too strong. I couldn't breathe. Black spots danced in front of my eyes as the darkness closed in.

Misha's words came back to me again, about how the loss of a good woman could kill a man. I thought of Sloane, of how much she meant to me. Of how much I loved her. And I knew, in that moment, that it was true. Somehow, I had always known that Sloane would be the death of me, one way or another.

My vision tunneled. I could feel myself slipping away. My chest burned with the lack of oxygen, and my body screamed for relief. I struggled to breathe, to stay conscious, but it was a losing battle. Blood pounded in my ears. Faster. Faster.

Dominic's grip tightened, and he leaned in close to my ear, his voice a low whisper. "I told you I'd be the one to kill you, Quinn."

Just as I was about to black out, I heard a gunshot, muffled like it was underwater. Shouting.

Dominic's hands went slack. I thrust my hands up and broke his hold, purely an instinctual reaction as I rolled over and away from him, gasping for breath.

Everything blurred. I shook my head to clear it and staggered to my feet.

Sloane, Connor, Grady, and about a dozen of the guys were in the mouth of the garage, guns drawn. Sal stood in front of them, shouting something. Sloane's gaze was fixed on me, her still smoking gun pointed at the ceiling. Her eyes were wide, her face was pale, but her hand was steady as she looked at me like she was seeing me for the first time.

Sloane came back for me.

She'd brought Connor. The guys. Christ, even my sister was there. Somehow, Sloane had figured it all out, and she'd come for me. The thought brought a new wave of adrenaline to my flagging body. I didn't know what this meant, exactly, but Sloane was *here*.

She had my back.

Just like I'd always have hers.

For a split second, it was just the two of us. Then time kicked back in.

Dominic tackled me from behind with a roar, slamming me into the ground. I landed hard on my injured shoulder, pain flaring through the joint. From my right, Sloane screamed my name. I bucked my hips and rolled out of the way, head-butting him on the way up.

The pain in my shoulder was white-hot, and I let out a grunt as I pushed myself to my feet. Dominic lunged forward, and I side-stepped, grabbing him by the arm and using his own momentum to throw him. His body slammed into the pavement with a dull thud.

Dominic rolled over and got back to his feet with a groan, and I felt a surge of satisfaction. He was hurt.

Good. I wanted him to hurt. I wanted him to feel the same pain he'd inflicted on me. I wanted him to pay for what he'd done, not just to me, but to everyone I loved.

He came at me again, but this time I was ready. I caught him with a hard jab to the ribs. I heard a satisfying crack as his ribs broke, and Dominic let out a howl of pain. But he didn't slow down. He kept coming at me, throwing punch after punch. I blocked as many as I could, but he landed a few good hits.

The fight had disintegrated into a street brawl. I ducked another hit and countered with a cross to the jaw that had Dominic staggering back, and in my peripherals, I could see both Connor and Sloane holding the crowd back, letting me go at Dominic. With a roar, I tackled him, propelling both our bodies out of the circle, over the concrete barrier, and off the edge of the parking garage.

We fell.

It was a short drop, broken by the construction debris that littered the ground. I landed on top of Dominic with a muffled grunt.

Rain came down in sheets and soaked us immediately. My ribcage screamed as I scrambled up. Dominic was a little slower getting to his feet, but the look in his eyes was pure murder. He lunged at me, but I sidestepped, grabbing his arm and twisting it behind his back.

"Where the fuck do you think you're going? We're not done yet," I snarled, driving my knee into his side. I heard a wet pop as his arm was forced from the socket, and Dominic screamed.

A right and a cross brought him to his knees. I slammed my fist into his face again, and again, and again. Dominic sagged to the ground. His face was a bloody mess. I grabbed him by the hair and yanked his head back, my voice a growl. "Give me one reason why I shouldn't end you right now."

"Go ahead. Kill me," Dominic choked. "I'm dead anyway, just like you."

I blinked blood and rain from my eyes. Thunder boomed overhead. Behind me, I could hear my clan shouting for me to finish him. To kill him, right here. Right now. Only Connor and my sister were silent, watching. Sloane looked like she was about to run to me, but Connor grabbed her shoulders, stopping her with a shake of his head.

Lightning split the sky. From the other side of the lot, the Italians stood silently. I could feel their eyes on me, waiting to see what I would do.

Dominic coughed, blood dribbling down his chin. He looked up at me, his eyes glassy. "Do it."

I stared down at him. He looked so pathetic, kneeling there, consumed with revenge yet knowing he was beaten. All but begging for a death I wanted to give so badly. I wanted to end him, to make him pay for everything he'd done, for all the pain he and his family had caused.

I should hate him. I should pity the person he'd become. But all I saw was a foreshadowed warning of my own future should I continue down this path.

I looked at Sloane, and our eyes met. Faintly, she shook her head.

With a snarl, I released Dominic and shoved him towards the Italians. "Not today."

Dominic slumped to the ground. Blood dripped from his nose. He looked up at me, hatred still twisting his face, but the fire behind it was gone. Instead, something else burned in its place. Fear.

Blinking past the rain, I caught Sal's eye. "This ends here," I said. "Our families, this fight? It's over. You stay on your side, and we'll stay on ours. This is my peace offering to you."

Behind me, I heard the click of rounds being chambered. My guys were prepared to back me up if Sal decided to push back.

He did not.

Sal nodded. "I accept your terms. Enough blood has been spilt on this soil."

"Good." Trying to keep my steps steady, I took a step forward and held out my hand.

For a moment, Sal looked surprised. Then, slowly, he reached out and grasped my hand. Our gazes met, and I could see the respect in his eyes.

The moment stretched on as we stood there, facing each other. Then Sal nodded once and stepped back, turning to the rest of his brethren.

I nudged Dominic's unmoving body with my foot. "Get this piece of shit out of South Boston and make sure he doesn't come back."

Without another word, the Italians picked up Dominic's body and carried it back to their car. Sal was the last one to leave. He turned back to me, his eyes unreadable in the darkness.

"There will be other fights," he said quietly.

"There always are," I agreed. "But not tonight. Not with us."

Sal nodded again. "I hope we never see each other again."

"Likewise," I said, meaning it.

As Sal turned to leave, I caught sight of Sloane pushing through the crowd of clan members. She walked towards me quickly, the expression on her face murderous.

I met her halfway, bracing myself for the ass-chewing I knew was coming. "Sloane, I know you didn't—"

Sloane didn't stop.

My jaw slacked as she barreled right past me and pulled her gun on Misha. "Give me one reason why I shouldn't blow your goddamn brains out right here. *Volkov.*"

25

Sloane

I HELD MY GUN steady, drawing a bead right between Misha's unblinking eyes. Or, Aleksandr Volkov, as his birth certificate read.

Volkov smiled lazily, seemingly unsurprised. "Sloane McTiernan, I underestimated you. You know you're the first one in years to figure it out?"

"Shut the fuck up," I growled, cocking the gun.

"Sloane, what are you doing—" Cassidy's voice cut off as Connor scooped her out of the way.

The second I pulled the gun on Volkov, the clan erupted, everyone shouting and trying to see what was going on. The Italians had just departed, the fight over, but the tensions were still high. Everyone was on edge.

Only Tommy stood quietly by my side, his eyes flicking between Volkov and me.

"You set me up," he grated out. "You led me straight into that ambush."

"No ambush," Volkov said. "I knew your men wouldn't be too far behind you. Although, it was a near thing. I really had to spell it out for your second-in-command, there." His eyes flicked to me. "What gave me away?"

Not taking my eyes off Volkov, I inched closer to Tommy. "You know that woman you saw the night of the crash, Tommy? She wasn't working for the Italians. Your boy Luca called me when he couldn't get ahold of you and Dominic left with half the compound in tow. The Italians don't have any female soldiers, and I doubt they'd take one on board, even if they were desperate. He identified the assassin as Natalia Andreyev, aka the Black Viper. One of the best in the business. Russian, in case that wasn't plain enough from her alias."

Tommy looked at me sharply. "Misha was in the car that night with me."

"Volkov was. There never was a meeting, was there?" I asked him, my gaze hardening. "This was all a setup, wasn't it? Right from the beginning."

"An opportunity," Volkov clarified. "Only later did it really begin to take shape. Once that mad dog Dominic's threats started getting under your skin, I saw an opportunity to even the playing field a bit."

"You mean pit us and the Italians against each other with the hope we'd take each other out," I spat.

Volkov shrugged. The gesture was so purely Misha I felt a new stab of rage drive through me. "I just fanned the flames. Tommy's need for vengeance did the rest."

"Hold on." Connor stepped forward, keeping Cassidy behind him. "You sent the photographs? Broke into our apartment? Set the fire at Lady D's?"

Volkov shook his head. "The photographs were Dominic's. But when they didn't prove to be...sufficient motivation, I saw the need to take matters into my own hands."

The crash. The fire.

"You almost killed Sloane," Tommy snarled. He barreled forward, but he froze when I grabbed his shoulder, stopping him.

"What about Tommy's father?" I asked.

At that, Volkov had the nerve to look sorry. "No," he said quietly. His eyes flicked to Cassidy, then settled on Tommy. "What happened to your father was unfortunate, but it was natural. I didn't have anything to do with it. Neither did the Italians."

When Tommy lunged forward this time, I didn't stop him. He hauled the Russian off his feet and slammed him into a concrete barrier. "Why should I believe a single goddamn word that's coming out of your mouth right now? You lied about everything else."

Volkov wheezed as Tommy's fist connected with his face. I was about to pull him off when Volkov raised a hand, signaling that he was done. Blood trickled from his nose, and I was pleased to see that Tommy had broken it. He grinned through the blood, and I felt my stomach turn at the sight of it.

"Because despite my manipulations, I like you, Tommy. I respect you. I would gain nothing by killing your father. Or you, Sloane." His eyes flicked to me. "I regret what happened at the bar. I would not have continued had I known you were still inside."

I didn't say anything. I couldn't.

"Sloane?" Tommy's voice was soft.

"He's telling the truth," I said finally. "Volkov looks out for Volkov. Murdering me or your father wouldn't have served any purpose."

Tommy looked at me, and I knew he could read the truth on my face. He released Volkov. "There never was any deal on the table, was there? You never intended to give us your contacts."

"I told you Volkov wanted the seaport. You should have listened."

"You *are* Volkov, asshole," I snapped. "We know your secrets."

Volkov shrugged. "You know one of them."

He looked up at the sky, still spitting drizzle. The thunderclouds had moved off, lightning illuminating a distant edge of the harbor. "If you are going to kill me, get on with it. Otherwise, let me go. The rain is ruining my jacket."

"I'm not killing you," Tommy said, looking disgusted. "You're not even worth the bullet it would take to put you down. I should, after everything you've done, but I won't. Instead, I'll offer you the same deal as the Italians. Get the hell out of South Boston, and don't come back."

Volkov's expression didn't change. If he was relieved, I couldn't tell. He straightened up, blotted the blood from his nose, and shot Tommy an impressed nod. "*Dasvidaniya*, Tommy Quinn."

"Whatever," Tommy growled. He was swaying on his feet, barely able to stand, but his voice was steady. "Get the fuck out of my city."

Volkov chuckled as he walked away, his hands in his pockets, his jacket flaring out behind him. He didn't look back, but I had no doubt that we'd be seeing him again.

The clan erupted. Half the guys were trying to pat him on the back, and the other half was trying to get him the hell out of there. Two rival gangs banished in one night. A line drawn in the sand over an olive branch.

It was going to be an interesting year.

I lost sight of Tommy as the clan descended on him. Connor took charge of the chaos, organizing the group into the remaining cars so we could relocate to a safer location. It wasn't until the cars pulled up at our warehouse in the shipping yard that I was able to see him.

Cassidy, predictably, was bossing him loudly, trying to get him to lay down while brandishing vague threats about broken ribs and brain injuries. The siblings bickered, each stubbornly refusing to give ground until Connor intervened, placing a calming hand on his wife's arm. "Let him go, love. Tommy's got some unfinished business to take care of."

"But—"

"He'll be in good hands." Connor looked at me and winked.

I felt myself blush. I looked at Tommy, who was watching me, his gaze unreadable. My heart skipped a beat, and I felt my body respond to his closeness. I swallowed hard, my throat suddenly dry. I'd spent the entire drive here worrying that Tommy was going to be hurt, or worse, that I was too late.

Now, standing here in front of him, I couldn't help but feel a little bit scared. Not of him, but of the depths of my feelings for him. I loved him. I think, maybe, I had always loved him, all along. All his faults, his bravado, his stubborn attitude. He was everything I'd ever wanted and never known I needed.

I was in love with Tommy Quinn.

Tommy looked at me, uncharacteristically shy and unsure. He was bruised and bloody and half dead on his feet, but when he opened his mouth to speak I didn't wait.

I threw myself into his arms and silenced him with a kiss.

Tommy's breath left him in a grunt as our bodies collided. He staggered backwards a step and wrapped his arms around my waist, pulling me tight against him. He smelled like sweat and rain and blood and adrenaline, and it was intoxicating.

His lips were warm and soft against mine, and he tasted faintly of copper. I kissed him hungrily, greedily, as if I was afraid he would disappear if I let go. Tommy kissed me back with equal fervor, his hands roaming my body, sliding under my shirt and across my skin.

"Sloane—"

"Not here," I gasped into his mouth. "Office."

We stumbled blindly towards the shipping office, not breaking the kiss. Tommy's hands were on my body, his fingers digging into my hips as he pulled me closer. His touch was fire, burning away my doubts and fears and leaving only desire in its wake. Briefly, I heard catcalls and whistles, but Tommy kicked the door shut behind us.

The sound of the door slamming closed echoed in the empty office. Tommy pushed me against the wall and kissed me hard, his hands gripping my hips as he pressed himself against me. I moaned into his mouth, feeling my body respond to his touch.

There was nothing gentle this time. A second battle had been waged, this one of our hearts as we kissed and bit, fisting hair and gripping waists and pushing hips together. It was frenzied, and fast, and everything I wanted.

I tore at his clothes. “I hate this jacket.”

“I hate your fucking attitude,” he shot back, ripping off my shirt.

"I hate your fucking mouth," as I devoured him.

"Not as much as I hate yours."

“I hate you.”

“I know.”

“I love you.”

Tommy froze. "What did you just say?"

I smiled and cradled his bruised jaw. "You heard me. I love you, Tommy Quinn."

Tommy's face split in a grin so wide it looked painful. "I know. I'm just glad you can finally admit it, spitfire."

"Asshole!" I tried to shove him, but he just laughed and pulled me closer.

"I love you too," he murmured in my ear.

He kissed me again, fisting his hand in my hair and pulling me closer. I could feel his arousal pressed against my stomach, and I moaned into his mouth as his hands roamed over my body, sending shivers of pleasure through my veins.

We finally made love right there on that desk.

We didn't even manage to get all our clothes off before he entered me, thrusting forward in a single claiming stroke. I cried out, my nails digging into his back as he set a brutal pace, pounding into me with an animalistic fervor. Our bodies moved in tandem, each thrust bringing me closer to the edge as he drove into me with a wild abandon I'd never seen from him before.

I clung to him, meeting his thrusts with equal ferocity. I screamed his name and felt his stomach muscles clench. Tommy growled, low and possessive. His teeth sank into my neck as he fucked me harder, driving me closer and closer to the edge.

Right when I was about to come he pulled out completely, stalling my orgasm. I twitched and gasped as he cradled me in his arms. "Tommy..."

"Shh, honey. I'm here. I'm not going anywhere." Slowly, he turned me around until I was bent over the desk. "I want to take my time with you. Just let me love you, Sloane."

"Always," I gasped as he entered me from behind.

This time, his pace was slow. Thorough. Fully unseating only to sheathe himself up to the hilt with slow, powerful thrusts that made my eyes cross. Filling me up completely, stretching me in ways I didn't know were possible. I felt every inch of him as he moved inside me, and it was both pleasure and torture.

I gripped the edges of the desk as Tommy made love to me, and I think I lost a little bit of myself in that moment. I gave it up to him willingly, along with my heart.

Tommy's hand slipped up my belly and to my breasts, teasing and pinching my nipples with his callused fingers. I whimpered, arching my back as he increased the pace of his thrusts. His other hand came up to lightly grip my throat, teeth nipping at the sensitive skin possessively.

"That's it, baby. You're mine. Come for me now," he panted in my ear. "Come on my cock."

His words pushed me over the edge. I cried out as my orgasm washed over me, wave after wave of pleasure crashing over me. Tommy groaned as he felt me tighten around him, his hips jerking erratically as he emptied himself inside me.

I slumped into his arms, and he held me close as we rode out our climaxes together. When we were spent and breathless, Tommy kissed me gently and pulled me close.

"You have my heart, Sloane McTiernan. I will love you until the day I die."

Our lips met, and this time the kiss was slow and gentle, full of promises. I could feel Tommy's heart pounding its truth against my chest, and this time, I knew he meant it. Tommy loved me.

And I loved him right back.

Epilogue

The lights from Temple Bar winked merrily off the River Liffey, mirrored in the dark water below. Live music floated out from the open windows of the pubs and restaurants that lined the street, the sounds of laughter and conversation drifting out into the night.

It was a perfect evening in Dublin, and I was enjoying every moment of it. I leaned against the railing, taking a deep breath of the crisp Irish air. A cool breeze blew in off the river, and I shivered, wrapping my arms around myself. Tommy's arm immediately snaked around my waist, pulling me close to him. I smiled, leaning into his warmth.

"Cold?" Tommy asked, concern lacing his voice.

I shook my head, smiling up at him. "No, I'm perfect."

Tommy's eyes softened, and he leaned down to kiss me. "You knocked 'em dead tonight, spitfire," he murmured against my lips. "I'm proud of you."

We'd just come from dinner and drinks with our new associates, courtesy of Callum McTiernan. After catching wind of our new scheme to steer the clan out of guns once and for all, my father wholeheartedly threw his weight behind our bootlegging operation. A few introductions from the old country and a week of smooth talking on Tommy's part had been enough to secure a few contracts and get our new business venture off the ground.

Tommy and I ruled the McTiernan Clan side-by-side, the King and Queen of South Boston. An equal partnership. It was unprecedented, and it pissed off some of our rivals, but it wasn't anything we couldn't handle. Times were moving on, and the clan was moving on with it.

Now, we had several associates spread across Ireland, England, and even up into Scotland. High tariffs meant a thriving market for smuggled liquor, and Tommy and I were more than happy to oblige. Business had been so good, in fact, that Tommy and I had decided to expand our operation and set up shop in Dublin as well.

Tonight, we met with our newest clients face to face for the first time. It had been Tommy's suggestion, a three-week tour of Ireland and the UK to meet with our clients and cement our relationship. I'd been more than happy to agree. It was about as close to a vacation as we were going to get.

The dinner had gone smoothly, but it was a relief to be finally alone. While we'd made strides to repair our reputation in the local community back in Boston, it would take a lot longer than six months to completely shake off the stigma of the past. Establishing local charities like Skip and Mary's Place helped to ease the burden a little, as well as beating the pavement and letting people know that the McTiernans were here to stay. Grady was a natural at it, and we had left the clan in his capable hands before departing for Ireland.

Life, of course, went on. Nearly a year after it burned to the ground, Lady Devine's was reestablished in a vacant building three blocks down from the original. Tommy and I bought the entire building with the profits from our first oversees shipment of bootlegged liquor. Kat now worked for us full time; unsurprisingly, she thought that the fact that Tommy and I were mob kingpins was 'wicked cool.' She and Grady got along like two peas in a pod, an unlikely yet solid friendship.

Cassidy gave birth to her second child, Rosaleen McTiernan, right on time, and she said that overall, the experience was a vast improvement over the first time. Little Rosie already had Connor wrapped around her little finger. My parents relished their role as grandparents and were already dropping hints about Tommy and me. I told them not to hold their breath—we liked our life just as it was, thank you very much.

As for Luca, he and Tommy talked regularly, now. Luca was kind of an unofficial go-between, keeping us apprised under the table of any Moretti activities that might blow back on us, and in return, Tommy was attempting to help Luca through some of the darker periods he was going through. I could tell Tommy was worried about Luca, but he was hopeful he could get through to him.

And Misha, AKA Aleksandr Volkov? We hadn't heard a peep from him.

Yet.

It had been a wild six months. Between setting up our new headquarters, navigating the Irish bootlegging scene, and fending off the occasional whisper of challenge from rival gangs, Tommy and I hadn't had much time to ourselves. Not that I minded. I'd always known the work would be grueling, but I loved every minute of it.

Besides, Tommy made sure to make it up to me every night when we finally got home.

Tommy's hand found mine, and I squeezed it as we walked along the river. We stopped to look out over the water, enjoying the peaceful night. I glanced up at Tommy. He looked so handsome in the moonlight, his eyes shining with love as he gazed down at me.

I reached up to touch his cheek, my heart swelling with affection. "You know, this isn't how I pictured things going."

"What do you mean?" Tommy asked, frowning.

I shrugged. "I didn't think it would be this easy, that's all. It feels like we're living in a bubble, here. Like, any minute now, reality's going to come crashing down around us."

Tommy's expression softened, and he pulled me close, wrapping his arms around me. "I know what you mean. It seems too good to be true, doesn't it?"

I nodded, resting my head against his chest. Tommy's heart beat strong and steady beneath my cheek.

"But it's real, Sloane. This is us, together. And we're going to make it work," he said firmly. His gaze swept out over the water, then flicked down at me. "Come on."

Tommy took my hand and pulled me down a winding cobblestone path away from the river. It was darker here, the shadows thrown into sharp relief by the streetlights, a soft ground fog starting to seep in. If I hadn't caught Tommy's sudden change in demeanor, I'd have thought it romantic.

Like a man on a mission, Tommy led me by the hand, his eyes scanning the walkway and dark corners, missing nothing.

"Where are we going?" I asked.

"Shh, come on. Keep up." Tommy's pace quickened, his grip tightening.

I did as I was told, hurrying to keep up with him. We didn't speak again, but I noticed his palm had gone sweaty. Finally, he came to a stop in front of an old stone archway. Beyond it stretched a length of green peppered with trees and flowers, backlit by the setting sun.

Tommy turned in a full circle as if searching for something. Fingers itching, I reached into my jacket and unsnapped the safety strap over my gun, sliding it into my hand. The weight reassured me, and I caught Tommy's wrist.

"What's going on?" I asked, my voice low. "Where's the threat?"

"The what—Jesus, Sloane!" Tommy pushed my hand down, hiding the gun from view. He looked around, eyes wild, checking over his shoulder to see if anyone had seen.

"What is wrong with you?"

"Put that thing away!" he hissed.

"But you're acting like we're about to be jumped. Are we being followed?" I asked. I still wasn't convinced.

"No. Fuck, no." Tommy dragged a hand through his hair and swore softly under his breath. "We're not being jumped. Look, just forget about it."

"Forget about it? What the hell is going on”

"Will you put that thing away."

"Not until you tell me what's going on."

"I'm trying to ask you to marry me!" Tommy shouted.

My jaw dropped. I'm pretty sure my heart stopped for a moment, only to pick up double time. Tommy's eyes were wide, and he looked like he wanted to throw himself off the nearest bridge.

From across the walkway, a flock of pigeons took startled flight. People passing by were slowing to stare at us, and I quickly shoved the gun back into my concealed holster, hoping wildly that they thought we were rehearsing some kind of insane, one act play.

"I was going to...I mean, that is, if you wanted to..." Tommy trailed off weakly.

His face was a dangerous shade of crimson, and he looked so miserable I couldn't help but laugh. "Oh, Tommy. You are absolutely hopeless."

I pulled him close and kissed him firmly. It was a long kiss, deep and unyielding, and when we broke apart, both of us were a little breathless. I cupped his face in my hands and stared up at him. "Only you would propose to me with a gun in my hand."

Tommy grinned sheepishly. "I guess that wasn't exactly the romantic gesture you were hoping for."

"I don't need romance," I said honestly. "I just need you."

"Is that a yes?" Tommy asked hopefully. “Because I can do it again. I have a ring and everything.”

I rolled my eyes and smiled. "Yes, you idiot. It's a yes."

Tommy's face lit up, and he crushed me to him in a bear hug. "Fuck, I love you, spitfire."

"I know, I love you too." I pulled back and gave him a serious look. "But, I swear to God, if you ever try to pull a stunt on me like that again, I just might shoot you."

"Promises, promises. I guess I'll just have to spend the rest of my life making it up to you." Tommy drawled. But there was a new lightness to his words, and I knew he felt it too.

"I'll hold you to that," I said, and I kissed him.

We were in this together, for better or for worse. All our flaws, all our imperfections made us who we were. Our lives were never going to be perfect, but that didn't matter, because we had each other, and that was all we needed.

"Come on, Mrs. Quinn," Tommy said, taking my hand. "Let's go get drunk and make some bad decisions."

"You're my bad decision," I replied, laughing as he pulled me down the street.

And he was the best damn thing that had ever happened to me.

THE END

CONTINUE THE BOSTON KINGS STORYLINE WITH THE MORETTI FAMILY...

Read Sofia Russo and Luca Mariano's story in Deadly Secrets, Book One of the Moretti Syndicate Trilogy...

A MILLION WAYS TO SHATTER

Still reeling from the aftermath of Cassidy's abduction, warlord Connor McTiernan has retreated to the family compound in Maine to give his wife time to heal. As the rift between them grows and the Italian threat looms closer, Connor makes a blood promise save the woman who owns his heart—even if it costs him his life.

Alfie Doyle has never taken life too seriously, but all that changed the day he met Emilia and fell head over heels for the quiet beauty with the razor-sharp tongue. There's just one problem, though—Emilia is the adopted daughter of Lorenzo Moretti, head of the Moretti Crime Family and sworn enemy of the McTiernan Clan.

When a vicious series of murders lands on the Clan's doorstep, loyalties are put to the test as Connor and Alfie find themselves caught in a dangerous tug-of-war between the families, wondering if they'll ever find sanctuary, or if their star-crossed love stories will end with tragedy.

Coming December 27th, 2024

PREORDER HERE

Exclusive Content and Sneak Peeks

WANT TO SEE HOW Alfie and Emilia's relationship began? Newsletter subscribers can download a free copy of *Saint*, a novella that takes place during the events of *Dark Empire* and sets the stage for the book 2, *Cruel Empire*. Newsletter subscribers can download a FREE COPY here.

Author's Note

FINISHING A NEW BOOK is a bittersweet journey for me, and Tommy and Sloane's story was no exception. In a way, it feels like I'm saying goodbye to old friends, the way this book tied up so many loose ends for these characters and gave new insight to their childhoods. Tommy and Sloane's story was probably the hardest for me to write, not in regards to angst (although there is plenty of that!) but with their individual journeys through shared family trauma and heartbreak. That being said, Tommy and Sloane have been hands-down my favorite characters to write, with Misha coming in as a close second – more to come from him, as well!

What's next? Sofia and Luca's story is the main focus for *Deadly Secrets*, the first book in the Moretti Syndicate Trilogy. These two are another pair close to my heart, and while their story is guaranteed to require many tissue boxes, I'm excited to help them find their HEA—they deserve it! Look for *Deadly Secrets,* coming August 2024.

So, although we are closing the chapter on the McTiernan Clan's story, we'll see these characters again in the upcoming trilogies in the overarching *Boston Kings Series.* I have big things planned for these expansion trilogies, so stay tuned—a trilogy featuring the Moretti Family AND a trilogy featuring the mysterious Volkov Bratva are in the works, as well as a couple related stand-alone novels. Keep in touch with me on Instagram, my website, and, of course, the best source of bookish news, my newsletter.

And of course, I would be nowhere without you, dear reader. Indie authors are a different breed, and every one of your page reads, purchases, ratings, reviews, shoutouts, and comments are greatly appreciated. Thank you, thank you, thank you!

If you enjoyed reading this book, please consider leaving a review. Reviews are fuel for my writing machine, and they help spread the word to new readers.

Thank you for reading!

About the Author

AJ Fallow writes dark, gritty contemporary romances featuring strong heroines and morally grey heroes. Her works contain strong themes, steamy romance scenes, and graphic violence. Please check the trigger warnings for each individual book, AJ's works are not intended for readers under 18.

AJ has been previously published under several pen names in romance, fantasy, paranormal, and horror genres. She is currently pursuing her MFA from Southern New Hampshire University, and lives with her family in Wisconsin.

Instagram: @author_ajfallow

Facebook: AJ Fallow

TikTok: @author.aj.fallow

Newsletter: Subscribe

Website: www.authorajfallow.com

www.ingramcontent.com/pod-product-compliance
Lightning Source LLC
LaVergne TN
LVHW050922080826
845145LV00001B/175

* 9 7 8 1 9 6 0 6 1 9 1 2 9 *